EVA TROUT

Elizabeth Bowen was born in Dublin in 1899, the only child of an Irish lawyer and landowner. She was educated at Downe House School in Kent. Her book *Bowen's Court* (1942) is the history of her family and their house in County Cork, and *Seven Winters* (1943) contains reminiscences of her Dublin childhood. In 1923 she married Alan Cameron who held an appointment with the BBC and who died in 1952. She travelled a good deal, dividing most of her time between London and Bowen's Court, which she inherited.

She is considered by many to be one of the most distinguished novelists of the present age. She saw the object of a novel as 'the non-poetic statement of a poetic truth' and said that 'no statement of it can be final'. Her first book, a collection of short stories, *Encounters*, appeared in 1923, followed by another, *Ann Lee's*, in 1926. *The Hotel* (1927) was her first novel, and was followed by *The Last September* (1929), *Joining Charles* (1929), another book of short stories, *Friends and Relations* (1931), *To the North* (1932), *The Cat Jumps* (short stories, 1934), *The House in Paris* (1935), *The Death of the Heart* (1938), *Look at All Those Roses* (short stories, 1941), *The Demon Lover* (short stories, 1945), *The Heat of the Day* (1949), *Collected Impressions* (essays, 1950), *The Shelbourne* (1951), *A World of Love* (1955), *A Time in Rome* (1960), *After-thought* (essays, 1962), *The Little Girls* (1964), *A Day in the Dark* (1965) and her last book, *Eva Trout* (1969).

She was awarded the CBE in 1948, and received the honorary degree of Doctor of Letters from Trinity College, Dublin, in 1949 and from Oxford University in 1956. In the same year she was appointed Lacy Martin Donnelly Fellow at Bryn Mawr College in the United States. In 1965 she was made a Companion of Literature by the Royal Society of Literature. Elizabeth Bowen died in 1973.

Elizabeth Bowen

EVA TROUT

OR
CHANGING SCENES

PENGUIN BOOKS

Penguin Books Ltd, Harmondsworth, Middlesex, England
Viking Penguin Inc., 40 West 23rd Street, New York, New York 10010, U.S.A.
Penguin Books Australia Ltd, Ringwood, Victoria, Australia
Penguin Books Canada Limited, 2801 John Street, Markham, Ontario, Canada L3R 1B4
Penguin Books (N.Z.) Ltd, 182–190 Wairau Road, Auckland 10, New Zealand

First published in the United States of America
by Alfred A. Knopf, Inc. 1968
First published in Great Britain by Jonathan Cape 1969
Published in Penguin Books 1982
Reprinted 1983, 1987

Made and printed in Great Britain by
Richard Clay (The Chaucer Press) Ltd,
Bungay, Suffolk
Set in Monophoto Baskerville

CONTENTS

TO

CHARLES RITCHIE

PART ONE

GENESIS

· I ·

OUTING

'This is where we were to have spent the honeymoon,' Eva Trout said, suddenly, pointing across the water. She had pulled up the car on a grass track running along the edge of a small lake. She switched off the engine – evidently, they were to gaze at the castle for some time.

Her carload of passengers was dumbfounded. Nothing of this had been mentioned before. The four Dancey children, packed in the back seat, climbed over one another to see better (the view was framed by the Jaguar's left-hand windows). Of their mother, in front beside Eva, more seemed required – Mrs Dancey, wildly craning her neck, brought out: 'Not in winter, I hope?'

'No – spring. There would have been daffodils.'

The castle, mirrored into the sheet of probably artificial water, did not look ancient. Nor did it look indigenous: though its setting was English, the pile resembled some Bavarian fantasy. Light-coloured, standing straight up out of the lake (there was no terrace) the façade showed with photographic distinctness in the now fading January afternoon. Its windows, many of which were balconied, one and all were made sightless by white shutters. Above the turreted roofline rose steep woods, sepia with winter: no smoke from any contorted chimney blurred the transparency of the trees. The only movement was in the foreground, where swans rippled the image cast on the water by zigzagging absently to and fro.

Though the Jaguar must have been nosing towards it for some time (along woodland rides, through tunnels of evergreen) the castle had only now come into view, with dramatic suddenness. And the same might be said of Eva's design. The Danceys had had no idea where they might be going to, or why: all they knew was, Miss Trout was taking them for an outing. For two-and-a-half hours, up hill, down dale, they had been rushing through cold scenery. What they'd been more and more earnestly looking forward to was a stop for tea: this was a sunless and sere day for pleasure motoring. It was some weeks, now, since Miss Trout had first invaded the vicarage, showering benefits on them, often mixed ones. How long, they wondered, would this go on for? For ever and ever? Perhaps not . . .

'Closed for the winter, evidently,' said Mrs Dancey. She hazarded: 'Is it in private ownership?'

'It was a school for a while. Not now – *no*; we should have had it all to ourselves,' the girl said, nonchalantly and grandly.

'Mother,' asked one of the children, 'may we get out?'

'May they get out for a minute or two, Eva?'

Eva did not reply; *she* was getting out. Having done so, leaving her door open, she walked round the car throwing all others open, with an air of largesse. January knifed through the heated Jaguar; a child sneezed as it battled its way to freedom, and Mrs Dancey, erecting her fur coat-collar and sinking so far as might be down into it, declared: 'I think *I*'ll stay where I am.' Eva did not reply; she had walked away. The children set off in the reverse direction – their mother, impaled on draughts, sent a whinny after them: two of them came back and banged shut the doors. Mrs Dancey at once lowered a window, to call out: 'All of you, better not go too far!'

Once alone, Mrs Dancey, who already had a crick in her neck, saw no further need to study the castle. Instead, here was an unprecedented opportunity to study Eva, at length and in peace, from a safe distance. Eva, one saw straight ahead, through the windscreen. The giantess, by now, was alone also: some way along the edge of the water she had come to a stop – shoulders braced, hands interlocked behind her, feet in the costly, slovenly lambskin bootees planted apart. Back fell her cap of jaggedly cut hair from her raised profile, showing the still adolescent heaviness of the jaw-line . . . No, it would not have done, pondered Mrs Dancey (meaning the marriage: what marriage? Any). Yet after all, why not? She's twenty-four. *Is* she thinking? Mrs Dancey thought not. Monolithic, Eva's attitude was. It was not, somehow, the attitude of a thinking person.

The girl looked round.

The watcher hastily lowered her eyes to the walnut dashboard, with its so many dials. She went on to close her eyes, only just in time – Mrs Dancey's favourite form of immunity was a feigned nap; and, sure enough, Eva *was* coming back! Purposeful strides could be heard returning over the turf made iron by black frost. They passed the car, not a pause, and continued onward. Going after the children?

Not yet inspired, torpid after the drive, the children stood about in a loose group, stamping their feet or blowing on to their fingers through Fair Isle gloves. Their bright gloves (Christmas presents), their suffering scarlet ears and the brass-yellow of the two girls' pigtails were the only touches of colour about the Danceys, otherwise clad alike, irrespective of sex, in sombre dark-blue berets and belted overcoats. In age they graded down from thirteen to seven: Catrina, Henry, Andrew, Louise. From time to time they communicated neutrally with one another, in their own manner, barely moving their lips. Had the lake been frozen, they could have slid on it; but it had not, yet, more than a margin of mean ice, nibbled at by the ripples caused by the swans. As for the castle, it looked, from here, as though cut out, flat, from a sheet of cardboard.

'Catrina!' now shouted the nearing Eva. 'All of you! Why do you stay so still?'

'Anywhere to go to is too far.'

'I say, Miss Trout –'

'– Henry, you must call me Eva!'

'All right. – Is that castle *bona fide*?'

'He means,' said Catrina, 'has it an inside?'

'No I don't,' said Henry, turning away.

'Could I pass my honeymoon there if it had not?'

'But you're not going to.'

Bright-witted little Louise chimed in: 'Or there couldn't have been a school in it, either, could there?'

'Yes, that school,' Andrew wanted to know, 'was it no good?'

'It was experimental,' Eva vouchsafed, in a large way, waving a hand. 'Boys *and* girls.'

'That has been tried before,' Henry pointed out.

'So then, what happened?' persisted Andrew. 'Were any drowned in the lake?'

'Or did they push each other out of the windows?' Louise supplemented. 'Or fall out of a boat?'

'There's no boat,' said Andrew in a discouraged tone. 'If there had been, we could have rowed across.'

'Not if the boat had been on the other side,' said Henry, again scoring a point.

'We could have walked round, then rowed back. – Was it sunk, do you think?'

'Anyway, that would have taken too long,' said Catrina, pessimistic as ever. She drew some shreds of Kleenex out of a pocket and wadded them together, to blow her nose on. 'Eva, how do you know about this school? *You* weren't there, were you?'

'For a while,' said their patroness. She said no more.

'So then what happened?'

'The school ceased.'

Henry, eyeing the structure with growing scepticism, inquired: 'Are there dungeons, for instance?'

With a fervour she seemed to reserve for Henry, Eva cried out: 'No, you horrible boy – nothing so insanitary!'

'I rather thought not,' said Henry calmly. He made as though once more to turn away, then did not – pressing home his advantage, he asked: 'Where *are* we going to have tea?'

Though small for his age, twelve, Henry stood out: topmost intelligent one of a family all rendered to a degree intelligent by poverty, breeding and the need to get on. His manner was particularly composed, and at times (as on this occasion) sardonic. Though Andrew was the handsomer of the boys, Henry's features, made delicate by precocity, gave promise of greater interest in years to come. His charm was nascent, perverse and a shade standoffish. Already he was qualified to deal with Eva: she could not boss him and he could mortify her – though unless unduly provoked he refrained from doing so; treating her, on the whole, as he might an astray moose which when too overpowering could be shooed away.

The word 'tea', not spoken aloud till now, made the others stare haggardly at Henry, and then at Eva – who gave out: 'Oh, some hotel, I suppose!'

'There weren't many,' Henry remarked, 'on the way here.'

Catrina, re-wadding the Kleenex, made further use of it. 'If there were, there wouldn't be tea if we're too late.'

'It's NOT late,' shouted their captor.

'It's getting dark, you know.'

It was. The inhospitable castle receded, already, into its ink-like woods, taking on a look of the immaterial – its reflection, even, fainted out of the lake, over which was forming a frozen vapour. No pathos invested the scene. There was no afterglow – there had been no sun. And the swans were gone.

Still ruminating over the school's fate, the children, swarming back to the Jaguar, looked behind them once or twice at the castle. Eva did not – she could not, now, wait to be off. Her boorish infidelity shocked the Danceys: one of them raised a voice in re-proof. 'If it's left like *that*, I should think it would soon fall down. Doesn't it belong to anyone now?'

'Oh yes, it belongs to my father's friend.'

'Alive, is he? It doesn't look like it.'

'*How*,' she retorted, 'could a thing belong to anyone dead?'

'What's his name, Eva?'

'Constantine.'

They packed back into the Jaguar – causing Mrs Dancey to start up, preternaturally wide-awake, frantically wanting to know: 'What time is it?' Cocooned in a rug, she had lapsed from the acted nap into true, deep slumber; which, guilty though it had left her, had done good. Mrs Dancey was permanently exhausted. For all she knew, now, this could be tomorrow. And where in the world ARE we? (She prayed to remember.) Anyway here was Eva, right back on top of one. Eva, as ever, extra heavily breathing, about to twitch the ignition key. 'Are you *all* there, children?' appealed the mother. Wherever this was, it was soon to be some-where else – for the Jaguar, stealthily purring, was creeping for-ward.

· 2 ·

MR AND MRS ARBLE

Though Eva these days all but lived at the Danceys', she did not live with them: her base, not too far from the vicarage, was the home of friends with whom she looked like making an indefinite stay. She was paying guést there. This had the approval of her guardian (in which was vested the office of trustee also) by whom any arrangement involving money had, still, to be authorized. For the big heiress was not, by the terms of her father's will, to enter into enjoyment of her fortune till she should be twenty-five. (That would be next birthday.) Meanwhile her welfare was, at least in name, the concern of Constantine, who charged himself with financial arrangements for it. Her wish to take up residence with the Arbles, Mr and Mrs, had, happily, suited Constantine's book. Indeed, the Arbles seemed to him just the thing. Their home, Larkins, should be remote from trouble. They solved a problem; he recompensed them, liberally, accordingly. He had a mind easily set at rest.

This was a part of Worcestershire largely given over to fruit farming. Larkins was set in plum orchards, of which acres extended on three sides. The house was itself built of plum-coloured brick. Square, two-storeyed, five sash windows in front (three above, two below) with a door in the middle, it was not unlike a house in a child's drawing. Its gaze was forthright. It faced on, though stood a little way back from, a lonely by-road.

Iseult Arble seemed destined to have Eva – destined, she some-times wondered, never to lose her? Everything had indicated Iseult. She and her husband needed the Eva money, to make ends meet – *could* they, otherwise, have gone on very much longer? She was a highly intelligent person, young still, of pleasing appearance and good character, as to whom there existed but one mystery: why had she thrown herself away? (She apparently had.) She should know how to deal with Eva, an ex-pupil. Iseult had been teacher of English at a first-rate, unambiguous girls' school attended by Eva eight years ago. Miss Smith, as she then was, had made an abiding impression. Eva had never lost touch with her. She remained an influence – all the more so by having incurred, it seemed, a lifelong devotion.

Iseult Smith had gone out of her way to establish confidence, for her own reasons – she proposed to tackle Eva's manner of speaking. What caused the girl to express herself like a displaced person? The explanation – that from infancy onward Eva had had as attendants displaced persons, those at a price being the most obtainable, to whose society she'd been largely consigned – for some reason never appeared: too simple, perhaps? Much went into the effort to induce flexibility. But Miss Smith had come too late on the scene; she had had to give up. Eva by then was sixteen: her outlandish, cement-like conversational style had set. Moreover – the discouraging fact emerged – it was more than sufficient for Eva's needs. She had nothing *to* say that could not be said, adequately, the way she said it. What did result from the sessions was, on the girl's side, awe for the dazzling teacher; also, Eva was left in a daze of gratitude. Till Iseult came, no human being had ever turned upon Eva their full attention – an attention which could seem to be love. Eva knew nothing of love but that it existed – that, she should know, having looked on at it. *Her* existence had gone by under a shadow: the shadow of Willy Trout's total attachment to Constantine.

The entire cut of the jib of Eva's father could have given the lie to that obsession; which had, in fact, waited to mark him down till he was into what seemed maturity. Big in height and frame and in a big way easy in movement, stalwart and open in countenance – though under-the-eyes pouches and a tic in the cheek declared themselves under the later pressure – he looked what he otherwise was: a business man fortunate in his background, a crack polo player, with a pretty wife. He had been popular. An apparent artlessness concealed the acumen, approaching genius, through which he had trebled inherited wealth. Possibly the genius side was the rocky side? It was in him to deviate: that, Constantine had unerringly sensed . . . Willy's child had not been the only defrauded one. His wife fled, two months after the birth of Eva. Mrs Trout was then almost at once killed in a plane crash. Willy's own death, twenty-three years later, was as abrupt, though in a different manner. It left Eva, a legacy, on the hands of Constantine till the Larkins solution came to be found.

After school Eva, accompanying her father on global business trips, had constantly sent picture postcards to Miss Smith from wherever she found herself. She obtained glimpses of Miss Smith when back in London. As a wedding present, she had sent an enormous, glitteringly fitted picnic basket from Fortnum & Mason's: the bride would have liked to exchange it for comestibles, but dared not; Eva often visited Larkins. Iseult Smith's abandonment of a star career for an obscure marriage puzzled those for whom it was hearsay only – but the reason leaped to the eye: the marriage was founded on a cerebral young woman's first physical passion. The Arbles had now been the Arbles for some years – so far, no children. Accordingly, room for Eva. She had had her way. Visits terminate, visitors have to go – she now was a visitor no longer.

What had deteriorated?

Today, the day of the castle outing, was running out. How fared the benighted Jaguar, over hill and dale? At Larkins, still no sign of Eva.

Iseult, having begun to look at the clock, did so each time with increasing hopefulness. The late are apt to be later – *might* not Eric, for once, be the first home? With each five minutes, this became more likely. Only when alone did Iseult betray, by dramatic extremes of attitude, the internal tension she felt at all times. Now she sat erect in a spacious fireside chair intended by nature to be leaned back in, just out of the ray projected by an Anglepoise lamp. She had finished working: her looseleaf notebook, the old French dictionary and the ultra-new French novel were shoved away on the floor, almost out of sight. Translations, one way of making ends meet (or meet more nearly) in the pre-Eva days, had been resumed as an exercise, a diversion – and, too, on the principle of letting nothing go. For, who knew? From day to day, there was no saying . . .

To think or not to think? Iseult, with a gesture more like an exclamation, thrust back her hair, which was dark and springy, from her high white forehead which was strikingly beautiful. By habit, she looked round the room she sat in. Anything she could do to it had been done; what it could do to her seemed without limit. The full-blooded, late-Victorian furniture had been Eric's people's. The carpet had been bought to last, and was lasting. The armchairs and settee to match had been borne home by Eric from an hotel auction during the trauma preceding marriage. The new grate, post-Eva, gave out its advertised glow. So far, the living-room was consistent – Iseult's own 'touches' had been less fortunate: thought-out low white bookcases, now in place, for all their content looked cramped and petty; block-printed linen curtains, skimped by economy, had between them strips of vacuous darkness – as also the room, in the main excluded from the Anglepoise's intellectual orbit, became what it least in the world was: spectral. She would do well to switch on the ceiling light before Eric entered: he liked to see. But the switch was away by the door. Nervosity wired her to her chair.

To atone, she listened. Along the road, both ways, and throughout the orchards – for how far? – there stretched nothing but a mindless silence.

Ultimately, his step *was* to be heard.

Eric never came straight in; he washed first. That meant three–four minutes. The wife grabbed round for a cigarette, lit it, drew on it twice – tensely. She then cast it into the fire and leaned back.

He seldom came in saying anything. He saw no need to. On the contrary, he came back into a room as though not conscious of having gone from it. Once he was there, he was there. He gave but one sign of having been far afield: invariably he brought back the evening paper. Quite often he quite simply sat down and read it. Who would have thought this man had been gone a day? – but that by what had happened, might have arisen, been done or not done during the day away, he was still to a certain extent pre-occupied. This evening, however, he said: 'Cold out' – for it truly had been. Also this was his way of letting her know that the warmth maintained in here made a grateful contrast. He lowered himself into *his* chair and looked across – she once more wore that terracotta cardigan, reputed to be Italian, still with a button missing. And something other was missing. 'Eva?' he asked.

'Out.'

'Where's she gone off to?'

'I couldn't tell you. – Anything in the paper?'

'How am I to say when I haven't looked?'

'I thought you sometimes looked at it on the bus.'

'No, I don't,' he told her. 'Fancy your thinking that.'

'Then look now.'

He stated, more than complained: 'Not too easy to see.'

Iseult, twisting round in her chair, readjusted the Anglepoise. 'Better?'

Anything but. The concentrated 75-watt glare was directed full upon Eric, transfixing him. From where she sat he looked like a searchlit building. The wide-at-the-top face, brows bent by a light but intent frown, faced her without a flicker – the jaws clamped by partly resistance, partly forbearance. Rusty fleckings stood out on the ash-grey irises of the open eyes. Electricity, making just more than lifelike the general ruddiness of the colouring, struck infinitesimal copper glints from stubble faintly beginning on cheeks and chin – clean-shaven, he was less so by the end of a day. The shape of the skull, hair flattened flatter than ever by just-now's wash-up, was cut out sharply, with an added solidity, against the dimensionless dusk behind.

So, for a minute. He then took evasive action, canting across the right-hand arm of his chair. 'Try and not monkey with that lamp,' he advised her, not for the first time. 'It does no good.' He got up, went to the switch at the door and bathed the room in normal illumination. Coming back, he asked: 'Ought we not to know, though – rightly? Or, at any rate, oughtn't you?'

'What are we talking about?'

'Where Eva's gone to.'

'Oh,' she said, looking up at the ceiling.

He went on: 'That was the understanding, *I* understood.'

'What understanding?' said she – still to the ceiling.

'When we took her on: that we were to keep an eye on her. What else are we taking all this money for? Already there's been that muddle about that marriage, and it would be only natural if that unsettled her. Just now, does she seem to you quite herself?'

' "Herself"? That would be difficult to say. One thing one can be sure of: she's at the Danceys' – or with them: where else would she be, these days? . . . What *is* the matter all of a sudden, Eric?'

'Not so all of a sudden,' he remarked – though as though to himself, or at least absently. He scooped up the newspaper, squinted along the headlines, then let it drop: instead, he perused his wife, across their hearth, at once warily and resignedly – the habituated manner, it might be said, of one who has yet to find the right answer. 'This,' he went on, 'has for some time been on my mind; but you and I seem to have never a chance to talk – I mean, as things are. She has the right to be with us; but there it is. There *she* is.'

'You are telling me,' said Iseult.

'And yet when she's not, there's come to be quite a gap.'

'We are never alone – you realize – except in bed.'

'That's putting it strongly! And for that matter, Izzy, what are we now?'

'Waiting,' said Iseult, 'for her to come back.'

'Then we'd better step on the gas and get this said. The Danceys – you mean at the vicarage? They're all right; they like her. But where's she going to turn to after the holidays? Those kids are going to have to go back to school; and if you ask me, they're the attraction.'

'Horrid little Henry?'

'Yes, *he's* sharp for his age. – The Reverend and Mrs Dancey are busy people.'

'You understate that, Eric; they are all but demented, from what I've seen of them – which is not much.' (Iseult, geographically a parishioner of Mr Dancey's, was not a churchgoer. He had called, but it had not been a success.) 'He always has such a blinding cold that he's really rather a menace on the roads, darting about in that vapoured-up little car; and she's muddle-headed and bleats like a worried sheep. Still, any port in a storm.'

'What d'you mean exactly by *that*?' he asked, with a genuine deepening of the frown. 'There's no storm here.'

'Storm or not,' said Iseult, 'Eva'd rather go anywhere than be here – now.'

'So out she goes. So what are you grumbling for?'

'I am not, Eric. *You're* the one who's been grumbling – "a gap", you say.'

'I'm sorry I spoke,' he said. 'But yet in point of fact, Izzy, I don't believe you. I can't believe you. The sun rises and sets on you, where Eva's concerned; always did, and surely it always will? She asked no better than to be under this roof. And you, *you* liked her – you must have done, or why did you interfere with her at the outset? There was some reason.'

She looked along the books on a chair-side shelf, sighing: 'Yes, I suppose so.'

'Not,' said Eric, 'that a thing always works out as one foresaw. – Or had hoped,' he added. 'And in that case, no use asking whose fault. A person – though that they were not to know – may actually never have had it in them to make a go of whatever it was that they thought they could. It had been a case of trying the wrong road. All the same, who's to say it was wrong to try? You can *but* try . . . However,' he ended up, 'that you and I have reason to know. Eh?'

'You prefer the garage.'

He had failed as a fruit farmer. Too much had been against him, beginning and ending with not having enough capital to surmount bad years or buy back mistakes due to inexperience. Always he had wanted to be a fruit farmer, or thought so. He had put his back, together with all he'd got from selling up a small business left him by his father, into the enterprise known as Larkins Orchards. Tremendous unsparing worker, he set out with what had not been unreasonable expectations – or, they were reasonable till Iseult fomented them. She had burned with them from the instant she fell in love. She never foresaw their marriage, its days and nights, other than as embowered by dazzling acres, blossom a snowy blaze and with honeyed stamens, by sun then moonlight, till came later – fruited boughs bowed, voluptuous, to the ground, gumminess oozing from bloomy plums. She had been a D. H. Lawrence reader and was a townswoman. By the end, he was lucky not to have come out worse than he did. They sold off the orchards but kept the house, which the purchaser did not want, a lopsided barn, a half-acre of land . . . Nor did Eric step off into a void: a garage-proprietor cousin of his in the local town happened to be looking round for a foreman – and Eric, it was to turn out, filled the bill. For this reason: Eric had profited, hands down, by his military service – he came out of three years with a mechanized unit a first-rate mechanic: clearly, he'd been a born one. (And good with men.) Possibly that should have been his line from the start? – from, that was, when he first came out of the army? He might have had a garage of his own by now, who knows? Anyway, no good thinking ... As it was, he nowadays daily caught the seven-thirty a.m. bus into town, intercepting it at the crossroads, and usually made it home on the six-thirty p.m. In the Larkins barn sat an old Anglia, bought when they'd sold the van – but if *he* took that, what was Izzy to do all day?

Never had she uttered a word about the loneliness. She had her brain, of course? The rate she did those translations at was astonishing, the more so when there she was with the house on her hands, *making* work, dating back to the Year One. Yes, looking back, that had been a bad patch. 'Go back to teaching again, for a while at least?' he had put forward. ' "Back"?' she had cried aloud. ' "*Back*"! – I never go *back*!' Dead-white in the face. That had shaken him, he piped down. Later, as things got no better and somewhat worse, some idea of W.E.A. lecturing or some such had come to be entertained. But that meant, out at nights, all over the country. When would they see each other? ... Then, just then, Eva had come along.

'Waiting supper for her?' he now asked.

'Why? – No.' She began to get out of her chair.

'No, look – stop a minute!' he interposed. 'No such great hurry.' So she settled down again, showing no feeling either way. (Her movements as housewife were those of a marionette: these days they were less frequent, and less compulsive – 'help' five mornings a week, and a shining Aga with one of those long-term ovens.) Eric continued: 'Speaking of the garage, you do know she's been on at me about that? She's got it into her head we could take her on there; and will she take "no" for an answer? – no, she will not.'

'That was quite unknown to me,' said Iseult calmly. 'As you say, it would never do.'

'No. We don't want another hand, and we don't take learners: that I've told her repeatedly.' He pondered. 'I see her idea, though, in a way.'

Iseult asked: 'What idea do you see?'

'You can't blame her for wanting to do something with herself, can you?'

'Eric, do I ever blame anyone?'

'I don't know,' he confessed, sombrely. 'That, I shall never

23

know. – But Eva,' he went on, with a change of tone, 'should have some outlet; or otherwise she'll run into some other trouble. Not much society round here – is there?'

'That,' Iseult pointed out, '*I* would hardly know.' She held a hand up, studied the finger-tips. 'And what would any society do with Eva?'

'Why not? – she's not defective in any way. And look at her future, look what's coming to her! We've no right to leave her playing cowboys-and-Indians – or *is* that all she's up to? You don't think she's going with anybody we've not got wind of? . . . Izzy, what do we know about that marriage?'

'Chiefly,' she said, exhausted, 'that it's evaporated.'

'Yes. But *at* the time,' he declared, 'we should have known more.'

Iseult drew up her shoulders, as though a wind blew. Then, looking down her Italian cardigan, she began, absorbed, to pluck at the tuft of threads in the place the button had gone from – bother it! 'Constantine,' she remarked, as from far away, 'seemed to be satisfied: he's her guardian.'

'Is he up to the job?'

'You should have it, probably?'

Eric's answer was: silence. He splayed his hands out on the moquette chair-arms, put the whole of his weight on them, bent forward, thrust himself upward out of the chair. He was going away? He turned his back on Iseult and went to a window. This Larkins living-room ran through the not great depth of the house, south–north: it had, therefore, a window at either end – the one to which he had gone was the back, or north, one. Outside lay the orchards – the lost acres. Through the gap in the curtains he stared out, trying to decipher the darkness. Nothing. He whistled at nothing, under his breath.

Iseult was frightened, defiant. She ventured: 'Sorry.'

'What for?' said he, in no particular tone, not turning round.

'For what I said.'

'Did you?'

'*Please*, Eric!'

'Nothing,' he mused, 'makes sense. I don't; you don't. You and I don't, too much, Izzy? She makes sense as much as anyone else.' He whistled again.

Too much . . . Iseult, with a desolate sob, a desperate one, re-
linquishing life, cast herself back as far as the chair went, head
slithering sideways against a cushion that slid with it. Thus she
remained: a carcase: only her hands livingly twisting themselves
together. 'Eric,' her voice began, like a voice recorded how many
years ago? 'Eric, Eric, Eric.'

'What is it, Izzy?'

'Come back – can't you come back? Come here.'

He did as she asked.

She unknotted the hands and flung one of them out beseechingly.
He half-laughed, sat on an arm of her chair, caught hold of the
hand and massaged it with his thumb. '*That's* a good girl – eh?'
Then, leaning lower over her rigid stillness, he restored the hand to
her, pityingly laying it across her breast as he might a dead
woman's. A tear from under a closed lid slid down her cheek. Her
lips struggled.

'No, but what *is* it, Izzy?'

'I didn't mean to be terrible.'

'If she's going to get on your nerves she had better go.'

'Then what would become of us?'

'We made out before,' he said, though with shaken certainty.

'No, we didn't.' She butted her head farther into the cushion.
'You know we didn't – I cracked.'

He considered that. 'Then need she get on your nerves?'

'Always there, always there, always there.'

'I know, I know, I know: but what about it? Old Eva – what
can she do to you? Or what *does* she do?' She turned again in the
chair – he received a sudden, as it were a stolen, view of her face:
its bereftness, its unresigned weariness of its exile. He took a leap in
the dark. 'Remind you of what you *could* do? – of what you used to
be, when you liked?'

Instantly the eyes opened. Tear-blotted as they were, they
dilated at him. 'What do you mean?'

'How can I tell you?'

'Don't go away from me – don't! I love you, I love you. What
does she do to *us*?'

'We're all right. – Smile at me, Izzy?'

'We don't make sense, you just said.'

'Well, nor we do. – But go on, smile at me, Izzy!'

She smiled like the girl she had been.

'So you see?' he said. Frowning lightly, intently, he moved her hand from her breast to put his in its place. This hand of his went about till it felt her heart beat.

She said: 'We never make love.'

'*What* . . .?'

He reached round her, got his hand under the cushion and raised up the cushion, her head and all. Feeling his breath on her lips, Iseult gave a final sigh, as though falling asleep.

Then, sharply, he turned his head away, listening sharply.

'– Eric –?'

'I'm just listening.'

'I know you are.'

They both listened. 'Yes,' he said, 'that's the Jag. Here she comes . . .'

· *3* ·

CLERICAL LIFE

The vicarage had witnessed various scenes of clerical life. Not old, it was elderly, landed on this village by a wave of ecclesiastical betterment in the 1880s. In many ways it was a dreadful building: narrow-visaged, four storeys high, topped by peaky gables. The windows were church-like, as was the porch. Internally it was no better: an ill-lit staircase climbed up a shaft in the middle, conducting draughts. Draughts also rose from between floorboards, causing the ascetic carpets to billow. There was no hope the place would ever be sold, allowing the Danceys to move into a bungalow, as did more fortunate clergy, for who would buy it? As Mrs Dancey said, 'If it had been Queen Anne . . .' The best to be said for it was, she thought, that at any rate it was not infested like Borley Rectory: no occult manifestations, which was as well, for the hollow plan of the house made home life already noisy enough.

For that reason, Mr Dancey's study was at the top. Amid starlings chittering round the chimneys he had wedged an attic with stuffed bookcases, from which his oil-heater drew a musty smell. He secured a degree of peace, not much, and least of all during the Christmas holidays, with indoor children at large in the rooms below or gathering for conference on the stairs. No door but his was ever shut, though some banged fitfully when a wind blew.

Yesterday's outing to the castle had emptied the vicarage, but for Mr Dancey; which he had found ideal. This, by contrast, was a terrible morning. All at once he came bursting out of his study, with a choked roar. 'Stop that!'

Silence.

Determined not to have worked himself up for nothing, he reiterated: 'Stop it, I say!'

'We have, Father.'

'Yes, I daresay,' he said, in a scoffing tone, not unlike Henry's. 'For how long?'

'We have to be somewhere.'

'What are you doing, for instance?'

'Waiting for Eva.'

'That reminds me, Catrina, I'm out of Kleenex.'

'You *can't* be, Father!' His elder girl, beginning to come upstairs, gave a bothered and busy toss to her yellow plaits.

'Yes, I can, and I am.' He gave the child an as nearly malignant look as his nature permitted. He revengefully told her: 'I'm down to handkerchiefs.'

'Goodness. How many?'

'Three. – No, four,' he announced, going through his pockets.

'Give them to me; I'll boil them.' Catrina held out a masterful hand.

'Hi, you can't take them all away! What am *I* to do?'

'That inhalant I gave you should dry your nose up.'

'It makes my eyes water.'

'Writing that book again?' She looked superstitiously past him into the study. Chaos reigned on his desk.

'I had thought of doing so.'

'Give me all of those handkerchiefs, then I'll get you more Kleenex.'

'What am I to do in the meantime?'

'You can contain yourself for a minute or two, surely, Father?'

Mr Dancey did not seem certain, perhaps rightly. At the very thought he had to repress a sneeze, which cost him an agonizing contortion. At forty-two, he would have been better-looking than any of his children were it not for the havoc wrought by his chronic affliction. His alive countenance had seldom a chance to be quite itself; vision, discernment and charity shone from it, but often as though through a blurred pane – inflamed eyelids, sore, swollen nostrils, bloated upper lip. There were few intermissions: when winter relaxed its grip he regularly started to have hay fever – April's first flowering currant bush set him going. He did not allow his handicap to worry him, as apparently nobody could do anything about it (he never was seriously ill) but it did exasperate him occasionally. Occupationally, his anxiety was his voice, which had taken to varying in volume as unaccountably as though a poltergeist were fiddling with the controls, sometimes coming out with a sudden boom of a roar, sometimes fading till off the air. The suspense induced was particularly noticeable in church, and was on the whole enjoyed by his congregation. One and all thought highly of Mr Dancey.

'What did you say you were doing?' he asked Catrina – in what dropped, without warning, to a conspirator's whisper.

'Waiting for Eva. We have been, most of the morning.'

'Perhaps she'll be taking you all out again?' he suggested, brightening.

'We hope not. Today we're rather exhausted.'

'You did not sound exhausted,' said Mr Dancey. He turned back into his study and shut the door, reopening it to shout: '*Hurry!*'

It was as Catrina feared: there was no more Kleenex, anywhere in the vicarage. Four outsize boxes consumed since January 1st! – an ominous opening to the year. For this luxury, since its discovery by Mr Dancey, was one of the few breaks in the family's abstemiousness: it sent household bills up worse than anything else. Resignedly the daughter slung on her overcoat and, having waited only to drop the handkerchiefs into the kitchen fish kettle to simmer, made off at a lope down the village street – long, here and there obsoletely pretty, and this morning made still more torpid by frozen mist. At the far end, Catrina was vexed to perceive the Jaguar contentedly sitting outside the post office, back turned obliviously to the vicarage. Then Eva walked out of the post office, looking *affairée*, larger than life in the frame of the humble door. She wore a Robin Hood hat and an ocelot coat and carried a mighty crocodile handbag. None of this gear had been seen before. Occupied in shovelling money into the handbag, she did not observe Catrina coming alongside. 'Good morning,' said Catrina sarcastically.

Eva succeeded in snapping the bag shut. 'Oh good morning. I am in quite a hurry.'

'Oh, are you?'

'Yes. I am going to London, to see my guardian.'

'Well, I like *that*!' exclaimed the aggrieved girl. 'Last night, you told us all to wait in for you this morning.'

'Last night I had not yet had his letter.'

'Henry,' remarked Catrina, 'will be furious.'

Eva heaved a sigh, though pleasurably. 'Will he miss me?'

'What Henry wanted to do was, go into town. Now it's too late; the bus will have gone – so there goes *his* morning!'

Eva shouted: 'How can I change – now? I have sent a telegram. He might never, never forgive me. I mean, my guardian.'

'You might have said, though. You could have telephoned.'

'*Oh* no I could not!' Eva now brought forth from under an armpit, and tugged on, a pair of immense gauntlets, ocelot-backed. Flexing her fingers inside them, she went on darkly: 'Telephone? To telephone was impossible.'

Cloak-and-dagger? Catrina deflated *that* by saying, merely: 'Is your hat meant to be crooked?'

'I don't know,' replied Eva, punching it straight. The long pheasant feather quivered like an antenna.

'*I* am in a hurry,' stated Catrina, looking away from Eva into a shop. 'Father, in fact, will be going out of his mind.'

'Give my affectionate greetings to Mr Dancey!'

The vicarage child (muffling, perhaps, a pang?) asked: '*Driving* to London?'

'No; to the train only. I wish not to be lost in the mists round London; I am not in the mood.' Staring at nothing, Eva beat the gauntlets together. 'My hands are gone cold, cold, cold. I am cold all over.'

'It's a cold day,' said Catrina, nose in the air.

'No, Catrina. Cold since I had his letter.'

'Why? He can't eat you; or can he?'

'Certainly *not*!' said Miss Trout. (The very idea!)

'What did his letter say, then?' pursued Catrina.

'Only it answered "yes," that he would see me if I was there today. No, it's not what he says; it is what I must.'

Catrina confined herself to stamping her feet, with a trudging though static movement. Eva mourned on: 'I am so AFRAID, Catrina.'

'Well, keep calm.'

'I cannot.'

'You never can, somehow.'

The distracted one ferreted under a gauntlet, laid bare her wristwatch. 'My train – my train!' She wrenched the Jaguar's door open, hurled in her handbag and, made bulky by finery, squeezed herself under the wheel. Hand on the still-open door, she informed Catrina: 'I cannot stay much longer where I now am.'

'O-oh?'

'No, I don't think so.'

'Have you had a row with them?'

Eva did not reply: she was starting the car. 'Most of your coat's hanging out,' reported the child. Eva hauled in the ocelot, then drove off.

White Kleenex, it was discovered, had run out – more on order, but what was the use of that? A choice between lemon and rose confronted Catrina. 'Neither,' she said, 'would be very appropriate for my father.' Everyone in the shop agreed fervently. 'Still,' she sniffed, 'needs must when the Devil drives.' She accordingly went away with a box of each.

· 4 ·

CONFERENCE

My dear Mrs Arble,

What is all this about? I have had a somewhat dismaying visit from Eva, since when I have half expected to hear from you. That I have not done so leads me to hope that the situation of which she spoke to me does not, in fact, exist outside her own fancy. That could well be possible. You must, I take it, have known of her trip to London; that you knew of its purpose seems less likely. If you suspected nothing, that reassures me – there may *be* nothing?

None the less, this was the first I had heard of there being anything but harmony at Larkins. And should this be the first you have heard, pray forgive this letter. Perhaps I blunder? Frankly, my own instinct would be to let whatever this is blow over, but Eva is to an extent forcing my hand. She desires to leave your keeping, and has told me so. Not only does she desire to, she intends to. To put it abruptly, she might walk out.

That, as I continue to see it, could be disastrous. I wonder, therefore, whether you and I had not better discuss this apparent crisis? That is to say, meet? I would come to Larkins, but that there would be Eva. If you could make it convenient to be in London, we might lunch? I could, I am certain, so adjust my engagements as to be free any day you may name. I would suggest that this be a day in the near future.

May I add, it would be a pleasure to me to renew our acquaintanceship.

Yours ever sincerely,
CONSTANTINE ORMEAU

This letter, far from being a blunder, acted like a tonic on Iseult.

It arrived in disguise: two sheets of deep azure monogrammed paper overflowing with his distinctive handwriting made their journey to Larkins inside a buff business envelope, the address typed. This precaution against the eye of Eva was not lost on Iseult, herself one of those few people who think of everything. She marked Constantine up for it. Also, the whiff of conspiracy was flattering. As, in the mood engendered, she read, read on, then read again, she found herself thinking surprisingly well of Eva. Yes, decidedly Eva rose in her estimation – the girl had precipitated *something*, which was what everybody needed. The long Larkins bog-down looked like nearing its end. What had Eva been up to? Iseult felt stirrings of that original vivisectional interest which had drawn her to her uncouth pupil. In the glow of knowing herself fallen in hate with (for what else was this?) she relived the year at the school, and the years after, during which this organism had so much loved her. She regretted nothing. Might it not be, she wondered, that she and Eva had only now arrived at their true bourne?

And the letter not only revivified, it was balm. Continuously being ignored by Constantine had mortified Iseult more than she admitted. 'Our acquaintanceship . . .' There had been one meeting: the half-day visit by him to Larkins, to assure himself as to its suitability as a repository for Eva, then talk money. He had been more than satisfied on the one score, she on the other. Since then, nothing. Made use of, made sure of, she had been written off: a former teacher, down there at a former fruit farm. Now the tune began to be different; or did it not? The reader felt herself smile. Also, the expert in English professionally analysed this document – what a way to write, what garlands of affectation! Yet, to give him credit, this was quite a performance. This mannered manner of his was not quite the thing, no. Yet the ambiguities in themselves had one sort of merit, a sort of promise – one was at least on the verge of the Henry James country.

She turned the letter over and over throughout the day on which it arrived. When Eric came home, she turned it over to him. He ingested it slowly. 'Well,' he pronounced, 'here's a kettle of fish!'

She agreed. 'A bombshell.'

'Not to me,' he declared. 'I saw how the wind was blowing – you remember, I told you.'

'No, never, Eric. You never told me.'

'The other evening, here in this room. Or tried to, but then you became upset.'

'Oh, *then*? I thought you were angry with me.'

'Yes,' he said, 'that's what comes of trying to talk. Can anybody wonder I keep my mouth shut? Apart from that, though, couldn't you see for yourself?'

'That she hated me?'

'The conclusions you jump to! – and that's a wicked conclusion. There's no harm in Eva. Even what it says here –' he gave an emphatic shake to the blue pages – 'even what this says gives no ground for that. All this does is, bear out what I told you: she's disappointed. She's had her heart broken, here. Isn't that enough?'

'Enough, it seems, to have made a tremendous scene of,' meditated Iseult.

'Yes, scared the guts out of *him*,' said Eric with relish. 'She had to let off to someone – other than us.'

'Still, Eric . . . going behind our backs?'

'She had the right, if she wanted to: she's his business. Why shouldn't he do something – or would that kill him?'

'I've no idea,' said Iseult. 'Give me back his letter.' She smoothed it, it being the worse for mauling, folded it, slid it back in its envelope. She then put to Eric: 'What ought I to do?'

'As things are? What he says, I suppose: see him.'

She, fatefully, hesitated. '*You* think I ought to?'

'As things are.'

'I suppose you're right. Yes, I'm afraid you're right.'

'I do grant, Izzy, it's a good deal to ask. All that way to London, then also back again – that monotonous train journey twice over, *and* the time it takes. Not to speak of the worry. However. See he pays your expenses.'

'*Eric!*'

He stared.

She covered her eyes, despairing. 'Oh, Eric – *really*!'

Constantine's head was aureoled as he sat down again, repeating: 'Yes, this has been more than good of you.' At his back was a window: January sunshine came in, diffused by fibreglass curtains. This office of his had (at least from where Iseult sat) an extensive view of nothing: it was near to the top of one of those crops of skyscrapers which spring up in Knightsbridge overnight. It seemed like him to operate from this area.

The handshake done with, she settled down to facing him: aslant to evade the sun, knees crossed, handbag balanced on them. She inclined her head, but said nothing. Constantine, opening an onyx box, offered her an Egyptian cigarette; which, leaning across the ormolu writing-table between them, he lit for her. He then, flicking his lighter shut, uttered an initiatory sigh. On the table, in addition to the cigarette box, a matching ashtray and an object which probably was an intercom, sat a box file with TROUT: XIV written not only on the back but on top. This meeting across an idealized office desk gave the occasion, at least now, at the outset, the character of an interview. 'Fortunately,' he added, 'it is less cold today. Less bitingly cold, that is – or a little less so.'

Iseult took a sip at the cigarette, then rested it on the lip of the ashtray in order to draw off her right-hand glove. The gloves, fairly fine black suede, were not lost on Constantine: undoubtedly they were new. There had, then, been a moment to shop on the way here? A less wise woman would also have chanced a hat bar; Mrs Arble had kept her head and stuck to her sleek-feathered turban, which – dating back though it might be a year or two – still was in good shape (not many outings, probably?) and showcased the forehead loyally: nothing like an old friend.

'You're well, I hope?' he asked with renewed concern.

'Very. And you?'

'So-so. This is a treacherous time of year.'

'Though spring,' she suggested, 'is more treacherous, isn't it? In winter one at least knows what to expect.'

'How true. Yes, that is very true.'

'Though Eva,' she had to admit, 'has a quite bad cold.'

'You astound me – how did she manage that? She seemed very warmly wrapped up when she came here.'

'I imagine she caught it at the vicarage.'

'Vicarage?'

'There, they are six-a-penny.'

'*That* should keep her quiet, at least for a while. Which, under the circumstances – you'd agree? – is something.' He glanced at the file, then away from it. 'I hope, Mrs Arble, my letter was not a shock to you?'

'I hope,' she returned, 'her visit was not a shock to *you*?'

He looked out of the window behind him, over his shoulder. So great grew his interest in the empyrean that he shifted, even, some way round on his chair. So intent, so 'held' was his attitude that Iseult stared also, past him, through the synthetic gauze. A helicopter, a kite, a suicide leap? – she found no answer. He slewed suddenly round again, back: she was caught off guard. With no particular candour, their eyes met. 'Between ourselves . . .' he began.

On his left, the room had a second window. The man had in consequence two existences: one rather cloudy in silhouette, the other in clear relief, side-lit. This other Iseult examined, during an interim. The blond, massaged-looking flesh of Constantine's face seemed, like alabaster or indeed plastic, not quite opaque, having a pinkish underglow. It padded the bone-structure beneath it evenly – nowhere were there prominences or hollows or sags or ridges. The features, though cast in a shallow mould and severally unremarkable, almost anonymous, all the same were curiously distinct. What was strangest about them was, their relation to one another was for the greater part of the time unchanging: this was the least mobile face one might ever have seen. Now and then some few creases came into being, to supply their owner with such degree of expression as at that particular moment he chose to grant himself – or occasionally (though this was rarer) there was a calculated levitation of the eyebrows. Anything of that sort was, though, almost instantly wiped away.

Colour entered the picture, though used sparingly. Lips, for instance, were the naive fawn-pink of lips in a tinted drawing. Less perceptibly pencilled-in were the eyebrows, lashes, the exhausted pencil employed being gold-red. And the same tone reappeared in the hair; well nourished, though back from the forehead. And the eyes? These too were in the convention: a water-colourist's grey-blue. If they glinted beneath their lids, this appeared phenomenal. They were to see with, chiefly.

Why this shadowless face, with its lack of and almost disdain for accentuation, should strike one on the instant as being memorable; how, so unhaunted-looking, it none the less conveyed its power to haunt, it was hard to say. He would be fifty? He was in good condition. Celerity, though its use was indolent, characterized his movements. One *can* not so much look youthful as lack age – as time goes by, a frightening deficiency. Most of all, about this ever-freshness of Constantine's (what had it fed on: life-blood?) and his guard of blankness, there lurked, somewhere, youth's most dreadful residuum: youthful cruelty.

'Between ourselves –' he repeated.

'Yes?' she asked, ready.

He burst out: 'What a heredity!'

'That is, Eva's?'

'Alas, who else's? You were quite in the dark, as to that? You had no idea?'

'I should have been told, perhaps?'

'One hesitated.' He drew the box file towards him, spread a band on its top and pronounced: 'Poor Willy!'

'Nothing you say will upset me,' she said objectively.

'I'm sure not,' he agreed – in an equivocal tone.

She asked, edgily: 'Do I give that impression?'

'You give a delightful impression, dear Mrs Arble. But it's not a matter of that, it's a matter of time. – There's a good deal *here*,' he went on, pressing down on the file as one might on a tomb, 'that I don't see that you and I need go into. Everything has some bearing, of course, on the situation that's now confronting us; but if we went into everything, where should we be? Well into the middle of next week. And by then our bird might have flown. No, the situation itself is the urgent thing. Though far from being the first of this kind of crisis, it is *a* crisis.'

'Distinctly.'

He sighed, this time with appreciation. 'You are highly intelligent. Such an alleviation!' He slid the file away to his right, dismissing it. It struck her to wonder if he had been embezzling. She exclaimed: 'Yet how I've blundered, apparently!'

'Mrs Arble, in any dealings with Eva intelligence if anything is a handicap. You are speaking to one who knows: *I* have found it so – but that is a long history.'

'Then may I ask –?'

'Do!'

'What made you send her to me?'

37

'There was also your husband. – He's well, I hope?'

'Very, thank you.'

'Moreover, you – as I'm sure you know? – were the sole, one person out of heaven and earth with whom Eva then wanted to be. When heart-whole, she's difficult to oppose.' He uttered a third sigh, his weightiest. 'As indeed was Willy.'

Iseult leaned forward, scrutinizing the table; she followed a scroll of the inlay with her eye. 'There *are* characters it is impossible not to disappoint.'

'A Trout,' he said, 'of any kind, is a liability.'

'Yet you took Eva on?'

'That was the least one could do for Willy.' Turning, he addressed himself to the intercom: 'The car.' She started to pull on, stroke on, the right-hand glove. 'I am taking you somewhere quiet, but not bad,' he explained to her. 'I think you will like that.'

Change of scene was, thanks to the chauffeur-driven Daimler, a matter of minutes, glided through smoothly. Huge creamy porticoes, lit-up little luxury shops were registered by Iseult. Newsflashes from vendors' corners, orchidaceous flashes from florists' windows. 'Not bad,' suggested the thought-reader, 'being back in London?' She gave a sphinx smile. He pursued: ' "Once a Londoner, always a Londoner" – isn't it?'

She disobligingly said: 'I grew up in Reading.'

'You surprise me.'

Once again, she found on reaching their destination, he had thought of everything. The chaste smallish circular table awaiting them, chairs facing, was in this place the only one of its kind; and as such must have been specially designated by telephone. All other tables-for-two ran along banquettes, whose springiness, by tilting each couple inward, made for a divan-like intimacy. All, whether lovers or not, had the air of being so; nor to this did any seem to object. Their contentment was shocking to Constantine: he could barely look at them. This distaste of his for female propinquity, manifest now that they were in public, to an extent lowered her spirits. Further quenched by the costly duskiness of the restaurant, she could think of nothing to ask for but a Daiquiri – what that was, exactly, the exile could not recall. It was chargeable, in any event, to Eva. Near by, on some other expense account, something or other was being *flambé*: up leaped more flame as in went more brandy. She watched. He asked: 'You are interested in cooking?'

'I was thinking.'

'Ah,' said her host resignedly.

'What was her mother like?'

'Cissie? She was delightful.'

'Oh?'

'Yes, indeed – dear Cissie. Such enchantingly girlish ways, so charming so often. So deliciously' – his eye skated lifelessly over his guest – 'dressed, always. One was devoted to her.'

'She does not sound very like Eva.'

'Not superficially. – Yes, in her day Cissie played quite a part.'

'Such a disaster.'

'*Oh* . . . Mrs Arble?'

'Her death.'

'Ah, yes. Yes, indeed: poor Cissie. Such an unspeakable end, not a cinder left. – But just a minute: shall we order, perhaps?'

Their waiter eclipsed their table with two large menus. '*Ris de veau*,' Iseult declared, looking no further. Constantine winced: 'You are quite sure?' 'Quite.' 'Then by all means stick to your guns. *I*' – he erected his menu – 'must deliberate.' Iseult seized the occasion to snap open her handbag, take out the mirror and give herself a subtle, steadying look. 'All in order?' he asked, round the barricade.

Iseult kept her head again. 'Of course, Eva –'

'– Just a minute: you would not say "no" to oysters?'

'No.'

'*No?*' asked he, assuming a tragic air.

'I mean, no; I would not say "no".'

'Then there we see eye-to-eye.' The wine waiter came. Constantine, showing more emotion than usual, received the list from him. '*You*,' he informed Iseult, 'would say Chablis, probably?'

'Chablis,' she said accordingly.

'If you don't mind, I fancy we can do better.' So did the wine waiter, an old accomplice . . . The host, finally, polished his face with a hand and looked round the restaurant. He recalled himself, saying, 'You were saying?'

'Eva, of course, can't remember her?'

'Alas. Motherless from the cradle.'

'So I had thought. Yet – this you may not know, Mr Ormeau? – she maintains she remembers hearing her mother shriek.'

'Quite impossible.'

'One would prefer to think so.'

'Eva,' he said austerely, 'entertains many fantasies – as did Cissie. Fantasies, one could say fancies, were Cissie's undoing. The hold they gained! Till the sad day came when *off* Cissie rushed.'

'Mrs Trout . . . left?'

'Hopped it. Bolted. Don't tell me you didn't know?'

'Nobody told me.'

'You're neglecting your Daiquiri: wasn't quite what you wanted?' She gulped the Daiquiri. 'Yes, well there you are,' he continued. 'One fine day, out of the blue. One was quite stunned. There we were left, *bouches béantes*, Willy and I. And worse was to come.'

'The plane crash?'

'*Rather* more than she'd bargained for! And of all places, over the Andes; or rather, on to them. So feckless, so very characteristic. Wouldn't Paris have done?'

'For what?'

Constantine's face went puritan. 'For what she was up to. A skite with a paramour.'

Iseult winced, in her turn – what a vocabulary! 'What a disproportionate end, though. It seems unjust.'

'So unjust to Willy. Such a horrid telegram: he was most upset. What a time one had with him! This may not sound credible, but he wanted to go belting off to the funeral. One dared not take one's eye off him. Day and night, I remember, we played shove-halfpenny.'

'What was done with Eva?'

'There was a nurse of some sort. I believe, a Latvian.'

'Now there's no longer a Latvian, Mr Ormeau,' – Iseult looked searchingly at him – 'what do *we* do with Eva?'

'You keep to the point so wonderfully – what indeed?' He invoked Heaven. 'Such a case-history, the poor dear girl – as I said to you in the first place, such a heredity! Also, I hate to remind you but this is January: April is all but on us. Come April, you and I turn Eva loose on the world. Restraint ended, further control impossible. At large, with not an idea. That fabulous wealth – *she*, who has never owned anything but a Jaguar! At liberty. When one thinks, you know, it's unthinkable! Rack and ruin –'

He broke off, looking about him pettishly. (Their oysters?)

'Necessarily?' meditated Iseult. 'I wonder ... I don't think my husband, for one, would share your view. He thinks highly of Eva.'

'Yes, so she tells me.'

'She's not quite without ideas,' said Iseult, nettled.

'Such as they are, I fear, they resemble Cissie's.'

'But Mrs Trout was "delightful"?'

'But *not* normal. – But AHA!' exclaimed the transfigured man, giving a sort of muted bound in his chair, 'here we are, don't you see?' Advancing upon their table came hosts of oysters. Salivating, he had to compress his lips: he leaned back, dotingly watching the feast set down. 'Fewer than these – you agree? – would be worse than none ... Delightful she could be, could have been. One so wished that she should be. But possessive, vindictive? – frankly, she was maniacal. Willy she wore to a shadow. Such scenes ... However ...' He not only picked up his fork but described with it a mystical circle, exorcising any and all ill-will from the vicinity of the oysters. 'One should say grace; *I* feel one should say grace!'

'Unfortunately, I'm an agnostic.'

Iseult's enjoyment of her oysters was at once methodical and voluptuous. The very first she swallowed wrought a change in her. Greed softened and in a peculiar way spiritualized her abstruse beauty, with its touch of the schoolroom. Eating became her – more than once she had been fallen in love with over a meal. She gave herself up, untainted, to this truest sensuality that she knew. Her nonchalance with the menu had been a feint; or more, a prudishness as to her deeper nature – of which the revelation was so surprising, so at variance with the Iseult that had been, as to be first intriguing, then disturbing, then in itself seductive ... How she ate, Eric had ceased to notice; and Constantine did not care.

She drank less attentively: that he did note. It was in fact enraging to watch wine vanishing steadily from her glass, as it was doing, repeatedly thrown away on her. 'Not too bad?' he was compelled to ask, raising his own.

'No. – Are you French, Mr Ormeau?'

'That has been wondered.'

'By descent, I mean. *I* should more have said, Scandinavian.'
He looked piqued. She added: 'But for your name.'

'Ah – yes. "Young, stripling or little elm". Elmlet, or elmling.
How that made Willy laugh!'

'But you can't,' went on the emboldened woman, '*be* French.
You've no psychological sympathy with love.'

'You interest me.' He let his wandering fork tip at and wobble
an emptied shell. 'That would be your finding, would it?' He
watched the shell rock back into equilibrium. 'On what grounds?'

'The way you speak,' she cried. 'The judgements you pass! Mrs
Trout annoyed you: was she, perhaps, annoyed? "Not normal . . ."
She ran away with a lover; that's wrong, but not so very extraordinary. Rash, not monstrous. Who's to know what she felt? Not *you*,
Mr Ormeau. In condemning her you seem to me to know nothing
at all. She made a mistake, possibly: passion makes for mistakes –
one can throw one's life away.'

Constantine raised an eyebrow. He did so slowly – as slowly,
looking the speaker over. 'One does not know,' he said. 'Or, I do
not – you do, perhaps?' All her story, all that made her his creature,
was summoned up. A prolonged inhuman condolence was meted
out to her. 'Cissie,' he said, 'did not live to tell the tale.'

Iseult showed spirit. '*I* still think her unfortunate!'

'You take the noble view. But one misapprehension of yours I
must clear up. Cissie did not a thing she did out of love. Revenge,
purely – I am sorry to tell you.'

'I don't follow.'

'I don't wonder! Here, Mrs Arble, we enter the zone of fantasy.'

She looked suddenly, speculatively, at him across the table, then
looked away – embarked on a train of thought. A feather, loosening
from the turban, flirted with one of her cheekbones – Constantine
felt at liberty to look elsewhere. She tucked the feather away. A
minute went by. The mountain of cerebration then brought forth
what could have seemed a mouse. 'Who was the young man?'

'Giles-Georgie-Gerald. At this distance of time, I could hardly
tell you. *He* terminated, poor wretch.'

'Are you sure?'

'No survivors. – Why?'

'I don't mean that. I mean, are you sure he'd existed? Was he
ever met, was he seen? *He* was not a fiction?'

'Mrs Arble? I'm a little at sea.'

'I was thinking of Eva.'

'Very properly, yes. But in what connection?'

'Eva's engagement. Eva's unspecified bridegroom – *that* mystery.'

'Mystery,' he said agreeably, 'was the word for it.' But his mind was elsewhere. 'What are they doing, what on earth are they up to – or not up to?' He cast about him accusingly. 'I've never known them so slow here; it's getting scandalous. Or your *ris de veau*'s receiving special attention, do let us hope! . . . Yes, but of course, yes: Eva's romance.'

'You believe there was one?'

'A trifle dreamed-up, perhaps. If you wish to know who Mr X was, I cannot help you. Ask her.'

'But you're her guardian. *You* didn't.'

'One felt some delicacy.'

'Your approval was necessary, wasn't it? You gave it?'

'It never came to that point, as frankly one rather felt it might not. *Ah!*' Leaning back, unstrung, he watched the trolley's advance. Vibrations of heat invaded the table; covers were lifted – one disclosure being that Constantine was to partake of woodcock. 'I hope,' he said kindly, '*you* will have no regrets.'

They ate.

Iseult drew breath. Ominously, she touched her lips with her napkin – back to the chase? 'But you were quite involved in this, Mr Ormeau. Some castle you own, you promised her for the honeymoon.'

'Castles in the air, castles in the air: what harm? Not, of course, that this castle does not exist: anything but! It's, *I* think, pretty. At the far end of nowhere. It made a delightful school – a school, alas, in ways ahead of its time. (You would have been interested, I'm certain.) Since then, wasted: really almost a tragedy. And the rates, oh dear! It was Willy's most generous gift; and was – you will know this? – Eva's first *alma mater*. Can one wonder her fancy wove its way back?' He took in conviction with every mouthful of woodcock. 'Eva is chronically romantic; that, I need hardly tell you!' He repeated. 'Chronically romantic. So much so that to isolate *a* "romance" –'

'I did not. I'm asking about her "engagement". At the time, it did rather perturb me. She was under our roof.'

'So she was. But as one saw, it blew over.'

'It seemed to me symptomatic.'

'I'm sure, rightly – how very acute you are! Exactly what superseded it, one wonders? And what may not supersede *that*? One will have to watch. Mrs Arble, our responsibility does not end with April. Or so I feel.'

'Do you?'

'I do. We must face this: Eva's capacity for making trouble, attracting trouble, strewing trouble around her, is quite endless. She, er, begets trouble – a dreadful gift. And the more so for being inborn. You may not realize for how long and how painfully closely I've known that family. The Trouts have, one might say, a genius for unreality: even Willy was prone to morose distortions. Hysteria was, of course, the domain of Cissie. Your, er, generous defence of Cissie won't, I hope, entirely blind you to how much of what was least desirable in Cissie is in her daughter. Eva is *tacitly* hysterical. – Has Eva been truthful with you?'

'Not lately.'

'Yours is the paramount influence.'

'No longer.'

'She rebels against it, I grant – but that's proof, isn't it?' He paused. 'You and I, Mrs Arble, are wicked people. We know, at least, what the form is. You and I cut ice. We effect *something*, and – do you know? – it's not always quite for the worse. Don't blinker yourself.'

Iseult gave a dizzied touch to her turban. She leaned back from the table; her skin glistened. 'Airless in here – isn't it?'

'Probably – Mrs Arble, you *must keep* Eva!'

She mutinied. 'I am sorry, I have done all I can.'

He raised, then touched, a barely visible eyebrow. 'You would not be entirely single-handed. Not quite unaided.'

'You mean there's Eric?'

'Such a delightful certainty! But you and *I* should, probably, keep in touch. Closer in touch than hitherto. Er – collaborate.'

Iseult took stock of him anew. Mere misgivings gave place to incredulity: he did not seem possible – did not seem likely, even. Nothing authenticated him as a 'living' being. A figure cut from

44

some picture but now pasted on to a blank screen. To be with him was to be *in vacuo* also. She said to him: 'Do you know, Mr Ormeau, I have actually no idea what you do. What you actually *do*, I mean.'

'I import.'

'Oh, do you? – Or, where you live.'

'In an hotel, principally. – What can I next tempt you to? The *profiteroles* here are not always bad; they go down easily, which we may be glad of. Because, we must put our heads together before we part. Don't you think so? Begin to concoct something . . .'

· 5 ·

TWO SCHOOLS

Time, inside Eva's mind, lay about like various pieces of a fragmented picture. She remembered, that is to say, disjectedly. To reassemble the picture was impossible; too many of the pieces were lost, lacking. Yet, some of the pieces there were would group into patterns – patterns at least. Each pattern had a predominant colour; and each probably *had* meaning, though that she did not seek. Occupationally, this pattern-arriving-at was absorbing, as is a kindergarten game, and, like such a game, made sense in a way.

The day of Iseult's absence in London was passed by Eva, hazily, in this manner. At Larkins, the girl lay abed with her heavy cold. A slight feverish drowsiness ran the hours together. From noon on, she was alone in the house (Eric at work, the morning woman gone home) but for her bedfellow: this was a princely cold. Could it be a descendant of Mr Dancey's? One might hope so. Best of all, she was no longer at bay – for so long, that was, as the cold lasted. Also the cold set up a moratorium; during it, no decision had to be taken, or indeed could be ... And, how if Iseult should never return? Suppose she vanished? – women constantly did so. *Then*, it would be unnecessary to leave Larkins.

She felt entrenched by being in bed. 'Stay where you are,' had been the injunction (Eric's). Any show of solicitude was heart-warming. Seldom in anything but rude health, used to but scanty attention when she was otherwise, she had set store by the hourly cups of tea brought by the woman during the morning. The last remained at her bedside, a cherished memento, scum on its dregs. And there was, too, a cloudy tumbler of water. This afternoon she ate eucalyptus lozenges, exhumed by Eric from the back of a drawer. He had searched for but failed to find a thermometer. There had ended his doctoring, but for 'Keep warm!' She believed herself to be doing so. A once-hot rubber hot-water bottle drew comfort from her Viyella thigh. The window was bolted. An electric heater gave forth a smell of scorched dust and ate up oxygen. Over her pyjama jacket she wore an anorak.

The window looked north. Some time ago, the distances of the country had been thinly painted by sunshine, but that was over; earth and sky had now the same unluminous greyness – which must *be* daylight, for it was waning. Indoors, Larkins mustered its evening shadows. The triumphing calm of its emptiness could be felt: no person troubled that calm by seeing or hearing, thinking or knowing. Only the kitchen would be giving ear to the tip-tap of the drip from the sink tap hitting the upturned plastic bowl. Only the living-room knew of the slow combustion going on inside the banked-down fire. The motherly chair by the fire would be rejoicing in having no unmotherly occupant. Nobody was down there – nobody to object, nobody to wince. All day, there had been no one to suffer whitely. Up here, one could have been going all out on one's transistor, full blast. Or one could have roller-skated . . . One lay in languor.

The bedroom – which, though called Eva's, continued to be like a spare-room, generally empty, in which an overnight bag has been unpacked hastily – began to darken. Round her, her belongings faded from sight. She owned a couple of hair brushes with her father's monogram; a miniature model of a ship's compass; a jugful of coloured pencils; the claw of a greater eagle mounted in silver; a still-inviolate Elizabeth Arden Christmas casket (from Constantine); a clay cat and donkey, examples of Dancey art, and the transistor, cased in apparent ivory. This last, with a gleam like a forehead's, stood by her bed – at a moment, she was constrained to reach out and touch it. She received a shock: *ice*-cold, the thing had become! Angrily ice-cold, colder than anger. Eva drew back her frightened, rejected hand, rolled over and lay on top of it, to console it. The tide of the day turned, against it and her; down once again on her came the enormous sadness which had no origin that she knew of. She cowered away from it under tangled blankets.

What are you doing, Eva, lying in the dark?

Lying in the dark.

Supposing somebody came in softly, saying, 'How is my darling?'

She *had* heard somebody saying, 'How is my darling?' – but when? where? Some other child had been present, a very sick one: 'Darling.' Eva searched through her store of broken pieces of time, each one cut out more sharply by fever, looking for an answer. The voice had come in as a door opened – but what door? where?

That Eva had been to two schools was little known. She so seldom spoke of the first that she could be taken to have forgotten it. Even Iseult (then Smith) had, during the great research, uncovered practically nothing on that subject – she had perhaps not probed deeply enough? Before being sent to Lumleigh, where Miss Smith was, the girl had, for just less than a term, been one of the twenty guinea-pigs at the lakeside castle.

At that establishment, she was to be pointed out as the donor's daughter. Her father had bought the castle to give to Constantine, whose heart had then been set on founding an experimental school in which to install a friend of his as headmaster. The considerable cost of the enterprise had seemed slight to Willy, should this serve to keep Kenneth elsewhere. Inspirational Kenneth of the unclouded brow and Parthenon torso was on the way to becoming Willy's nightmare: two hundred miles out of town would be just the place for him. Kenneth together with Constantine had envisaged the school as in Surrey; but nothing doing. 'Take it or leave it,' said Willy (whose, after all, was the cheque book). 'Castle, or nothing.' Vainly Constantine froze. 'Nice lake,' had declared Willy, grinning like a dog, 'for water sports. Jolly surroundings, scenery, Nature, so on. Far from the madding crowd.' Though in the throes of a jealousy aggravated by chronic mistrust of Constantine, Willy was not unscrupulous – boys, he would not have signed over like this for a single instant; but in a mixed school could Kenneth get up to much? The mixedness of the school was the whole idea. Kenneth, combining vision with bashful hedging, went into the matter with Willy at large and at length. 'Co-education could have averted so many . . . tragedies.'

'You were not co-educated, I take it?'

'Alas,' sighed Kenneth, none the less looking wonderfully complacent, as well he might.

'Don't think me dense,' said Willy, 'but where do you plan to get these various kids from?'

'There will be only too little difficulty about *that*.'

'Aha. And from families who'll pay up? I'm not going to carry this thing, you know.'

'But *naturally* not!' cried Kenneth. 'What an idea!'

'Ken,' Constantine said to Willy, 'knows half the world – you don't seem to grasp.'

'One hopes,' confessed Kenneth, 'to cast one's net fairly wide. *Not* have distinctions of class –'

'– And then who'll pay up?'

'*Or* of race –'

'– Go to the British Council.'

'Sometimes,' Constantine said to Willy, 'you make me sick.'

'Why?' asked Willy, whitening. 'I'm sending Eva.'

So the girl went. Her goodbye to her father was stoic, as no doubt was Jepthah's daughter's. For the first time, she was to be exposed to her own kind: juveniles – a species known to her so far only in parks in the distance or hotels fleetingly. At the castle, inevitably, she did not shine. At fourteen Eva was showing no signs of puberty, which discouraged the matron or house mother, a Hungarian lady; and her negative emotional history made her unlikely material for Kenneth. Her companions supplied in abundance what Eva lacked; they were wealthy little delinquents who knew everything. One and all they'd sized Kenneth up at a glance and were matey in their manner to him accordingly. Exactly how he proposed to run this racket, it was going to interest them to see. Should he give trouble, they were prepared to blackmail him. Boys and girls alike, these children were veterans, some having run out on, others been run out by, a succession of optimistic schools. Bribed into coming here by distracted parents, they might stay on if that were made worthwhile.

A wish to have such children kept off one's hands and deterred from out-and-out criminality, with few questions asked and at almost any price, had been noted by Kenneth, with sympathy, in the course of his travels, and been had in mind when he conceived his school. This seemed the least he could do for so many people who had been wonderful to him – abroad, chiefly. Set though the sun might on the Union Jack, it remained under contract to golden islands, coasts, lakesides and terraced mountains re-empired by Kenneth's abounding friends, whose dominion extended from palm to pine. Only one shadow fell: parental dementia. Could a well-wisher not put things right? As for the children, here was where genius came in! With the young, he was almost psychically understanding – he'd been told so. He could do anything with them. Genuinely, he was certain he had a mission.

The castle turned out, after all, to be just the thing. Better than Surrey – Surrey might not have done. Here, one was virtually in outer space: in these woods, no one but poachers minding their own business and couples abed in the bracken. Live and let live. 'You were so *right*,' he wrote, in his generous way, to Willy. To be absolutely frank, one did not miss Constantine. Everyone here adored one, which was dizzying. There were dramas, naturally.

The school opened its doors one blazing September. Kenneth's haul of children were coloured only by having rushed about naked on private beaches – the race experiment having, so far, aborted. So had the one with class: young proletarians made one peevish by being difficult to get hold of – the State was too fussy about them, a real old auntie. One had to keep out of tangles, so far as might be. With that in view, the forewarned Kenneth had also had to look out about education. Once a school was got wind of, down came inspectors – one might not think so, but this was a fact of life. Kenneth was therefore assisted by two B.A.s with former teaching experience. He'd selected them carefully. This particular two were lucky to find themselves here or indeed anywhere, as he very nicely let them know that he knew. 'We're all re-born *here*!' he'd assured them, giving one then another vital hand-clasp and dividing between them one of his famous glances, at once frank and hush-hush. 'All the same, steady does it!' ... The B.A.s, whose frantic respectability fortunately fascinated the children, taught routine subjects, the more inspirational being reserved for Kenneth. The children had no objection to anybody's trying to teach them anything. They drifted amiably into the informal classrooms overlooking the water and sat waiting.

Of situations going on in the castle, still more of the castle's itself being a situation, Eva was unaware. She walked through everything, straight ahead, as a ghost is said to walk through walls. Perpetual changes of milieu attendant on being the Trout daughter had left her with no capacity to be homesick – for, sick for where? – and after life with distraught and high-voltage Willy all here seemed calm as the little lake. As for her comrades, she took them with equanimity. She was senior to any of them (in actual age) by a month or two; one of them was taller than she, the rest rather miniature: even the smallest seemed wondrously physically complete to Eva, who had been left unfinished. So these were humans, and this was what it was like being amongst them? Nothing hurt. From being with them, she for the first time began to have some idea what it was to be herself; but *that* did not hurt, so deep-seated was her acquiescence. She took for granted that these others had the blessing of being 'ordinary', which caused her to study one then another of them, for lengths of time, ruminatively rather than inquiringly, with her cartwheel eyes. She attempted to take in at least something of anything that was said. But one and all they affected her very little. She loved the castle.

She did not bring out the worst in the other children, who on the whole were nicer to her than nicer children probably might have been. 'Trout, are you a hermaphrodite?' one did ask.

'I don't know.'

'Joan of Arc's supposed to have been.'

'Never established,' one of the boys put in. 'How could it be? *Elle fut carbonisée.*'

'Then canonized,' said one of the other girls.

Eva pondered. 'I'd like to be Joan of Arc.'

'That's what we're asking,' said the first speaker. 'And *she* heard Voices.'

'I don't hear Voices – do I?'

'That's what we're asking.'

If Trout was wanting, only look at her father – imagine sinking one sou in a dump like this! What did he expect to get out of it: uranium? Or was he after the Kettle-drum (Kenneth)? Yet the children themselves found the dump rather *simpatico*: a novelty, abounding in unsophisticated pleasures, such as being on the roof in the dark harkening to the owls and answering back; or doing a Dracula up from balcony to balcony; or setting an Oedipus-trap for Tusks (one of the B.A.s; the other was Jones the Milk) by arranging an effigy of his mother in his bed; or insisting on the Kettle-drum's taking them all to church, twice a Sunday, to a distant edifice known as The Chapel in the Valley, which meant three taxis as overflows for the beach wagon, when *he* said he felt

51

nearer God in the open air or when contemplating some Greek object. What would the dump do when they all were gone? – fall down? Already the cellars were full of fungus, and you could chip bits off the ornamental stucco with a nail file.

Eva fell in love with the castle at first sight, in the shimmery amber weather of her arrival; but remained true to it when later autumn harshened the trees and dead leaves clotted and marred the lake – mist, those evenings, made a greater and wraithlike lake into which melted the lighted windows. No great gales, that year; only a soughing and undulation along the skylines and, at nights, a whimpering in the tortuous chimneys as though young lost souls had come into harbour. Winter, when it came, only tightened the place's hold on her heart. How the short days glistened in the transparent woods! Indoors, you might often hear the whir of a bird which had found its way into the heated rooms and was casting its shadowy wing span this way and that. The corridors and the staircase, lit from tea-time onward by hanging lanterns, became more friendly than any Eva had known – alone, she patrolled them: a by now almost effaced pattern was stencilled over their terracotta walls. Down the perspectives were many painted doors – some of them were unreal, they did not open. This hollow core of the castle was fanned through by a resinous smell of fir cones being consumed: in the grand saloon, a fire was kept burning at each end. In *there*, however, she did not often go, liking better to picture (or recollect) the gorgeousness being given by the flames to rush matting and scattered rattan furniture. The saloon was the common-room. It was seldom empty. She had not, strictly, any-where of her own.

To mark her status, the donor's daughter had been awarded an octagonal vaulted chamber with a balconied window and lake outlook, holding two beds only – the second was that of a fairylike little near-albino who had for some reason been christened Elsinore. This child's washed-out beauty gave her an air of age: she was eleven. Elsinore wrote and re-wrote the same long letter, which she read aloud, then tore up, then began again: fury made her still whiter as she worked away, denouncing her mother, deriding her stepfather, and praising love – she had been reft from the Japanese butler's son. Elsinore wept at nights, sometimes stormily, out of thwartedness, sometimes piteously, out of sensuous desolation. Her sobbing orchestrated her room-mate's dreams; and perhaps caused them? But towards dawn the Juliet ran out of tears, and slumbered grimly. Her silence would – then – wake Eva, who asked no better.

For, this was the hour. Through the curtainless window day stole in, fingering its way slowly, as though blindly, from thing to thing. Redness, though still like a watered ink, began to return to the top blanket, under which lay outlined her body. This redemption from darkness was for Eva, who had witnessed it nowhere else, a miracle inseparable from the castle. Her bed had its back to the window, but a looking-glass faced it – in that, she could see existence begin again. Seeing is believing: again, after the night of loss and estrangement, after the malicious lying of her misleading dreams in which she was no one, nowhere, she knew herself to be *here*. Here again was the castle, and she in it . . . At the beginning, when the sun still rose early, striking the lake, the lake had telegraphed brightness up to the ceiling – when a swan furrowed the water, a golden dance had gone on over the ribbings of the vaulting. Now, winter made the sun late for breakfast. But to unhasp the window and step out for so much as a minute on to the balcony launched into waking earthy air was enough to tell one that, behind the scene still dark as the darkest celluloid, day was about the place.

As would be the daffodils – 'You wait!' The many-ness and splendour of the forlorn castle's daffodils was a legend. Few looked upon them, but those few carried the tale. 'Round and round the pond, up the woods, down where there used to be that garden – everywhere! Year after year I think, "Well, I never!" and so will you do.' Mrs Stote, the prophetess, spearhead of the party of local women induced by Kenneth to come in, when they could manage to, and clean up a bit, let go of her polisher-mop to extend her arms, graphically, for Eva's benefit. 'Yellow as Technicolor! They'll surprise you – miss,' she added, as an afterthought. Mrs Stote spoke of Kenneth's little community as 'the school' to Kenneth only, and only out of civility. School, my eye! This was a Home, if ever she saw one, and moreover a Home for afflicted children. Nothing said or done by the inmates, consequently, caused her to turn a hair. There you were, you took the rough with the smooth. This big Eva seemed no worse than a little dull – now, why had *she* had to be put away? Anything you told her she took an interest in.

Mrs Stote had related to Eva the tense story of the herons being driven out by the swans, which meant bad luck, and of how the rooks had deserted, which meant worse. To which the girl had replied: 'There are still the owls.'

'*Ah.*'

Eva now asked: 'When are the daffodils: in April?'

'March, they come.'

'April,' said Eva, longing for a concession, 'is my birthday. April 21st.'

'They'll be dying down then.' Mrs Stote stooped to retrieve the mop.

'I wish I could imagine them,' said Eva.

'How can you expect to? – you've never seen them.'

'I've seen daffodils.'

'I daresay you may have.' Leaning her weight on the frail mop, Mrs Stote looked about, before going back into action, at the spaces of unpromising floor. 'But *these* you'd never believe in unless you saw them.'

'But,' Eva discovered, 'I *do* believe in them!'

Which was as well, for she never saw them.

Nor, by that March, was there anyone left to see them, other than Mrs Stote coming in to caretake the emptied premises. Long before daffodils came, the school was no more – gone, leaving no trace of itself but some wear-and-tear, sunbursts of colourwash and a shot or two at a mural, various installations, some not yet paid for, and one proof more (were that needed) of the unconquerable unluckiness of the castle. To start with, Elsinore walked into the lake – she did not drown, but on being pulled out went into convulsions. That sparked off other mishaps: waves of food-poisoning thought to be due to verdigris in the *batterie de cuisine* (copper, taken on with the castle); an attempt on the virtue of Jones the Milk by one of the girls; outbreaks of arson – nothing went very far – and two escapes (or, wayward departures). What was most distressing was, boredom began to set in – crises failed to amuse the children; they had plenty at home. They had relied on this castle to be respectable, and told Kenneth so – several spoke to him sharply. His rocket-like aesthetic evenings became damp squibs. In this humid, sunless, listless, rotty-smelling December, a further nightmare was the approach of Christmas – for which almost everybody was to remain here. Kenneth had thought of striking a pagan note, but under the circumstances would that do? . . . The police came; though only (so far) to check on bicycles. One had been stolen, or something.

Elsinore got no better. She withdrew into coma. Sickness not having been envisaged, there was no sickroom; she continued, therefore, to lie in her sad bed distant only from Eva's by the width of the window. Elsinore, destitute now of tears, had in her fragility and her piteous stillness the look of a thrown-out fledgling salvaged too late – eyes turned up under the purplish membrane of their faint lids, hair moistly wisped over the only just whiter pillow. Could she be dying? – the doctor finally sent for said so little. 'Such an unhealthy little thing, poor thing,' complained the Hungarian lady, angered. 'And as for you, Eva, where am I to put you? No other place at all, in this small castle.'

'Thank you, I'd rather stay with her.'

'It may be, she goes to hospital – but to hospital where? Oh, that stupid doctor!'

'Don't,' pleaded Eva, 'take her away!'

'Not that she is sick *badly*,' said the Hungarian lady. 'But all the same . . .' She sized up Eva, disparagingly. 'You are not nervous?'

'I am accustomed to her,' the dolt said.

'*You* must not touch her, Eva: you understand?'

Eva locked her hands together behind her back, in token of abstinence. She nodded.

'You call me – yes? – should there ever be anything. Though I am very busy. All this is terrible for Kenneth!' lamented the Hungarian lady (who *did* adore him). She rolled her lustrous, emotional, heartless eyes. 'He has this beautiful nature, so is imposed on. Never should he have been sent this unhealthy child, who also was trying to go to bed with a Japanese boy, I am sorry to say.'

'She wants her mother, I think.'

But nobody heard. The spike heels of the matron or house mother went clickety-click away down the sounding stairs.

So the watch began. No longer did mornings transform the room, a perpetual makeshift curtain having been thumb-tacked over the window, to hide the lake – now, only a lightening of the fabric on which stood out a cabalistic pattern spoke of the duration of the short spaces, too like one another to be days, between night and night: whatever the hour by the clock, nothing made the ceiling less of an umbrella-shaped canopy of shadows, which multiplied within it, as do cobwebs, as time went on – though, *did* time go on? The octagonal chamber, outlook gone from its window, seemed more locked-up round its consenting prisoners than if a key had been turned in the door, and, made medieval by the untimely dark, began in a cardboard way to belong to history. Though set in the middle of the castle, whose unreal noises could be heard, the place was as though levitated to a topmost turret. What made Eva visualize this as a marriage chamber? As its climate intensified, all grew tender. To repose a hand on the blanket covering Elsinore was to know in the palm of the hand a primitive tremor – imagining the beating of that other heart, she had a passionately solicitous sense of this other presence. Nothing forbad love. This deathly yet living stillness, together, of two beings, this unapartness, came to be the requital of all longing. An endless feeling of destiny filled the room.

There were few intruders. Back came the doctor, on guard, mistrustful, knowing more than he said. At irregular intervals the house mother, silently turbulent, 'saw to' Elsinore, or, hauling the child's head up, tried to pour consommé between the inert lips. Eva went downstairs only when, chancing to be remembered, she was sent for to go to a lesson or a meal. Sometimes, on such occasions, her place was taken by the boy who had pulled Elsinore out of the lake and been riddled by self-analysis ever since – 'She knew what she was doing, but did I? A reflex. It was disgusting. What fundamentally am I, a Boy Scout?'

'Oh, no,' Eva grew used to saying.

He then would gnaw at a thumbnail. 'Look what I've possibly done to her – she *may* live, you know! Look what she's done to me, though; jumping me into this. *Her* decision was rational, tiresome little thing . . . Look at her – Ophelia's illegit!'

'Oh, no.'

Often, however, leaning over the bed he not unkindly blew at a downy wisp of Elsinore's hair; whereat the child's head rolled, as though facelessly, his way. Then the afternoon came when he said to Eva: 'Her corrupt mother's been sent for; didn't you know?'

'No . . .'

'That's the buzz today. You never hear anything up here.'

With the coming-into-the-room of Elsinore's mother, all here ended. From that instant, down came oblivion – asbestos curtain. Whether Elsinore died or lived no one told Eva. Not told, she became unable to ask. Nor did she ask what ended the school in the castle so suddenly, so silently and so totally.

Several likely scandals Kenneth had kept at bay, but an unexpected one was the wrecker. 'One cannot,' he sobbed to Constantine over the telephone, 'think of everything!'

'One had better be able to, next time,' replied his sponsor.

'Such a stab-in-the-back!'

'Nobody's pinning anything on you, so far, are they?'

'Not so far as one knows; but one never does, does one? Everything's frightfully threatening. That filthy doctor –'

'Listen: post Eva home – first thing.'

'What's poor Willy going to think of us?'

'I'll square Willy. Then get the others out, while the going's good – it *is* still good, for a day or two? – Then you blow.'

'Mayn't that look rather fishy?'

'This is fishy.'

Eva, Willy considered, had had enough schooling for the time being. He took her to Mexico, where they were joined by Constantine; then, business calling him to the Far East, dropped her off with a Baptist missionary family in Hongkong, reclaimed her, left her in San Francisco with some relations of his chiropodist's, caused her to be flown to him in New York, flew her from thence to Hamburg, where he picked her up later and asked her if she would like to become a kennel-maid, decided it might be better for her to go to Paris and was about to arrange things on those lines when she said she would like to go to an English boarding-school: one for girls. Two years having elapsed, his daughter was on the eve of being sixteen.

'What d'you want to do that for?' he asked, though absently.

'I should like to learn.'

'Why didn't you think of that before?'

'I did, Father.'

'Then why didn't you say so? You're a bit old for that, now, I should have thought.'

'I *should* like to.'

'Then just as you like, dear girl,' sighed Willy, fondly and indeed

57

more than that – with a sort of wistful, spectral imitation of the far
more he would have liked to feel for her (and perhaps might have?).
The best he seemed able to do for her was, begrudge her nothing.
'I'll find out. That's to say, that shall be arranged.'

So it was; in the face of strong opposition. Willy had understood
that girls' schools would be looking about for girls, but far from it.
They fought like wildcats to keep his girl out. Lumleigh was the
first to weaken, so in he got her . . . Eva awoke one morning to find
herself in a white, airy dormitory.

This was a rainy, blowy, bright-green late spring. The girls wore
their regulation oilskins, yellow, going from class to class, for much
of the school went on in huts in the garden – enlightened huts,
consisting so largely of glass that in them you still felt outdoors, in
the gusts of petals from the new-planted cherry trees, cream, pink,
crimson. Eva's attention did not wander once a lesson began:
steadily, earnestly, emphatically, and so searchingly as to appear
reproachful, it remained focused on whichever of the teachers held
the floor. Some of them found it mesmeric. Miss Smith did not.

Supremacy set apart this wonderful teacher. She could have
taught anything. Her dark suit might have been the habit of an
Order. Erect against a window of tossing branches she stood move-
less, but for the occasional gesture of hand to forehead – then, the
bringing of the finger-tips to the brain seemed to complete an
electric circuit. Throughout a lesson, her voice held a reined-in
excitement – imparting knowledge, she conveyed its elatingness.
The intellectual beauty of her sentences was informed by a glow;
words she spoke sounded new-minted, unheard before. With her
patient, sometimes ironic insistence upon fact, as fact, went what
could be called her opposite capacity – that of releasing ideas, or
speculation, into unbounded flight.

Fearless of coming to an end, she allowed pauses, during which
she thought, or picked up a book and turned over a page abstractedly, almost idly. Meantime, there was suspense in the
glassed-in classroom; nobody stirred.

One afternoon – before, even, the rain had had time to cease –
the sun burst out, taking advantage of the recreational half-hour
following school tea. It (the sun) caught Eva halfway along one of
the brick paths intersecting the lawn. Then Miss Smith was beheld,
coming straight towards her in one of the school oilskins – which,

too capacious, enveloped her semi-transparently like a tent of yellow lit from within. The vision advanced on a shaft of light blinding to Eva. Instinctively making way, the girl side-stepped off the not narrow path. Her foot sank into the lawn with a deep squelch.

'That's not necessary!' called out the other.

'I'm sorry,' said Eva. She got back on to the path.

'I'm not royalty.'

'I could not,' Eva explained, 'see.'

'No – this *is* dazzling, all of a sudden!' Miss Smith, bringing to light two books which she'd been keeping for shelter, while yet the rain fell, under the oilskin, came to a standstill not far from Eva, casting round her a look at the brilliantly glistening grass and despoiled cherry trees quivering with prismatic drops. 'There should be a rainbow?' She threw a glance round the sky.

'No?' said Eva, sharing the disappointment.

'Are you in a hurry?' Miss Smith asked. (It had not seemed so.)

'I only was looking for a snail.'

'You collect them?'

'This was for nature-study.'

'It's not urgent?' Eva shook her head. 'I am glad we met, then. – How are you getting on?'

'I am trying to,' said the girl, with a touch of passion.

'You listen very intently. But I really wanted to know, are you glad you're here? – or does "here" seem strange, still?'

Eva examined the path's brickwork; then, down to its very roots, some near-by grass.

'Or perhaps that is rather a question?' asked Miss Smith.

'Anywhere –' Eva began. She began again: 'Anywhere would seem strange to me that did not.'

'Eva, do look at me! – not away.'

'The sun's in my eyes.'

'Yes, of course it is,' the other said quickly, penitent. 'Let's both go the way I'm going, shall we, then we shall both have the sun behind us.' So they began to. Ahead stood the pleasant house with nothing to hide: the original Lumleigh Court, now the school's headquarters. Towards it, ahead of the walkers went their two shadows: Eva saw nothing else. Miss Smith, too, saw them – 'Yes, we're like coming events! But,' she went on, 'what were you saying

59

before? Anywhere would seem strange to you that did not . . . what?'

'Seem strange.'

'That is a complicated thought.'

'To me,' said Eva, expanding, 'nowhere does not, by now – a little.' But then she thought of the castle. 'Or almost nowhere.'

'How *steamy* it all is, suddenly!' cried the other. Oppressed, stifled, she moved apart from Eva. 'Tropical. You've been in the tropics, have you? – I know you've travelled.' Sweat came out on her forehead. 'Will you hold these' – she thrust the books at the girl – 'and help me out of this?' She tugged at the oilskin. Eva, demented, clutching the books, one-handedly tugged at the oilskin also. Miss Smith got herself out of it, but let Eva carry it, saying: 'Thank you.' Adding: 'They're suffocating, those things. I'm better now.'

'Are you delicate, Miss Smith?'

'No; made of steel. Only, I'm claustrophobic.' She left the warning to sink in. They walked on. 'Why,' asked Miss Smith retrospectively, 'did you say, "by now"? I wonder whether that means that you've travelled too much? Satiation could give you that feeling of unreality.'

'Have I that feeling?'

'You've been trying to say so. You go everywhere with your father, somebody told us – there is only your father?'

'Only my father.'

'He must miss you,' speculated Miss Smith, gently.

Here came the nice house. And in a way already they were half into it – their shadows were entering the veranda, which had a tessellated pavement of red and slate-blue; for Lumleigh Court, though surrounded by the contemporary, was Victorian. The veranda, for a wonder, was empty – nobody there to perceive, by Eva's expression, that the world now came to an end. Or did it? 'We can go in through the dining-room,' said Miss Smith, addressing herself to a french window. Though you mustn't make a habit of this, Eva!'

'Am *I* coming in with you?'

'Aren't you?'

They went through the house to the library; *it* was empty. 'What are books for, I wonder?' mused the teacher of English. She replaced her two, then drew from their different shelves three others, which she'd made for unerringly. 'What they are not for is to be simply gazed at!' she told Eva; who, moving from section to section of the bookcases, was doing exactly that, though with steadfast awe. 'Do you ever read?'

'I am frightened to.'

'I see. Could you ever get over that?'

The girl took out a lovely morocco volume and nursed it, looking upon it sorrowfully. She said nothing.

'If you were read aloud to? Stories, at the beginning? Poetry? Shall we see what happens?'

'Miss Smith . . .?'

'I think we should try, don't you?'

'Miss Smith . . . how can you be so good to me?'

Then a girl came in. This first manifestation took place at five ten in the evening, by the library clock.

To anyone looking back (Eva never did) there could have seemed to be something occult about the pact entered into. Yet all belied this: the affable wide window, young May beech branches fanwise in country jugs, blond woodblock flooring solidly underfoot . . . Nothing hidden except what was in the books. Something disembodied Miss Smith; neither then nor later did Eva look upon her as beautiful or in any other way clad in physical being. Miss Smith's *noli-me-tangere* was unneeded in any dealings with Eva – who *could* have touched her? In fact, at that time, that particular spring at Lumleigh, the young teacher was in a state of grace, of illumined innocence, that went with the realization of her powers. They transcended her; they filled her with awe and wonder, and the awe and wonder gave her a kind of purity, such as one may see in a young artist. No idea that they could be power, with all that boded, had so far tainted or flawed them for her. About Iseult Smith, up to the time she encountered Eva and, though discontinuously, for some time after, there was something of Nature before the Fall. There was not yet harm in Iseult Smith – what first implanted it? Of Eva she was to ponder, later: 'She did not know what I was doing; but did I?'

The month of May ended by being summer. One of Eva's impediments was, any written work. 'Well, leave it!' Miss Smith decreed, sweeping it all away. 'That can come later. It panics you – doesn't it? – out of all proportion.'

'For ever leave it?' asked Eva dolefully.

'No, no – just till you're clearer.'

'My handwriting's clear, though?' the girl said, brightening.

'Copperplate! Who taught you?'

'Governesses.'

'I thought so. How many of them?'

'Many,' said Eva, after reflection. 'Whenever we came to a new place where we were to remain for more than some hours, my father would telephone down for one, doing so only later for a stenographer. He took care to.'

'What stupendous hotels.'

The Trout girl scented mockery. She went on defiantly: 'Yes, they could also obtain a horse for me, a masseur for my father's friend, a hypnotist to allow my father to sleep.' She capitulated. 'Is that *only* why I am extraordinary?'

'You're not. – I *should* like you to think, though. You have thoughts, I know, and sometimes they're rather startling, but they don't connect yet.'

'Are they startling?' asked the gratified owner.

'They startle you, don't they? – But try joining things together: this, then that, then the other. That's thinking; at least, that's beginning to think.'

Eva fitted her knuckles together. She frowned down at them. 'Then, what?'

'Then you go on.'

'Till when?'

'Till you've arrived at something. Or found something out, or shed light on something. Or come to some conclusion, rightly or wrongly. And then what? – then you begin again.'

'Why, however?' Eva asked, not unreasonably.

Miss Smith whirled her fingers over her forehead: a parody of despairingness. She laughed aloud, an abandon which was endearing. 'Honestly, how can I tell you? It's what is done, Eva. Try –'

– A clanging began.

'That,' Eva said sanctimoniously, 'is the chapel bell.'

She was all for observances. Also, the routine here acted as a conveyor-belt, smooth and ceaseless. High scholastic standards not only did not alarm her, she was fervently for them – latitude being allowed her on the grounds of her being partly foreign (this no one queried) and partly handicapped: in what particular or for what reason she was to be taken to be the latter was not gone into. Part of Lumleigh's good character was that it invariably made room for a 'case' or two – what could better have demonstrated the school's fearlessness? Eva was therefore assimilated, without surprise, by her good-mannered if not enthusiastic companions, whom she was slow to distinguish one from another. Floppy clean hair, smelling of the school shampoo, oblong wristwatches, Connemara pullovers and a habit of humming seemed to be universal. The pullovers seldom came off, for the girls were *frileuses* and this was an English summer – when they did come off, under them were striped shirts, all of them tailored to the same pattern. And under the shirts? – again, similarity.

The five co-existers with Eva in the white dormitory did what they could to put her into the picture. Guidance was offered, in sentences beginning, 'I shouldn't –' or 'I don't think if I were you –' Having done their utmost, they then went on as though (which they would have preferred) she were not there: not by *them*, for that reason, was it brought home to Eva, the monstrous heiress, that she was unable to speak – talk, be understood, converse. They were to be shaken by one discovery: this coaching Eva was having from Miss Smith? Crucial examinations now lay ahead for several of these girls, who worked till they squinted, but had one of them ever been singled out? As one, however, they put envy behind them. The sessions must, they decided, be therapeutic. But, Miss *Smith* . . . How far could compassion go?

That Eva also wondered – till slowly credulity overtook her. Then, through one after another midsummer night, daylight never quite gone from the firmament, cubicle curtains round her like white pillars, she was kept amazed and awake by joy. She saw (she thought) the aurora borealis. Love like a great moth circled her bed, then settled. Air came to her pillow from hayfields where, not alone, she had walked in a trance, or the smell of the rushy and minty and earthy wetness of moments at the fringe of the stream returned. The silence of buildings and of the garden was now and then disturbed by a sigh.

Her spirit struggled under this new belief, as though for breath – it was too much for her. 'I cannot!' she once cried out to the sleeping dormitory. By day, she went about haggardly. Her countenance with its look of subjection, bewilderment, fatalism, took on more and more the cast of her father's. The alteration in her came to be noted.

'I hear you look as though you had seen a ghost,' said Miss Smith one evening, examining Eva to see if this were so.

'Am I complained of?' the girl asked – for her, quickly. 'Would they send me away?'

'What should anyone send you away for?'

'What would *become* of me?' clamoured on Eva, senselessly.

Miss Smith, with the flat of her hand, made a to-and-fro movement to calm the air down. 'Everyone knows, and admires, how hard you're trying – indeed, *I* know! Only I know how hard. Perhaps, too hard? – I believe I am tired too. We mustn't exhaust one another, Eva.'

'I am so very sorry,' the girl said, though in a strangely remorseless tone.

'I don't think you really are; and neither am I.' Miss Smith leaned back, considered what she had said, but did not emend it. She sat at her table, on which stacks of exercise books supplicated, open, for attention – those topmost, exposing their lines of writing, were weighted into position by broken fragments of marble, from what tomb or temple? This being Miss Smith's one room, there was against one wall a divan on which it was to be taken that she slept. At the pillow end of it, crooked downward like an inquisitive stork, an Anglepoise lamp stood – not yet lit. Books were mustered in the low white shelves provided by the school: to whom or what they, the books, belonged was an open question. But for a cherry-coloured cardigan – which, tossed away, had fallen short of the divan on to the floor – and Miss Smith herself, little betrayed the fact that anybody inhabited this room. 'Are you coming nearer the surface, I wonder?' her voice asked. 'I want you to.'

'Yes. I am.'

'Yet there are sometimes times when I think you would rather go on being submerged. Sometimes you cling to being in deep water. What are you afraid of?'

Eva might have said: 'That at the end of it all you'll find out that I have nothing to declare.' She did not, of course – instead, she stooped (she was sitting on a windsor chair, by a window) and pulled off one of her mocassins. She began to pluck, with absolute concentration, at one of the beads embroidered on to the leather: this one was working loose on its thread.

'Where does that horror come from?' asked her teacher.

'Albuquerque. – You are dragging me up from the bottom of a lake, Miss Smith?'

'Nobody's "dragging" you. Come up of your own accord, or stay where you were.'

'I am very heavy, however,' the girl said, twisting hard at the bead.

'I shall fine you sixpence for each time you say "however"!'

'My father will have to send me more pocket-money!' The bead came away – for whichever reason, Eva gave a deep-in-the-thorax laugh. Then: 'What,' she asked, 'is the matter with "however"?'

'Oh, it's pompous, it's unnatural-sounding, it's wooden, it's deadly, it's hopeless, it's shutting-off – the way *you* use it! It's misbegotten!'

'Like I am,' pointed out Eva, manoeuvring her foot back into the mocassin. This, which took time, kept her face hidden. 'Why do you care for me?'

Miss Smith drew her chair closer in to her table. She lifted one of the chunks of marble, analysed one or two of the lines of writing, put the weight back. She gave half a smile and said: 'What a question!'

'One thing,' declared Eva, 'I *have* done.'

'Well – what?'

'Learned that religious poem.'

'*Religious* poem?'

'It is to God, I think.'

'Oh, one of the metaphysicals. Say it, then.'

Eva agonized. 'I don't know whether I can ... I shall say the end.'

'*Go* on,' said Iseult patiently.

'. . . But thou art Light . . .' began Eva –

'– But thou art Light, and darkness both together:
If that bee dark we can not see,
The sunn is darker than a Tree,
And thou more dark than either.

Yet Thou art not so dark, since I know this,
But that my darkness may touch thine,
And hope, that may teach it to shine,
Since Light thy Darkness is.

O lett my Soule, whose keyes I must deliver
Into the hands of senceless Dreames
Which know not thee, suck in thy beames
And wake with thee for ever.'

The anxious voice stopped.

'Yes,' said Miss Smith, noncommittally – tolerantly, if anything.
She looked about. 'How right for this time of day. I wonder . . .
Does it make sense to you, Eva?'

'What it says? Yes.'

'Curious that it should have caught your fancy. *I* like it. You see
how pure language can be? Not more than two syllables – are
there? – in any word.'

'I don't know,' admitted the helpless creature.

'Count, some time.' Miss Smith picked up a pencil and tested its
point, idly, on her thumb. 'It's a pity you began in the middle.
Still – thank you!'

'How,' Eva asked unforgivably, 'have I made you angry?'

'That's the last thing I am; but I *am* busy.' The teacher waved
round her demanding table.

'Why should I not understand that poem *now*?'

'Or indeed at any time? – All I do wish,' Miss Smith added,
lightly, so lightly that it became dismissingly, 'is that I understood
you.'

'*You* not understand me? – that cannot be possible. All that I
know of me I have learned from you. What can you imagine that I
would hide from you, *could* hide? What C A N you imagine?'

'Don't, don't, don't be so rowdy!' enjoined Miss Smith, in what
was, in reproving contrast to Eva's, an unaccented and extra low
tone. She nursed her forehead. 'No wonder we're both worn
down.'

'I am so sorry,' said the inflexible girl. 'But – you care for me?'

'As much as I can.'

'Then that is enough.' Eva rose from her chair to go. She stared
down the room. 'Don't you want your jersey,' she asked, 'that is on

the floor?' She edged past the table, retrieved the cardigan, brought it back as an offering. Miss Smith, shivering absently at the idea of needing it, slung it across herself, knotting the sleeves, 'And your lamp?' said Eva. 'Will you not soon need your lamp, that is by your . . . sofa?'

'*No*; I don't like anybody else carrying it about.'

Eva made for the door. Hand on the handle, she stopped, though not turning round. 'Do you know, I have never wept, never cried? Not once. Not as a child, even. I cannot. I am unable to, for some reason.'

'Have you wanted to?'

'Not till tonight. I am so happy.'

'Go downstairs quietly; other people are working.'

'This will not end, Miss Smith?'

The other, folding her arms under the knotted, dangling sleeves of the cardigan, obdurately and honestly said nothing. It could, too, be that a current had started up in her and already was racing her elsewhere.

'I am not mistaken,' said Eva, 'being so happy?'

'Time's very long,' answered Iseult Smith, whom it had not yet troubled. 'Very long, very dangerous – how can *I* tell you?' She looked past the chair left empty, out of the window: the garden chestnut trees, no longer in flower, were beginning to darken, with night, with summer. Trembling with her wish to work, she began to gather the stuff towards her. In a minute, she would be bringing herself her lamp. Gratitude to Eva for being gone, or all but, made Iseult Smith, for an instant, turn to the closing door a face already become unearthly. Before, quite shut, the door became part of the wall, Eva glimpsed that involuntary beauty.

Iseult Arble came back tired from London. Carrying nothing, she made her way from the train, along the platform, heavily and slowly, as though laden. Make-up staled and caked on her face by the long day gave her the feel of wearing her own death-mask. The feathered turban irked like an iron circlet. *There* stood Eric. 'Safe back?' – he did not stay for an answer. They got out of the station, into the Anglia. 'You know, you should rightly have stayed the night,' he told her, 'while you were about it, and done a show –

pity we never thought of that.' ' "Show"?' she said. 'Lunch was a show in itself.' 'He did you well, then?' 'Yes; oysters and so on – Eric, do you mind if I don't talk now?' 'All in, are you?' 'Well, *look* at me!' 'Can't see you, just at this minute.' (They sat side-by-side in the dark, rattling back to Larkins; he driving. Mist, at freezing-point, curdled under the headlights.) He added: 'That's always a nice hat, though.' 'Yes, you've liked it for years.' He grunted a laugh, then couldn't refrain from asking: 'Anything arranged – I mean, sorted out?' 'Eric, *do* you mind if I don't talk now?' 'Sorry . . .' He set the screen-wiper going.

They rattled onward.

She asked: 'How's Eva? – oh, no, you wouldn't know: you've been out all day.' 'No – in point of fact: having the car with me, when I got out from work I nipped back to Larkins, to have a look-see. She's getting on all right.' 'Sneezing? Playing her transistor?' 'Not that I know of, no. A bit drowsy; still got a touch of fever.' '*Fever*, Eric – how on earth would you know?'

Eric said: 'She was wandery in the head. There she was, lying all in the dark – then she made me jump. I went soft on opening the door, but she must have heard it; she shot up in the dark and what do you think she said? "How is my darling?"'

'That made you laugh?'

'No, not so specially. Should it?'

'I don't know.'

He manoeuvred the car over an icy patch, in silence.

Iseult, some minutes farther along, said: 'Strange.'

The car made its usual turn down the Larkins by-road. 'And so how,' asked Eric forgetfully, '*was* our Mr Sincerely-Ormeau?'

'Eric, do you mind if I *don't* talk now?'

'O.K.; but half the time you keep asking. Just as you like, though, Izzy – it's all the same to me.'

'Yes,' she said. 'Yes, I suppose it is.'

They reached Larkins, ran the car into the barn and let themselves into the house by the kitchen door. They listened. Tip-tap went the drip from the sink tap on to the upturned bowl. Otherwise, nothing. They went through to the foot of the stairs and listened again. 'Asleep, by now,' said Eric, 'I shouldn't wonder.'

'She *is* there, is she?'
'What are you talking about?'
'No; but she could be gone – could have got away.'
'You must be crazy, Izzy. The girl's ill.'

· 6 ·

SATURDAY AFTERNOON

'How should I sell a Jaguar?'

'How did you buy one?' asked Henry Dancey.

'Constantine did so for me.'

'Couldn't he hawk it round?'

'No – you stupid boy!'

The unruffled Henry went on: 'Then what about Mr Arble, his garage and all?'

'Not under *these* circumstances,' said Eva heavily.

At that, Henry's delicate features, which had hitherto had something of the remoteness of the Samurai, lit up. He indulged in a smile of slight speculation. All he remarked was: 'Well, I'm afraid you have rather come to the wrong shop.' He looked objectively round the vicarage drawing-room.

He and Eva were seated at either end of a long lean sofa draped in a cretonne cover, facing the fire – a captious February wind puffed smoke back again down the chimney. The room behind them showed signs of exhaustion, like Mrs Dancey; but also bespoke, by its very scars – tracks trodden like field-paths across the carpet, veneer chipped from furniture and the hard-used look of the cabinet wireless in the window – the inexhaustible energy of her brood. Mental avidity showed in cascades of books on the general table and tattered mountains of periodicals on chairs. It was a saying of Mrs Dancey's that she liked a room to look lived in, and this did. It also was unmistakably one of those homes there is no place like; and Henry in no way detracted from it pointing out that it offered no likely mart for a Jaguar.

The vicarage was, this Saturday afternoon, singularly silent – Mr Dancey upstairs constructing two sermons, Mrs Dancey gone into town with Louise to have the child's gumboil dealt with.

Catrina and Andrew had biked to a meet that morning and were not back yet. Henry, who weekly-boarded at the grammar school twenty miles away, enjoyed the prestige of a visitor during days at home: he preferred to do nothing and if possible go nowhere, and was allowed to. Eva's hopes of securing him should she happen into the vicarage on a Saturday were well founded.

'Though I daresay,' he decided, 'I could find out for you.'

'That was what I had thought,' said Eva in a self-congratulatory tone.

'I might even act for you. On commission, of course.'

'*What*, Henry?'

'That is the done thing. Anything else would be unheard of.'

'All right,' she grumbled.

Henry said briskly: 'You want Larkins kept in the dark about this transaction?'

'They know nothing of what I do!'

Henry looked sceptical.

She swept on: 'And must never, Henry – *never*!'

The boy took thought. 'What about your guardian? You were going to split to him – or Catrina thought so.'

'Never as to the Jaguar. Or, Henry, as to where I am going now.'

'As you don't know yet, you hardly could have.'

'Constantine, *above all*, must discover nothing. Is all this clear?'

'Fairly,' said Henry reluctantly.

'Can you not understand me? This is nobody's business – my own Jaguar.'

'Registered in your name: yes. That ought to be quite plain sailing. But shan't you miss it?'

'Yes!' cried out Eva. Thumping her chest with a fist, she rocked towards Henry. 'Goodbye to it is horrible anguish – no other ever will be the same.'

'Then, why?' asked Henry, in his logical fashion.

'Now I shall tell you –'

A virulent puff of smoke caused an interruption. Both coughed: Henry with some distinction, Eva rackingly and persistently. Experienced, Henry dug about in the sofa, extracted shreds of Kleenex from its interstices and handed them to Eva to mop her eyes with. Doing so, she told him: '*What* I shall tell you –'

'– I don't expect you need. You're doing a bunk?'

She was thunderstruck. 'That was extremely secret!'

'You shouted it at Catrina outside the post office, weeks ago. We've wondered why you're still here.'

'Oho – you wondered, you and Catrina? Thank you. There was first my cold, which became bronchitis (never a word from *you*, Henry!). Then, I thought. When I go, I must pay for somewhere to be – till I can, I cannot. Is that quite clear to you?'

'You mean to live on the proceeds from this Jaguar?'

'Only till April. Then ALL my money!'

'You'll be rather a millionairess,' said Henry slightingly. 'Can't you hold your horses till April?'

'My horses, Henry?'

'Stick it out at Larkins? They haven't eaten you so far. Feb., March, April . . .' He ticked them off on his fingers. 'Just look –' he directed Eva's attention to a scraggy quartet of purple crocuses which had managed to bloom from a bowlful of stones-and-water atop the wireless cabinet – 'spring's in the air!'

'*I* know what I am doing – you stupid boy!'

'If I'm stupid, why ask me to sell your Jaguar?'

'Because I have to obtain a house.'

'Oh. To reside in?'

'How should I obtain a house?'

'House agents. Where do you want it?'

'Wherever farthest from here. By the sea, I think?'

'You could hardly get farther away than that. We shall quite miss you.'

'Shall you? – oh, shall you really, Henry?' She gazed his way, monumentally shaken. 'You'll come and stay, however?'

'That may rather depend. – What size?'

'Of a size for me,' she said in her lordly way.

Willy-nilly, Henry was fired by the project. 'Then if I were you,' he exclaimed, 'I'd go all out! – a lounge-hall and a sun lounge and a swimming pool.'

Eva, on the other hand, sobered down. 'How am I to go there, without my Jaguar?'

'You go by train. Once you get there, you buy a bicycle . . . But stop a minute, what are we thinking of? There's that castle, that noble castle we all had a good look at – inhabit *that*!'

'No!' she thundered, banging her eyes shut.

'Just as you like,' said Henry – bored, remote again, looking the other way. He so far relented as to ask: 'Though, why not?'

'No "why"; simply because, *not*.'

'It might,' he conceded 'be dull there with no bridegroom.'
She said nothing.

'And, of course, it belongs to your wicked guardian.'

'They would know!' she cried, in great agitation, bumping up and down on a broken spring in the sofa. 'They would guess – they would go and look for me there.'

'You want,' he said, brightening up again, 'to elude pursuers?'

'You shall know where I am.'

'Thanks,' said Henry resignedly. He examined a point in the air (as it were, the future) from this then that angle. 'I am to cover your tracks?'

'That will be so kind of you.'

'– Psssssst!'

The injunction was hardly necessary. Echoes resounded round the hall. Battle was being given to the front door, which objected to opening on principle. The attackers won – Mrs Dancey and Louise triumphantly kicked off overshoes on the indoor doormat. Mrs Dancey's enthusiastic progress to the foot of the staircase could be followed: she shouted up: 'Alaric, we're back!' From above, silence. 'Louise was *very* brave! (Your father can't hear, I expect, because of the wind.)'

'What about my shilling?'

Now, Mrs Dancey addressed herself to the drawing-room door – ajar, as ever – though not as yet coming round it. 'Who's in here, I wonder?' she soliloquized. She liked to prolong suspense. Family life abounded in the unexpected, than which she valued nothing better. 'Henry, probably?' She entered. 'Yes, there you are, Henry. *And* Eva!' (Eva rose, and was kissed.) 'How very nice that you're here, but what sad news! – Henry, the fire doesn't seem very happy: you could have kept it up, dear?'

'It has not yet eaten what it was given, Mother.'

'No? Too damp, I'm afraid.'

Louise, who had followed her mother into the drawing-room, sucking away at the crater of her gumboil, argued: 'It can't be quite out; it's still busy smoking.'

'Never mind. – Has anyone put the kettle on?'

'Catrina,' complained her brother, 'seems to be still given over to blood sports.'

'Will you, then, Louise dear – if you're feeling able to? (She's been very brave.) – Eva, aren't our crocuses cheerful?'

'Yes,' Eva agreed. 'May I stay to tea?'

'We should not dream of letting you go! Particularly as I happen to know – as I know *you* know – that there isn't anybody at home at Larkins. Mrs Arble was on the bus with us, going in.'

'I thought,' said Henry, 'they had a car of sorts.'

'It is being decarbonized, I believe she told me. By chance, she was on the seat just in front of us, so we had a word or two – she was very friendly. But, Eva, this is the saddest news!'

'What?'

'Why, that you're going away! – Henry, did you hear? Eva's leaving Larkins. Almost any time, any day, Mrs Arble says. She and her husband are, naturally, so sorry.'

'*I* could have told you they knew,' said Henry to Eva. He and she exchanged an inimical glare.

'Henry's dazed,' said his mother.

'Anything but,' said Henry. 'What I can't see is, how anybody can be such a complete ostrich as some are.' He made it clear that this reference was to Eva – who, Amazon at bay, drawn up on the hearthrug, glowered in return.

'Dear Eva, *you* would rather have broken this news to us? What was I thinking of!' cried Mrs Dancey. 'Still, let's all sit down quietly, now, till the kettle boils.' Happy to act on her own suggestion, she dropped luxuriously into a declivity of the sofa. 'Come, Eva – come and be lazy too!' Eva complied: settling herself into place beside Mrs Dancey she stuck out her long, strong legs, in fancy stockings. Henry turned away and damningly left the drawing-room. From the grate, during a lull in the gusts, yellowish coal fumes twisted their way up. With shy suddenness, the mother said to the orphan: 'You won't be lonely, where you are going to?' The orphan went rigid all over. Mrs Dancey withdrew. She exclaimed: 'What pretty stockings, so scarlet! Someone knitted them for you?'

'Who should?'

'No, I suppose not. What a clever shop, then.'

'Mrs Dancey, I heard of cuckoos at school. *I* am like one?'

'No, no – except that they fly away. I have often wondered what it feels like being an only child; I have never been one and never had one – Catrina was only an "only" for such a short time. Do we sometimes seem stupid to you, Eva?'

'No.'

'So wrapped up in ourselves? You are so . . . independent.'

'Henry is independent.'

'Yes; and they all of them are, in their own ways. But that's somehow different. It must be strange, there being only oneself. Nobody with one, no one at all like one . . . How I wish I had more imagination! Yet now you're going away, it all seems too late – I shall always be sorry. Where *are* you going?'

'That is not yet decided.'

'I see. I shall pray for you, if you don't mind. And remember, won't you, that we love you here and here is always a home. You'll come back?'

Mrs Dancey, so saying, for the first time braved looking straight at Eva. The head of the one addressed hung down obliterated by hair. Out of the hair came a groan: 'But I lie to you!'

'By nature, you are as honest as the day!'

'But what becomes of anyone's nature, Mrs Dancey?'

Louise came in, saying saintedly: 'Tea's ready.'

'Dear, find Henry and tell him to tell Father. – Are the macaroons out?'

'Out of what?'

'Out of the bag. – We bought macaroons, Eva.'

'What am *I* to do?' wondered the wonder-child. 'I can't bite on anything yet, and that dentist said, particularly, for me not to drink anything hot.'

7

CATHAY

The house obtained by Eva, on North Foreland, was called Cathay. It had a lounge-hall and a sun lounge, though not a swimming pool. Built around 1908, it had been modernized in the earlier 1920s; the sun lounge, added by a voluptuary of the 1930s, had since been blown out by a bomb but made good as war damage. Cathay, to be let furnished, had for so long and for so long unavailingly been on house agents' books that it had by now faded from all but one of them. Only Denge & Donewell, a firm still modest, newly established, still on the hunt for business, had latterly charged themselves with Cathay – their now great emotion on getting rid of it would have roused misgivings in any client but Eva. From all she heard of it, Cathay sounded exactly what she was after. And, in a way, it was.

Eager to take up residence, she did so before anything could be reported about the Jaguar, which awaited developments in hiding in a lock-up round the corner from Henry's school. No acute crisis arose from this hanging-fire, £273 11s. 7d. having been discovered to be her bank balance, residuum of more than one quarter's unspent allowance. She sent the cheque for the one month's rent in advance, then drew out what remained in the bank in cash and brought it to Broadstairs on her person. She was met at the station by Mr Denge, small and, on this occasion, anxious. At three o'clock on a Tuesday afternoon in what now was March, not many passengers were alighting; from those there were, he picked Eva out by elimination. At the far end of the platform, against the sky, she stood in lonely importance. She wore the ocelot – yet somehow the cut of the jib of the massive coat made her less feline than paramilitary: she brought to mind Russian troops said to have passed through England in the later summer of 1914, leaving snow in the trains. Mr Denge, hat raised, moved in with caution. 'Miss Trout? Welcome!'

'Welcome,' said Eva absently. She was occupied in counting pieces of luggage – of the seven, one was a transformation suitcase and one a duffle-bag; the rest, corded bundles or mesh bags distended by objects wrapped up in newspaper. She had never transported luggage by train before. Her transistor she grasped along with the somewhat larger reptile handbag wondered at by Catrina. Mr Denge was in luck; he secured a porter; the three of them made their way to the firm's car, a conservative Rover, and loaded up. Mr Denge threw the car convulsively into gear. 'Must we go far?' asked his client, as they drove off.

'No distance!' sang out the professional optimist. 'You are not familiar with our part of the world, Miss Trout?'

'No. That is why.'

'*I* see,' he said, accustomed to doing so. 'You will find we are rich in associations, not to speak of celebrities past and present. Charles Dickens –'

'– Yes. Where do I buy a bicycle?'

'Now, immediately?'

'Yes.'

Mr Denge altered course. 'And, Miss Trout, groceries? This is your opportunity. I take it you *have* brought with you your plate and linen? As we pointed out in ours of the 23rd, those you provide. We trust that was understood?'

'No. What are they?'

'Ha-ha – sheets, and so on. Spoons and, ha-ha, forks.'

'How should I possess those?' asked Eva moodily. 'Must I buy them? Are they very expensive?'

'Not necess*a*rily. Had I foreseen, I'd have brought Mrs Denge along – had she been available. Tuesdays however are ladies' bridge afternoons; one of many social occasions in which you may find you would like to take part. Broadstairs is also animated in the evenings, more rather than less so out of season, when, less overrun by visitors, we are more exclusive. You will find in the better part of the town hotels with an international cuisine, not to speak of restaurants. Those, Mrs Denge and I and our little circle frequent, on occasions – that is, from time to time. Mrs Denge would, I think I can guarantee, be happy to introduce you, and not less, to assist you with any shopping . . . Meanwhile, just this and that, to carry you over? Miss Trout, though not having had instructions we took it upon ourselves to have gas re-connected, also the electricity. Water, needless to say. We took no steps, however, with regard to the telephone – that, *you* have to apply for.'

She flew into a panic. 'I WON'T have one!'

'*I* see.'

They obtained the bicycle (which Eva had roped, forthwith, to the back of the Rover), one pair of floral sheets and their pillow-cases, a tricolour bath towel, a spoon, a fork and a knife, such groceries as Mr Denge and his friend the grocer considered basic, a bottle of milk and a swiss roll. Mr Denge darted to and fro under Eva's feet. 'Any oranges, Miss Trout, apples, dates or bananas?'

'No. I have spent enough.'

'*I* see. In that case, nothing of any kind to, ha-ha, drink?'

Eva did not reply: she had crossed the street to examine a Mr Micawber cream-jug. 'Now,' she announced, looking round for her charioteer, 'I want to go home.'

'*Home?*' cried he, fearing all was lost.

'Where is my house?'

The Rover turned out of town. Their way, on the left palisaded by terrace houses, then trimmed by villas, on the right was accorded glimpses of sea. Mr Denge grew more tense as Cathay neared. 'You are going,' he said, summoning all he had, 'to be delighted. Cathay is a house of character.'

'Are there rats, mice?'

'We've had not a complaint on *that* score, I can assure you!'

'I understood they inhabited empty buildings.'

'You were quite misinformed. Are you nervous, Miss Trout – nervous of rodents?'

'No. I am fond of animals.'

'You have no dog?'

'No – but I might.' (Why not?)

'No friend like a dog. But professionally speaking I ought to warn you – they cause damage.'

They now entered a region of grass-verged roads with eroded surfaces, which gave the impression of being obfuscated. Nowhere was anybody about, or any other vehicle in motion. Though bald on its sea frontage, along the cliff-top, the promontory had inland an intense secretiveness, everything being sunk within bastion hedges impossible to see through or over. The forceful growth of the hedges had here and there burst open the wooden fencing beneath; and this same sappy-leafed evergreen which composed the hedges also bushed up gardens, smothering as it flourished. This was no arboretum: sycamores stunted and now leafless and birch strangled by ivy put up a losing fight. From amidst this rose semi-mansions; each with its balconies, mansards, gables and windowed turrets turned, like an ever-expectant sunflower, to the absent sun. All were silent, some shuttered, some boarded up. 'Many people,' said Mr Denge, 'are away.'

Though sunless, the sky was large with the light of spring. Gulls skimmed inland. The chalk-white lighthouse stood apart on a tumulus of its own.

The Rover wound down a road and bumped to a stop. Mr Denge got manfully out, heaved open a gate, got back and drove through on to an asphalt sweep. In the cracks of the asphalt persisted wintry weeds. This was Cathay: Eva lifted her eyes to it. Spacious, as promised, it was not yet falling down. Above a porch with deep ornamental eaves were leaded windows between exterior plumbing. 'We are now on the north side,' said Mr Denge. 'The more desirable rooms face the other way.' The derelict garden ran south also: the English Channel appeared in gashes, some of them largish, between back-views of dwellings edging the cliff. The sea was sheeny as steel today.

Eva, on the return from a swift reconnaissance, let Mr Denge let her into Cathay. He immediately plonked his hat down, in a proprietary manner she did not care for, on a refectory table – the first of Cathay's appointments to meet her eye. This interior, the entrance or lounge-hall, was a darkling salmon-pink where it was not beset by oak just too black to be old. Antlers and ironwork (candle brackets) studded the walls. One breathed a musty aroma – at once dear to her. 'Trifle stuffy in here?' murmured Mr Denge. He made free with one of the windows, throwing it open.

Eva could not, now, wait for him to be gone. Walking decidedly away from him, she set out on a tour of the reception rooms. These opened into each other, through flattened arches, and had many bay and some subsidiary windows, of which some were blotted out by the evergreen pressing congested foliage against their panes.

The sun lounge, plastered along the southern front of the dining-room, had been so very unfortunate in this matter that it now more resembled a charnel arbour: there was nothing to sit on in it, and no wonder. The double drawing-room was furnished: carpets and parquet were dotted with brocade-clad armchairs and sofas, trefoil-shaped tables and standard lamps with tiltedly-worn shades. You could see that everything had its history: chair-backs wore grease-darkened circles where heads had rested, and chair-arms, tables and flooring not only were mapped by wandering stains but abounded in small charred troughs burned by cigarettes ... In some other life, Eva had been shown a knocked-about doll's-house (had it not stood on a veranda, somewhere?) and knelt down to look deeply into its dramatic rooms. She had desired it. She was the more won over, consequently, by what was now round her – and the more elated. *This*, she possessed.

There was a *manoir*-style dining-room suite. The new proprietor worked on stuck sideboard drawers till they jerked open, corks rolling about inside them. The contents of the china closet were three odd saucers and four chipped cocktail glasses with crowing cocks on them. From the kitchen, Eva retreated: Mr Denge, last heard of dumping the luggage, had got in there and was trying out matches on gas appliances. Bangs resulted, one being a loud explosion – gun-shy, Eva made for the upper floor. Here were more bay windows, folded-up triple mirrors and stripped-down large beds still smelling of something. Mr Denge ran her down, finally, in a black-tiled bathroom she was admiring. 'All in excellent order, so far!' he was glad to report.

'Thank you,' Eva said unforthcomingly.

'Now I'm just running round making certain there are no air-locks.' He applied strength to a tarnished bath tap, which coughed twice then had a haemorrhage of dark-rusted water. 'That will *run* clean, in no time.'

'And also hot?'

'A little tiff with the heater – you may have heard me? – but I've got it alight. Now better left, I should say, to its own devices.'

'*I*, now, also,' pointed out Eva, 'should like that better.'

'Whereas the refrigerator, a later model –'

'– Thank you. I expect that you must be going?'

'Toilet in order?' He reached past Eva and gave a tug to a

chain. The resultant roar, cataclysmic, stampeded Eva, who pushed nay fought her way violently past him, shouting: 'This is enough! Go – go away at once! You take liberties!'

Mr Denge was no less outraged. He went crimson. What could or did she imagine, this she-Cossack? Cautionary stories raced through his brain. Fraught though his calling was with erotic risks, nothing had so far singled him out. A frame-up? Blackmail? This could be the end. This could be all round town. He should not have bought sheets with her without Mrs Denge. Mrs Denge was right – 'You never know,' she often was known to say. But at other times she was equally known to say: 'Whatever's the matter with you? – she can't eat you.' You could not win.

'You make too many noises in my house,' Eva, from a distance, deigned to explain.

'Just as you wish,' he stuttered, like a choked engine.

She indicated her one, imperative wish with a large gesture. 'Out!' it wordlessly said.

He put a finger in to loosen his collar. 'I had *been* intending to ask you: fuel?'

'No. Not now.'

'The heating-system requires –'

'– Have you set free my bicycle, my new bicycle?'

'Miss *Trout* . . .?'

'Have you untied my bicycle from your Rover?'

He stuffily said: 'It is in the hall.'

'Is there no garage for my bicycle?'

Mr Denge, in justifiable silence, brought out a key labelled 'Garage' and, at extreme arm's length, handed it over. Eva saw him off as far as the top of the stairs – bob, bob, bob went his head on its downward course. At the turn, he revengefully said: 'Well, *good* afternoon!'

'Stop! – one thing you must show me!'

'And what might that be?'

'How a kettle is boiled.'

There was no kettle. There was certainly one on the inventory, Mr Denge said, but by an oversight that was in his office. The kettle was in his office? No, the inventory – this would be seen tomorrow. Meanwhile, could Miss Trout make do with a saucepan?

'From that, how am I to learn how to boil a kettle?'

Once he was gone, Eva wheeled out the bicycle and rode figures-of-eight on the asphalt sweep. She experimented with the four-speed gear, tested the brakes and tried out the bell. This was a springlike evening, the dusk falling – when and if she took her thumb from the bell, birds, temporarily astounded, began to flute again. No other sound came from any part of the promontory . . . Becoming hungry, finally, she dismounted. Having installed the bicycle in its quarters – as new to it as hers, tonight, were going to be to her – she then homegoingly turned indoors.

The bay window at the seaward end of the drawing-room contained a love-seat – originally, a gilded one. Fetching provisions, she brought them to this camp. She drank milk out of one of the cocktail glasses and repeatedly brought the knife to bear on the swiss roll: still more, an abysmal contentment filled her. Day darkened over the Channel, the skyline vanished – then, at a moment, the window at the other end of the room sprang into diaphanous, distant illumination: street lamps along the twisted, bosky, misty and empty roads coming alight. The faint shape of the window, enmeshed in branches, was cast over far-away chairs and parquet.

Eva was glad, later, of this ghostly give-off from civilization, reflected likewise upon her staircase; for it, only, lighted her way to bed. She was able to find no switch that turned anything on.

Three mornings later, a letter dropped noisily into the wire letter-cage.

No letter could be from anybody but Henry . . .

Dear Eva,

  Not a nibble so far, I am sorry to tell you. But don't be alarmed, I shall get things moving. A rich widow is what I am looking out for, and I think a boy here has an aunt who is. But also how would it be if I advertised, in a cryptic way? If so, send me the cash, please. How long can you hold out? No hue and cry after you so far, from what I hear or rather from what I don't. I did not go home last week-end (a match, we won) but Mother said nothing when she wrote. If the police were digging for your bones in the Larkins garden, she would have told me.

How are you getting on in Old Cathay? Don't let Denge & Do-
theboys stick you with any extras. What make of bike did you go
for? I shall be interested to hear. No more now, but will write
when there is anything further to report.

Yours truly,
HENRY

Eva read this, then crammed it into a pocket. At the minute,
breakfast was what concerned her. Mr Denge, though preserving a
wounded silence, had sent out a kettle by special messenger; but no
instructions came with the kettle. Nor, for that matter, had she yet
had the nerve to try anything on with that angry gas-cooker. She
drank gulps of water straight from the tap, polished off remaining
digestive biscuits, then set off, as was becoming habitual, for
Broadstairs, cycling zigzag head-on into a Thanet gale. Over two
thick jerseys she wore her anorak. One of the mesh bags, empty,
lightheartedly flew from a handlebar – its return home would be
more sober than this.

In Broadstairs, she chose a picture postcard for Henry. It
depicted North Foreland (though where, alas, was Cathay?). She
wrote on it, stamped it, posted it. No sooner was it into the box
than a qualm seized her: how if this card fell into enemy hands?
What a give-away, what a clue to her whereabouts . . . Had she
but known, those had been already established – with little trouble.
In her precipitate flight from Larkins she had overlooked papers
wedged far back into her bedside drawer: these comprehended
drafts (in the hand of Henry) for the Eva side of the Eva-Denge
correspondence, including the 'clinching' letter, plus the ardent
replies of Denge & Donewell, headed, of course, by the firm's
address and particulars. Intermingled were various notes from
Henry on the subject of taking over 'the J.' and the basis on which
he was to receive commission when the J. should be, as was to be
hoped, disposed of . . . Iseult had gone straight to the drawer like a
hawk to water. What, if any, should be their course of action had
gone on being debated between the Arbles. Agreement had not
been reached. That had not prevented an action's being independ-
ently taken.

Today, Friday, on her return from Broadstairs some time in the
afternoon, Eva was greeted by Eric in the Cathay garden.

Now she owned it, the gate was let stand open. She'd come sailing in and was on the point of dismounting when he appeared round a boss of evergreen at the side of the house. She fell off the bicycle on to one foot; slowly, she disentangled the other before bringing herself again to look at him. She did so, this second time, with appalled credulity. A yellow sprig, *her* forsythia, was shamelessly in his buttonhole. He wore a check tweed jacket, the more jubilant of the two he had. 'Quite a nice bit of property,' he conceded, 'you've got here.'

She looked elsewhere.

'Not much of a welcome,' he said unreasonably.

Gripping the bicycle, she told him: 'You've come to take me away.'

'Take *you* away?' – really, he had to laugh! He came nearer, inspecting the gaping shopping-bag. 'What have you been buying up, half the town?'

'Milk, and . . .' She was overcome by amnesia. 'I don't know . . . How *can* you be here?'

'Can't you get milk delivered?'

'Where is, is, is – is Iseult?'

'Where should she be? – Can't we go on in, Eva? I've had this garden.'

'First I must put away my bicycle.'

He took part in the ceremony – not happily, for now it was that the useless void of this garage, nothing inside but a garden fork, tore a cry from him: '*Where's* the Jag? What's that little so-and-so done with it?'

'It is safely somewhere.'

'Much you care,' he said bitterly.

Eva flinched under that injustice. She answered nothing.

'You're funny in the people you trust,' he nagged.

They moved out of the garage, and Eva locked it. 'How did you come?' she asked.

'Drove: how else? For the better part of the last night.' At the thought, he yawned.

'*I* was obliged to come by expensive trains.'

'Hard luck,' said Eric sardonically.

'Then, where's the Anglia, Eric? I never saw it.'

'You weren't meant to. (It's round there, round the corner.)'

'Oho. If I saw it, I'd run away?'

'Well . . .'

She led the way back to the house, and into the hall. 'Look!' she invited; looking about, herself, with infatuation.

'Baronial,' said he, preoccupied – he threw an arm round Eva, pulled her to him and kissed her. Her cheek was wind-burned. 'No harm?' he asked, letting her go.

She showed no opinion, either way.

'Glad to see me?'

There was no saying, apparently.

'You dealt us a knock, you know. You gave us a fright.'

'*Now* come,' she said, in an almost siren tone, 'and look at the sea.'

'I've seen it.'

'See it out of a window.' She walked away through an archway, so he followed.

Eric took in the drawing-room, saying nothing. Its disreputability was what chiefly struck him. On top of that, the whole place was filmed with dust and, if not cold yet, made stale by used-up sunshine. Round the bay window were copious strewings of crumbs: at those, he could not restrain himself – 'You'll be bringing mice in.'

'"No," Mr Denge says.'

'He's the big noise round here?'

'He was noisy, but he is quite small, though.'

Talk ran out. Absently, to establish communication, he put a hand on Eva's anorak shoulder: they stood lined up, staring out to sea. 'Well, *I* don't know,' he decided after some minutes.

'Did, did, did – did Iseult send you?'

'No. My idea.'

'She'll wonder where you have gone to?'

'She knows – naturally.' He took his hand from the shoulder – but then seemed lost, dissatisfied and unanchored.

Eva, in an unlikely bout of perception, due perhaps to feeling herself a hostess, put forward: 'We might sit down?' There seeming little to choose between the large tarty chairs, he settled at random. Eva made for the love seat. Picking crumbs from the wicker, she began to brace herself for a question. 'How *did* you learn where I am?'

He told her. Eva was mortified. She exclaimed: 'Henry will say, "How stupid!"'

While hating to side with Henry, he rubbed salt in. 'You can't get a grip on things. *I* could have done the job for you, if you had to do it – I don't mind saying. Instead of which, you give me a slap in the face. There *I* was, you could always have come to me. There I was, all the time. – What was wrong with me?'

'Being my keeper.'

'I don't work for loonies – I've got better to do.'

'You married my keeper.'

'Look, leave Izzy out of this. I don't know what's gone wrong between you two, and I'm not asking. I could have cared for you – I *do* care for you, Eva!'

'I think,' she said – in extenuation – 'I had perhaps a peculiar upbringing.'

'Don't think I blame you; I'm only telling you.' To emphasize what he was saying, he turned full round at her – there she sat, twisted against the window, keeping fanatical watch on the Channel skyline. Uncomprehending? Dumb, anyway, as a rock. Over *his* nerves spread a kind of petrification. He rebelled, got up and strode across to her. 'You're my girl, you see – in a way. Or you could have been.'

'Never,' said Eva positively, 'have I been anyone's; so how could I be?'

'Come on. You were your father's – weren't you?'

'No. Always Constantine. Has, has, has – has she told him?'

'Where you've got to? Don't know – I couldn't tell you.'

'Oh, oh, oh.' She dragged a fist slowly across her eyes.

He thought up a remedy. 'Come on out!' he commanded.

'*Out* of my house?'

'We could go for a spin. It's as cold as the tomb in here!'

It had come to be – the sun had moved off. In the emptied chill, bronze radiators were mocking, inactive p   sences. The elaborated fireplace of the dual drawing-room sent out, only, a breath from soot which had sifted on to its hearth-stone, during how long a time, since when? '*How* you don't die . . .' he wondered. 'This is winter, to all intents and purposes.'

'Oh no: March. March is spring.'

'Isn't there anybody to fix things up, anybody in charge?'

'Mr Denge has gone,' Eva told him, with the utmost complacency. Her euphoria had for Eric, for the first time, almost an overlap of insanity. How she did live beat him – he shrank from asking; for how, and still more *where*, might not asking end? How had she fared, these three–four days; what had the hours done? She had found two primroses; they gazed at him from a cocktail glass on a window-sill. And a gull's bleached skull and some razor shells and some others, beach gleanings, were set out on one of the trefoil tables. And so what? A recidivist, Izzy said. He had started walking about, and he kept going – like a man kept living by being marched.

'Oh, very well,' Eva agreed, 'we will go out.' She stood up. 'Where?'

Eric consulted his wristwatch – his heart sank: still an hour to go! An hour to go till the hour anything opened: six o'clock. Till lately a fairly abstemious man, he was that no longer. Since Eva'd lit out of Larkins he had taken to putting it down steadily: all round, he was the worse. And the worst was now. That parting set-to with Izzy; that night-long drive; that wait in the garden; Cathay, Eva – all at once all that, everything, rose and hit him. He thirsted sorely. He craved, like an alcoholic. His need was whetted by the sight, through the arch to the dining-room, of a cellarette . . .

'You wouldn't,' he said, 'have anything in the house?'

' "Anything"?'

Making his right hand into a glass, he jerked an imaginary drink down: eloquent dumb-show. She caught on, but only to shake her head.

'That's that, then.'

'How should I know, Eric, that you were coming?'

'Don't ask *me*: *I* didn't know myself! Thought of it once or twice, then thought "Better not" – and I'm not so sure I was not right.' He blinked at her out of a haze of fatigue and doubt. 'But the trouble was –'

'Yes?' asked Eva attentively. To concentrate, she had brought herself face-to-face; and there stood, searching his eyes red-rimmed by want of sleep, the bouts in the pubs, the havoc wrought in him by the journey, with that mooselike fidelity known to Henry. 'Yes? – what was the trouble?'

'Don't keep on,' he said restively.

'But please, Eric!'

'*You* were; if you must know!'

'But that,' she declared with a sweeping superiority, 'was silly!'

Eric got hold of Eva by the pouchy front of her anorak and shook her. The easy articulation of her joints made this rewarding – her head rolled on her shoulders, her arms swung from them. Her teeth did not rattle, being firm in her gums, but coins and keys all over her clinked and jingled. Her hair flumped all ways like a fiddled-about-with mop. The crisis became an experiment: he ended by keeping her rocking, at slowing tempo, left-right, right-left, off one heel on to the other, meanwhile pursing his lips, as though whistling, and frowning speculatively. The experiment interested Eva also. Did it gratify her too much? – he let go abruptly. 'That's all,' he told her. 'But mind your own business, next time.'

'Yes. – What shall we do now?'

'Get the car and *go* for a blow. Why not?'

They sought the Anglia. Round the corner, it was run up on to a grass verge. 'Neighbours?' asked Eric, quizzing the hedges. She had no idea. 'If you have,' he reasoned, 'they're dead.' The Anglia, having gone through this enigmatic maze at an awed crawl, quickened on entering open air – passing the lighthouse, they swooped down the loops of the road to Kingsgate Bay. One grade above sea-level, two great white-painted lions outside a great white closed house looked across, watching the tide go out. Not a ship in sight – and the road, in the bright boundless chill of the salty evening, was vacant also. Even the wind had gone. The outgoing water sucked and dragged at the wetted edge of the beach, but you could not hear. – 'This where you found those shells, Eva?'

Some way ahead, to the east, like a kind of beacon, the Captain Digby crowned the sawn-off headland terminating the bay. Now, building and cliff were one in an hallucinatory afterglow: B–A–R was able to be deciphered. (*Half* an hour to go.) Eva, not aware of the Captain Digby, was trailing a look through the back window at what they were leaving behind them: Kingsgate Castle. The crenellated mock fortress, flint-hard in silhouette, rode forward over the waters towards France. She could by no means behold it often enough.

'You did not say much,' she observed, 'when we passed that castle.'

'In point of fact, I didn't say anything.'

'Why, though?'

'I was not sure what to. Didn't know how you felt about castles, these days.'

'Oh, because of my honeymoon?'

'More or less, yes.'

'But Eric, I made that up.'

'Oh, you did?' he remarked, somewhat unconcernedly. 'Try not to do that again, though; you had us worried.'

He had been slowing the car down; he now stopped it, got out and crossed the road to the railing overhanging the beach at no great height. Looking over, he examined the beach. What he saw – what perhaps he had hoped to see? – then sent him rapidly down some steps. There was driftwood lying . . . Eva came hard after him, shouting: '*Wha-at?*' He shouted back: 'This could make you a fire!' They started gathering. Once, straightening his back, Eric looked round him, getting the scene by heart. He and she were alone on the crescent beach but for gulls coming swinging in to see what went on. The eternal shingle skeined with eternal sand was strung and clotted with dunglike seaweed; bedrabbled seaweed slimed some exposed rocks proceeding outward like stepping-stones to nowhere. A last-summer's child's bottomless bucket, upturned, could have been jettisoned by expeditionaries from some other planet. A colourless haze was gathering out at sea. 'You know what?' he shouted, '*I* wonder you didn't pick on the moon!' No answer from Eva's foreshortened back-view. By the end, they had not done too badly. Opening the boot of the Anglia to stack the stuff in, he calculated: 'This should do for tonight.'

'For how long,' it struck her to wonder, 'is your holiday?'

'"Holiday"? – fancy your thinking that. No, one day is what I contracted out for, and that's this one – or was,' he said, looking round at the dusk.

By six o'clock they were far from the Captain Digby, careering inland over the darkening Thanet flats. Continuous nameless soil and vast lost sky engendered in Eric a wish for the bright lights: at their first stop, he accordingly sketched out their coming evening. He should like soon, he said, to eat somewhere posh – why not? Because, said Eva, that would be very expensive. And so what? – that was for him to say, he was taking her. ('And drink *that* up; or don't you know what it's for?' She'd been given a shandy; he stuck to beer – so far.) She said, there were two nice places down by the harbour: both gave large helpings, she went to them turnabouts. He dared say she did; but had he come all this way to eat fish and chips, did she think? He didn't mind telling her, he had not. This once, what was wrong with beating it up? What *had* she against the classier part of Broadstairs? She was not got up for it? Not exactly, perhaps . . .

'I by no means am,' said Eva, seizing on this.

'Still, what of it? They'll never see *us* again.' Eric, leaning sideways against the bar, prospected Eva from top to toe. 'Anyway, you'll do. You're a handsome girl – got a comb, though?'

He at last got to the bottom of her objection. All scenes of classier Broadstairs night life, noted for international cuisine, must be shunned by Eva. *There* might be Mr Denge.

'Well, that *is* silly.'

But could he shake her? No. So the harbour it had to be – after more stops.

They pushed their way, eventually, into the steamy café. Of the few tables, none was now quite empty: Eric and Eva got themselves on to bentwood chairs, facing each other, alongside another couple doing the same. She looked about, amicably. He picked up a bottle of sauce and stared hard at it. 'Well . . .' he said, noncommittally. The adjacent couple were eating, so said nothing. There was a hissing of urns, a sizzle of pans, a banging-about of crockery, with, as additional background, background music. 'Still – for the best, who knows?' he aloud reflected.

'What did you say, Eric?'

'I said: "Least said, soonest mended".'

'*What?*'

'What I'd been otherwise going to say to you –'

No good. Overheated in here, Eva was peeling down to one jersey. She flung discards behind her over the back of the chair.

8

MIDNIGHT AT LARKINS

Iseult flexed her fingers over the keyboard. She angled the lamp lower over the typewriter, to see more clearly what it was about to tell her, then set to:

'So he's gone. An hour ago? more, less? I didn't look at the clock. What does he tell himself he is going to do, argue her back? So he told me. He dissimulates all the time, most of all to himself. At all events, another page is turned over. I never believed for an instant this would not happen – yes, I *did*, I believed it would not happen. How inconceivable oneself is. One would say mad, but that I knew what I was doing. But to know what one is doing without caring, is that to know what one is doing? I murdered my life, and I defy anybody to defend me. I should hang for it.

'But at least I am living as no one else does, an existence without *fundamental* tedium. Money or not, we need not have had Eva here. I am glad we did. The antagonism she's sparked alive between him and me, for one thing. The passion I had for Eric was becoming less than a memory, now it's more than one. That kind of passion at its height can wipe out anything that's an obstacle. In this case, the obstacle was my life, as it was – and was to have been, and the "I" I had been. So . . . I did not implicate him in the crime; he was not aware of it, he would not have approved it. What he has had to do is, live with its outcome. I now see, he had wanted me as I was. He wanted me because I was *not* his kind. I was beautiful, the death of me dulled that out. I'd excited him because I seemed set apart. My bookishness and my being a teacher fascinated him like a Pythic mystery. Therefore, I murdered for nothing. Not so good.

'Eva then came along. Eva reappeared. From the moment of moving in she made herself felt – yet how? Under this roof she's gone steadily back, back, back till of even the Eva there was there is not a trace. Was that vengeance on her part? But what for? I am not loving by nature, she knew that – did she not? What I thought could be possible in her, I can't remember. What was I like at Lumleigh? I can only imagine, I wanted to see what I could do. Or wanted to see whether there could be anything I could *not* do? What I did do was reckon without Eva: her will, the patient, abiding, encircling will of a monster. I should have been warned. There were danger-signals. Her stepping out of my path, when the sun came out, in that subservient way. My breaking out into that sweat when we had to follow our joined-up shadows. Blind I was, not to see. She was as stuck in a groove on the subject of love as probably that other victim her father. I suspect victims; they win in the long run. She went on wanting to move in; in she moved. She took Larkins over. Those consuming eyes and that shoving Jaguar. Yet she has had her use. If Eric has now gone after her, I sent him. Eleven-forty. Twenty minutes to midnight. How far will he have got to? A long trail. "Only take care," I said, "not to fall asleep at the wheel."

'Eva's good at conspiracy, who'd have thought it? Living around with those two, she learned their ways. What an ambience to grow up in, a hated love. What isolation round them. Yet I think highly of Constantine, he's without false sympathies. Only now and then a crocodile tear. I doubt whether any cruelty is gratuitous, and certainly it's not expended for nothing – it constructs something. Evidently C. is a satisfied man. Evidently he was attached to that wretched Willy, evidently he understood him as no one else did. Attachment to prey I imagine must have about it some sort of equivalent of tenderness. I imagine Willy's capacity to suffer was inexhaustible: such a being probably can attach a tormentor to him more lastingly than most of us could attach a lover. Willy had that spectacular business acumen; is it possible that Constantine admired him? That could account for C.'s fidelity in cruelty. Willy from all they say had a large-sized temperament. A continent for a great part given over to marsh and jungle but with sources of wealth. Interesting, having the whole exposed to one. Rewarding. How do I know this? – because I know it. Blast Constantine for his insolence in that restaurant! Yet he saw me and used me as a confederate. He was not wrong to. I am *capable de tout*. I am soiled by living more than a thousand lives; I have lived through books. I have lived internally.

'Conspiracy, the air natural to her. At Lumleigh, she could make an encounter seem like an assignation. That simpleton Eric. Anyone could have told him. He is not indifferent to her, who says he is? *I'm* not indifferent to her, which is what is galling. For, for her I'm over, I'm a thing of the past, and what's that to Eva? Her dramatic orbs are turning another way. Or were. Now off she flies like a wee bird out of a window, and he goes after her. – I forgot, *I* sent him.

'Eva, Constantine. She behaves as though he petrified her, but I wonder. Exactly what did go on? No doubt she connects him with her father's suicide, and no doubt rightly. Yet I doubt that C. either meant to bring that about or envisaged such a catastrophe as possible. Scandal apart, the thing was against his interest. I should think he never foresaw there could be a snapping-point. One infinitesimal cruelty too many? Willy revolted – that, after all those years, must have jolted C. as much as anything else. What Willy did left nothing more to be said. In a way, a master-stroke. C. left shackled to Eva, that walking monument. How much she knows, how incriminating what she knows is without her knowing, how is he to find out? Tenterhooks. His shuffling of her off on to us, lock, stock and as near the barrel as could be, his incessant anxiety not to see her, to have as little to do with her as possible consistently with that awful legal relationship is accounted for. Distaste, fretfulness, boredom are all he *manifests*. But – ? She gets anything out of him that she wants, I've noticed. Jaguar, loan of the castle for that supposititious honeymoon, so on, so on. Now the end's in sight, though. He's about to be quit of her. April, the birthday girl takes over her all. Her fortune. Willy's mountainous money – no, I don't think, though I own that I once thought, that C. has been up to anything with *that*. C., it stands out a mile, was more than provided for. Yet no wonder one wondered – how uneasy he was! What would become of that money were Eva gone? She never will be, be certain. She is eternal.

'"Frankly", he kept beginning. In more than half a mind, each time, to *be* frank. Each time, abhorrence of me stopped him. All the same, across that insulting table what was going on was a sort of inverse courtship. He was wooing me to return his intense dislike;

his idea, perhaps, of coming to terms? Intimacy, of a kind? I was more his, actually, than he took account of. Read my mood he could not, but the fact was I'd have shrunk from no detail of his horrible life. There was nothing he could not have said to me or shown me. In effect I said so: a blunder, he is censorious. Yet that did not put the lid on it quite finally. He went on tantalizing himself with that word "frankly", then turning away, sucking those lips in. What was he hankering to come out with? That complacence with which he gourmandized wasn't genuine – very nearly, almost, but not quite.

'That was January, this is March. Not a word since, not a word thought necessary. I had my orders. That ghastly beauty of London. To what size do I go on blowing up that photograph? Imagining oneself to be remembering, more often than not one is imagining: Proust says so. (Or is it, imagining oneself to be imagining, one is remembering?) How I should like to play that scene over again: I should get a better grip on it next time. Now the situation's taken this further turn. Will he act on my letter telling him where she's gone to? Ought he not to? Ought I to egg him on to?

'What's it like at the sea? Fresh air, after the inland? Near where she is on the map are the Goodwin Sands, the mariners' peril. There's a German poem about them, a schoolroom poem likening them to a snake. *"Sie trieben sich langsam, satt und schwer wie eine Schlange, hin und her."* Similarities? Though I conclude she went there for no other reason than to be gone from here. So tomorrow (today, in a minute or two) what a surprise for Eva. Or may it not be? *Was* it by accident that she left those papers? Yes, I'm light-headed with anger, how should I not be? Come, Iseult! Come on, Iseult Smith – your gemlike flame! The horrible thing about intelligence is its uselessness. Will there be spray on the windows, will there be anything to eat? I ought not to say Eric dissimulates; more he tries to conceal his extreme honesty, knowing it to offend. "I ought to go," he told me, "I should go. I have got to go." Shining armour . . . *I* sent him? – let us be FRANK, like Constantine. I sent him by scepticism. "Do go," I said, unbelievingly lighting a cigarette. That did it.

'That exasperating drinking, I could not do with. – Time, now? Midnight, exactly midnight. The Equator. Tomorrow's today. We dawn on a better world, like a Chekhov ending. Dope. This could be the moment for *me* to go. This is a moment handed me on a plate. Yes, but the car's gone to the sea. No car: no matter, because I am not going. No intention of going. Here I stay, *ils ne passeront pas*. I married, this is my marriage. This is my crime, I intend living it out. I can't turn back, the path has grown to behind me. What was I once? – who cares. What can I never be again? Intact.

'Shall I go to bed? Touch is everything. Touch is a leech. Go up and lie by a cold pillow, hearing nobody breathing? Better keep on at this, these are words at least. Eric has a soul, I think? Yes, no query: Eric must have a soul. Shall I ring up the vicarage and ask what that is? What a flurry in the middle of the night, what a lot of sneezing. But shouldn't a parson answer a sick call?

'Eva is unable to weep, she told me.'

· 9 ·

A LATE CALL

Anybody looking in at a window – though who should? – would have seen how fire transformed the room, had he known it any other time. The piled-up driftwood now it had caught alight was burning ethereally, excitably, with a brandy bluishness. The fire was fed: as spar after spar fell in, incinerated and glowing, in were flung more. There was something devotional about this attendance upon the fire by the two persons crouched on the rug in front of it. They seemed unified, and not by their awe of the element and their task only. The zestful blaze, which was still so youthful that it illuminated rather than warmed the hearth, played on two primitive faces not far apart. Now and then hands collided, or shoulders touched.

The dimensions of everything had altered. Furniture, amorphous in the distance, was uncertainly lit by a standard lamp – which, off in a corner, out of the perpendicular, had the air of one street lamp surviving in a ghost city. A parcel shaped like a bottle was on a table. Stark night-filled windows served to mirror the room.

Not a curtain was drawn across, for not one would stir. Against this resistance, Eric had pitted himself in vain – the taffeta rotted by sea damp split at a touch, the runners were rusted on to the rail. The shortcoming had never affected Eva. 'But anybody,' he had objected, 'can see in.' She assured him, they had the promontory to themselves – and so it sounded; therefore he too forgot. The Cathay universe took the homecomers back again into its absolute, unassailable empty hush; which after the bedlam of the café smote upon them the more commandingly. Taken over by it, they kept their voices low. Stealthily they had carried the driftwood in, like two thieves carrying loot out. The bringing-into-existence of the fire had been gone through with, jointly, in fervent silence; what was burning now burned as softly as silk, with at the utmost a sigh, never a loud one. And a sigh, at last, emanated from Eric also, 'Do you know what? I wish I didn't have to go.' 'No,' agreed Eva, still more rebelliously. Once a car could be heard going slowly by, turning and coming past again, still questing; but it either found what it sought or went out of hearing. They less than listened. Between themselves and the roadway ran, like a fortification, the dense hedge.

Yet the car left a psychic wake. Eric remarked: 'In a way, I lied to you, Eva.'

Extending the palm of her right hand to be read by the flames, she leaned over the fate-lines in it uncomprehendingly. 'Yes?' she asked, with no great concern.

'I did come to fetch you away.'

'That I saw. I said so.'

'What about me, after all? At Larkins, the bottom's dropped out of the world. It's like nothing, nowadays.'

'Then *you*,' she said irrefutably, 'stay here.'

'Ha-ha – yes. Walk out on my job?'

'Here we could set up a garage. A splendid garage.'

'I hear you say so.'

'Or airfield, considering all my money. A charter airline.'

'What do you think I am?'

'Or helicopters even, for the time being.'

'Stop it, sweetheart – you're silly. You only hurt me.'

'What did you call me?'

'Sweetheart. We've had a good day, haven't we? A day in a million – wouldn't you say so?'

'Now,' she said, 'you desert me.'

At that, he was rent by a cavernous, groaning yawn, which finished its way out through him in a string of shudders – fatigue, rage, frustration, nervous despair. He was left as though he had vomited. 'I'm quite tired,' he vacantly told her. 'Imagine I'm looking forward to tonight, going on the road again? Look at last night. Keeping on keeping going, that gets on top of me. Who'd have thought it? – not what I was, I daresay. But that damned black desert everything is when you can't see it, that damned black desert. *And* alone again . . . You still wouldn't think of coming?'

'*Back?*'

97

'All I meant was, for the ride. No – you wouldn't do that?'

Eva only replied: 'You should sleep first.'

'What – here, you mean?'

'You would be wise to, Eric.'

'Forty winks, eh?' The temptation gained on him. A voluptuous stupor, like a fume through the brain, more than half overcame him – he battled, turning the matter over. 'I don't know . . .' he told Eva warily. 'You could be right. I expect I could use an hour.' Back came the shudders.

'I would wake you.'

'*I* wonder!'

'You say to me "Sweetheart", then don't trust me.'

'I wonder . . .' A twitch ran over his forehead. 'How late is it?'

'See,' said Eva impartially.

Steadying the wrist wearing the watch, he endeavoured to: spectral delusive firelight danced about in reflection over the watchglass. Eric had to lumber on to his feet and go away to the lamp to obtain a verdict – she watched even this degree of departure woundedly. 'Might be worse,' he reported. 'Just five to ten. O.K. then, Eva; you can give me an hour. To the minute – I *mean* an hour. Got that?'

'Give me your watch.'

'Where's yours?'

'It remained in the train.'

He wondered muzzily: 'Why d'you go taking it off?' He unstrapped his watch like a man already asleep – his captor came over and took it from him. 'Now, where?' he stood waiting to know. 'Up?'

'Yes. There are many beds.'

'One is going to do me. The first I come to.'

'Some you can't find, the rooms being in the dark.'

'Come on up with me, then – my girl. You had better show me.'

She was at a turn of the stairs, on her way down, when the bell rang. This could only be the front door's. Its hoarse rasp was totally unfamiliar: it had not occurred before, it had had no cause to. The bell sounded angered – no doubt by the assumption, indeed Eva's, that like almost all else in Cathay it was out of order. In return Cathay, long untroubled, was appalled by the bell – the

Stygian service quarters, most affected, went on as though stung by a hornet. Elsewhere, the baronial woodwork crepitated; vibration made any electric candles left in their sockets between the antlers appear to flicker, as might the genuine kind. The owner was no less outraged than was her property; halting, she looked down the stairs aggressively. This attack from the bell – but who had attacked the bell?

Mr Denge?

No – *his* methods were more circuitous; also would he not by this time of night be encompassed by Mrs Denge? A telegram? Day-and-night life with Willy had taught his daughter that telegrams detonated at any hour. If so, what sender? Henry, to say he had sold the Jaguar? Elsinore, saying she had not died? . . . Or was it the dead themselves who were at the door?

The bell, mind conscious of right, sounded again. It drilled deeper, this time. It intended never to cease.

To thwart it, Eva went down and opened the door.

'Good evening,' said Constantine, from the depths of the porch. On the gloom which consumed the gloom of his London overcoat his face hung like a phenomenon: subluminous. 'Some little delay? Your château is large, of course.'

'This was unexpected,' said Eva dauntingly.

'Rather late,' he agreed. 'But one saw you were still about.'

'*How* did you see?'

'Lights in your charming drawing-room. Might one come in? – it's draughty out here. I shan't keep you long.'

'How long have you been out there?'

'You have no sixth sense? If you don't mind, I should like to parley *in*doors. What do I want? – a word with you, just a word or two. Now come on, Eva, don't act the Iron Guard! Of course, a girl must be careful, all on her own. You are on your own?'

'Yes – Constantine.'

Eva stepped back; Constantine crossed the threshold. 'Yes . . .' he said, registering the interior. He investigated the refectory table, felted with dust – there, one did not put down one's hat. While he faced the problem, Eva snatched the hat and suspended it from an antler. And the same fate, he foresaw, was to be his overcoat's. Still (all things considered) wonderfully forbearing, he explained: 'I had trouble finding Cathay. My taxi driver maintained it did not exist, and one drew a blank wherever one stopped to ask. One can only think it has faded from human memory. – A *bois dormant*,' he added, though in parenthesis, as they approached the drawing-room. 'Otherwise, one had hoped to be with you earlier. A hurried bite at the Albion; one is staying there – unfortunately, less than a glimpse of Broadstairs. All really rather a rush, which does not agree with one.' He brought out a small Fabergé box and swallowed two pills. Eva watched the box back to his pocket; it had been Willy's.

'Still,' he said, 'here one *is*. Enter the Wicked Guardian. – May a chair be sat in?' No word. He sat down; Eva did not. Elbows spread-eagled slackly over the chair-arms, head back, lids lowered, he let a minute elapse: dosage being given a chance to begin to operate. His lack of objection to his surroundings, or at least his neutrality in regard to them – as in a ship's saloon or hotel lobby – made clear, they were much as he had envisaged. By so being they gave him, if anything, satisfaction. That 'Yes' of his, in the hall, was to be his exhaustive comment upon Cathay, whatever more of its marvels might be to follow – no further reaction must be expected or tribute wrung from him. His ostentatious unseeingness of her drawing-room could hardly more have roused the ire of Eva. She saw it as very much more than slighting: perverse, an evident policy, contrariety. And it occurred to her also that worse was possible – the room was *not* new to him, having been viewed already. 'Viewed'? Better to say, spied in upon!

Posted near his chair, she inquired: 'Are you deteriorating?'

'No, I am sorry to tell you – in what way could I?'

'*You* eat pills now.'

'Ah. But one always carried them, Eva, don't you remember?'

'Much fades from human memory. Not all, though.'

'True.' The minute now being over, Constantine unhooded his eyes at Eva and levered his torso into the upright. Instantly, his attitude had about it something judicial and puritanical. She was addressed by the Bench. 'Is it *your* aim to fade from human memory? From the way you've been going on, one supposes so.'

Eva ruminated. 'Oho,' she finally said.

'Your friends are more than concerned, they are distraught.'

Meritorious, she reminded him: 'I have soon been found.'

'Naturally,' he returned. 'As you always will be. To vanish takes what you have not got; so better put *that* illusion out of your head. However, that is beside the point – your whereabouts, at this time or any other, give far less cause for anxiety than your, er, state of mind: as to that, there *is* increasing alarm. And dreadful distress is felt, I need hardly tell you – what are you compelling us to begin to think? What conclusion may we not have to come to? Your behaviour's seldom been normal; that's been allowed for – we now face the possibility that it's something worse.' He paused. 'I am sorry, but there you are.'

'Are you so very sorry?'

Constantine laved his countenance with a hand. 'It's good of me,' he pointed out, 'to have come.'

'In the middle,' she asked indignantly, 'of the night?'

'To dry-nurse you is not my métier, at any hour. But crisis made this imperative – one had no choice.'

'Then how was it good of you? Crisis, what?'

'Are you aware that you cause uneasiness locally?' She looked blank. 'Round here,' he explained, with some patience. 'In this vicinity.'

'I do not.'

'That's what's come to my knowledge.'

'I do not. Only to Mr Denge.'

'Listen. Mrs Arble, seriously disturbed, was on the telephone to me this afternoon. She had just completed another long-distance call, the substance of which she relayed to me – one could hardly wonder. She got through, it seems, to the house agent named in the correspondence you left at Larkins, for the perfectly natural and simple reason that she wished to be certain you *had* arrived at Cathay. "Yes, indeed," she was told in what struck her as a peculiar tone. She went on to say, she trusted that all was well? The reply was so very evasive that, sensing trouble, she felt it devolvent upon her to know everything. She explained herself as *in loco parentis* to you – even so, she was met by an extreme caution, an, er, agitated professional discretion that hardly could, she says, have been more alarming. Largely from what was not said in so many words, she gathers that this agent has cause to doubt that you are fit to be tenant of any house, or should stay in this one unless under control. What, she asked, had given him that impression? He disclosed, under pressure from Mrs Arble, that a violent outbreak had caused him to flee the premises, into which you then barricaded yourself, *as* violently; that a messenger subsequently sent out by him with a kettle had turned tail, leaving the kettle to its face, on being grimaced at "hideously" from a window, and that no further sort or kind of communication has been had from you since; though sallies into Broadstairs, in incomplete control of a powerful bicycle, have been reported. Not the least of this unfortunate agent's fears are, that you may blow Cathay up by tampering with, er, intricate gas appliances, or burn the place down – he scented pyromania in your excitability when he struck matches. Nor, Mrs Arble inferred from a less-than-hint, was that the only mania he scented. – One does not know,' Constantine said distastefully. 'In short, his impression was . . . instability. He has since been – can one wonder? – consumed by worry, not knowing what to do or whom to contact. He confessed himself glad to be speaking with Mrs Arble.'

'Nice for her, also,' commented Eva – sole sign of having given ear to the recital. During it, she had gone away to the table which constituted her little marine museum; she now was pushing shells about, with a finger, into a pattern surrounding the gull's skull. 'And it is *today* she was anxious? *Today* she telephones? Oho.'

'Why "Oho"?'

'Because, "*Oho*".'

The shells and Eva were some way off to the right of Constantine, and not only that but slightly behind him: to keep her within direct range, as he required to, he had now to shift not only his own position but, he found, that of his chair. Some magisterial status seemed lost in consequence. The exertion, too, added petulance to his manner. 'Why,' he complained, 'have you turned against Mrs Arble? That, I asked you last time, in London: you would not answer. What have you got against her? What has she done?'

'I change,' said Eva, considering that enough.

'All at once, though, this insensate hostility!'

'Not all at once.'

'You are not – now – jealous of her, for any reason?'

'I change,' she repeated woodenly. 'May I not?' She swept the shell-pattern to pieces, forsook the table and walked back towards him, echoing: 'May I not?'

'But you, you see, change convulsively. Chaotically, without rhyme or reason – as no one else does, Eva; as no one else does. It's dismaying to watch. That in itself suggests some kind of . . . disorder. Constant in nothing?'

'In one thing I am,' she declared, looking straight at Constantine.

He gave an odd, gratified pout, then at once abolished it. 'But you must take care,' he put to her, extra softly, 'or how might this end? And we must take care of you. "Instability" is a kind word, as words go; one prays one may not be driven to any other. But people are harsh, Eva; other people are harsh. You know you will be conspicuous, with this money. The world will be only waiting for you to blunder, to crash, to be cast on its tender mercy. Watch yourself, I implore you. You cannot for ever stay as you are, locked up with your demented fantasies and invented memories, and not show it. And you do indeed show it. At every minute, you're giving yourself away . . . why so frightened, for instance, just now, when you came to the door?'

'I was not – was I?'

'Terror was written over you.'

'How was *I* to know it was just a murderer?'

'There you go,' he said – not wholly displeased, though.

'Also I was annoyed; that was *my* bell. That was all it was.'

'Unless it was guilty conscience?'

'*You let me* ALONE!' shouted Eva. '*I*'m not my father!'

'Thank God,' he mused, 'Willy's out of this. It would have killed him.'

'And let God alone!' – she added: 'I would advise you.'

'Perhaps you are right,' said Constantine. He cast about for some more biddable subject. 'Your delightful fire,' he mentioned, 'has gone out.'

An airstream still came from the hearth, the sea salt had left behind it a sweet acridity; but that was all, but for livid quivering ash across which had fallen a charred spar. The ecstatic blaze had fled back into the nothing that gave it being: it might never have been. Eva betrayed no feeling; she shrugged her shoulders – going across, she aimed one kick into the ashes' heart. Sparks answered, momentary crimson glints like suspicions, and those she studied. 'How,' she demanded, turning from them to Constantine, 'do *you* know this was a delightful fire?'

'Surely a fire is, at this time of year?'

'You're cold, I suppose?'

'One is stoical. Late-comers can't be choosers.'

'On the contrary, you came the hour you chose – the hour you like! The later the better, to torment in! *I* know your voice in the nights, keeping on, on, on. I have heard through walls.'

'You had curious dreams,' said Constantine.

'I did not,' said Eva.

An inevitable pause.

His hand by habit rose to his face – one more imaginary ablution? Not this time. His countenance needed nothing; it was at its best. It presented Eva with one of its masterpieces of non-expression – lightly sketched-in eyebrows at rest above lids at a heavy level, eyes unreflective as a waxwork's but less demarcated, hueless segments of glaze holding pinpoint pupils. And the lips, contrasting in their slight moistness with the matt finish of the surrounding flesh, were at rest also, lightly lying together as they might in a smile, though smile they did not. The now neutral shape of that deadly mouth was what held Eva's regard for longest. She had seen Constantine 'vanish' before now, but not 'at' her; the performance always had been for the benefit of Willy – who could act back in no way.

Not so his daughter. Conjuring from a pocket a voluminous Hongkong handkerchief, printed with dragons, she flagged it at Constantine, whipping the air between them, vociferating: 'Stop *that*! *I* won't have it!'

A slight smile formed.

'*Stop* that!'

'Willingly; but what? I'm altogether mystified.'

'No, you're not.'

'Negative,' mourned Constantine, 'after negative. One arrives nowhere: can you do no better? Some statement, Eva, really you do owe. One came to give you a hearing – you find that "torment"? One had hoped to know at least what you think you're doing – if, indeed, you have thought? For how long, and, if one may venture to ask you, for what reason do you propose to remain in a state of siege here? Is this, er, obsolescent pile to shelter you long? How soon, so far as this is foreseeable, is your next fugue liable to take place? Might one have some assurance, my dear good creature, that you're less, er, *adrift* than might have been feared? You may not be able to grasp this, but – one worries. We all worry.'

'*You* need not. I shall come for my money.'

He rapped out: 'And see that you do turn up!'

'Suppose,' she said, eyeing him, 'I was dead then?'

'Then, what a kettle of fish! And not a farthing for me in it – that you realize? As must be known to you, Eva, I had my cut.'

'Still, you'd prefer me dead,' decided the heiress. She was stuffing the handkerchief downward into the pocket. 'Silent for ever, in my tomb.'

'Ah, yes. Marble, ivy, an angel.'

'*I* was not joking.'

He retorted: 'Then you should see a doctor.' He'd had enough. She'd become infernal to him by not sitting down, by pacing about, by (to his eye) melodramatically standing. She now metamorphosed into an outsize ninepin more or less demanding to be knocked over. 'Or more precisely, be seen by one: a psychiatrist. Mrs Arble's right, I'm afraid: in her view, this should have been years ago. I admit, I've opposed the idea –'

'– I should talk to this doctor?'

'– I feared the disturbance, feared what it might precipitate. I had reason to – remember, I knew your mother. So I've hesitated; "treatment" can be so drastic. Was I mistaken? Now, I begin to wonder.'

'Mad would be probably better,' said Eva promptly. 'What the dead said sometimes is later listened to; but to what the mad have to say, who would ever listen? Better – for you.'

Constantine meditated. 'If they *could* dislodge that obsession, that one obsession!' He half-glanced over his shoulder, as it were to confer with someone behind him, or at least to share, so mitigate, his distress. 'One would wish to help you, Eva,' he said, returning. 'One would like to help you.'

Once more, she was not where she had been. 'Oh, yes?' she called back, careless and airy – elsewhere. By chance, a step or two off the hearthrug had carried her into sight of her reflection; across the room, in one of the windows. 'A handsome girl,' had said Eric. A handsome girl . . . There, indeed, was Eva! One felt reinforced. The Evas exchanged a nod, then stayed rapt in mutual contemplation. This could have lasted, how long? – had not Constantine, right out of the picture, come to what at least was a physical decision: with one of the co-ordinated movements he still commanded he extracted himself, in one, from the armchair and stood up. On the rebound, the chair lurched back on its casters over the bumpy parquet. Eva turned to see what was happening to her furniture. 'Going to go?' she asked, almost disappointedly.

'Thinking of going, yes.'

Deep in the thought, he did not yet act on it. His route out, through the arch to the hall, through the hall to the porch, waited; but was cold-shouldered. He steered a course, instead, southward, down the length of the room to its terminal – the bay window, now contained in the gloom which contained the Channel. Brought to a stop by the love seat, he there stood fixedly, gazing outward. 'Lights at sea,' he remarked. 'It's a pity,' he said, continuing to observe them, 'that things are going so badly between us, Eva. They need not have – we are unnecessarily lonely. There was a time when they did not. You won't remember, but as a child, once, you took me out for a walk with you in the snow. "*You* come," you said. In the Dolomites, was it? The edge of a village. The shades of night were, anyway, falling fast. It was evil snow, not deep but more coming down. Our tracks vanished. Any light we saw had as little to do with us as those lights out there. The whole thing was peculiar, all wraiths and spirals. You wore a hood. Suppose I had kidnapped you? – there've been odder stories. As it was, no story; simply, we had our walk.' He added: 'More has been buried than you know. Try not to malign me entirely, as you've come to do; it's rather a pity to. There might have been something to be said for me . . . I'll see you, then, April 21st?'

'Yes,' she said – inattentively.

He asked: 'Listening?'

But not to him. Activity had broken out on the floor above. Headlong stridings alternated with frantic pauses. Something – a shoe being put on? – was dropped, something shoved back, something knocked up against. All of this being magnified by the hollow desuetude of Cathay, there was nothing to do but hear: one had no alternative. Constantine underlined each thud by impersonating somebody hearing nothing: he continued his scrutiny of the Channel. Eva, demoralized, sucked her cheeks in. A door could be heard being bullied open. Short work was made of a corridor. A resounding sound of descent began on the stairs. – 'Ah,' sympathized Constantine, '*here* we come!' A silent countdown began. Eric then, as expected, entered the drawing-room. Still in some disarray, hair bent by the pillow, tie not more than slung on, he made straight for Eva, stating: 'You never woke me.'

'What time is it?' she wondered.

'For God's sake, that's what *I*'d like to know! For all I know, this could be Sunday week. You pouched my watch. No, you've let me down nicely! – sweetheart,' he added bitterly.

'*My* fault.' Constantine, turning round in his distant cavern, brought himself and his personality into prominence.

Shock foundered Eric, sent him silly all over – he recoiled exaggeratedly, laughing loudly. 'What, company? Then this is Sunday week, then?' His levity angered Eva. 'No,' she answered quellingly, 'only Constantine.' Her guardian, courteously coming forward, tendered: 'You may not remember me?'

'I can't say I saw you.'

'We met fleetingly. You looked in – I think, on your way out? – in the course of a visit I paid to Larkins. Such an enjoyable day: I hope all's still well there? Since, I've remained in contact with Mrs Arble; she and I have Eva in common. She's spoken of me?'

'From time to time,' said Eric, with marked reserve.

'You know, then, my, er, relation to Eva? – or say, my function?'

'You run her money. – What's happened? You haven't lost it?'

'My dear *sir*!' expostulated Constantine, entertained.

'Well, I couldn't think what else could have brought you down here all of a sudden like this, at this time of night, breaking in on Eva. She doesn't keep late hours.'

'No?' said Constantine. 'No,' he repeated pensively. 'But she stretches a point in favour of you or me. We're to be envied – but for one mishap: the fire's gone and gone out. See? I condole with you, as with Eva. Tragic, almost. Nothing but messy ashes.'

'Can you wonder,' said Eric, less as a query than in a generally condemnatory tone.

' "*Les plus belles choses ont le pire destin,*" you would mean to say?'

'Sorry, I'm not with you. – *I* must be going!' Eric now flung at Eva, who responded in no way. She was there, in so far as she had not budged; fatalism, made incomplete only by a leaden objection to what was happening, having, throughout the foregoing dialogue, rooted her where she had been at the start. Lack of pleasure in being a *casus belli* was apparent in every line of her hangdog attitude. She from time to time looked torpidly round her violated drawing-room. '*Eh?*' nagged Eric. Eva so far bestirred herself as to say to him, doubtfully: 'Really going?'

'Yes; and don't just stand there, give me that watch back! – or what have you done with it?'

She searched her person, with signs of wakening anxiety. 'I hope it's not stopped, Eric. I can't hear it.'

'It's not a grandfather clock!' When she brought it forth, he snatched at it, once more marched to the lamp with it. There his scowl unknotted. 'It's still today.'

'That *I* could have told you,' said Constantine. 'What a pity.'

'All the same, time I was on the road.'

'Quite my last wish,' sighed Constantine, watching Eric intently buckling the watch on, 'would be to drive you out. *I* was on the point of going, Eva can tell you. You consider my visit ill-timed? Well, so it's proved to be; but then, my dear, er, chap, how was one to know? What brought me down here, you ask? What brought you, I fancy: concern for this shocking girl. Need to find out how she *is*, after all her tricks. Too, too well, one discovers; better than she deserves. Seldom has she looked bonnier, has she, really? Indeed, transformed: when I first came in, just now, she quite took my breath away. Sea air suits her, one can only imagine. – Now don't hang your head, Eva, you modest violet!'

'Somewhat big for a violet,' was Eric's caustic remark. 'Can I drop *you* off anywhere?' he asked Constantine.

'That's extremely kind; but I have a taxi waiting.'

That did galvanize Eva. '*All* this time? That may be most expensive.'

'You may find it so,' answered the callous one. 'Well, one must be tearing oneself away. *You*' – the incredulous Constantine turned to Eric – 'are really doing so, also? Too bad, that seems. However, in that case we fare forth together; or do we not?'

'I don't mind,' Eric said – gone dead to it all. He spat into a hand and smarmed a side of his hair back. He squeezed his eyes shut, to store them up for the journey, then re-opened them to spare one hard look for Eva – who reacted by shifting her balance, discomposedly, from one to the other foot. All at once, he could play it. Bravado. Going over to Eva, he struck her, with titanic joviality, on the shoulder, a blow that could have felled an ox. 'So long! Take care of yourself! It's been nice seeing you!' He got himself from the room.

Constantine followed – having intoned: 'Then, April?'

Both were gone – as unforeseeably, barbarously, as they'd both come. Not a trace left, but for damage to Eva's frame, and, still there on its table, the wrappered bottle. *She* now yawned: so dismissive a yawn that it distended her rib-cage to cracking-point, just not dislocating her jaw by the grace of heaven. She checked on the silence, waiting another minute before going out to make fast the porch door. She then double-locked, grinding the key round twice. She waggled bolts into long-forgotten sockets, wheedled the ball end of the door-chain along its groove. Surveying her work as an absolute, she was not content yet – a barricade should have been added, had that been possible.

So far as she thought of anybody, she thought of Henry.

A SUMMER'S DAY

Iseult stood by herself in the Dickens room in Bleak House, Broadstairs – by herself, that was, but for the inhabitant. This was a June afternoon, that June. She had reasons for coming. She was in the course of translating a fresh French re-evaluation of Dickens, *Le Grand Histrionique*, which, she'd made known to Eva, had rather fired her. Less revolutionary than it had been said to be (who could be revolutionary, by this time?) the evaluation had sent her back to its subject: he did inflame her. She was now in a state of total immersion in his works, and letters. Great significance surrounded the Broadstairs period. 'As I *shall* be there,' she had written, to Cathay, 'and so, near you, could we not meet? Just as you like, of course.'

Eva'd raised no objection. She was to come for Iseult, here, and afterwards take her to North Foreland. This plan, engineered by the visitor, cut out what would have been the nerve-rackingness, all considered, of being met at the train, and, still better, ensured that the meeting, when it took place, did so in the presence of a third person (virtually). Iseult had brought in with her a jotting pad, some books, and a brochure acquired down in the hall; these she placed on a corner of the table and did not, after all, look at again. Nobody else, to her relief, entered the room or, so far as she could hear, the house – which, though posted up over the humming town and crowded sands, was filled by a disembodied, insipid silence.

This room was designated 'the study'. It showed no more signs of studiousness than does any in which maniacal creativity has gone on. It was small: a semicircle breaking out into a lantern window. No fireplace: heat generated itself? The window, seeming large out of all proportion, hung out into the air, straight over the sea but for a tiny apron of garden, and was filled inside by a platform on which table and chair stood – an arrangement, surely, very precarious, should the man, excited, suddenly shove his chair back? Surely the peril would be distracting? – sufferance of it did not seem workmanlike. As against that, the platform brought the top of the table level with the otherwise too high window-sill. So it cut both ways – if, indeed, it *had* ever been here in his day? Practically nothing now in the room had, all having been assembled by later piety. The chair was as verifiable as anything, having found its way here (let's hope, found its way *back* here) after an auction at Gad's Hill or somewhere else. This chair, very lately vacated, existed in a picture hung on the wall near it: 'The Empty Chair' – Gad's Hill, June 9th, 1870. The day of the death. A wooden (pearwood?) armchair, with carved back, wicker seat (damaged) and castered feet. A white rope was now, very properly, tied across it.

Sir Luke Fildes, one of the sought-after reproductions of whose painting this on the wall was, also gave authenticity to the table – apparently? This on the platform here was identical with the one in his picture. Its massive woodwork was dulled by just less than a century. Its leathered top (which was to be touched) was worn, blotched, scabbed and eroded; doubtless by sea air. Though, by what else? This was a table which had been written at.

You could edge round the table, at either corner, to see farther out of the lantern window. Iseult did so. In his day, all along the top of the cliffs between here and Kingsgate there had been growing corn. Corn, then, in the under-the-window triangle now garden. 'A ripple plays,' he wrote and she recollected, 'among the ripening corn upon the cliff, as if it were faintly trying from recollection to imitate the sea; and the world of butterflies hovering over the crop of radisheed are as restless in their little way as the gulls are in their larger manner when the wind blows. But the ocean lies winking in the sunlight like a drowsy lion – its glassy waters scarcely curve upon the shore –' And another letter: 'It is the brightest day you ever saw. The sun is sparkling on the water so that I can hardly bear to look at it.' And another, June letter – in here, framed on a wall: 'I am in a favourite house of mine, perched by itself on the top of a cliff with the green corn growing all about it and the larks singing invisibly all day long.' He liked corn young, he liked green corn.

So today was, but for the corn gone and the butterflies with it. Butterfly-like sails, however, danced out over the dazzling water. Scarlet, yellow – blue most of all prettily, in that they were a blue other than the sea's. Sun made them quiver like little flames. Were larks singing? – impossible to hear them. Iseult turned at that point, and went away into the next-door bedroom. She wanted to see what the waking eyes saw. These windows looked west, along Viking Bay. The sands, not quite obliterated by people who ran about them or lodged upon them like coloured beads, were tawny, deeper than coagulated honey. (Who wishes silver sands?) Donkeys did business, nimbling along jogging solemn riders. Topping the crescent of low cliffs, 'this pretty little semi-coloured sweep of houses tapering off from a wooden pier into a point in the sea . . .' In the early mornings, light would have lightly lain on them, making them pearls.

Yet *this* was in itself a forbidding house – in contrariety to what was all round it. Out of his own contrariety, he sought it. 'Tall, solitary,' it was later to be admitted by a biographer, 'the house in question is a square, sullen structure – hard and bleak.' One thought of it as beheld from; beheld, it was truly a Dark Tower. Fort House was, rightly, its name in his time – under that name it saw him out. The addition which blandified it into a mansion, trimmed round the skyline with crenellations, was yet to be – so, for many years, was the whimsy which then re-christened it. He knew himself to be living in *a* bleak house, for all the family fun and the summer gambols. 'Bleak house' escaped, disloyally, from his consciousness. It struck him then as excellent for a book title. *Bleak House*, with its genial Hertfordshire landscape, was gestated here. That was what got him out – not the German bands (as complained of) or meandering fiddles. Having done with *Copperfield*, 'I sit down between whiles to think of a new story, and, as it begins to grow, such a torment of desire to be anywhere else but where I am; and to be going I don't know where, I don't know why, takes hold of me that it is like being driven away.' So he was. So that was the end of this.

Horrible sea storms used to beat about. Seven miles out lay the Goodwin Sands. (Yes, the Goodwin Sands.) Weeks after a cattle ship came to grief, bloated animal carcases, many of them burst open by putrefaction, 'tumbled and beaten out of shape, and yet with a horrible sort of humanity about them' continued to be washed up on to Viking Bay. Flaubert, reflected Iseult, would have been interested. Henry James, less so. What, now one came to think of it, *had* James, that Dickens really had not? Or if he had, what did it amount to?

She returned to the study. Still empty, still not so much as a footfall. It now affected her like an all but bursting bubble of afternoon: radiant. She paused on its floor with a sense of being in beauty – and she was right. Her new dress was lovely: pinkish, diaphanous as the day demanded, becoming to the young woman she still was. Incongruous for a train outing? – for all its fragility, it was uncrushable (this science had done). Voluminous, it had the good sense to fall down severely round her in classic folds. The garb of a votaress, with a touch of the ball gown . . . On the wall near 'The Empty Chair' hung a small (rare) photograph of Miss Ternan, the inevitable eighteen-year-old, 'the young friend'. Iseult investigated the porcine smile, with its refined look of dreamy gluttedness. '*I* should have been old for him,' she thought. 'At any age, always – but what a pity.' She turned and looked into one of the showcases.

Early editions. Faint paperbacks set out in a grubby fan: *Bleak House* in shilling monthly parts. Others. All-in-all, what a literature – of what? Longing. The lyricism of forgetfulness. The nightmare of the frustrated passion. The jibbering self-mockery of the 'comic'. The abasements of love. The unplumbable panic of the lost man, the incurable damnation of the forsworn one. Helplessness. Hair fetichism. The turning of persons into pillars of salt. A bunch of roses despairingly cast on to a river, to be carried away. A sickening scene with a schoolmaster in a City churchyard. This was the man they lived for, the man they died with. Commemorated in ashtrays, cream-jugs. 'He took our nature upon him' – *no*, that was Christ. What a blasphemy; or rather, how nearly! An agnostic, she sometimes felt, had the worst of both worlds. A bust of the man – the confused, pouched, violent, raddled-looking face in its hirsute bedding, artistically distraught – stood on the showcase. Yes, histrionic certainly.

The glassy sea was soundless; but the sound from the sands was not altogether sealed off by the big window.

Still, nobody else visited the house – no one came in to look at the dead man's table. Outdoors, everyone was too happy. Out there it was too glorious, too fine!

The step at last to be heard was Eva's. Like many big-framed persons she trod other than heavily, though, like many disorganized ones, with deliberation. In this case, she either procrastinated or – thinking herself before time – dawdled, stopping to look in at other doors. Finally, she filled this door with herself in what was simply and plainly a cotton frock. Peonies were stamped over her, and a summer stand-in for the crocodile bag, plastic simulating white patent leather, was slung from a shoulder. All exposed parts of her were equally sunburned; her hair had bleached somewhat. Shod in red canvas beach shoes, she from toe to top was the local girl, enlarged – or could have been, but for being Eva. This was the first time Iseult had seen her since her accession: April 21st last. She looked well on it; *bien portante*, Constantine would have said.

It took Dickens to not be eclipsed by Eva. The girl had clearly come in with no such intent; on the contrary, deference gave her expression the glaze associated with school chapel, and she seemed uncertain whether, in these surroundings, to greet Iseult in a secular way or not. This nonplussed her – not too badly, perhaps.

'Well!' exclaimed Iseult, kissing her hastily.

'Did you have a good journey on that train?'

'Very. Then I found my way here.'

'I *would* have met you.'

'I know, Eva; but I liked this better. I wouldn't for anything have missed this place; it is so . . . extraordinary. So gimcrack, so ghastlily cheery, so hand-to-mouth, so desperately inordinate, so unscrupulous, so tawdry – so formidable. Genius: only just not a cheat – isn't it?'

'What a lot you have thought.'

'I had just time to. – *You* found your way here?'

'I come in here when it rains.' Eva turned to the wall and addressed herself to 'The Empty Chair'. '*I*,' she said, 'have sat in that.' She turned to check on the chair on the platform.

'You had no business to!'

'One can untie the cord, then tie it again.'

'Are you glad to see me?'

It appeared to Eva, everyone asked that. 'Yes,' she said compliantly. 'Why have you come, though?'

Iseult, for emphasis, disregardingly smote the top of the chair. 'Eva, you can't not know why I am here! To *see* you and thank you. Writing's hopelessly distant. That letter I wrote – we both know? – was feeble; I don't think I tried to make it anything else. To be so completely *bouleversée* made me half angry; that may have come out, perhaps? I can't imagine anything more unforeseeable than what you've done, or – and this I hope you realize? – less *required*, in any possible way. As you must know, after you'd left Larkins and we'd had to face it you wouldn't be coming back, Constantine wound up everything, more than fairly. "Compensation", he called it. We had nothing whatsoever to complain of. We thought no more – why should we? But then, this . . . this almost blow you've dealt us of generosity. Ought you to have? Should you have been allowed to?'

'That,' declared Eva, 'was not, now, for anybody but me to say.'

'Are we wrong, I wonder, to take advantage of that?'

'*I* wished,' said the girl, 'to make compensation.' Hands locked behind her, she leaned up against the showcase, wobbling its ornament.

'But, Eva: what Constantine paid us off with was your money – his last act on your behalf, before handing over. "Compensation"? What further kind can you mean? Or I mean, for what?'

'There was some damage,' the girl pronounced, after one of her ruminative pauses. 'My cheque was to *you*, Iseult.'

The other wheedled her hair back from her forehead. 'But such a sum. Such an enormous sum, you know!'

'I know,' the donor agreed, with a certain glumness.

'I'm glad you say that!' cried out Mrs Arble, as exultingly, as impulsively, as Miss Smith might have. 'If you'd said, "Not to me," I think I'd have wanted to send the cheque back – or wanted to want to. Not that I could, now; I've paid it in.'

'I saw,' said Eva. 'So what now are you asking me all these things for?'

'You may well ask,' admitted Iseult.

'So . . .' said Eva conclusively.

'Eva, *Eva*, though: there were faults on both sides, which means I daren't think how many there were on mine. That damage, can one assess in money? Out of the question! Which is fortunate,' laughed Iseult, 'or where might *I* not be? Can't we, you don't think, ever begin again? I'd be happier if that money could be a present – do understand! – a present purely and simply. A considerate thought. A generous gesture – anything!' Iseult laughed again, extravagantly. 'A *pourboire!*'

'A *pourboire*,' said Eva, 'is a tip in a restaurant.'

'Yes, I see,' said Iseult, with no particular inflection. She bowed her head, acceptingly, then folded her arms, consoling the elbows. She slid a look under her eyelids from chair to table. '*Here's* an authority, anyhow,' she gave out, to herself not Eva. 'Who knew better what one can come to, or be brought to? Not one bad passion got through his net – not a sliver of grudge, not a minnow of resentment got by him! Well, well, well ... Am I wrong to have come?' she still longed to know. She requested herself to smile, and quite soon did so. 'I wanted to see you, wanted to *see* you, Eva. And so wanted to see Cathay, to see where you are – while I cannot imagine that, you seem more gone: that I mind, you know.'

'Let's go there!' Enthusiasm all over, Eva could hardly wait to be off.

'One thing more: I feel bad about Mr Denge.'

'You wish to call on him?' asked the girl socially.

'No, *no*! – Bad, I mean, about ringing him up that day. But I did want some word of you; I was at the end of my tether. Constantine said you felt I had been malicious.'

'Oho, did he?'

The Jaguar waited under the house, over the harbour; where, masterfully inserted into a park long placarded FULL, it was not flanked by the space due to it. Doors could barely open; one got in crabwise. Eva then masterfully reversed out. 'Nice,' Iseult said, smiling along the dashboard, disposing her summer skirts, 'to see this again. You are glad it's back?'

'Oh, yes,' said the owner dismissingly.

The fact was, the relationship had been broken. The Jaguar, homing, had had the chagrin of finding itself superseded by the bicycle. There are absences which are fatal, this had been one of them. And the car had a stain on its character, having involved Henry in an ethical duel with his father, when all came out. 'What possessed you?' Mr Dancey had wanted to know, worried. And he'd been angry. 'You've been unsuccessfully mercenary and extremely silly. As far as I can see you could be in jail.' 'I'm a minor,' said Henry, though slightly shaken. He looked down his nose and added: ' "The woman tempted me".' 'Adam,' said Mr Dancey hotly, 'was a cad.' 'I don't think,' said Henry, 'that comes well from a clergyman. And I'll tell you who is a cad, Mr Eric Arble, shoving his oar in: this was between me and Eva.' 'Mr Arble,' said Mr Dancey, 'was very nice, really. He merely rightly felt that I ought to know – he himself would have liked to, he said, in my place.' 'Tastes differ,' said Henry. 'And what signs does *he* show of becoming a father?' 'I dislike you when you are heartless,' said Mr Dancey. So it went . . . If Henry were out of temper, one could not blame him. Disillusionment settled down on the whole affair. He wrote it all off in a letter to Eva: 'Your dreary motor-car is being ferried back to you. It leaves tomorrow. Hope it will like North Foreland.'

Henry's epithet stuck. This unfortunate Jaguar, though now for nearly three months on Thanet, had got to know little of the locality. Going well when given a chance, it remained dispirited. Eva, negotiating the thing through Broadstairs' sometimes pretty and sometimes so-so though today radiant streets, threw out: 'I shall be getting another.'

'Larger or only newer?'

'Mm-mm,' Eva replied, or rather did not.

'How unfaithful you are!' said the other, very lightly indeed.

'This is our way,' said the girl, turning out of town.

. . . So this was Cathay? Stepping about the asphalt, from the cracks in which flowering weeds now sprang, in her shapely white shoes, Iseult looked from various angles up at the pile. 'A millionaire residence – I had never seen one. May I look at the garden?'

Roses run to briar had spread so far, they even engaged themselves with the evergreen. Roses conventional years ago, it was wonderful they had kept their power to bloom, even so fitfully as they did: pink, crimson, ivory with gold centres. Some, yesterday's, showed their stamens only, their petals scattered like the petals at Lumleigh – but those were cherry ones. The grass they flecked had grown into seeded hay, sheeny pinkish bronze – evergreen stood about in it like dark islands. There were moon daisies and, here and there, scarlet flickers, forerunners of what would be hosts of poppies. No flowers otherwise. In colour the garden was outdone by the Channel beyond it blazing its peacock blue. Heat made interposing houses send up a quiver. Eva, casting an eye over her domain, was just so far aware of imperfect order as to say: 'I have been busy indoors.'

'You housekeep?'

'No. Electricians.'

'Still, this is quite a garden, as Eric told me.'

'How is Eric?'

'He sends his love, of course!'

'Come into the house.'

'Just a minute, where are the Goodwin Sands?'

Eva did not know. So indoors they went.

Extensive re-wiring was in progress, though at a halt. Drums of copper casing obstructed the hall, also stacked with cartons of every size. Panelling having had to be taken down, dislodged antlers and art ironwork mingled on and under the refectory table; and portions of the staircase were cut away, leaving oubliettes, over which cables flowed upward towards the gallery. Nothing was at its best. 'It's a pity,' said Eva, 'you came today.'

'I'm sure,' said the visitor manfully, 'you are right in tackling this. Old, defective wiring can be dangerous.'

'Nor was it only that. It was inadequate.'

Once into the drawing-room, one saw why. In here had been activity; there was much to show for it. Outstanding examples of everything auro-visual on the market this year, 1959, were ranged round the surprised walls: large-screen television set, sonorous-looking radio, radio-gramophone in a teak coffin, other gramophone with attendant stereo cabinets, sixteen-millimetre projector with screen ready, a recording instrument of B.B.C. proportions, not to be written off as a tape-recorder. Other importations: a superb typewriter shared a metal-legged table with a cash register worthy to be its mate; and an intercom, whose purposes seemed uncertain, had been installed. What looked like miles of flex matted the parquet. Electronics had driven the old guard, the Circe armchairs, into a huddle in the middle of the floor: some were covered in dust-sheets and some not. Glaring in upon all this, the June sun took on the heightened voltage of studio lighting. All windows were shut.

'Well, I must say, Eva!'

'Yes,' said Eva contentedly.

'You understand all these?'

'I am learning to. – Will you have tea, Iseult?'

'I don't think so, thank you. A drink later?'

'My computer will be going into the dining-room.'

'Oh, really, Eva, how *can* you need a computer!'

'It thinks,' said the girl, looking aggrieved. 'That is what you used to tell me to do.'

'When,' asked Iseult, mastering herself, 'will it be arriving?'

'Not yet. Afterwards.' As she spoke that decree, a look of infatuated preoccupation passed over Eva's face. Something or other, still more tremendous, must be afoot. Had it occurred to her, even she could not at once have everything? – what other project, rival and/or incompatible, now got in the way of the computer? Onlooking at Eva, Iseult received again that puzzling impression of gained weight – exactly physical, or exactly not? The always ample and giant movements, slowed down (or could that be simply the heat?) gave signs of having prestige for the girl who made them: she rated herself, all she did and was, decidedly higher than she had done. She was in possession; in possession of *what*? Astronomic wealth, and its so far products in here, rationally should have supplied the answer: they not only failed to, they somehow did not begin to . . . Iseult Arble inwardly shrugged her shoulders. She seated herself (there was nowhere else) on the love seat – to discover she had as neighbour Eva's well-known ivory and now mute transistor. 'The nose of this,' she said, 'must be out of joint?'

'No. *It* can be carried from place to place.'

'I so well remember . . . I wish I could see this room as it was before. It's not easy to picture it that evening – for instance, where did Constantine sit?'

'What evening?'

'When you had so many callers. You and Eric got a wonderful fire going.'

'Who told you it was so wonderful, Constantine?'

'Eric, I should think? – This could have been quite a romantic room, "When day is done, and the shadows fall", as the song says. – You don't think you could re-decorate, once you've got things settled? – And as quiet, Constantine said, as a desert island. Eric's not, as we know, very observant, but Constantine spoke, when he wrote, of the friendly atmosphere.' (What he exactly *had* said was, 'They seemed relaxed, and on the best of terms.') 'That's the same hearthrug? Yes, I should think it must be. Are those burns where wood fell out of the fire?'

'No. Those are ancient burns.'

'One does not,' said Iseult, with a kind of gasp, 'need a fire today.'

Eva walked away, along the long line of instruments. She set one going. 'Shall I record us?'

'Not on any account!'

'It has recorded, "Not on any account". And it now records me saying, "it has recorded, 'Not on any account.' ".'

'Then stop it,' said Iseult drily. She ostentatiously waited till that was done. 'How curious, yes, how very curious, Eva, if you'd had that thing years ago, when I knew you. What should we think of the playbacks, I do wonder?' Leaving the love seat to the transistor, she also walked away (two could play that game), ending by vanishing into the dining-room. She could be heard unhasping a french window. 'What's this beautiful dark cool green cave out here?'

'The sun lounge.' Eva followed her into it.

'Couldn't we sit here?' The brightly light-riddled darkness was almost tropical. Eva brought two *manoir*-style chairs out of the dining-room and placed them facing. 'What a voracious, powerful plant,' Iseult said, looking out through the glass into the depths of the evergreen pressed against it. 'Can I have something to drink? – is there any ice?'

'No.'

'Then I don't think I will. – How short time is; so soon there'll be my train. Still, I've seen Cathay – "See Cathay and die!" ' went on Iseult with a wild smile.

'You have not seen all,' said her regretful hostess.

'No. I have not seen the upstairs rooms. But it didn't seem as if one could *go* upstairs, today. I shall have to imagine them. How shall you go to bed, when the time comes? Somewhere downstairs one can wash, I expect?'

'Yes. When you have caught this train, shall you be going straight back to Larkins?'

'I am spending the night in London.'

'With Constantine?'

'Really, my dear good *Eva*. – I am going to a Lumleigh re-union.'

'You used not to.'

'This year I thought I would. I have new clothes. – Eva, I'm glad I came; I hate to be going. Do you believe me? Dickens is our witness, I did ask you, "Can't we begin again?" *Can't* we? You have no notion how Eric misses you. For instance – couldn't you possibly come to us for Christmas? Like you once used to do; I think very happily. And even Christmas seems very far ahead, far too far ahead for Eric. Why, if you do come then, it will have been seven – no, eight, nine? – months since he's seen you. A long time.'

'Nine,' said Eva, looking up at the evergreen.

'Then at least, Christmas?'

'Christmas is in December?'

'It is usually. – Why? Is there anything else you think of doing?'

'In December I shall be having a little child.'

· II ·

INTERIM

Department of Philosophy,
University of Wyana,
Wilson,
Wyana

My dear Mrs Trout,

Your vanishing in the customs was a dislocation; after our hours in the air it left me twice over brought down to earth. What happened? I continue to wonder whether it was mischance, or could be intention. There at my side one minute, gone the next. Other planes with their quota of baggage having come in, the hall overflowed; chaos engulfed you – am I to fear you were not sorry it should? Must I conceive it possible I became a person you considered it better to shake off? I assure you, I had thought no further than that we share a taxi into the city, and during the ride consolidate as to some particulars before saying goodbye. That we should part under such conditions as rendered it likely we met again was not surely an inordinate wish. Our conversation had seemed not more than suspended by the touch-down. Is it never to be resumed?

I launch forth this letter to an address from which you already may have departed (short, you said, was to be your stay in New York) leaving no other behind. The Drake Hotel will no doubt redirect it back to me in due course. I foresee the day of finding it in my mail. Knowing for sure it has missed its mark, what shall I then feel? Chagrin? Relief? Resignation comes to me all too easily. I am addicted to it; hence incapacity in my non-mental life. Resignation is not experienced, it is undergone. Much is required to shock me out of it. Your vanishing may have administered that shock; how lasting are its effects to be, I have yet to know. Resignation tries to regain its hold on me even now, as I write. Do I already look on this letter as doomed to have as its reader myself only? More than half, I write for my own eye; yet what I write may by some remote fortuity reach yours. That is a possibility, and a possibility I should be wrong in leaving out of account. How what I write will strike me, should it return, I cannot compute. Weeks may have elapsed when it reappears, I may by then be a different man (though I do not think so). How it may strike you, that is, in a certain eventuality, is for me still more open a question.

I am resolved as to one thing, I shall preserve this letter when (or dare I say if) it makes its way back, as sole tangible proof of your existence. *You* occasioned it; could that have been so had you never been? (This is the address which will unfailingly find me, but may not reach you.)

That the primitive object of your journey might as the journey approached its end drive out every other consideration, I am able to see. Your coming reunion with your child – That the time, the place, the circumstances remain unknown to me (for you touched on none of them) does not lessen my attempts to envisage it. Such attempts are perpetual, at the cost of disturbance to my otherwise method of mind and habits of work. I perceive the cause of this. Mrs Trout, to learn that you are a mother affected me abruptly and very deeply. Do not misunderstand me when I say, my initial reaction was surprise. You diverged, you are not to know how widely, from the mother-image hitherto entertained by me. Your lengthy and unencumbered physique with its harboured energy more seemed to me, and not at the first glance only, that of the dedicated discus thrower. The then total reversal of my ideas could not be without some emotive effect. Now, still, viewing the fundamental you let me know of, I am the more in awe. I myself am debarred from knowing what it must be other than figuratively to have given birth, to have brought forth. There is, there can be, no intellectual analogy. Bring into being that which was not, one can. Bring into being that which of its own volition proceeds onward from what when brought into being it first was, one cannot. You have the better of me. Let me give the full weight it has for me to the statement: *You have offspring*. I see that no separation for you can ever have negatived that fact. Though how, by a motherhood so imperative as yours, separation was tolerated I do yet wonder. The duration and cause of it you did not reveal. Your child is a son, still infant; no more is known to me. Had we shared the taxi, it is not quite inconceivable I might know more.

Whether you are to be lost to me or not, I shall not, I so far find that I can not, cease to relive our passage across that oceanic sky. As a concept, 'the hand of fate' is distasteful to me; I mislike the anthropomorphic. I do defer, however, to the mathematical probabilities of chance, to the point of holding those could determine. The sickness (virulent bowel infection, attendant fever) which, first interrupting my Descartes research in Paris then condemning me to hospitalization, delayed by weeks my return to this University to the very great inconvenience of my Department, I now see as inevitably designed. Not otherwise would my flight have been late October. I have asked myself whether post-convalescence can have accounted for the state of, if not hyperaesthesia, intensified sensory awareness I was in when, some minutes after myself, you boarded the plane. You did not altogether seem to me credible. In the seat allocated to you being immediately over the aisle from mine, I cannot but see design again. Thanks to the mid-fall low in passenger traffic other places in your row remained unclaimed, enabling you to spread your belongings round and me to continue to have uninterrupted view of you. Your nonchalance, that of the habituated air traveller, at the outset perceptibly was disturbed by difficulty in finding room for your feet in the space accorded by Economy. You looked to be in expectation of something other; I surmised this might be your first trip at the lesser rate. Having accommodated as best you might, you then turned to a bag at your side and took out an apple, which you then ate. No clue to you was offered by reading matter, there being none in evidence then or later; entire engagement with your thoughts, together with reliance on them to engage you up to New York, was to be presumed: would an onlooker have been human had he not speculated as to their nature? Your impressiveness, my impressionability about matched. The extent to which you riveted my notice I was at pains to conceal, lest it offend – I need not have troubled, nothing of your consciousness was to spare. We did not, you may remember, fall into talk till some forty-five minutes after the take-off, when you lost an apple. Escaping from others in the bag it cleared the edge of the seat the bag was on and symbolically bounded towards me across the aisle.

Before returning it to you, I wiped it off. I expressed a hope it might not be bruised. You liked bruised apples, you told me, you liked the taste.

I think of myself as resistant to disclosures. I have had overmuch of them; they abound on the campus, beset the faculty club, are all but unavoidable in close work with students. At the best, I should say I suffer them. Never have I sought them, or sought to make them. Yet, in this case? Why should I not say, in yours and mine? Can I forget the manner in which you (literally) regarded me, when you did so at last? Your eyes – Mrs Trout, it is true to say – *rested* upon me when I returned the apple. I felt contemplated. Your gaze gives size to what is contained within it: I was. The momentousness of our journey stemmed for me to a degree from that. Yet there was more. As I recollect, we talked. Did we not? – do not think me ironical. In my academic capacity I give forth constantly, when not to my students then to my colleagues; existence would be insuperable without that. What a gulf between that and our intercourse. To you I *spoke*, Mrs Trout, to a comprehension latent within your silence. You in return granted me observations which to one not in key with you could have seemed enigmatic: each was, on the contrary, *you* revealed. The exactitude of your diction, its slow purity –. What you in words told me remains one in my memory with the far more you caused to appear. Our first phase terminated when drinks were served, a dividing going-and-coming adown the aisle. You selected a syrup you let me buy you.

Lunch trays descended, you reacting to yours less negatively than I to mine. Followed, the no-hour: the ever to me enormity of an airborne post-noon. An unreal torpor fills the pressurized air; bodies abandon themselves to daylit slumber in contorted attitudes of death. Awake or asleep, Mrs Trout, who is not afraid? There is mistrust. Nerves register, exaggerate, at this hour the stealthy continuous tremor of the plane. Outside, the glare: inimical, contemptuous, landmarkless, unabated, unchanging. The nullity of speed, the nullity of height. We accept that we move; do we know? – what evidence have we? Enough, to remain sustained. Shall we, shall we not? The terrible onus is on the plane, elongated the longer one looks along it to an all but hypothetical vanishing-point. One is within a directed pencil. Yet the onus is on the passenger, his vigil. No longer the critical individual but one alert lest he cease to be. The wailing or sobbing of an infant in the silence or imitation of silence becomes intolerable: how if we all gave voice? This time, in addition and no doubt due to my late sickness, I was onset by a sinister physical volatility; foreseeing my coming tension I should maybe have eaten more of my lunch, or taken spirits before it or drunken wine, but to spirits and wine I in part attribute my disaster in France. I was right out at my lowest ebb, Mrs Trout. It was then that I let myself look across. You, your repose was absolute. Needless to say unfeigned, for you feign nothing. It was basic. The sight of it moved me strongly (I did not yet know you to be a mother). Your head being back and lips widely parted, I judged you might be asleep. That, strangely (if so, forgive me), did not deter me from crossing the aisle, saying, 'Mrs Trout?' The one compulsive act of my life, to date. 'What?' you said, rolling your head around. 'I have the horrors,' I said. You put out a hand to the seat at your side and removed the apples. I took their place.

Your home by the sea. It seemed to me I visited its calm great rooms with their elemental outlook, 'opening on the foam of peril-ous seas –' Other though my subject is, my resort and irrational sustenance has been poetry; under its influence I perceived your echoing oaken gallery, your traditional kitchen, your garden leafy and green through every season. I would say I transmutedly entered them. I beheld your setting with such clarity, you in it, that it was saddening to picture it you gone – desolate it can only be. Yet, Mrs Trout, that was not a valid sadness, due to the ambi-ence in which it was felt by me. There is substantiality where *you* are, and, recollect, I was then beside you. I identified with your cycling trips, your work on your shell museum (do you project a catalogue?) your marketing in that ancient seaport. This home, you lately quitted with some conflict. You propose returning there with your little boy ultimately – how ultimately, I wonder? Your present stay in the States is likely to be for about how long? It may be you do not yourself know. I should be glad to.

You lost both parents. The I understood still recent end of your father was unexpected, I hope not shocking; the dolor you manifested forbad my asking. You had been all to each other, due to the early extinction of your mother. A plane wreck, total. I blenched, maybe? 'Not *here*,' you assured me, pointing downward through the flooring at the Atlantic, 'the Andes.' She was on a pleasure trip. She was young, lovely? You, what joyous memories you were robbed of. Left with a broken father without heart to re-marry, seeking in friendship such poor cheer as he could. Too bad, Mrs Trout, he was not to hold your child on his knee. You drew strength from sorrow. Little has come my way. Greatly, grievously even, I am your junior, but for the years. Bereavement has not yet touched me; coming so late as it will, shall I deeply feel it? (I have both parents, resident in Ohio near to my married sister and her family.) Have I been spared, or by-passed? – I fear the latter. Am I to atrophy, have I in part done so? Already do I enact what I fail to feel? Emotionally, am I parasitic? Could that have been otherwise, could it still? I have it in me to sorrow? – or have I not? Tell me.

Before marriage, what was your family name?

Putting that question, I touch the verge of an area I retreat from. Should I pursue this, this letter may do better never to reach you. Shall I speak plainly? I am unable to conceive who, or what in manner of being, or in some senses wherefore, can be Mr Trout. I repeat, unable; reluctance I might have mastered. Yet he must be posited. On your marriage finger you have a signet ring, I should say a male one. You are a mother, that cannot be without cause. This I brood over. Whilst we were yet in the air, this did not concern me. It did not present itself. Sublimation occurred. The desolation facing me in the customs hall set going what I have been prey to since. This is not fit matter for thought, I find thought rejects it – I do not think; I revolve, I do not proceed. Mr Trout assaults my sense of all possibility. The idea of such an association as your bearing his name has to comprehend is I do not say painful I do say foreign in connection with you. As a being you are auton-omous. Absolutely, it was as that you struck me. Your being not or other or less than that is, I have to tell you, wholly out of accord with the image of you less formulated *by* me than formulated *for* me by its own forcefulness. Other than you appeared, you are not reality – I continue therefore to doubt you are other than you appear (or, were other than you appeared). Was Mr Trout await-ing you at the Drake Hotel? If so, why did he not come to the airport? Or can he have been at the airport unbeknownst to me? Can it have been he who removed your child? – does he claim a share in its origin? One question more I feel free to put, as your friend: is Mr Trout pursuing a course of conduct which would have been objectionable to your late father?

Of two courses open to me, on leaving the airport, I not only did not attempt to adopt but did not consider adopting either. A speedy taxi could have delivered me at your destination not only not long after, maybe before you. Or I could have called the Drake. I should like to tell you delicacy deterred me; what did was pessimism. *Cui bono?* And I was sore, Mrs Trout. I could have had my card sent you attached to flowers. I do not know if you use them. Cordiality might not have been out of place. I should tell you, I was for twenty-four hours longer within New York reach of you, at Columbia, checking on Descartes detail in unedited sources privately made available by that University; but did nothing. I regretted knowing which your hotel was, lest the knowledge impinge upon me destructively. When, on the plane, you let fall your hotel's name, I asked, was the Drake familiar from other visits? 'No,' you said, adding, 'That is why.' What then, I asked, had led you to opt for the Drake, out of many others? You were fond of birds, you said. What then sprang to my eye was a green-neck, doubtless masculine symbol, afloat on a pond on a farm of Ohio boyhood. For reasons open to be established (I have not undergone analysis) I more than once pelted stones at it. None hit it.

Paralysis has passed over. Back here, I found you awaiting me, Mrs Trout. Had it ever been your impression that *I* defaulted, you are more than avenged. You can be denied no longer; I am faced by totality of recall. I endure it in the semblance which is my office, on the campus I could once have traversed blindfold but which now gives me to hesitate when I seek my way, and in the constricted apartment in name mine. In the faculty club I find myself prone to abeyances, lacunae. These, not unnoted by those who know me, are I find attributed to slow re-adjustment after my drastic sickness, and are tolerated in consequence with kindness. My work, I am able to tell you, is not affected. I found much to be dealt with, and am doing so. I drink additional milk to regain weight. Seemingly back where I was, I shall no doubt be so. What alternative is there? But what did you bring about? – and where are you now?

Poetry is latent in the banal, I have often maintained. It now comes dangerously near the surface. The impedimenta on this table I write at, in this office, files, folder, books, memoranda, paper cutter, pins and clips in their tray, and not only those but coats on the rack in the cafeteria, the desk I stand at to meet classes, the lamp at my bedside, all make felt a stormy inner existence. Inanimate, rarely vegetable, mostly mineral, they none the less put me in danger of Animism. I know I am most beset when I see what I do not, an apple rolling.

Mrs Trout, do I destroy this, or do I mail it? It may not reach you. Which is to be desired? – I am not certain. In either event, I remain as below inscribed,

Yours,

PORTMAN C. HOLMAN

[*This unclaimed letter was in due course returned to the sender, Professor Holman, nothing further having been heard of the addressee since she telephoned cancelling her reservation.*]

· *12* ·

COFFEE SHOP

Silent Night,
Holy Night,
All is calm,
All is bright . . .

It was late November, some days after Thanksgiving. Eva, en-
cumbered by a large gift-wrapped parcel, made her way into the
coffee shop. She was glad to.

A ferocious wind off one of the Great Lakes tore through the
city, bouncing the Stars of Bethlehem, clawing at garlands, setting
festoons, transparencies and Noël streamers a-writhe tormentedly
as they swung from the many filigree arches anxiously creaking
over the avenues. All the way down perspectives, a flapping twisting went on amidst jewel illuminations; as it might be, angels blown
off course. Here or there, flying fragments of tinsel caught at the
stripped-down boughs of the kerb maples, harassed enough.

It was evening. Though early homegoing traffic already piled
up at intersections, waiting on stop-go lights, nothing drained off
the crowds perceptibly. Glass-built stores, floor upon floor, were
transparent ant-heaps; through their whirling doors gusted out
renditions of sleigh bells. Stores cast slabs of synthetic daylight on
to the sidewalks: not a soul was unseen. In or out, being buffeted
bothered nobody: phlegmatic masses of people, flowing like lava,
contrasted with the aerial agitation. The hundreds now in two-way
procession exhibited not more than three makes of face, as though
with regard to this city and its environs the invention of the
Almighty had given out. And these three makes of face in use were
not unalike, all being weatherproof, sizable though coming in different sizes, innately wary. One great stalwart teeming family, roots

Nordic. Not animated, adults nevertheless gave off a collective sound of some volume, while children escaped on roller skates, blew on squeakers or aimed guns at each other with lifelike pops. Bright the night was (or the evening). Calm it was not. Eva, having completed her one purchase, had had enough.

This coffee shop, true to the Middle West, was, though blameless, obscurely lit like a dive or nightspot. In the assuaging raspberry-tinted darkness, Eva's sentiments homed to the piped-on carol. Ignoring somebody seeking to direct her, she ploughed through the gloom with its density of assembled women, whose hands, busts, throats fitfully did appear, though those only: all were decapitated. For this reason: each of the tables sat at had a downturned dwarf lamp simulating an oxblood toadstool – above lamp-level (for these first minutes) visibility nil. Each lamp showed just enough of its table to show it not only taken but full to complement; the marauder would be lucky to come upon one place vacant. She was, she did. Inserting herself, she squared off what had been a trio. These three were presences only in glints and glimmers: one wore octagonal spectacles, one a dangly charm-bracelet, the third was smoking. There was a rustle as they resigned themselves. (She was their penance for sitting on – they had done eating, plates held nothing but smears; they were starting in over again with coffee.) Gloves, purses were whisked punctiliously out of the Eva area. She, stooping, lodged her bulky, slippery parcel upright against a leg of her chair. Righting herself, drawing a breath, she pulled off her gauntlets. She left a forgotten hand lying, in outiine, under the lamplight.

All *was* calm . . .

'Trout,' said a voice from across the table, a voice so tiny it should have been tiny-printed, 'isn't that you?'

It was Elsinore.

She had hardly grown. Inside the haze of thistledown hair her waif beauty was as it had been, not child's or woman's. The silver fox cape smothering her shoulders, the brilliants studded into her ears might have been borrowings from an acting box. She sat slidden down, face back as on a pillow, shadow giving her temples their known bruised look. She wore frosted lipstick, more frost than colour. 'To think,' she said – to nobody. Fatalistic.

Eva, in the same tone, said: 'How did you know?'

'Your hand.'

The other two looked at Elsinore, then at Eva.

Now with time to be mystified, Elsinore said: 'What are you doing here, Trout?'

'What are *you* doing?'

Elsinore only gave an ethereal, feckless giggle. She knocked one cigarette out and lit the next. 'I never did die,' she remembered, 'wasn't that funny?' The interest of her companions became ardent; Elsinore, yielding under the pressure, sighed: 'I should like you to meet the girls. – This is Trout,' she made known to them, 'we were room-mates a while ago. – Trout, this is Joanne. She is Joanne Hensch. – That is Betti-Mae. She is Betti-Mae Anapoupolis.'

'Hi!' said the girls in unison.

'Hi!' said Eva.

They were young matrons. As such, they materialized rapidly and became complete, to the last detail – more so than Elsinore, who between them still wavered like ectoplasm. They obtained an immediate grasp of the situation. Joanne, turning on Eva her brimming octagons, only wanted to know: 'At school in the East?' Betti-Mae, jubilant, rattled her lucky bracelet. 'Elsi-*Nora*, isn't this your evening! *And* to think you nearly never came out! Now, you two, you'll have the world to speak of. – Forget us.'

'Do that,' said Joanne.

'We'll be quiet as mice.'

Joanne, before going into oblivion, had a remaining matter to clear. 'You're visiting here, visiting with . . .?'

'No. I –'

'– Don't tell *me*, just a stopover?'

'Yes,' said Eva.

Betti-Mae protested: 'For heaven's sake!'

Elsinore made a muddled, feathery gesture, signifying, she could no more. At this present moment, she wanted out. All had become beyond her – she shook her hair. Stopping on the way for a sip of coffee, she slid down, down again, face dropping back on the pillow that was not there. Her cigarette, miscarrying to her mouth, scrawled round and entangled itself in her fox fur. Eva hallucinatedly watched this – she then stared hard, disbelievingly, at the table, then, in the same manner, round the half-seen coffee shop. All swam, curdled, thinned, thickened, was blotted out. Her jaw *had* weight, for she felt it drop. Silence roared in her ears; cold-hot-cold tightened her forehead. In exterior space, there was someone saying: 'She's not sick, is she?'

The tower room in the castle, the piteous breathing. The blinded window, the banished lake. The dayless and nightless watches, the tent of cobwebs. The hand on the blanket, the beseeching answering beating heart. The dark: the unseen distance, the known nearness. Love: the here and the now and the nothing-but. The step on the stairs. Don't take her away, DON'T *take her away. She is all I am. We are all there is.*

Haven't you heard what is going to be? No. Not, but I know what was. A door opening, how is my darling? Right — then TAKE *her away, take your dead bird. You wretch, you mother I never had. Elsinore, what happened? Nobody told me, nobody dared. Gone, gone. Nothing can alter that now, it's too late. Go away again.* WHAT ARE YOU DOING HERE? *Better not —*

— Betti-Mae came through, on another line. 'Hi? — take it easy. *I* had come-overs, one time.' Joanne suggested: 'She should probably eat.' Joanne signalled a waitress, who gazed through her. 'That waitress is tense this evening,' said Betti-Mae. 'She already mistook my order.'

'She's a Moravian.'

'She once had a drinking problem.'

Eva acted. She reached across for the menu with an unexpected vigour which made her chair quake: the surprised parcel heeled over, pitching under the table on to their feet. Soft, uninjurious, it was heavyish — 'My, how you ever carried this!' After an all-in kicking-match, dive and scuffle it was laid hold of, hauled back to Eva, who, feeling some explanation owing, said: 'It contains a bear.'

'Trout,' Elsinore said faintly, 'what do you need a bear for?'

'A little boy.'

'I have three babies,' Elsinore said pensively. She referred to the others: 'Don't I?'

'She's a wonderful mother.'

'Yes; I married a salesman.' The boaster giggled. 'Mother always told me I had a downward trend.'

The girls looked down their noses into their coffee cups, which they raised with a rotatory motion. No opinion was voiced.

'Elsinore, where's your mother?'

'She's there, I guess.'

'*Where?*'

'Wherever she is.' Elsinore blew ash off the fur. 'This was hers,' she mentioned. She plucked out a scorched hair or two. 'You see? – dated. She had it mailed me; that was the last I heard. No, she cabled her husband died of cerebral haemorrhage. Trout,' she went on in her fated monotone, 'I owe you my wonderful life, don't I? – Trout,' she told the girls, 'pulled me out of a lake, one time.'

'*That* was not me.'

'Funny, I always thought.'

'Elsi-Nora, how did you get *in* that lake?'

A giggle. 'That was my downward trend. – Yes, that crazy castle: Trout, didn't your father build it? Those hooting ravens.'

'Elsinore, those were owls.'

'To think. Next I went in a clinic. – Where's that little boy you have, or didn't you say?'

'What?' fenced Eva.

'The boy your bear's for.'

'I am about to fetch him.'

Elsinore, with an instant air of complicity, at that withdrew her quivering gaze. Liberated, Eva proclaimed: 'I'm hungry.' She cast about.

'That waitress,' prophesied Betti-Mae, 'is never going to come if she sees you see her. She delights to pounce – you better be ready.'

Joanne asked: 'Do you have to carry that bear far?'

Eva, wrapped in the menu, declared: ' "Shirred eggs: sweet corn: asparagus points" – that I should like.'

'That's slender,' said Betti-Mae.

'She can add pie. – *Do* you have to carry that bear far? Your little boy's here in this city, in which part?'

'No.'

The waitress pounced, the order was given.

'In this city,' specified Elsinore, 'I would not know who there is. I'm alone mostly; Ed's back between-times. Telly gives me migraine – I look out of the window. Time flows, since I got me those three babies.'

'Elsinore, triplets?'

'No, they're normal. – I know what I don't do; in summer, swim; when it freezes over, go on the ice.' She extended a semi-transparent finger, aimlessly, to the oxblood lamp. 'Here I am though,' she meditated, sceptically regarding it. 'To think. You have to be some place, don't you, if you're living?' She said, without rancour: 'This is a handsome city, better than most would get for princip'ly mortifying their mother. To think of you, Trout, you and that mixed-up castle. That time, I wanted nothing but to be back on that island we then had: they wouldn't have me. Do you recall? – I almost forgot. How was I?'

'At the beginning, you wept.'

'Did I do that?'

'Night after night.'

Elsinore marvelled. She then asked: 'Which was the time you were all the time there?'

'Later.'

'I didn't know a thing. – You never did pull me out of the lake?'

'No. That was someone else.'

'Then I don't know what. Then how did I know your hand? – Who did you marry, Trout?'

'He was no good.'

'That was too bad,' said Elsinore. She knocked one cigarette out and lit the next. 'Well, girls,' she told them, 'we had our talk.'

In time, the waitress pounced back with Eva's order. 'She got it correct, for a wonder,' said Betti-Mae. 'But it eats me you never went for a T-steak. You don't have those, East.'

'They do,' Joanne said, 'but they're fibrous. They are kind of anaemic, you wouldn't know them – Excuse *me*,' she flashed at Eva, 'but that's the case.'

Elsinore exerted herself. 'Trout doesn't come from the East, she comes from England.'

The girls ignored the niggling distinction. It was decided, they sit on while Eva ate – that caused a spectacular, singular failure of appetite which dazed her no less than it astounded onlookers. Co-ordination broke down between her and her fork. Lumping rigidly forward, head low, sideways over the plate like a furtive dog's, she swallowed as though with a throat obstruction. It pained the girls to see such a poor performance. The music, through with 'Jingle Bells' and 'Adeste Fideles', swooned into 'I'm Dreaming of a White Christmas'. 'We just fixed our storm windows,' Joanne said. 'Did you all? – Elsi-Nora, till when do you have your sitter? Quarter of ten? Then we'll stop by at Betti-Mae's, then we'll walk your friend back.' She addressed herself to Eva. 'To where would that be?'

'Please,' said the other huntedly, 'that is not necessary!'

'*We're* friendly, you're about to discover!' Warningly laughing, Joanne captured Eva's wrist in a handcuff grasp. 'You ran into trouble when you ran into us. Didn't she, girls?'

'She did,' Betti-Mae agreed, if a shade abstractedly. 'If you're through,' she confided to Eva, 'we should leave. I have Dad on my mind. He's Herk's Dad, making his home with us. My problem is this – Herk's on the town tonight with a visiting fireman, and if Dad is left overlong he becomes morose and goes roaming groaning around rousing my children; therefore I should be glad if we had our checks. – Where has she *now* gone off to, for heaven's sake?'

Closing in round Eva, the girls got her out of the coffee shop under guard.

The Anapoupolis home was some blocks downtown, on this same avenue. They re-entered the maelstrom. Under walloping decorations the crowds were thinning; beset, two homegoing Santa Clauses held their beards on, their garbs ballooning. The Great Lake wind, bored with no more than blowing, had since last met become aggressively cold: one was glad to be out of it, into the subfusc lobby of a building moribund by this city's standards but still foursquare. Bear and all, they packed into the elevator.

Byegone and recent Anapoupolis family cooking cohabited in the closeness of the apartment, superficially freshened by floral air spray. Betti-Mae headed through a draped arch, vivaciously shouting: 'You have company!' Mr Anapoupolis senior, compact as a toad though degrees more human, probably, sat upright under a beaded lampshade. His skin, back to half of the skull, down into the dewlaps, was curd-pale; currant-black eyes shot forth, magnetically, through pince-nez. A dark ex-business suit continued to brace the shoulders into a business alertness, maintained *in vacuo*, but left belly to downward-ripple, despondent, and thighs to spread. He terminated in tiny, impatient, pointed-toed feet. He indicated, might he be excused from rising? – absolute lack of wish to could be posited, rather than inability. He bowed round, re-adjusting the pince-nez. 'Ladies,' he said, 'I am pleased to see you.' It was much to be doubted whether he was. Far from being morose, he'd been deeply occupied burning into the stock-market pages of the *Chicago Tribune*; irrelevant parts of the newspaper were strewn round him. – 'Here,' Betti-Mae reminded him, deftly advancing Elsinore, 'is your Girlie.' Elsinore stood confronting him in a chained way, a doll-size Andromeda, then sat down out of reach. He seemed content that this should be so. 'So she is,' he agreed, according his Girlie a lascivious but unambitious lick of the lips. He turned elsewhere, appeased. 'How-do, Mrs Hensch: Hermann well?' Now, he inspected the third visitor. Betti-Mae, in hasty aside to Eva, asked: 'Is "Trout" your given or your family name?' 'Family.' 'Dad, this is Miss – excuse *me*, this is Mrs – Trout.'

'Ha!' said he, slowly electrified.

'Hi!' tendered Eva.

'She formerly knew Elsi-Nora, wasn't that wonderful?'

Mr Anapoupolis hoisted round in his chair to the best angle from which to view the exhibit. 'T–R–O–U–T?' he said searchingly. 'Where d's she come from?'

'Elsi-Nora says England.'

He dragged off his pince-nez, polished them in a fury, nipped them on again, sited them upon Eva. '*You* by chance related to the financier?'

She gave him one of her measuring, blank looks, to which she saw no reason to add anything.

'Weren't you though, Trout, once?' wondered Elsinore. 'Or did I dream that up like I did those ravens?'

'How came,' Joanne keenly wanted to know, 'he built that sensational castle, if that was not so?'

'It was there,' said Eva. 'May I have a glass of water?'

The room was peculiarly hot: an antique steam-system, jacked up by the patriarch during his children's absence, sizzled and boiled through metal near by his chair, and not only that but was active elsewhere. One felt built-in also: a great wave of saleroom furniture of nostalgic interest, neo-Second Empire in character, having come to rest here, as had bric-à-brac. Betti-Mae had inserted one or two pieces, such as a coffee table, with laminated surfaces; these did little. Cut velvet and crannied giltwork harboured more dust than energy could extract, and this dust baked. 'It is certainly parched in here,' Betti-Mae assented. She searched about for the air spray but failed to find it. 'I was about to serve beer, or alternatively *ouzo* – you don't want water?'

'Now that,' went on Mr Anapoupolis, not relaxing his ocular grip on Eva, '*was* a mysterious thing. Set up a worldwide panic, when the news broke. Shook the market. That man had interests everywhere. False alarm, all O.K. Never been stabler. O.K., then – why d'd he do it?'

'Why did he what, Dad?'

'Take his life,' he snapped. 'Wasn't out on a limb. That beat comprehension. *I* ask, why should he?'

Eva stared away, at the bronze clock with prancing horses: the clock had stopped. The inquisitor went on, with cheated avidity, tinged by disparagement: 'Somehow thought, you might tell me.'

'She's embarrassed,' Joanne said.

He was not budging. 'Trout's not a usual name except for a fish. More than that, she closely resembles him. Could be his daughter.'

'Dad,' rhapsodized the daughter-in-law, 'the way *you* got around, one time, didn't you! The high-ranking contacts you made, the persons you knew!'

The old man, with some scorn, told her: 'I knew his picture.' He snorted. 'I followed his story' – the pointed feet executed a tiny, static, impatient dance. Excitement ran out; he showed signs of bladder unease. 'Ladies,' he announced, 'you'll have to excuse me.'

'There is a horrible old Greek,' Elsinore said, not more *sotto voce* than usual, as Mr Anapoupolis left their midst.

'Hermann's father did that. That age, they do.'

'*What* did Hermann's father, Joanne?'

'Discourse on the past. They become confused. – But wasn't that quite a coincidence?' Joanne asked Eva. 'Was that ever your relative?'

'Yes.' Eva went to the dead clock, prised its glass face open and stood moving the hands round to imaginary hours. Their hostess melted from view, gone for the beer. 'Elsinore,' said Eva, over her shoulder, 'in a minute I have to go. I must get back; I expect a long-distance call.' Elsinore, to give reason for saying nothing, brought her lipstick out, faced into a mirror and, hand not trembling, added frost to her lips.

'In connection,' Joanne pursued, 'that important call would be, with fetching your little boy?'

'No. – Yes.'

'You going far to fetch him? An air journey? Exactly what's the locality?'

'I don't know yet.'

'*My* . . .!'

Mr Anapoupolis rejoined them. He detoured by Elsinore, mock-pounced, licked his lips longingly more than lusciously, shook his head resignedly, sought his chair. As a wolf, he was finished. 'And how are you ladies doing?' he asked generally.

'*I* just had a shock,' admitted Joanne. 'Mr Anapoupolis, would you believe this? – this Mrs Trout is fetching her little boy and does not out of the whole earth know where he now is. Maybe in the East it's different, maybe in England, but I do have to admit that surprises *me*. Any such uncertainty would about kill me. Or am I neurotic? If so, tell me.'

No: Mr Anapoupolis did not think so. He himself took an exceedingly grave view. He arraigned Eva: 'What do I understand?'

'I'm to be told,' said Eva defiantly.

Elsinore sighed, in support: 'A long-distance call.'

'Be that as it may' – he knifed 'that' through with a gesture. 'What voice do you expect to hear on the telephone? A voice known to you? Have you proof your child is in proper hands? If he was, have you reason to know he has not passed out of them? Much goes on in this country, I am sorry to tell you – nor dare I say it is limited to this country. Of kidnapping, with extortion, I need hardly remind you; moreover, ma'am, there could be various persons for whom your family name spells top-bracket wealth. *At* a cost, your child could be likely to be recovered. But there's a racket more deadly – are you aware? There's a black market in infants, unknowing babies: are you conscious they can be purchased, they can be traded? *Are* you aware, those who cannot by law adopt, due to ineligibility, become buyers? Are you aware that this is a market in which demand has come to exceed supply? Have you ever conceived, ma'am, the means resorted to that demand may be met? – How old is your child?'

'Three months,' Eva replied – having thought rapidly.

'*The* age,' he declared, in a dooming tone.

'And,' moaned Joanne, 'not just to leave him around but then to propose to smother him with that outsize bear.' She averted the octagons from Eva.

'This network I speak of,' Mr Anapoupolis went on, in awesome crescendo, 'does not hesitate to traffic in snatched babies, when those to be got by bargain have given out. This network asks astronomic prices – as well it may. It is organized on a scale which could be admired. It deals with clients happy to ask no questions; or, should they ask, wanting the happy answer – which is supplied. And not only does it operate, with diabolic impunity, from coast to coast, it has machinery in continents other than this. It has agents in many an unsuspecting city, contacting and able to be contacted by means of passwords, code signs. It is absolutely expert in frontier-running. You pay down money, it goes ahead. It gives you first-rate service; it fixes, fakes. Birth certificates, visas, details of origin, blood-group documents. You've got no trouble coming. You've got your little baby, same as you just gave birth to it personally, in a high-class hospital. You're all set, everything taken care of. What was the one thing you had to do? Put down money. You –'

'– What did I miss?' Betti-Mae wanted to know, coming in with the tray. She eased the tray down. 'You're tense in here.'

'He's only been curdling our blood!'

Elsinore said: 'The things they think of to do.' She yawned.

'Now, Dad! – Been scaring you, Mrs Trout?'

'No,' said Eva, 'thank you.' She had in fact been listening with marked imperviousness. 'But in a minute, I'm sorry, I have to go.'

'She expects a call.'

Overheard, that drove Mr Anapoupolis frantic. 'Ma'am,' he expostulated, launching forward his torso at Eva with great earnestness, 'you, of all people, should hear me out! Before you take that call, I am warning you. I must draw your attention to what you may, not unlikely, be up against. You desire to see your child again?'

'Oh, yes.'

'Then I must impress upon you, proceed cautiously. Double-check. Query all you are told. You may be about to hear he's sick, he's down the street with a neighbour, his aunt stopped by and took him away, a hitch has arisen as to bringing him in, or, should you go fetch him, a hitch will prevent his being there. Nor could that be all: so great can be inhumanity, you *could* be informed, he all at once passed away. Shed no tears, make no bones – take action instantly! He could have been snatched.'

Betti-Mae wondered: 'But why should that be?'

'You missed the feature,' Joanne said. 'Herk's Dad's been illustrating to us how they purchase babies.'

'You don't say! – *I* should call that degraded.'

'It's pathological.'

Mr Anapoupolis all at once switched sides. 'Ladies, it behoves you to make allowance. Nature dowered you with maternity; some she did not. Law is also capricious, debarring many who would have wished authentic adoptive parenthood. Where a primitive need is devouring, it is baulked at peril. Those perils we see. Exploitation: a vile, a filthy way to make money.' He again grabbed off his pince-nez, again polished them – doing so, blinked reflectively. 'Money, it surely makes,' he had to concede.

'And to think,' murmured his Girlie, '*you* never thought of it!'

'Now, now, now!'

His daughter-in-law, making passes over the tray preparatory to serving what was on it, chanted: 'The evils Dad has laid bare! What beats Herk and me is, how he's taped the vice rings. The research he's done. Now he has leisure days, he delights to probe. – Don't you?'

He looked at her with some venom.

Eva rose, saying: 'Good night. Thank you very much.'

'But these girls count on walking you back!'

'Thank you, no.'

'You want me to call a cab?'

'No, thank you.'

Elsinore too had risen. She picked up her cape and huddled it round her, over the wispy black dress – also out of an acting box? 'Elsi-Nora,' the girls asked, 'what are you doing? Your friend doesn't need company, she just said so.' Elsinore's frosted lips moved desperately; not a sound came from them. She stared across, in appeal, at the old man. Mr Anapoupolis took over. 'Let her go,' he commandingly said, referring to Eva. '*She* can make her own way; she's an able woman, out of an able family – though I don't say she's not an unfit mother. Let her get back and handle that call: it's of vital importance. That is the Trout heir. And you, Girlie' – he beheld with compassion, comprehendingly, his thistledown plaything – 'you go down with her. Tell her bon voyage. See her on to the street.'

Elsinore and Eva went down in the elevator. Elsinore knocked her cigarette out and lit no other.

No one was in the lobby. Elsinore ran ahead, to the glass doors, to make certain the avenue still was there. She came back and flung herself against Eva: the bottomless, nocturnal sobbing began. '*Take me with you, Trout!*' The ungainly tear-wetted fur slithered and heaved between their two bodies. '*You never left me, you never left me before!*' The despairing clutch upon Eva, round Eva, was not to be undone till, most of all despairingly, it undid itself. 'No,' reasoned Elsinore, 'you can't have me come with you, and I can't go. No, however could I?' She buried her forehead in Eva, then pulled it back – looking down, Eva saw the purplish membraneous eyelids, the cast-out fledgling's. The terrible, obstinate self-determination of the dying was felt also. Eva cried out: 'Elsinore, *don't – don't*, will you?' Both of them froze together. Then Elsinore shook again: a consuming giggle. 'O God. You forgot the bear.'

'Yes!'

'Trout, what about that bear?'

'It could smother him . . . How big are your children?'

'Big Boy's the biggest; he's rising four. – He'd be happy to own it.'

'Thank you then, Elsinore.'

'To think,' Elsinore observed, for the last time. In a now rational manner, she shook her hair. 'I need a cigarette,' she said, 'and they're up there – so I guess I'll leave you.'

'I shall be back,' swore Eva. Not a gleam of belief lightened Elsinore's lost but composed countenance. The floor of the lobby widened between them. Elsinore, top-heavied by her mother's equipment, totteringly in balance on spike heels, stood in the elevator as in a showcase: its tarnish framed her. She waved, playing up to the daydream. 'See you!' The door slid to.

Eva forged her way up the avenue, a mild gradient – fur cap and gauntlets flattened under an elbow, hands thrust down into greatcoat pockets. Her stride was resolute, yet the turmoil that was everywhere was within her. Between bouts of the wind came an ululation such as used to be heard in the castle chimneys. Tomorrow was a banged-about Bethlehem star, yesterday a writhing un-ravelled pattern. She rebelled; she did not know against what. Stopped at an intersection, she lost her armour, mindless speed – a waiting thought leaped on her. 'I don't know her married name, don't know where she lives: so now gone she *is*. *Or*, do I go back?' She looked behind her. 'NO: I could miss him, I could lose him. I could fail him by never knowing so never coming. I could be late by a minute, they'd snatch him back. I *could* lose him for ever: the old man said so ... You came back too late, Elsinore. I cannot. You came at the wrong time.'

Lights changed: she headed on up the avenue, scowling with haste. A flying wisp of tinsel caught in her hair and would have clung there but that she plucked it out.

Entering her hotel, she veered near the desk. The alert clerk hailed her: 'Hi, Mrs Trout!' 'Anything?' said Eva. 'A call came in for you, five minutes back. No message. Caller will call again.' He gave her her room key. 'Good night, Mrs Trout.' 'Good night.'

Up in her dumb, lit, sealed room, Eva stared at the solid curtains. She paced the carpet. Going by, she shut the door of the bathroom lest there be ears there. Three pictures hung on the walls; she analysed each. From the under-shelf of the bed-table she took the Gideon Bible; she put her thumb in it. '*This is the law,*' she read, '*of the burnt offering, of the meat offering, and of the sin offering, and of the trespass offering, and of the consecrations, and of the sacrifice of the peace offerings –*' The telephone rang.

'Hi,' said the voice, 'you back again? You there?'

'I'm here.'

'You all by yourself?'

'All by myself.'

'Do I have your name?'

'Trout. – Eva.'

'That is correct.' A pause on the line, then – 'Dog in the ditch,' the voice said.

'Cat on the wall,' replied Eva.

'All set. Tomorrow.'

'Where do I go?'

'You got a pencil? – you want to write something down?'

PART TWO

EIGHT YEARS LATER

· *I* ·

VISITS

Eight years later, Eva and her little boy, Jeremy, boarded a Pan-American Boeing 707 at O'Hare Airport, Chicago. Destination: London. This was to be Jeremy's first transatlantic flight, and, at the end of the journey, first view of England – both prospects filled him with elation. While they awaited the take-off, he looked perfunctorily at the comics on his knee, but all the same, every now and then, with uncontrollable eloquence up at Eva. Each time he did so, she gave him a meditative smile, which he, having watched her lips for an instant, returned. Each of their interchanges was marked by this sort of gravity, which they had in common. He was a beautiful child, fair hair cut straight across a wide forehead, eyes with a sky-like power of varying between grey and blue. His skin, though unfreckled, delicate and fair, looked healthy. His features were to an extent in the Trout cast, having an openness which had been Willy's and was Eva's; yet his alikeness to her, at moments striking, had about it something more underlying, being of the kind which is brought about by close, almost ceaseless companionship and constant, pensive, mutual contemplation. Whether the boy would be tall, it was not yet possible to say; at present, he was average for his years. He was dressed in rather a British manner, cream silk shirt with a blue tie, short grey knickerbockers. Eva looked orderly in a Neiman-Marcus suit, also flannel grey. The two were travelling in comfort, indeed style. Others glanced at them favourably. There was no professor.

The lights trembled. The jet moved forward along the runway.

'Here we go – Jeremy! We're off!'

He put his hand in hers.

At the London end, they had reservations at Paley's Hotel, Gloucester Road, sw7, recommended to Eva as a good family one.

It was. The mahogany lift, massive ivory woodwork, Turkey-carpeted corridors had all the solidarity she hoped. They had a suite at the top; they came in late, so it was not till next morning that Jeremy saw out over the horizontal city, green-misted by its many, many trees – this was mid-April; spring, too, had arrived in London. They had lunch at the Zoo, then went to Madame Tussaud's. The evening, they spent in their suite, looking at pictures of London in colourful books which had been bought. The following morning, at the hour ordained, round came the chauffeur-driven Daimler. They were off again – this time, into Worcestershire.

The boredom, for Eva, of being a passenger was mitigated by showing Jeremy England. Lambs, elms, cottages, colleges (they passed through Oxford). He missed nothing. From time to time, dread of the impending day overcame her; the aware child, at such moments, went supine against her, shoulder to shoulder. They stopped for lunch at Evesham, roast beef, apple tart, afterwards walking some way along the river looking at boats. 'You'd like a boat of your own?' He certainly would. 'A seagoing boat, with an outboard engine?' Still better! . . . Just after three o'clock, the Daimler drew up outside Larkins.

'You stay where you are, a minute. Then I'll be back for you.' So saying, Eva got out – then, halted.

The short front garden was, as it never had been, tightly and brightly planted: wallflowers of every shade from lemon to wine blazed out their heady though velvet smell. The five sash windows facing the roadway wore, today, a look of feverish polish, and were crisply nylon-curtained within. The door in the middle, crimson since time began, was cobalt blue . . . From inside the car behind Eva, her little boy drank in this promised, promising house – so houselike, so red-as-a-plum, so square within its fairyland orchards. He watched Eva lag – why lag? – up the clean white cement path between the wallflowers. He saw her unable to find the doorbell, then at last discover *a* bell, and at last press it. Jeremy held his breath till the door opened – in it stood a stoutish put-about lady, in tight bright red. A colloquy followed, punctuated, on the part of the red lady, by stolid, irrefutable head-shaking. Throughout, Eva stood like a ramrod. She turned away only after the door had closed in her face. She then came slowly down the path to the

Daimler. The chauffeur sprang to attention – she got in again. 'Jeremy, they're not there now.'

He looked unutterably reproachfully at Larkins.

'They've gone away,' she said. 'She says, nobody knows where.'

The chauffeur remained at attention. 'Where now, madam?'

She sat there stupefied, stony. 'I don't know.'

The expressionless man waited. 'Yes, I do,' she admitted. 'Go to the vicarage.'

'You know where that is, madam?'

'Yes, I do.'

So they went there.

The gothic portal stood ajar, by about three inches, indicating, 'Out, but back in a minute.' Eva gave it the traditional shove; it brushed heavily inward over the doormat. Indoors, the cramped-up dusk was deeper than ever – she gave her habitual stumble, crossing the threshold. She got her vicarage voice back – '*Anyone there?*' From out of the drawing-room, a widening segment of sunshine entered the hall. Henry appeared, in the form of a young man.

'I thought,' he said, 'that sounded rather like you.' He looked past Eva. 'Who have you with you?'

She said to Jeremy: 'This is Henry Dancey.'

The boy came forward, hand out. He and Henry shook hands.

Back again in the drawing-room, Eva settled into her former place, at her particular end of the long lean sofa, Jeremy seating himself beside her. Henry retrieved a book he had left face downward, making a note of the page before he closed it, and went on to tuck it under his elbow. He then stood, in balance, one foot on the seat of the sofa at his end. There was a different cover, pomegranates and birds, not roses and loops – the fruit had become, by this time, not less washed-out than the flowers had been. April absolved the fire from being lit.

'Well,' said Eva.

'Well – indeed!' replied Henry.

'This,' said she, with a touch of the ancient truculence, 'was a surprise?'

'Nothing,' said he, with recourse to the ancient tactics, 'surprises me absolutely. – Mother,' he added, 'will be sorry to miss you; she's away for two days. Where have you been?'

Eva drew a dangerously deep breath.

'I mean,' he interposed hastily, 'more or less?' He could not have a full recital, he was not up to it. 'Where, for instance, have you immediately come from?'

'Larkins.'

Jeremy made a diversion; slithering off the sofa he looked with excited desire out at the garden. 'May he go out?' asked Eva. 'He would enjoy that; we have been much in cities.' Henry unlocked a reluctant, half-glass door, too ecclesiastical to be called a french window, and the child rushed out into the flowering currant bushes. 'How nice he seems,' Henry said, coming back. 'On the silent side; but we talked him down, I expect?' ·

Eva said nothing.

'Yes, of course,' Henry agreed. 'Larkins.' A slight reluctance began to invade his manner, as though he felt himself somewhat under a handicap – as one is when constrained, by civility, to discuss a novel or play which has not impressed one, bored one in so far as it did do anything, and in any event stays related to years ago. He was resigned, however. He did his best. 'I hear it's tremendously chic, now?'

She cried out: 'Henry, where *have* they gone?'

'They're not "they" any more, for one thing. They broke up.' He stopped and looked speculatively at Eva. 'You broke them up, it was thought?'

'I did *not*,' she declared, staring him out.

'You cut and ran, so how would you know?'

'How should *I* do a thing like that?'

'I've no idea,' said Henry, more than detached.

'When,' she asked, more uneasily, 'did this happen?'

'Ages ago.' He made an extra effort of · recollection. '*We* weren't supposed to know anything about it. About the time – I should say? – that you took off. After all, they could do as they liked; they were in the money. He probably bought a business somewhere else. (The man he was working for here was his cousin, wasn't he? – he might tell you?) Mrs Arble made a beeline for France, and as far as anyone knows may be there still. Past that, I can't help you, Eva. France is quite large, in its own way, and I barely knew her. She never took to me. You got rather a dusty answer at Larkins, did you? Mrs Thing takes a low view of her predecessors. She's got it into her head that they kept a brothel.'

'Was Jeremy,' she asked angrily, 'blamed for this?'

'You mean, was Mr Arble blamed for Jeremy? I believe so, in some quarters. – I don't know, really.'

'Then that was wicked,' she said. 'There was nothing, *nothing*.'

'Oh, good!' exclaimed Henry – relief was manifest. He could not, though, restrain himself from saying: 'Then how did you come by Jeremy?'

'That is my business.'

'Not by the usual means?' he proceeded rashly.

'That is *my* business,' said Eva, never more quellingly.

'"You stupid boy" – eh?' said he, with the best of grace – seldom more engagingly. 'What's Jeremy doing, I wonder?' He strolled to see. 'He has found the ash-heap; now there is a rich dig, layers of civilization – it's been a dump since we came.' With a kingfisher-like flash of the personality, back he came, to cast himself on to the sofa in his corner. 'You find *us* where we were,' he reminded her, 'at any rate. Why we still are and whether we always shall be, I can't tell you. One sop, though: Father's a rural dean. – Do you find me changed?'

'No.'

'Oh. – You're looking handsome, Eva; age suits you.'

'I am not so old as that.'

'You are twice my age.'

'No I am *not*, Henry.'

'You may not be now, but you were; and so that's indelible. The day of the gallivant to the castle I was twelve, and you were twenty-four. What a crew we were.'

'You remember that day?'

'Now I come to think of it. – Of course, though here in one sense we're gone in another: we children, I mean. Fledged and scattered. Catrina's just qualified as a P.T. instructress, which exactly suits her: bossier than ever. (Mother's now with her, settling her into digs. Unwantedly, I'm certain, but there you are.) Andrew got himself into Haileybury. If all shapes well, he'll be a chartered accountant. He has a tremendous effect on girls; he's away now with several of them, sailing. I am at Cambridge.'

'What is Louise doing?'

'Louise died.'

His face, for an instant towards Eva, showed a curious whitened hardening round the eyes. He watched her make a cumbrous, resisting movement, twisting her head about. – 'How *could* she?'

'I know,' he said. 'Not exactly the type, was she? Bright as a button. And she need not have. There was incompetence. I shall always mind very much. She was my familiar.'

'That, Henry,' said Eva, not only humbly but with a timidity lost for years, 'I never knew.'

'You never noticed. She was, always.'

She was left to blurt out: 'I'm sorry I asked.'

'Not at all. I made you, I led you on to. – You see, I hate telling people.'

Jeremy's shining head appeared, in the window. He indicated, he wanted now to come in again. 'No,' Eva said, 'he must open the door himself.' Henry went to investigate. 'No, he can't,' he reported, 'his hands are full.' He admitted Jeremy. The boy straightway tipped his handfuls of treasure on to the rug at Eva's feet, then crouched down, absorbedly starting to sort things out – half of a mangled teaspoon, a minute wheel off some minute toy, the crushed empty shell of some wild bird's speckled egg, three or four slivers of splintered mirror, particles of Woolworth willow-pattern, flower-pots, Crown Derby and, not least, one orange wooden button. Could his hands have held more, more would have been deployed. What there was, he was making into a pattern. From above, the comparative adults looked on. 'You've not done so badly, Jeremy,' remarked Henry.

Work continued, the boy not once looking up. He fingered about with collector's passion. 'Takes after you,' said Henry to Eva.

'You never saw my shells.'

'I was never asked. – What you did go for was pencils of every colour . . . Jeremy still doesn't say much?'

'No,' agreed Eva.

'*Jeremy!*' Henry persisted, loudly.

Not a flicker. Over the happy head, Eva confronted Henry. She did so steadily. She said: 'Yes.'

A deaf mute.

Pity mounted in Henry into a wave of hate. He could not contain it. He said: 'You were sold a pup.'

She might have heard him no more than did her child, but that, with the old hopeless motion, she dragged a fist, bumping, across her eyes. He went on, one might have thought triumphantly: 'You can't get your money back; you're wrong with the law.'

The fist dropped, tumbling into her lap. He said: 'You mind so much?'

'Mind?' she said. 'Mind that *you* are so cruel?'

He flinched. More unnerved if less desolate than she was, he said: 'I am awfully sorry, Eva.'

'How can you *be* so cruel? You might be Constantine – worse.'

'I don't know what came over me. You don't understand me. I don't know that I understand myself.'

Jeremy put the slivers of mirror into sun-rays surrounding the orange button; *his* patterns made sense. He then looked up. 'Yes,' assented Henry, quickly, 'that's pretty clever.'

'Or, all the time have you been like Constantine?'

'*That* veteran?'

No longer having it in her to be aghast, she said dully: 'You don't mean you know him, do you?'

'Certainly,' said Henry. 'That is, I've met him.' Deeply glad to gear down again into narrative, he took up a preparatory new position – leaning, this time, lightly against the chimney-piece, hands in pockets, one foot trailing over the other, on which he stood. The pose put him back some way into equilibrium. Each of his ways of standing, youthfully mannered, had at the same time about it its own authority: each gave emphasis. Now, the nonchalance he enacted quite soon returned to him. 'Yes,' he went on. 'He came round here, still questing after the Arbles. They, she, gave him the slip, apparently. He had not seen his way to letting the matter drop. He was more thrown out, I believe, than he cared to show. Or just pique, was it? He made himself more than agreeable. He was urged to stay to tea, and gratefully did. Mother looked on him kindly, thought him "lonely". *I* thought he was rather moulting, poor Wicked Guardian. The one he did hit it off with was Louise – she was still here then. They talked about snow.'

'Was it snowing?'

'Anything but. A nice warm September. A year-and-a-half ago. – You know, Eva, you gave him such a build-up. I would not exactly say one was disappointed . . .'

'Then that was all, then?'

'Yes, so far as I know. To me he said he was anxious to visit Cambridge; but I didn't think that would do. He might be a bore. Invitations to lunch were issued, but disregarded. – Have you seen him yet; I mean, this time?'

'No.'

'Shouldn't you? That might cheer him up. – Talking of tea, I wonder where Father's gone. He repeatedly goes out, but never comes in. In the absence of everyone else, we're keeping house: he and I, I mean.'

'That,' Eva dreamingly said, 'must be very nice.'

'No, it isn't. Father cannot abide me.'

He was wrong, she was certain! 'But, *Henry?* – he so much loves you.'

'That is the trouble. He doesn't like me.'

'He was most proud of you.'

'That is the trouble, also. – There was quite a dust-up, you know, about your motor car.'

'You're so like to each other!'

'You put your thumb on it. Father is sublimatedly heartless. – Never mind; I think I will boil the kettle.'

'Take Jeremy with you, will you? He might help. – *Jeremy!*'

That was not to be. Unmistakable sounds proclaimed Mr Dancey was back again in the vicarage. 'Father,' called out Henry, 'we have company!' 'Good!' replied Mr Dancey evenly: none the less he continued along the hall, and started upstairs. His step lacked resilience. More loudly, Henry took further trouble. 'It's *Eva*, actually.' On the staircase, an instant and total pause. Then: '*Eva?* – why ever didn't you tell me?' Mr Dancey turned and came down again. He entered, unhesitatingly exclaiming, 'My dear child!' both hands extended.

Jeremy got to his feet, to see who this was. Eva came, magnetized, round the sofa. 'Mr Dancey, I hope you are not angry?' They met midway. He put his hands on her shoulders, holding her for inspection. 'You *haven't* changed,' he said. 'I am very glad. The only pity is that my wife should miss you; just now, she's away.'

'Eva knows,' said Henry.

Mr Dancey brought Jeremy into focus. 'And who's this?' he said – not without apprehension. Eva replied by advancing Jeremy, beautifully – the child looked mildly up at the clergyman. Eva said to him: 'This is Mr Dancey.' The two shook hands. 'First visit to England?' asked Mr Dancey. Jeremy smiled.

'In a manner of speaking,' said Henry, 'her little boy.'

'Mr Dancey,' said Eva, argumentatively, stoutly, and yet beseechingly, 'there's nothing wrong about Jeremy.'

'Nothing,' he said, regarding the child with pleasure, 'that *I* can see. – Henry, what about tea?'

'I think, lies were told?'

'So often they are, unhappily. – And all this time you've been where? Did I hear, America?'

'Yes. We . . .'

'Then I do truly envy you. An exciting, I imagine an endless country. Here, we –'

'I am going,' cut in Henry, 'to boil the kettle. Eva, better tell Father, or there'll be bother later.'

'I dislike,' Mr Dancey said, 'being talked across. I am not yet senile.' Henry went to the kitchen. 'What did he mean, though?' went on his father. 'What am I to be told?' Jeremy made a diversion by towing Mr Dancey to the hearthrug, to admire the masterpiece. 'He's clever,' guaranteed Eva, following after. 'Only, what Henry meant is, he does not hear and does not speak.'

The startled man said: 'I should never have known.' He looked the more intently down at the pattern. 'Sight to me is the thing – the thing above all things. And more seeing eyes than his I have seldom seen. And they must be, or he couldn't have made this.' Mr Dancey, spotting a fragment of Crown Derby, ejaculated: 'The last of a wedding present! Twelve of everything – inconceivable now! . . . But surely, Eva,' he said most earnestly, 'in these days, and in that progressive country you've been in, something could have been done, has been done: what *is* being done?'

'Everything! – that is to say, very, very much.' Eva spoke with a passion that yet had somewhere in it a hint of evasion. 'But Jeremy doesn't like it; he doesn't want to. He not only doesn't co-operate, they all tell me, he puts a resistance up. He is angered by what they attempt to do to him. It upsets him. He would like to stay happy the way he is.'

'Many of us would; but that's not the thing. – Oh come, Eva, who would not wish to speak?'

'*I* have never wished to. What is the object? What is the good?'

'Or, hear?' he continued – changing his ground. 'Crass as sound can be, imagine a soundless world! No, this child has come into your life, however he did, and you must *not* doom him. I do mean "doom"; you doom if you acquiesce. You dare not,' he added, abating the verb a little by his compassion. 'There cannot – some-where? – be someone who cannot help, cannot handle him. I cannot believe you have yet tried everything: try everything! Search Europe.' He looked at her sadly and said: 'You're a rich woman.'

'I will think,' she assured him.

'Talk to my wife. – You'll be back, I hope?' He put down a finger and very slightly altered Jeremy's pattern, then conferred with the boy, sideways: 'Is that still better? – Henry,' he told Eva, 'thinks I am in favour of resignation: I am not. I most bitterly am not. I abhor loss.'

'Mr Dancey, I was so *very* sorry . . .'

'For what now?'

'Louise.'

'Yes – we are one less.'

Henry stood in the door, saying: 'Tea's ready.'

'Well, you were very quick,' said his father, disparagingly if anything.

'I started the kettle off from the hot tap.'

They went into the kitchen, where tea was. A Dutch check cloth askew on the scrubbed table: a loaf, lump of butter, a hacked-about gâteau, less than a plateful of fancy biscuits, a pot of jam. 'You should officiate, Eva?' said Mr Dancey, indicating the teapot. She retreated, askance. 'I had better,' suggested Henry. Grace not being said at tea-time, they sat down.

Henry, transfixing Eva, said: 'Last time you were here, there were macaroons.'

'Eva will make allowances,' said his father.

'I don't mean that,' the son said, turning away. Returning, he said: 'As a matter of fact, I *had* thought there were more biscuits.'

'I am the explanation,' said Mr Dancey. 'I ate several at two o'clock in the morning.' Jeremy looked about with admiring inter-est at pots and pans. Eva addressed herself to her host: 'I am so happy to see that your cold is gone!' It was not – the reminder was most unfortunate. Crisis having suspended it, he'd forgotten it: in a flash, now, out came the Kleenex, to meet a cataclysm. 'Never for long,' he gasped at her, strangulated, contorted. His smile appeared, like a premature rainbow, but then vanished – the blubbered upper lip, the runnels worn by watering eyes, the raw red glaze round the nostrils pushed their way back again into prominence. 'Plus,' he managed to say, 'an allergy. It's the flowering currant.' 'Could you not,' asked Eva, 'have them cut down?' 'Spring would not be spring without them, nor would the garden.' Mr Dancey rocked forward, squeezed saturated Kleenex into a ball and flung it towards the bucket under the sink – blind though the shot had been, there it landed. He brought out reinforcements. His ivory other self, his fine-carved son, sat, meanwhile, vindictive with love, rigid, withheld, furious – it was Henry who suffered the shattered vanity. With each year, this the more galled him. Something could have been done, something could have been *done* . . . Mr Dancey drew an experimental breath, counting up to ten silently, tensely. Yes: a lull! He returned to the world, on factual level. 'There've been changes here,' he told Eva, 'that's to say, growth. Three new shops, as you may have noticed; not yet a supermarket. Many more council houses. The Grange has become a chicken farm; Major Allsporth died. And' – he continued, in the same voice – 'Larkins, of course, has changed hands also: that you would know.'

'Anything but,' interposed Henry.

'Really?' said his father, with some irony.

'She has just been all the way round there, taking her child, only now to find they had flown the coop. She was dumbfounded.'

'Might we not let Eva speak for herself?'

'Why don't you call me "my dear boy"?'

'Because you are not.'

'You are using a "dear boy" tone. – Still,' said Henry, weighing around him the big brown teapot, seeking customers for it: no empty cups yet? 'Go on, Eva.'

She said carefully, as though in a court of law: 'I received no word from them. Not a word, ever.'

'Had you written? . . . No? Then how should they know where you were? – *we* had no idea.'

'I wrote to her from Chicago, before flying.'

'A little late? To be out of touch does damage,' said Mr Dancey.

He withheld himself half a minute, perhaps in prayer, before adding: 'Where there is not damage already.' He looked consideringly at Jeremy. *Could* one proceed with this in front of a child, hearing or otherwise? – it seemed unfitting.

Jeremy's presence, since they had sat down to table, was never not to be felt. Eva, habituated, was least aware of it. There he sat, enthroned on a cushion brought from the drawing-room, on a level in every sense with the rest of the company. His manner of eating and drinking conveyed a pleasure which was in itself good-mannered – he was not greedy. This did not, though, occupy him entirely: at intervals, he turned his candid attention from face to face, from speaker to speaker. Each time, it moved onward only when sated, which happened sometimes sooner and sometimes later. The effect was not so much of mere intelligence as of a somehow unearthly perspicacity. The boy, handicapped, one was at pains to remember, imposed on others a sense that *they* were, that it was *they* who were lacking in some faculty. Henry, of course, most nearly stood up to this; even he showed signs of an uneasiness inculcated, possibly, by a nascent rivalry? What Eva's little boy knew, what he always had known, and, still more, what he was now in the course of learning, there was no knowing. There was a continuous leakage, and no stopping it. A conviction that the vicarage tea table was bugged, if on an astral plane, gained increasing hold on father and son. One might wonder why this did not inhibit them. It did not: on the contrary, it increased their recklessness with regard to each other. None the less: 'Eva,' asked Mr Dancey, 'are you quite sure Jeremy cannot lip-read?'

'Only mine,' she said. 'And those he need not.'

Henry said: 'Extra-sensory.'

'I cannot,' burst out Mr Dancey, 'go to Larkins – and I do go there, these days I have to – without misery. There's a terrible painfulness, to me, about that place. What happened there, those last months before they left? Could a hand have been held out? – I shall always wonder. Could daylight have been let in on the situation, whatever it was? – I shall never know. Those two were remarkable people, with staying-power. They did not see their way to going to church; the deplorable thing is, their successors, the present people, are keen churchgoers, active in parish affairs, yet I never find that I can like them so much. A marriage, Eva, does not simply break like a china cup; it ends when it has been infinitely corroded. Perhaps the Arbles spared each other the worst by parting, but why, why, should it have had to come to that? They had surmounted so much.'

'For instance?' said Henry.

'More than you or I have. – The fruit farm disaster. Their to the outer eye very great incompatibility. Their continuing childlessness. They were people of courage; that stood out – what could *not* be surmounted? Don't think I am blaming you, Eva. At the worst, I suppose you were their mischance – that you should make your home with them seemed right, natural: and so it could have been? I shall never come to the end of my own penitence, felt so much too late, and so unavailing. They were not my flock, God help them – they were my neighbours. What is the good of one? – what's the good of it all?'

'What you are suffering from,' diagnosed Henry, blinking at his reflection in the glaze of the teapot, 'is guilt, not penitence.'

Mr Dancey, bored, said: 'Just as you like.'

'The distinction's rather important, I should have thought. Penitence is a reflex, guilt is a state.'

'I will make a note of that.'

'I do not feel guilty,' Eva remarked – unheard.

Mr Dancey gave a furious push-away to the gâteau, which had reached his end of the table, as though suspecting some effort to buy him off. '"Beareth all things, believeth all things, hopeth all things, endureth all things . . ."' he boomed out.

'That comes well from St Paul,' said his son, 'I have always thought. Egocentric, and took a most blinkered view.'

'At times, *I* find him trying,' said Mr Dancey. 'But as an assessment, that's idiotic.'

'Wrote like an angel,' said Henry, tipping his chair back.

'If you're going to condescend, you had better go.'

'Jeremy's first view of British family life. – Eva, what became of Cathay, is it still there?'

'Oh, yes. I bought it. Making those innovations, to rent it, merely, became unsatisfactory. – Many of those,' she said moodily, 'will be by now obsolete. Yes; we go there next week.'

'To find what, I wonder. May not moth and rust rather have broken in?'

'Mr Denge is in charge.'

'Wasn't he rather a pill?'

'That was overcome.' Eva handed her handkerchief to her little boy, to wipe jam from his mouth with. The kitchen window, which was behind Henry and faced out on the street, was slowly filled as the Daimler slid into view. 'Yes – now we must go,' she declared. She turned to her host. 'Thank you, Mr Dancey, for your great kindness, also your hospitality. Jeremy, thank Mr Dancey.' The boy slid off the cushion, made his way round the table.

'A short visit.'

'It is a long drive.'

'You were good to come; I am really most deeply touched, and so will my wife be – cruel, she should have missed you. Eva, may I tell her you'll come again?'

'Yes,' said Eva vaguely – she was looking at Henry. 'Shall you be here?'

'If not,' he said leniently, 'you can come to Cambridge; I could show it to Jeremy. – Yes, we've begun again. More or less where we left off; not, naturally, quite.'

· 2 ·

INDICTMENT

23.4.67   *Merry Monarch Garage,*
Nonest Street,
Luton,
Beds.

Dear Eva,

Well it was strange to hear from you after all these years,
though I am not so sure that you should have written or gone
out after my cousin for my address. It was a mistake of mine to
rely on him. Well did he know my wishes, I should have thought.
I left there seeking a new start. Was thinking of Canada or
Australia when I chanced to hear of this going in Luton. On
investigation it proved to be just the thing. To cut a long story
short, I am doing well. Little other news, since you kindly ask.

Yes, since you do ask you did make trouble. What else did
you expect? You went out of your way to. The state Izzy came
home in I shall never forget. I respect the fact she did not go
crazy. Not a word I swore would she listen to. What you led her
to think was the case got her on the raw. She was not blind, saw
how I'd wanted a kid all that time while where she and I were
concerned none came along. (I have now two, Diane, $5\frac{1}{2}$,
Trevor, 4. Their mother is a Norwegian.)

You incidentally injured my reputation. I am not harping on
that, just telling you.

No, I have no idea where she now is, any more than you
have, so no use asking. Yes, France was where she went off to,
not a word since, never did she do anything by halves. This is
not altogether convenient, as due to the turn events have taken I
wish to contact her with a view to obtaining my legal freedom.

In this one way she is treating me thoughtlessly. In other ways she treated me more than fairly, considering the bitterness she felt. She for instance divided with me a cash present you had recently sent. She also left with me this typewriter, which stands me in good stead for office work, correspondence, etc. She intended to go for an Olivetti on reaching France. It seems curious sometimes that after all those years when she was my wife I have nothing left of her but this typewriter. Looking back, she was above me in all ways. As for me, the worse things went, the more I cared for her. By the end, we seemed nearer than at the outset. So go on, Eva, you puzzle that one out!

The disappointment you were to me, but why drag that up? Life is too short. At a time, I do not deny I was fond of you. That day we had, by the sea and so on, could have gone on to be a wonderful memory. Then subsequently you let that be all fouled up by the construction afterwards put on it. That was the finish, Eva. However could you? Doubtless your Mr Ormeau also injected poison in Izzy's ears, and for him I perhaps ought not to hold you liable. However enough of that, at this late date.

Otherwise, I should have been all for your having this little boy, and am glad to hear he is such a nice little chap. He should be an outlet for you, and steady you down. The best news would be you were getting married. Placed as you are, I agree you need to look twice. Reliability is the thing to go for. I was fortunate, coming across this nice girl. We are well suited. We found a nice maisonette, but are looking about for something having a garden. In time I shall regularize the position. What I won't have is anyone rocking the boat. I appreciate your saying we ought to meet for old times' sake, but do not see my way to that. I am kept busy. So there it is, Eva. At risk of hurting your feelings, I must ask you not to arrive in Luton.

Yours ever,

ERIC

The recipient made little of this letter – she laid it beside her plate for attention later. So far, this was not being a good morning. Jeremy, in one of the paroxysms which were the inverse of his angel nature, had flung a potted gloxinia out of the window, just not decapitating a Gloucester Road pedestrian. Sympathetic though the hotel was to family life, protests had had to be registered, in the public interest – a note on a salver, a plaintive telephone call. Still sadder, the gloxinia had been a gift from the management. The boy now lay on the floor, unappeasedly drumming with his heels. Eva, a quilted robe over her pyjamas, presided over the breakfast trolley. Their suite had a sort of un-willing, provisional look of permanence: more and more cultural picture books, a scooter, boxes of crystallized apricots, a telescope, a cageful of budgerigars, and so on. The silver-mounted claw of the greater eagle had reappeared. Here they still were. What next?

Cathay was not the answer. They had visited it, having notified Mr Denge, requesting the key be left for them at the Albion. Jeremy, cantering from room to room, raising reverberations he could not harken to, had twitched sheet after sheet from the covered fetiches. All stood immaculate, byegone, mute as he – disconnected. Time had stood still in them. Elsewhere it had not. Mutilation, a rush job, had been wrought on the evergreen; last-minute lopping and chopping by Denge employees had left the sun lounge desol-ately sunny, the drawing-room shorn of conspiratorial crepitation against its windows. Not even dust remained. Rooms had been aired out, nothing came back to fill them. What had been had gone. Cathay, emptied, had at the same time been by an evil paradox bled of that imperial emptiness once its. Unmeaningness reigned. Again, a case of an absence which had been fatal. Eva went half-way up the staircase, lost heart, came down again. ('What to find, I wonder?' Henry had meditated.)

At the foot of the stairs, Jeremy stood wondering at the antlers. At sight of him she swallowed a sob. 'No,' she cried, 'come along, come *along*!' He stood his ground a minute, bewildered, resisting – Larkins over again? Where, then, was to be the promised land, the abiding city? She prevailed; they withdrew, conclusively locking the door behind them. She swooped him (there being already an-other Jaguar) down to sea-level, Kingsgate Bay. Glossed by April sun, it looked like a postcard. The bereft boy looked from the Channel to her: what about his boat? Back in Broadstairs, they sat down to tea in the Albion; she then rendered the key back to the hotel office, where she demanded the telephone. Denge & Donewell.

'Miss *Trout*? Welcome!' cried Mr Denge.

'Thank you. We are back from Cathay.'

'Everything shipshape?' asked he, with justifiable confidence.

'Very. It is a pity we cannot stay, but we cannot.'

'No longer alone, Miss Trout?'

'Oh no. I now have a little boy.'

'*I* see. – I trust you had a pleasant time in America?'

'Yes, but I had to dissolve my marriage. I have therefore returned to my maiden name.'

'*I* see.' He so far recovered himself as to let her know: 'In actual fact, Miss Trout, I had no idea you –'

'No, I expect not. It was very sudden.'

'Dear me. Ha-ha. No bones broken, I hope? *Next* time, my dear Miss Trout, look before you leap – eh? However, all the more fortunate, is it not, that you have your old home to return to, waiting and ready. Exactly the place, I should say, for your little lad. What age might he be?'

'Seven or eight. – I shall not, though *be* returning, I am sorry to say.'

The line recorded sincere shock. 'Surely that is not definite, Miss Trout?'

'Yes. I should like you to sell Cathay.'

'Now, immediately?'

'Yes, please. Put it back on your books, without loss of time.'

He allowed himself one prolonged groan, then one more try. 'But absence,' he wheedled, 'makes the heart grow fonder. It's completely unheard of that it should fail to. An eternal verity. Give yourself time, Miss Trout. Think how much has gone into that residence, years of upkeep. Are you not being impetuous? – if I *may* say so, impetuous once again?'

'No.'

'You resided there very happily.'

She agreed.

'You propose to remove those various . . . installations?'

'No, they stay with the house.'

'You will not,' he told her revengefully, 'see your money back. I must ask you to realize, Miss Trout, that not *everybody* . . .'

'That is up to you, Mr Denge. You must do your best.'

He blew his nose, by the sound of it. 'I am somewhat wounded,

I must confess. All these years, you may not know with what loving care –'

'– Yes, I am sure. All was very shipshape. – Thank you,' she added vaguely. 'Now I must go. Goodbye.'

'Just a minute – if these *are* your instructions, kindly put them in writing.'

'I should naturally do so.'

Eva and Jeremy tore back across Thanet, taking the London road. He, leaning an elbow out of his rolled-down window, with eyes at their widest scanned the enormous sky. Once he pointed out an ascending (and singing?) lark. Jeremy's silentness, usually, had manifold eloquent variations, outgoings, clamourings and insistencies, queries, ripostes. It took much to tie the tongue of his mind. But this evening he was in a silent mood.

Back to Paley's.

Since then, days had gone by.

Ashy spring rain had been falling, this dubious morning, but now ceased. Eva yawned, rang and had breakfast removed – it dawned on her later that Eric's letter must have been also carted away. All the budgerigars loudly burbled and chittered. A trough of low pressure, a negative feeling of bother, impended over her. Constantine would be coming to tea at five: how best fill the intervening day? What next phase in Jeremy's education? 'Get up,' she said, 'we are going to Richmond Park.'

She telephoned down and ordered a picnic lunch. She adverted to one of the fauna books, leafing it through. 'Deer,' she said, 'there'll be deer there,' – indicating a picture. He got up, to eat a crystallized apricot. She walked away from him slowly, to have a bath. Doldrums.

The afternoon was enervating, green, steamy. Smells of refreshed dust fumed from the Richmond grass. The deer shrank back on to their bosky hillocks, little of them was seen. Still exhausted after whatever crisis had brought about the murder of the gloxinia, Jeremy fell asleep in the Jaguar, which ever more aimlessly trailed through spaces. Eva complained: 'This is a beautiful park.' She stopped the car, bent over and kissed his forehead. She drove on, saying: 'I thought we were going to walk.' Lovers were out, dogs were off the leash. 'Tomorrow, I take you to the Imperial War Museum.' Some dream made the boy give a violent start. As so often happens when one is dissatisfied so keeps on trying, they stayed too long.

Constantine, therefore, was already awaiting them in the lounge at Paley's. He began by forgiving them – 'Nothing like air and exercise. This is Jeremy?' He and the boy shook hands. Constantine, that over, seemed at a loss: no suitable word could be framed to address to the youngster.

'You need not say anything,' she said easily, 'he can't hear. Jeremy's deaf and dumb.'

'Ah. – Yes?'

'Shall we have tea upstairs?'

'Quieter? – Yes.'

It was not, in fact, noisy in Paley's lounge.

This first meeting after the eight years gave promise, so far, of passing off with admirable triteness. On their way up, Constantine sang the praises of the hotel. 'Exactly where I'd have advised you to come,' he told her. 'Law-abiding, very quiet at nights. Seldom a difficulty, I remember, about a taxi.'

'Oh, you've stayed here?'

'No, not stayed. – I find an increasing charm in this part of London.'

They entered the Trout suite. 'Yes, how very nice. – But could those little birds go into the bathroom, Eva, or wherever you think fit? They are pretty, but would be pleasanter stuffed. I have – you remember? – a phobia about chirruping.'

'So you had. – Jeremy, take the budgerigars away.' He did so. 'Stupid of me,' Eva acknowledged.

'As one used to say, "Much fades from human memory",' said he, with indulgence bred of affection. 'Well . . . Eva.'

She telephoned down for tea, then said. 'Yes, Constantine?'

'Simply, I'm glad to see you.'

'I am so glad.'

'Glad I'm glad to see you, or glad to see me?'

'Oh, both.' Jeremy came back, and made for the apricots. '*Don't*,' she cried, 'greedy! Tea will be coming.'

'Little boys who eat too many sweets get spots,' said Constantine, addressing this generality to Jeremy. 'Or did in my day.'

'Jeremy doesn't.'

'Evidently,' he said, approvingly, 'not.' He transferred his gaze, without loss of a single drop of its content of benevolence, to Eva. 'Time has treated you kindly?'

To reverse the query, how had time treated him? One saw no particular or outstanding answer. Eight years, for one thing, were but a sliver in relation to his presumed age. He had formed the habit of living, of being Constantine, and habit itself had formed an undintable surface. Henry's reported impression, 'moulting', at this moment seemed to have been a biased one or, an exhibition of that *dégagé* spitefulness by which youth betrays original sin. Constantine was not to be thought of in terms of plumage, like him or not. Display had never been his method of working. His physical smooth collectedness, imperviousness, his look of being once and for all assembled, and staying thus, accounted in great part for his effect on others, whether or not diabolical, and, with that, for his extraordinary lastingness in their memories. The history – or was it the legend? – of his cruelties had as source his huelessness, his 'vanishingness' when to be vanished from could be torment, his semi-deliberate, semi-reluctant pouting enunciation of (it might be terrible) words used. Not an extravagance, ever – he had nothing to shed. What had he to lose? Yet, *was* he reduced? This touch of the genuine he was showing . . . A plea, almost? A plea pleading not to be too late?

She did not reply.

'I'm thinking,' he suddenly said, 'of selling the castle. If you don't want it?'

'No,' she said, startled. 'No – not now.'

'There's been an offer. Some community industry. Weaving, pottery, so on. Highly innocuous.' One cheek crinkled, somewhat disreputably – he ran a hand up it lightly. 'What an affair that was!'

'How is Kenneth, I wonder?'

'I'm unable to tell you. – The roof is going.'

'It's gone on being empty?'

'But for occasional summer camping,' he said with noticeable sentimental reserve. 'But you, Eva: how did your travels go?'

She was about to tell him when in again rolled the trolley, now with afternoon tea on it. – 'Was there a letter left on this?' 'I'll inquire, madam.' – She returned, to give Constantine ample benefit of the recital flinched from by Henry. San Francisco, quite a spell there. Indianapolis. Cleveland. Dallas. Seattle. Kansas City. Brooklyn – no, not New York. Last lap, Chicago. Finances (of interest to her once trustee) had not been difficult, thanks to the extensiveness plus the solidarity of the Trout interests.

'Chiefly,' he commented, finally, touching his handkerchief to his forehead, 'you seem to have opted for big cities.'

'Chiefly,' agreed Eva – herself exhausted.

'As more anonymous?'

She did not appear to know what that might be. 'I was seeking for specialists, for Jeremy.'

'Of course. But you made – or renewed – *some* contacts, I should imagine? Your father's daughter . . .'

'Oh yes,' said the father's daughter. 'But you see, I had in addition those of my own, of long ago, formed by me while waiting about for Father. In many cities. Kind friends to return to, of many sorts. Should I need anything, I was shown where to go.'

'Nothing, I hope, that Willy would not have approved of?'

'Was my father particular?' she asked Constantine.

'Very, on your behalf.'

'Jeremy, Mr Ormeau has no tea-cake.' Jeremy flourished the lid off the plated hot dish. Eva Trout looked into the teapot, and went on to replenish it with hot water, before reminiscently nodding – 'For me, no underworld.'

'What since?'

She selected a buttery quarter of tea-cake and bit deep. Masticating, she remarked: 'I have now no guardian.'

'Wicked or otherwise.'

The sun came out. Jeremy, whom Constantine did not rivet, went off to seek his malacca cane. New as a possession, indeed his latest, this as a near-antique had been priced accordingly: its silver band, just tarnished enough, bore the florid initials of some dandy, dead or if living senile. Elegant, as was the boy, it was too long for him; he made surprising play with it in the course of the energetic stroll now set out upon, round the room, round the tea trolley, round the other two. Constantine took the hint. 'How,' he said, 'if we all went out for a turn?'

They did so, south along Gloucester Road into Hereford Square. The square, an oblong, lies open to Gloucester Road on its east side: at this hour, going on six o'clock, it had the perfect clarity of a set piece. Westering sun excluded by roof-tops, one was the more in a tank of brilliant, water-coloury half-light, not yet dusk. Railings which once caged in the verdant privacy had been immolated to a forgotten war: over the hedge sheathed in wire-netting lolled lilacs, their plumes in red-purple bud, and laburnums not yet quite ready to drip yellow. 'Shortly, this should be pretty,' pronounced Constantine. 'Not too bad now.' Nice-looking cars were parked all along the kerbs under the balconied stucco houses, spotlessly painted white, cream, pearl. 'The soul,' he said, admiring the façades, 'of normality. We are outsiders, Eva.' The square, as though inhibited by their presence, seemed dead-still, at this otherwise social hour.

He burst out: 'I wish you would give up lying like such a trooper!'

She asked: 'How do you know I do?'

'My dear girl, that's unavoidable – it sticks out a mile. All of us know.'

'Are *you* truthful?' In the course of a lifetime (hers) this point-blank question had not, for some reason, come up before. She put it to him with unspoiled interest.

'Yes,' he said. 'Curiously enough.'

'What do you mean by "all of us"?'

'Your, er . . . circle.'

'Constantine, what were you doing at the vicarage? – Stop that, Jeremy!'

There still were railings topping the basements, and Jeremy, having naturally brought his cane, was voluptuously rattling the cane along them. The remorseless din was the more so for being discontinuous – front-door steps interrupted the railings. 'He enjoys,' asked Constantine, raising his voice above it, 'doing what he can't hear?' 'It's the vibration.' 'Ah. – Well, stop him; or they'll call the police in.' Jeremy didn't desist; she caught up with him, in two or three strides, and shook him. Jeremy bore no malice; he slanted away from Eva across the roadway to peer through the hedge, which was patchy and eaten-looking, into the interstices of the glades within – voluminous golden privet and speckled laurel, serpentine walks, overtopped by ash, sycamore, lime, plane, poplar, already leafy enough to enhance the mystery – with the rigid, addicted intentness of a voyeur. Eva said: 'I wish he could play in there. Might that not be arranged?'

'I should think not.'

'Why not?'

Constantine, halting at a locked wire gate, read aloud from the notice-board there posted. '"No bicycles are allowed. Tricycles are allowed on the paths only." – That would never suit *you*, Eva, you reckless tricyclist. – "Ball games and dangerous pastimes not permitted." Dangerous pastimes? No place for any of us.'

'No. What *were* you doing at the vicarage?'

'Which vicarage?'

'The Danceys'.'

'Of course, of course. – I thought for a minute,' he said, with a shade of consciousness, 'you meant the clergy-house. – Yes, I looked in there. "They might always know at the vicarage," locals told one. A kind welcome, though a forlorn hope. You heard about that?' he asked, not ungratified. 'In point of fact, I was acting for your friend Arble.'

'*What?*'

'Yes.' They walked on, towards an extra-vermilion pillar-box at the south-west corner. 'He is increasingly anxious to trace his wife, or hear of anything that might lead to her. Still feels the spoor might be picked up somewhere about in the Larkins neighbourhood, but cannot face going back there – *you* may know why? He's in really rather a fix, so applied to me.'

'But he can't bear you, Constantine.'

'So he makes clear. One all the more saw what a fix he's in.'

'He has a Norwegian companion,' Eva said sternly, 'and two children. Their names are Diane and Trevor.'

'Yes, very probably. – Oh, you are in the picture? Might one ask how?'

'He wrote to me.'

Constantine raised an eyebrow.

They reached the pillar-box; Constantine slapped the top of it, meditatively. They then turned about and retraced their steps. Jeremy was still, always, gummed to the hedge, though he now looked through at a different point – children were playing inside there, where there was grass. 'How did Eric get hold of you?' Eva wondered. 'And when was this?'

'A year-and-a-half ago. By the simplest method, walking into my office. He contrived to suggest that he had a right to – there was more than a touch of the injured husband. He over-estimates (that is to put it mildly) such influence as I ever had on Iseult. He can't get it out of his head that I know where she is – or ought to, or might. Innately suspicious, is he not – to the point of mania? What else he may have contrived to imagine, I didn't ask – it would have been fatal to laugh. In he marched; his predicament, he explained to me, being one not suitable to put down in writing. It appears, his Norwegian young lady came over here in the first place as an au pair girl, and was in that capacity somewhere about in Bedfordshire when romance hit her. All then was forgotten. Her permit expired, unnoticed and unlamented. By continuing without "papers" in this country she's landed herself and could land Eric in a position which could be fishy. The cohabitation can hardly be passed off as a social visit; it's been too unusually protracted, not to speak of having been blessed with children. Luton, which they find very congenial, has so far minded its own business; but any outbreak of nosiness and there could be trouble. Trouble on quite a scale: "law courts", "getting into the papers". Marriage lines (he holds) could right the matter, like magic. Marriage lines therefore are required. Only one hitch: your friend must get his divorce. But how, without the assistance of Mrs Arble? "Isn't it seven years, or more," I put to him, "since she walked out? You could bring desertion. You go straight to a lawyer." He jibbed at that – terrified like a blackamoor. *Sans* Mrs Arble, he cannot proceed one inch. The Macbeth type. Goes to pieces – as he did at Cathay that night. "*You* go on," he said, "you try." (Meaning, find her.) "You ought to, you should if anyone can." So, Eva, that has become my object. One has time, at times – I do also admit, he interests me. Like so many stalwarts, he has a *louche* streak. – You are well out of him.'

She began: 'I never –'

'Oh, come, Eva!'

Up in one of the drawing-rooms, somebody was picking out a tune on a piano. Something about the faultiness made it lyrical. The plate-glass of the sash window was slightly lifted; muslin curtains swelled in a breath of evening out of the trees. Tulips in a bowl, in the earliest, prettiest phase of a dying agony, had twisted open till they became orchids. At any moment, might not a petal give up the game? The two on the pavement watched to see what would happen. 'You know,' Constantine told her, 'it's time you married.'

'No. Why do you say that?'

'You can't continue with this . . . this harlequinade.'

'Jeremy is not a harlequinade.'

'No; but he bodes no good the way he's going.'

'Today he's not his best,' she said vulnerably.

'Get him a father. – Wouldn't you,' asked he – referring to their surroundings, this enclave – 'like any of this? There is much to be said for it.'

'Would you?'

There being no reply, the young woman earnestly examined her former guardian, in what might be a new light. So thorough became the scrutiny that he, with a gesture, protested: 'I'm not proposing! – Though, curiously enough, you could do still worse.'

The tune went on being picked out on the piano.

'You mean,' she said, 'I could come to a full-stop?'

'You don't feel your life is lacking in . . . purpose?'

'Again you are trying to frighten me. I should have stayed in America.'

'Don't be stupid, Eva. – Why are you not at Cathay? What's gone wrong there? Can you never take root?'

'You are like Mr Denge.'

'I am very fond of you.'

Leaving behind the house which begat the quarrel, they brought themselves to one of the square's two junctions with Gloucester Road – here, traffic assailed them by roaring by; they beat a retreat. Out of the distance Jeremy came towards them, trailing his cane. He signified, he was bored with Hereford Square. '*Once* more round,' urged Eva, 'and then . . .' Inspiration failed. Constantine filled the breach: 'Then, if you won't think worse of me, I should like a drink. There is a bar I remember in your hotel.' They stood grouped close in to the parapet scarred by its vanished railings; a dangling spray of laburnum trailed over Eva's head; she reached up and angrily snapped off the budding thing. A trifle on edge?

'What are you going to do about that boy?'

'You mean, he can't come into the bar?'

'No. His future, his schooling. His disability. – He's your heir, I suppose?'

'He might understand you,' said Eva. 'Please do not, Constantine.'

Giving on the bar at Paley's is an anteroom to which bar service extends. Here crimson sets of mahogany and mahogany crimson; there is an amplitude of armchairs, wall sofas and miniature tables. The Trout party, not having this place entirely to themselves, settled for the corner most out of earshot and made free with that, pulling the chairs about. Constantine's magnetism ensured that Eva's shandy and his brandy and soda were with them promptly – Jeremy's Orange Crush took longer, having to be sought for in some non-alcoholic region of the hotel; but the child atoned for earlier ups-and-downs by a display of seraphic patience.

'I hope,' said Eva, 'the budgerigars are not miserable in the bathroom.'

'They must take the rough with the smooth,' said Constantine. 'Most of us do. – Yes', he reflected, dandling his glass, 'what an agreeable afternoon that was.'

'*This* afternoon?'

'That afternoon at your friends the Danceys'. He, my host, I'm sorry to say was out; but *she* disentangled herself from some deep dream and was most understanding. It hardly needs to be said that we spoke of you: veiled but one could feel rather intense anxiety – might you not have sent them one postcard, Eva? – and helpless, rather meandering speculations. Everything very natural, tea in the kitchen. The undergraduate son seemed a trifle sticky; but there was a delightful child . . .'

'You talked about snow.'

'Then she still remembers?'

'I don't know,' said Eva. 'She's dead.'

Constantine looked away, down a length of corridor. A twitch ran over his forehead. He said: 'A pity.'

'I was there last week. Otherwise they were well.'

'The wall's very thin.'

'What do you mean?'

'Between dead and living. One has begun to feel that. – *You* might not, yet.'

'I'm sorry I said you were frightening me.'

'Did you? – in that case, perhaps I was. When, in particular?'

'Saying I had no purpose.'

'I don't think I *said* so, did I?' he said with exemplary mildness. 'I think I asked whether you did not possibly feel a lack of that. In your life, that is; that is, as you're living it. Er, social purpose. Spiritual content.'

It was beyond Eva to remark – as Henry might have? – 'That comes well from you.' She did not, at least, do so aloud. Her astoundedness, and her totally nonplussed stare, which had in it just a hint of the cryptic, the nearest she ever came to the sardonic, did, however, to an extent convey that. Constantine, for his part, did not merely note her reaction; he seemed to bathe in it. It was as desired – she had not disappointed him. He was in humour for it. 'I surprise you, do I?' he mused. 'The fact is, Eva, my, er, angle on many things has been a good deal altered. My, er, values have been reorganized, since I last saw you. The result of a friendship.'

'Oh.'

The Orange Crush came: Jeremy sank his nose in it.

'Yes. – Tony,' expatiated Constantine, with evident pleasure in the sound of the syllables, 'is Tony Clavering-Haight, a young East End priest. Anglican, naturally.' Putting his glass down emphatically on the glass-topped table, he veered full round, unblinkingly, upon Eva before going on to add: 'Of the highest principles.'

'I am so glad to hear that.'

He blinked once. 'What do you mean?'

'So glad you have a friend.'

'Yes,' He drew a breath, leaned back, picked up the glass again. 'So am I, Eva.'

'Then that is nice, Constantine.'

'Tony,' he sighed up at the embossed ceiling, 'will miss the castle. He and I have fallen into the way of taking summer parties of lads there, camping – his youth club lads. To that he devotes his holidays: absolutely selfless. But last summer turned out to be really rather too much; the rain streamed through. – Really it's just as well you don't want it, Eva. A pretty penny that roof is going to cost. Even Willy'd have jibbed, I think. This year I must negotiate for a barn somewhere – less of a setting, but there one is.'

'Where does Mr Clavering-Haight live?'

'Where he works, in a clergy-house. Absolutely austere. Not that it's too bad there; it rather grows on one. Should you like to come there, one afternoon? By the way, he is Father Clavering-Haight. "Father Tony",' Constantine fondly reported, 'is what he's known as. Which makes one smile; he seems hardly more than a boy. Yet his influence . . .'

'Yes,' said Eva, elsewhere. Gone was the Orange Crush, not a drop left, and Jeremy was now on the go again: there were danger-signals. 'Go up,' she bade him, entrusting to him the key to their suite, 'and see how the budgerigars are.' He hopped off, vanished into the lift. 'Oh,' she found, too late, 'he's forgotten his walking-stick: *he*'ll be miserable!'

'No,' said Constantine, 'he'll fall on those apricots. In a way, this agonizes me . . . Eva, there is *one* thing I should like to know: did you knowingly, did you willingly, take on a handicapped child?'

'Why,' she touchily said, 'do you say "take on"?'

'One assumes that was so,' he returned dismissingly. 'When you took him on, did you know him to be as he is?'

'How should I? He was a little baby.'

'I see. – In a way, I am rather sorry.'

'Sorry for who?'

'Rather sorry that that was the way it was. *Not* an undertaking, embarked upon. Not, er, a self-dedication . . .'

'Oh *really*, Constantine!'

'All the more, I should like you to talk to Tony. I'd like him to have a chance to study the boy. I can think of no one more fit to grapple with this. There's such a thing as exorcism, you know.'

Eva rolled her eyes at Constantine, but said nothing.

'There are dumb devils – a frequent case of "possession". Apart from that, it would do the child no harm to see something of the East End: its realities. You keep him in Cellophane. You make a plaything of him; at best, a playmate. He may well go on hugging his disability, it's a form of immunity. He does well with it – you make life too charming for him: an Eden. High time he was cast forth from it; as things are, that could only be done across your dead body. None the less, he has a Black Monday Morning coming to him, I shouldn't wonder. – For instance, what's to become of him when you're gone?'

'*You* tell me Jeremy has a devil?'

'No, no, no: don't be so flatfooted! Another shandy? No? Well, I do intend to take you to tea there. Afoot there are various burning projects which might fire you – have you ever begun to consider how much you *could* do?'

'Subscribe, you mean?'

Constantine waved and said: 'It's not merely money (though, do you propose to keep yours under your mattress?). You have, or could have, very great "drive", Eva. You have unusual, many would say phenomenal, force of character. Er, dynamic energy, seeking an outlet. In fact, you –'

'– Yes. Once you said I was mad.'

Constantine pressed a bell embedded in the mahogany for, again, bar service. 'You wore me down, I can only imagine,' he said, returning. 'Willy wore me down also, often ... What are your plans, for instance, for next week?'

'One day we are going to Cambridge, to visit Henry.'

'You have reason to think so?'

'Yes. I received a postcard.'

· 3 ·

EVA'S FUTURE

'Or,' Henry said, 'you could cut a dash. Why not?'

The Cambridge day was nearing its end. Up here in Henry's college, on this side overlooking a lane, he and Eva were keeping watch for the taxi which was to carry her to the station. Visit by Jaguar had been banned by Henry, with no explanation, so far, other than: 'No, I don't think that would do.' The taxi was not, actually, due for some ten or twelve minutes more. This ancient room which he shared with another man, Parker, by now looked exhausted by hospitality. From a beam crossing the low ceiling depended a mobile, the property of Parker – of its owner nothing had been seen; possibly Henry thought he would not do, either. Stacks of records, of which some had been played from time to time during the day, were understood to be Parker's; his taste was catholic. Books of Henry's, overflowing from his share of the shelves and not to be contaminated by Parker's, had for this afternoon been deposed from chairs and littered the floor. Jeremy was somewhere out on the staircase.

Like so many conversations which might make history, this, on the really rather momentous subject of Eva's future, had waited to get itself going till the last minute. 'You not only could but ought to,' Henry pursued. 'What is to stop you? And you know, Eva, in a peculiar way that's what you're rather cut out to do. As you're conspicuous anyhow, why not be conspicuous on purpose?'

'Oh,' she said emptily. 'Well, go on.'

He intended to. 'Be,' he told her, 'sensational. Get hold of a house, and I *mean* a house. A spectacular London one. If you can't find one that's spectacular, have it made so. Launch out. Fill it with people.'

'What people?'

'Those known as "people".'

'Where are those got from?'

'You'd need promotion. I could promote you, up to a point.'

'Then, what?'

'You could promote me.'

Eva looked torn, dubious. 'Yes, but more serious courses have been suggested. I should not like to be lacking in social purpose.'

'I'm pointing one out to you, you silly!'

'Yes, Henry; but as I have just been telling you, my attention has been drawn to the good of the world. I could, for instance, foundate a research institution on deaf-and-dumbness, in memory of Jeremy.'

'"Foundate" isn't a word, and he's not dead yet. Yes, I should think you *have* just been telling me! My blood boiled,' declared Henry – who had, throughout, not appeared to be other than at his coolest. 'Do-gooding sharks! Wasps round a jam pot! Headed by your infatuated guardian. And if he imagines he's going thereby to better himself with Tony Clavering-Haight, he's gravely mistaken, let me tell you.'

'Constantine isn't trying to.'

'Oh, isn't he.' A pause. The promoter-to-be contemplated his subject – who, against this backdrop, mullions, embrasures, so on, profile sharply over a shoulder and arms folded, had a heraldic handsomeness. 'I wonder,' he speculated, 'who ought to dress you. I could find out.'

'You are worldly, Henry.'

'Only out of impatience,' he said impatiently.

'Would you like me better . . .' she began, then did not know how to finish.

'That's beside the point!' he cried, snapping thumb on finger. 'The main thing is, I'm projecting a role for you. Can't you see? Don't you want one? You ought to – I want one for you.'

That was all, then? Eva, left heavy-hearted, looked about at the books dispersed on the floor with something of the hopeless, regretful reverence which had been hers in the Lumleigh library. Stooping, here and then there, she retrieved some, which she built up into a cairn. It wobbled and fell.

'Leave those *alone!*' ordered Henry, peremptorily. 'No – I'm sorry, Eva.'

'*I*'m sorry,' said Eva, straightening her back, wiping together her chidden hands. 'Yet this was, this has been, such a happy day.'

'I don't think it went too badly, do you? Pity it rained when we were on the river, nothing is wetter than a punt. – And don't tell me Jeremy now wants a punt of his own; one could see that. – What did you think of Jocelyn?' (An undergraduate who had joined them for tea, then gone away gracefully, when indicated.)

'Oh, I liked him.'

'Good. He was an experiment.'

'What's Jeremy doing, I wonder.'

Henry did not pretend to. Taking up one of the more trickily balanced yet authoritative of his standing attitudes, he narrowed in her direction his lambent dark eyes. 'You know, Eva, one about you is, you're a trend-setter. I mean, your proclivities are infectious. You vanish; everyone does the same. Well, not everyone, but look at your friends the Arbles – gone like smoke, leaving not a rack. Even your guardian's ducked down into that clergy-house; since when,' Henry said, with a shade of pique, 'nothing more has been heard of him. – And there's another thing about you, Miss Trout: you leave few lives unscathed. Or at least, unchanged. You don't know a rather long poem called "Pippa Passes"? No, I expect not. We were reared on Browning, owing to Mother. This girl only had to pass by (though as a matter of fact, she did more than that, she sang away at some length under people's windows) to leave behind the most dynamic results. In a way you're a sort of Pippa – though in reverse.'

'*I* don't sing.' said Eva mistrustfully.

'No; and *you* don't have an improving effect. Pippa diverted people from lust and villainy, and exactly one or the other of those two things, or both sometimes, do rather seem to spring up where you set foot. Don't feel I feel this reflects on you. Ethically perhaps you're a Typhoid Mary. You also plunge people's ideas into deep confusion; that is, so far as they ever had any. You have only to pass –'

'– Yet you advocate my taking a house in London?'

'Oh, all the more so! – Pippa, of course, marked people down in advance; she designedly went and sang under *their* windows. She wasn't nearly as artless as she was thought. You are artless; that is the awful thing. You roll round like some blind indeflectible planet.

Sauve qui peut, those who are in your course. I shouldn't think there's anybody you've ever gone *out* for, is there? Other, of course, than Jeremy (and after all, when you did that you had yet to meet him). – Otherwise, no one?'

Eva turned away to examine the mobile. She seemed unconscious that a reply was sought.

'Unless me,' he said – as though in parenthesis.

Looking with fervour, with passion almost, into the geometry of the mobile, Eva uttered no word. She nodded, however.

In a room below, someone opened a window and shouted down to somebody in the lane.

Henry, never rendered speechless by agitation, indeed very much the reverse, now burst out: 'What I *cannot* get over is, your having gone through life never having heard "The lark's on the wing; the snail's on the thorn". Not on a calendar, even? It's incredible.'

'Much is.'

Jeremy, losing his way on the dark staircase, battered and banged on the door – the third he had tried – before getting a grip on the handle. Having let himself in, he defiantly out-stared Henry (though so far, everything between them had gone swimmingly) before making possessively for Eva, whom he leaned up against. A residuum of panic was about him; his hair still was in rats'-tails, at every angle, after the towel-scrubbing given it on the return from the rainy river. He extracted from Eva's pocket a blackcurrant jujube, which he went on to suck. 'That should do him good,' she observed, 'if he *has* caught cold.'

'Why should he? I don't – and *I*'m far more highly organized!'

'I know, Henry.'

Appeased, he said: 'I'm afraid that sounds like the taxi.'

It was the taxi.

'Goodbye?' said Eva.

'I'm seeing you off, naturally.'

On their way to the station, she sat locked in an anguish nobody could explain – across her, the other two played cat's-cradle with the cord off a cake box. She could not endure this day's being over. Fixedly looking ahead, past the driver's ears, she cast no backward glances; she could not bear to. Nor did she need to; the beautiful agonizing mirage of the university was inescapable from. This was a forever she had no part in. The eternity was the more real to her for consisting of fiery particles of transience – bridges the punt slid under, raindrops spattering the Cam with vanishing circles, shivered reflections, echoes evaporating, shadows metamorphosizing, distances shifting, glorification coming and going on buildings at a whim of the sun, grass flashing through arches, gasps of primitive breath coming from stone, dusk ebbing from waxen woodwork when doors opened. Holy pillars flowed upward and fountained out, round them there being a ceaselesss confluence of fanatical colours burningly staining glass. Nothing was at an end, so nothing stood still. And of this living eternity, of its kind and one of its children, had been Henry, walking beside her.

Now, like an executioner, he would be consigning her to the train. Then, turning back again into his world of learning, emptying her of hope. Here in this Cambridge taxi, haunted by May Week lovers but more by the many intellects it had carried, Eva was set upon by the swamping, isolating misery of the savage. Already they were in the brick streets. Over her knee, swaying occasionally with the swervings of the taxi, Henry's two sets of fingers stretched the scarlet cord tensè for Jeremy. Was he indeed made of flesh and blood? She ached for him with the whole of her longing being. Was he capable of knowing? – she thought not. During the declaration, she had faced into nothing but the mobile. Later, the whiteness, the look of protracted shock which had accompanied his speaking to her of the death of Louise had appeared to be faintly there. It was now gone – he recovered quickly.

'I sometimes wonder,' said Eva, for no knowable reason, 'where Iseult is.'

'She'll turn up.' As Henry spoke, the taxi was slowing down. 'Here we are – I'm afraid.' He and Jeremy disentangled their fingers from the cord.

'Might you, might you come to London, Henry?'

'If we could find your house.'

She prepared the way by making a round of the more illustrious London agents. To be less sceptically shadowed while doing so, she disembarrassed herself of Jeremy by sending him daily to Primrose Hill, where a needy sculptress would teach him to model. Sometimes Eva, sometimes a car-hire car vouched for by Paley's took him there. The sculptress, when required, kept him for lunch. The organization which had produced the sculptress had other activities up its sleeve, should Jeremy come to tire of clay – he not only did not, he would not be parted from it; he gummed up Paley's by bringing lumps of it home wet. Eva fared less happily; as house-huntress she had entered the field late; everything to be looked upon as desirable had by now been snapped up for the Season. Anything still going was, it was made clear, in the white elephant category. She viewed white elephants. One she liked, but feared it might not please Henry – strategically, it was ill-situated; vast, it was made so over again by being decorated with slabs of mirror and by everything buildable-in being built in. Its commodiousness was solid and satisfying, as was its opulence. Personnel difficulties (servants) were hinted at as a reason for its remaining empty; there would be further difficulties with Henry. In this one London interior, Eva 'saw herself'; on the *grand escalier*, reflected, she permitted herself for an instant to strike an attitude. There was a ballroom, dripping with chandeliers. Value for money . . . But more and more did she know, it would not do. She returned to Paley's the sadder, and this continued. One day, however, Father Clavering-Haight took action. He paid a morning call.

House-hunting having lapsed, she had slept late and was not yet out of the quilted robe when they telephoned up to know if the cleric would be acceptable. His card preceded him, on the salver – as to his identity, when shown in, there even without that could have been little doubt. 'I hope,' he said, far from hopelessly, 'this is not tiresome? Constantine said if I was in this part of town, and in point of fact today I happen to be.'

He was a tall young man, elongated by black, agile. His narrow-oval countenance could have been Byzantine but was contemporary – the Jeremy-like fairness of its colouring was set off by the genuine shell rims of his spectacles, so roomy as considerably to widen the face at the top, at the same time magnifying his gaze, which unrestrictedly wandered about within them, though not dreamily. The lenses were convex: blind as a mole without them? His mouth had a marked look of effectuality. He went on: 'I hope you're well?' in a tone implying that no one had any business to be anything else.

Eva, taking this to refer to her dressing-gown (which the robe was, under another name), replied: 'Yes; it is only that I am late.' She had been walking about; seating herself, she arranged the skirts of the robe over her knees into folds which flowed solidly to the carpet, erected her spine against the back of the chair, disposed her hands waitingly in her lap, wrists crossed – combining thus the formality of one having decided to grant audience with the deference owing to his cloth. 'Please, sit down,' she bade him. Father Clavering-Haight did so, at a small table on which was a litter of correspondence (Eric's letter, by the way, had turned up) and one of the boxes of apricots, lid half off. She inquired: 'Are you coming to see me, or are you coming to see me about something?'

'Both,' said he – surprised, but adjusting. '*You* are what I have come to see you about, chiefly. That is, if you have no objection?'

'I think,' she pointed out, 'I might have been asked.'

'I rather agree. I never believe in shock tactics,' he told her. 'Where is the boy?'

'He is out modelling.'

A misunderstanding, though momentary, threatened to bring down vials of wrath: Father Clavering-Haight's forehead went deep shell-pink. '*Monstrous* clothes?' he demanded. 'Kiddy-capering in front of the camera? The road to narcissism – you wish that?'

Eva could not be bothered. 'This sculptress lives near the Zoo, he's been doing animals. This week he's doing a head of me.'

'Oh, that kind,' he said, mollified. – 'Look here, what always makes you so hard on Constantine?'

'All was pleasant,' said Eva, 'the other day.'

'There goes a sad man, you know. An autumnal character.'

'Oh.'

'I don't like the way you say that. That affair with your father was less discreditable than various thises-and-thats that made hay with Constantine at one time or another, over the years. We've had most of that out. Yes, rather a ghastly past, by his own account. Poor chap. – May I eat one of those?'

For a short time, an apricot kept him quiet. She watched him wipe stickiness off his fingers on to a snowy monogrammed handkerchief. 'I shan't have much lunch,' he mentioned, 'I am meeting a Buddhist. – What there was between him and your father at least lasted.'

'Yes, till my father killed himself.'

'Two sides to that story. You judge harshly – quite apart from the fact that no one has any business to judge at all. You have no idea what goes on.'

'Yes I have,' said Eva.

'Your attitude,' he made known to her, tucking away the handkerchief, 'has disheartened Constantine. He is the brooding type.'

'Very probably that is his bad conscience.'

He heaved his shoulders. 'Yet,' he declared, 'he's fond of you.'

'Yes,' agreed Eva. 'And I do not mind him so much, now.'

He looked about, as though seeking evidence. 'Where are those birds you apparently had?'

'With the porter's wife.'

Fitting the lid back on to the apricots, properly, he proceeded: 'Anyone else you resent?'

'What should make you ask?'

'Wanting to know.'

'Yes. I resent my teacher.'

'We're not speaking of the subsequent Mrs Arble?'

'Then you do know.'

'*That*'s a business, apparently, that nobody can make head or tail of. What – exactly – took place?'

'She abandoned me. She betrayed me.'

'Had you a sapphic relationship?'

'What?'

'Did you exchange embraces of any kind?'

'No. She always was in a hurry.'

'Good,' said he, ticking that one off. 'Then in what way – I should rather say, in what sense – did she inflict these supposed injuries?'

'They were not supposed.'

'What did the unfortunate woman do?'

'Everybody,' remarked the incensed Eva, 'it seems, was unfortunate but me.'

'Get yourself out of the centre of the picture. What *did* she do?'

'She desisted from teaching me. She abandoned my mind. She betrayed my hopes, having led them on. She pretended love, to make me show myself to her – then, thinking she saw all, she turned away. She –'

'– Wait a minute: what were your hopes?'

'To learn,' said Eva. A long-ago tremble shook her. 'To be, to become – I had never been.' She added: 'I was *beginning* to be.'

He remarked, with enthusiasm: 'A gifted teacher.'

'Yes. Then she sent me back.'

'Sent you away?'

'No; sent me back again – to be nothing.' Eva uncrossed her wrists, freeing one hand; this, in the form of a fist, she brought down not hard but with a dreadful precision, as it were hammering a nail in, in one blow, on to a point in her quilted lap. 'I remain gone. Where am I? I do not know – I was cast out from where I believed I was.'

'God –' began Father Clavering-Haight, for the first time. Having begun, he ceased; or perhaps waited? 'Why,' he put to her, 'do you imagine she acted in this way?'

'I only *imagine?*'

'No,' he said, looking about the table, tugging the letters from under the box of apricots, shuffling them absently through, as he might documents. 'Suppose she did: can you imagine why? What made her – have you any idea?'

'I became too much.'

He told her: 'You were a problem.'

'Because of what?'

'Don't revert! – as you say, you became too much. Also she married: you took exception to that?'

'Oh no, never at the beginning. First, I was always glad to be in their house – I even looked on it as home. As you know, I had Constantine put me there. Only then, I saw that she hated me, hated the work she had feared to finish. And I who was that work, who had hoped so much – how should I not hate her? She saw. Twice over, she could not abide me there. I became a witness. How she had cast away everything, she had seen me see.' Eva came to a stop. She smoothed out the dint in her robe left by her fist.

He leaned sideways, to see from another angle. 'You say, "She cast away everything". Why did she?'

'Oh, all for Eric.'

'So then, you annexed her husband?'

'No I did not, eventually.'

'You had a good try, though. Love or revenge?'

'At that time, I was anxious to start a garage.'

'You afterwards led her –'

'– Have you,' broke in Eva, greatly exasperated, 'nothing but scandals to think about in your clergy-house? I understand you to be devout and busy.'

'You were misinformed,' said Father Clavering-Haight. This was lost on Eva. He laid aside irony with a forbearing sigh. 'Did it never occur to you that you might pity her?'

'It did so only the other day.'

'Better late than never.'

'*I* am in love.'

He took no notice.

'Get,' he said, 'those resentments out of your system.'

'Oh yes. By what means?'

'Pray.'

'I'm unable to.'

'That we shall have to go into. – Though not this morning,' he added, with a glance at his watch. 'Then I tell you what: think about something else.'

'I more and more do, *now*!' she exclaimed – transfigured. She continued: 'You do not ask who he is.'

Father Clavering-Haight's brow clouded. Their conversation had owed its speed and efficiency, so far, to having been mapped out: *this* came under no heading. So far as he could be thrown out, this threw him out. He specialized in iniquity: off his subject, he objected to being impounded as confidant. Eva sank in his estimation, and he showed it – he looked again at his watch, this time less regretfully. 'Should I?' he asked, with secular languor. 'Would that convey much?'

She considered it ought to; she came out with all particulars, more with zeal than coherence, ending up with: 'And knows you. – Or certainly, knows about you.'

'That's just possible. But I'm sorry, I haven't been near Cambridge,' said the unwilling celebrity, 'for I don't know how long, one way and another. No, can't place him. – Unless he's been to any of our Retreats?'

'I should not think so. His father is already a clergyman.'

'But you can't mean this is serious?' asked the priest, really almost seriously concerned, examining Eva as though a question of sanity were at issue. 'A nebulous undergraduate of twenty ... *Do* you think that would do?'

'No. But ...'

'There is no "but".'

'I am not so old,' she said.

'Old enough, I should have thought, to have more sense.'

So, she decided to change the subject. 'Constantine says you are absolutely selfless.'

'Not absolutely. Everything is comparative. *He*'s had a try for the better, from time to time – pity that school got off on the wrong foot; it embodied a certain idealism. Now the camping has been a flop, as he may have told you. Dicky drains from the beginning, now dry rot.'

'The roof, he said.'

'The roof was the least. I am all for a barn, as I always was; but from the point of view of the poor chap, you see, yet another set-back. "Say not the struggle naught availeth," I told him.' Heaving his shoulders, he went back to the agenda. 'Talking of boys –' he began, in a threatening tone.

'Yes?' asked Eva, re-crossing her wrists.

'*Your* first charge must be the one you made off with. When you did that, you did the most awesome thing – did you then realize? If not, I suppose it's dawned on you since? You know what you're up against, do you?'

'Jeremy? Yes.'

'You incurred him – humanly speaking – by criminality. Regard yourself as wholly committed to him. Anything else you may want you may have to sacrifice. There is no way out of that. You have no option. The circumstances are dreadful: he's in your power.'

'No, Father Clavering-Haight, I am in his. Jeremy'll never let *me* go.'

'Retribution. I'd like to have had a look at him.'

'You believe in retribution?'

'Not for a minute!'

'Then why –?'

'I don't know,' he admitted, colouring, mortified, 'it came out ... Well: sorry I missed him. Nice to have had a word; that is, the equivalent. Just *conceivably*, I –'

'You are very kind,' she murmured correctly. He slid his eyes round in the spectacles, but let that pass. 'If,' she went on to propose, 'you would stay for lunch, I could have him at once returned.'

'No,' he said, charmingly standing up. 'Pity; but next time – I must be off to Harrods. Told you, I'm meeting a Buddhist. Think all this over, won't you; then when you're ready come and make your confession. Tuesdays or Fridays, or one could make an appointment.'

'I should have thought, I –'

'Far from it. Anyway, off the record: this is my day out.'

'What shall you do, with this Buddhist?'

'Steer a course, I expect, through the V & A, where there are various things; look in on my mother, who's in Harrington Gardens; finishing up at the six o'clock, Brompton Oratory.'

She objected: 'That is a Catholic church.'

'My dear *girl*,' he exclaimed, 'what a way to talk!'

On that note of indignation, he went away. Eva at once dressed, then made for the restaurant, where she fell on the *plat du jour*, Lancashire hotpot, being in the grip of a nervous vacuum. Gradually, her fork slowed down. She reflected, frowned. She sent for a glass of wine.

Since Cambridge, she had till this morning conversed with nobody. The irruption of Father Tony could not, had he known, have been more cunningly timed. What was this lack she had felt? – it was foreign to her. How came it that she could feel it? The fact was, since the return to England her mistrust of or objection to verbal intercourse – which she had understood to be fundamental – began to be undermined. More than began; the process had been continuous. Henry, Mr Dancey, Constantine, Henry again, and now finally Father Clavering-Haight: each had continued the other's work. Incalculable desires had been implanted. An induced appetite grew upon what it fed on.

She was ready to talk.

Did this make her traitorous to the years with Jeremy? – the inaudible years? His and her cinematographic existence, with no sound-track, in successive American cities made still more similar by their continuous manner of being in them, had had a sufficiency which was perfect. Sublimated monotony had cocooned the two of them, making them near as twins in a womb. Their repetitive doings became rites. Harmony had been broken in upon only by the tussles with ear-and-speech men, or women, to whom she faithfully took him. (She *had*, so far as she knew, tried everything, everyone. Jeremy and his rejections came out victor, each time, as she'd told Mr Dancey.) Each time, what lessened the force of the disappointment? Insidiously, something had compensated. She had felt, and had come to feel more, each time, exonerated by having at least tried.

Yes: during the at-large American years, insulated by her fugue and his ignorance that there could be anything other, they had lorded it in a visual universe. They came to distinguish little between what went on inside and what went on outside the diurnal movies, or what was or was not contained in the television flickering them to sleep. From large or small screens, illusion overspilled on to all beheld. Society revolved at a distance from them like a ferris wheel dangling buckets of people. They were their own. Wasted, civilization extended round them as might acres of cannibalized cars. Only they moved. They were within a story to which they imparted the only sense. The one wonder, to them, of the exterior world was that anything should be exterior to themselves – and *could* anything be so and yet exist?

Moments of joyful complicity had abounded. Sunrises with Jeremy capering naked on Eva's bed like Cupid cavorting over the couch of Venus. Horseback dashings out into forest fires of fall colouring. Mimicries and secret signals. Stinging of their same faces by spray from cataracts too loud to be heard even by Eva. True, Jeremy looked more deeply into some of the images than she did. Torn skies, curdled waters, hieroglyphic smoke he had had a particular way of scanning: seeking for portents? – if so, rightly.

The return to England, bringing Jeremy with her to face the music, had been a step taken by Eva for his advancement. That was to say, that was how she saw it. She had been brought to it by sighting premonitions of manhood in his changeable eyes. High time for Jeremy, scion of Willy Trout, to be other than a rumour. She had not computed the cost for him of entry into another dimension. What he had been thrust into the middle of was the inconceivable; and the worst was its not being so for her. He was alone in it. Void for him, this area was at the same time dense with experiences which by claiming her made her alien, and it could be possible that he hated it – it could not be possible that he hated her. He could not but know her to be exhilarated. The music he'd watched her nerving herself to face now stirred her. Were they to be sundered? – there was a very great inequality in their roles. Unlike the little Lord Fauntleroy, Jeremy had not landed here as a future earl: little awaited him but curiosity, sentiment roused by his looks and by his being, whether or not in the usual sense, a lovechild, and what childhood least relishes, compassion. Over all, he was regarded – and must sense this – as the latest, in some ways the most outrageous, while at the same time the most thriving, of Eva's peccadillos. And, so far, he had been denied a home. That England was to provide one had been implicit. What an error, to grant him a glimpse of Larkins, an afternoon's habitation of Cathay. Eva had broken a pact, which was very grievous.

Does one love more when things go badly? From what Eric said, it could seem so. Never till now had the love between Eva and Jeremy had more dissidences, yet been more mutually imploring. Never before now had she felt him to manacle her – perhaps he had not?

His beguilingness and the manners she had taught him were underlain by hostility to strangers: what was he coming to see *her* as? Yesterday, calling at Primrose Hill for Jeremy at the end of the afternoon, she had penetrated into the studio-shed in which he was at work on the head of her. This was the first view of it; she had not sat to him. It was a large knob, barely representational – only, he had gouged with his two thumbs deep, deep into the slimed clay, making eye-sockets go, almost, right through the cranium. Out of their dark had exuded such non-humanity that Eva had not known where to turn. There stood the sculptress, noncommittal, beside her. Jeremy, in one of his silent silences, cryptically stood away from his work. The sculptress, a person of some integrity, did not say that Jeremy was original; all she did volunteer was: 'He has *something* in mind – he's feeling his way.'

– More wine! Hers was a table for two: something was suddenly trying to sit down opposite her at it: tragedy. Twisting away, she started looking about for her at related-looking parties and couples at other anemone-decorated tables in Paley's dining-room (for such the substantial, dadoed crimson interior, nothing but daylight on its napery, managed to appear, rather than a restaurant: it was not febrile). What would it have been like to have had the enjoyment of aunts, uncles, cousins? These existed; but both sides of her family had violently quarrelled with Willy on account of Constantine, raising heaven and earth, writing insulting-denouncing letters and wielding threats, in efforts to get Eva away from him, out of contamination-range. Some even charged him with Cissie's death, that having arisen from her flight. After Willy's death, most of them had attempted to re-open relations with Eva, offering her a home, and so on. Consort with her father's enemies? Never. Yet, a pity. She had first been withheld from, then forfeited her birthright of cricket matches and flower shows. Unaided, she was beset by the quandaries of the rootless rich, for whom each choice becomes a vagary ... From afar, her study of happy families became what Iseult would have called 'consuming'. To solace her, a waiter came to know, what next? Gooseberry tart?

Nothing had been heard from Henry. Not a word, not a post-card.

'Madam, you are wanted on the telephone.'

The page stood at her elbow. Her heart stood still. 'Oh?' she asked, suffocated by hope.

'If you would like to take the call in Box 3?'

Eva slowly imbibed the last of her wine, before saying: 'Where is it from: Cambridge?'

The page, in a wary tone, said: 'I could not say, madam.' In a still warier one, as though loth to connect himself with anything so menacingly improbable, he said: 'You are wanted by a Miss Smith.'

Inside Box 3, Eva raised a receiver already speaking. '*Eva?* – good. How are you?'

'Very well.'

'So am I. I was glad to hear you are back. What are you doing? – what are you going to do?' asked the former teacher.

Eva said: 'I do not know where you are.'

'That is perfectly simple, I'm in Reading.'

'How do you know where *I* am?'

'Constantine. This is nice; I wanted a word with you. When we said goodbye, I'm afraid I was in rather a state,' Miss Smith continued, not only lightly but as though speaking of last week. 'Partly the heat – it really was blazing, that day.'

'No. My conduct was shocking.'

'Rather extreme, perhaps,' said the other in her most Lumleigh manner. 'But how remote it all seems, doesn't it? I hear you're selling Cathay? Well, it had a short life, but on the whole, I suppose, really rather a dramatic one.'

'Eric,' said Eva ponderously, 'is looking for you high and low.'

'Yes,' said Miss Smith, with a sort of enthusiasm, 'to get rid of me. I *should* have thought of that; I thought I had thought of everything, as I do usually. We parted on wonderfully good terms. On the whole I am grateful to you, Eva; if it hadn't been that it would have been something else. We could never have lasted . . . What are your future plans?'

'Why have you stayed away so long?'

'Why did you, if it comes to that?'

'Henry says my proclivities are infectious.'

'Henry? Oh, Henry Dancey? My heavens, yes; he must be almost grown up.'

'Yes, almost.'

'Imagine that,' said Miss Smith.

'You left Eric your typewriter,' said Eva.

'Fair's fair. I took his revolver.'

'There was no firearm in Larkins?'

'As he'd say, "Fancy your thinking that!" Why did I take it? A Hedda Gabler complex. – Talking of that, I hear the *amie* is a Norwegian.'

'How did Constantine track you down?'

'He is not a bloodhound. I rang him up.'

'He did not,' said Eva sternly, 'report that.'

Three pips sounded. 'This must be that,' said Miss Smith swiftly. 'We could always meet, though – now I know where you are.' She hung up.

Eva came out of Box 3.

What a performance . . . Was Miss Smith even now asking herself how it had gone? There had been a vivacity not there formerly . . . Had this *been* Miss Smith, or was she dead and somebody impersonating her? (For what reason: money?) X certainly had documented herself faultlessly: not a trick missed. But yet in another way she had fallen short, betraying an insufficient grasp of the character, its ins-and-outs. She had somehow falsified it. X could have known Miss Smith only superficially: it surprised Eva to realize how well *she* knew her. Something – who was to say what, exactly? – had not rung true. The voice's inflections, even, had been, if not quite parodied exaggerated, over-stretched, harshened; more than once a hollow ring had been given them. The Lumleigh intonations had been winners, give X that! – had X, possibly, been at Lumleigh? All the same: no. Try as X might, she had not convinced. She almost deserved to.

Had Constantine fallen for this? From the way he'd been ladling out information, one might suppose so. Going back to Box 3, Eva had a call put through to his office. Characteristically, he was out at lunch. Therefore, her stride made long by deliberation, weighty by doubt, she paced and re-paced Paley's spinal corridor. She went halfway up in the lift, came down again – then, near a sand-filled column inviting rejection of cigarettes, was galvanized. A further possibility had occurred to her – the impersonator of Miss Smith had been Miss Smith, a deceased person purporting to be a living one. Not that she necessarily was in her coffin; no, she could well be walking about in Reading. ('Charles the First walked and talked half an hour after his head was cut off.' You put in a comma somewhere, then that made sense but was not so interesting.) But, she had given an impression of dissolution. Or, if not of that, of a volatility amounting to it. An impression of upborne, gas-filled flight, cable cut, ballast cast overboard. Miss Smith was tied to ordinary earth no longer; in some way she eluded the law of gravity. What had she undergone to attain this state? Had she struck some bargain? There was something alarming about her at large thus. What did she want? – What *could* still be wanted? What had she had in mind? – if she *had* a mind?

Or had it all been a trick played by the wire? Alone with a voice, shut up with it, you are fooled by what can be its distortedness. Eva's could be an over-excitable ear, so long-lasting having been its desuetude. Might the ear not seem to have registered what it had not? Anyhow, what a slippery fish is identity; and what *is* it, besides a slippery fish? If Miss Smith had not rung up Eva, nobody else had: 'X' could be counted out. What *is* a person? Is it true, there is not more than one of each? If so, is it this singular forcefulness, or forcefulness arising from being singular, which occasionally causes a person to bite on history? All the more, in that case, what *is* a person? Eva decided to see by examining many. She telephoned for the Jaguar and drove it to the National Portrait Gallery, of which she had heard.

She had trouble in parking anywhere near. As against that, one entered without paying. Of its scattering of visitors, most were foreign; Eva being partially so also. Directed into a lift, she began where the scroll began to unroll. Echo-deadening acoustics increased the hush of pilgrimages over the solid flooring. These portraits went back in history no further than the point where they could be taken to be authentic: one made one's start with the Tudors, which comprehended the Reformation. This had been an age in which ends were dire: she learned from small placards adjoining the gold frames how very often, if not invariably, initiative, recalcitrance, ambition, ill-spent beauty or indomitability carried their possessors to the block, or, in cases of bishops, to the stake. The over-clever had perished along with the over-brave, not deterring others from doing likewise. Brittle bejewelled fingers and cobweb lace ornamented the surface only: one was in an internally maniacal, autocratic, dolichocephalic labyrinth. Inexorable pupil-darkened eyes, fumily burning and set in high up, and energetically compressed lips stabbed at her by reminding her of Henry's . . . She went through a doorway into the Stuart area of betrayers and betrayed, of whom the majority, less taut than those in the rooms before, had a free-flowing lavishness and engagingness. Their look of importance – for it was evident that important they were – was etherealized by a graceful, in some cases a glowing, in others a melancholic pensiveness, which made not the youths only appear young. Fatal was to be the division between their fortunes, yet who could guess? Foreknowledge of destiny, or destination, was not easily read into these faces, to which a family likeness had been imparted – though here or there in a physiognomy framed in showering curls and set off by satin were caverns measureless to man, or shadows cast by gathering frowns over eyes a degree, perhaps, too far-sighted. Whatever *did* happen, Eva from now on felt herself getting away from the smell of blood. She had a sensation of greater amenability, of betterment. Divines, for instance, as spiritual ferocity decreased with Eva's chronological progress, could be fiery without having to enter fires; thinkers and other originals died in their beds, none the less respected, and exile came to be the severest fate meted out to all but the most unlucky careerists . . . Next, one reacted to an invigorating, outright bravura, set off, for some reason, by Good Queen Anne, though outlasting her. Eva was drawn, more, to the military side of the Age of Reason: surely never had so many glorifying attitudes been struck? Swords were at the moment of being drawn, battle-clouds rolled between parted draperies, carmine hued the cheeks of bellicose admirals. And opulence was as evident as the victories, though rendering nobody inert. Statesmen looking hardly able to contain their potential oratory contended for wall-space, as the decades went on, with actors gesturing with olympian confidence, and men of letters who had adorned the age were fitted into all the interstices. The periwig's giving place, early on, to bunched-back tresses was accompanied, so far, by no diminution of authoritative vitality. Eva enthusiastically followed the King Georges, I, II, III, IV, over the threshold into the nineteenth century. In that, she instantly felt displaced. She turned round and went back the way she had come.

She did not intend, however, to quit the National Portrait Gallery without having achieved her aim; the less clear she became as to what that had been, the more systematically she stood by it. So, after a lingering last look at Lord Southampton, she went down in the lift – it being on the ground floor, she learned from a custodian, that Victorian notables awaited her, in hosts. And so they did, lantern-jawed, dark as crows. Eva tried to indoctrinate, or at least inspire herself, by studying philanthropists and social reformers, among whom were women – the sex had travelled a long way since its upstairs appearances as brocaded consorts or pearly-bosomed companions each with a sparkling eye to the main chance. After some sobering minutes it struck Eva that she might, now, look up her former Broadstairs neighbour, and also the (from everything Henry said) powerful progenitor of 'Pippa'. Both were at the advantage of being shown here as depicted in youth. Browning looked bothered already; Dickens, fresh as a daisy, lightly emphatically whirled round on his chair. A beardless boy . . . So was Henry. And why not?

But, upstairs or down, they *were* all 'pictures'. Images. 'Nothing but a pack of cards'? – not quite, but nearly enough that to defeat Eva. She could no more – she retraced her way to the foyer and sat down on an unfriendly bench. No, no getting through to them.

They were on show only. Lordlily suffering themselves to be por-
trayed, they'd presented a cool core of resistance even to the most
penetrating artist. The most martial extroverts, even, nursed their
mysteries. Each was his own affair, and he let you know it. Nothing
was to be learned from them (if you expected learning that nothing
was to be learned). In so far as they had an effect on the would-be
student, it was a malign one: every soul Eva knew became no
longer anything but a Portrait. There was no 'real life'; no life was
more real than this. This she had long suspected. She now was
certain.

None the less, this had been a sociable afternoon. And it had set
the mind at rest as to one matter – there is no hope of keeping a
check on people; you cannot know what they do, or why they do
it. Situations alter for no knowable reason – as though a game
continued while you were away from the board or have left the
table. See what had taken place during Eva's absence: lovers
became indifferent to each other, enemies friends or at least con-
federates. One plot unravelled, another knitting. Realignments,
out-of-character overtures, fresh fancies budding from hoary
boughs. Yet here the personae were, as before. As ever.

Eva yawned from reaction. A slight gooseflesh crept over her, in
the stony foyer; leaving the bench, she dawdled out of the gallery
into open sunlight: Charing Cross Road. Its cataracting glaring
velocity made her blink, after the twilit arrestedness of history.
This now was the rush hour striking up. An ant-hill of aimful and
desperate fevers. From where *she* stood, how many minutes to
Primrose Hill? No good being too soon, fetching Jeremy; bad, on
the other hand, to be tardy. And above all, ruinous (after yesterday) not to fetch him herself – that she shrank from the studio and
its gorgon inmate would be suspected. She side-angled past Foyle's
windows on her slow way to where she had left the Jaguar.

Timing proved perfect: just after five Eva drew up at the sculptress's door, half-heartedly painted yellow. (The woman still
occupied what had been the parental home, but let off the top half;
she retained use of the garden, into which projected the fateful
studio.) Eva rang, hard, then got back into the car. Her wait
prolonged itself to three, four minutes – she began to beat a hand
on the wheel. Then the door opened. The woman, who wore today
more than ever her look of hallowed stupidity, mystical-bovine,

was sexlessly belted into a monkish overall with thrown-back cowl, out of which rose a neck corded with tendons, supporting a head which might have been sculpted by herself – or rather projected, begun upon, then abandoned. 'Oh?' she inquired in her unfocused way. 'I didn't imagine it could be anybody. Then, you are wanting something?'

'Jeremy, only.'

'Oh, but he's gone, you know.'

'But that is impossible. I did not send for him.'

'But your friend came for him. You would know, she told me.'

'No. I have no friend.'

The woman received this extreme statement with apathy, merely saying: 'Then I don't understand.'

Eva broke out of the car, on the off side, and came round the bonnet saying: 'I have forgotten your name.'

'Applethwaite, simply.'

'Miss Applethwaite, when was this? – how long ago?'

'I should think, an hour. About an hour *I*,' the woman explained, with the melted smile of a martyr out of the flame, 'was working.' More directly addressing Eva than she had so far, she pointed out: 'And still am. She interrupted us both; but he then went away with her willingly; I assumed he knew her. Usually it's hard to make him break off, but all today there had been some kind of hitch or disturbance. He lost his way with that head, I think, since you saw it . . . Could she be some friend he has made unknown to you?'

'No. He is not confiding. Nor is he ever out of my sight, except when here, where I thought him safe.'

'Then,' said the woman passively, 'it is quite a mystery.'

'No. It is quite simple. He has been stolen.'

'I expect,' said the woman, in an unaltered tone, 'you had better come in, hadn't you, and sit down?' She hypnotized Eva into entering a front room, of some sort – Eva saw nothing. The woman, locked in dubiety or in some kind of travail, stayed at a distance – attempting, possibly, to recall Civil Defence directive as to handling of bomb shock? She resorted to fishing out of her garment a veteran packet of cigarettes – she shook one out, offered it, uncomplainingly waited for some reaction, then took it back and lit it herself. The two or three pulls she took on it boned her up: resistance began to formulate. 'But you know,' she told Eva, 'if you had any reason to think anything like this was liable to happen, you should have told me. In that case, I would not have accepted Jeremy. I undertake to in so far as it may be possible teach children, not bodyguard them. This was unfair to me.'

'What did she look like?' asked Eva, rousing herself.

'I can never describe anyone. Words do not connect, for me; I am visual purely. And tactile, naturally.'

'That does not alter the fact that he is gone.'

'Breathe,' advocated the sculptress suddenly, visited by at least a fragment of recollection, 'deeply. Deeply and slowly. You will be all right.'

'Had she dark hair, very white forehead?'

Hard put to it, Applethwaite queryingly knocked on her own forehead with a thumb-knuckle; *she* breathed deeply. 'The hair was dark, but worn in a bull fringe coming low down, like a Knossos dancer's or in a Zola film, so that one could not see what was underneath. One was not meant to? It was as though to hide something, some disfigurement, scar or burn or a birthmark. It overhung the eyes, and they looked dilated. The rest of the face had been made to look pale; whether it *was* pale I cannot say. Remember, I only saw her for a minute.'

'You lost little time in letting Jeremy go.'

'Miss Trout,' said the woman, more with regret than passion, 'that is an intolerable remark.'

'This is an intolerable thing.'

'You have to realize that I was working. Then, it is difficult not to be lost to everything.'

'How long could it take to travel from Reading?'

'I do not know where it is, I have never been there.'

'No, I suppose not. You are not helping me. – You did not notice her hands?'

'The nails were painted, but listen. She wore bracelets. – Miss Trout, have you some enemy?'

'I don't know.'

The sculptress again proffered a cigarette. Her spatulate fingers, unexpectedly lively, were deeply mahoganied by nicotine – they started tapping about her, over various surfaces, unrewardedly hunting for something: matches? During the interregnum, Jeremy

appeared to flit like a marsh-light across the invisible room. Un-
tensed by coming upon the matches, Applethwaite said: 'He and I
hit it off. That happens so rarely. Jeremy was remarkable. One
wondered what he thought, what he might have said. *You* must
have wondered?'

'Nothing was lost on Jeremy,' said Eva.

'Miss Trout, you ought not to speak of him in the past tense.'

'You did.'

The woman said lifelessly: 'I did not intend to.'

Eva, faltering in every part of her body, became afraid: perceiv-
ing some sort of ottoman or divan she got to wherever it was and
let herself drop. The thing was against a wall, to which she was
able to turn her face, at the same time muffling her mouth with
both hands. Then, gradually loosening her fingers, she said between
them: 'If he *is* in the past, there is no future. He was to be everything
I shall not be.'

The woman rebuked Eva. 'This is too soon.'

'What is too soon?'

'This – this abandonment. It is premature. What real reason is
there why harm should come to him?'

'Is it not harm being in evil hands?'

'Do you,' inquired Applethwaite, looking with abhorrence towards her telephone, 'wish me to let the police know?'

'*No!*'

'I do not want to, but might it not be advisable?'

'No, it would not be advisable. They would ask questions.'

'There is nothing to hide?'

'This is not the first time Jeremy has been stolen.'

'Ought you to communicate with your lover?'

'Henry is not.'

'Or former lover. The boy's father.'

'There is no such person.'

'You know, this will ruin me,' interjected the sculptress, starting
moving about and across the carpet, in her sere and it now seemed
penitential garment, with a masochistic, doomed, acquiescent
smoothness, as though taking part in an *auto-da-fé* procession of
one. 'Whatever happens. Sooner or later. When that agency hears
of this, it will drop me. No more pupils; what do I in future live
on? I have never been "recognized"; I have been passed by.

"Applethwaite" would have been a name to have made, I have sometimes thought, just the *kind* of name; but no one has ever heard it. No one has heard of me. My work means nothing to the world; I try not to let it mean more to me for that very reason. – Why, I wonder?' she went on, in the same monotone. 'Or, why not – what is it that has not happened? Why has nothing put a stop to the blindness, their blindness that I am right in the middle of? It makes me no money, naturally – my work – and not only that but what I need for it costs money, so that if I have none I cannot go on. Apart from rent from above' – Applethwaite nodded up at the ceiling – 'I have nothing to keep going on but rich children, and who will send those any more to where one was taken from? No, this is the end of me. Still, it cannot be helped. – Can it, Lucius?'

A cat answered: rearing its head up, it stretched open its mouth to the widest. Its eyes were slits. Brindled so darkly as to be blackish, it had been sleeping, flat, on a blackish chair. The woman gathered the cat up and held it splayed against her concave chest – with a hind paw, claws out, it scrabbled for foothold in the region of the monastic belt. She fitted a finger under the paw, resisting its violent downward mistrustful thrusts. Doing so, she asked Eva: 'You never felt he could become an encumbrance?'

'*What?* I don't understand.'

'You might not want to. The little boy, I mean – as he is.'

Only slowly, to Eva, did the import of the outrageous question come seeping through. So righting her attitude on the ottoman, or divan, as to rid it of the indignity of collapse, she said: 'You say this to justify your own carelessness.'

'Lucius does not encumber me; but then, he is an animal.'

'Are *you* human, Miss Applethwaite? At such a moment as this? – you must be infernal. I not only don't understand what you say to me, I do not understand how you dare say it.'

'One dares to wonder – always, I suppose,' said Applethwaite vaguely, studying the fur on the skull of the cat. She added: 'I did not do more than that. But you may be right; I should not have asked you. As you say, at this moment – but then, it was *this* moment which made me ask. I am not unfeeling; I feel solicitude for you. I have no future, for reasons which I have told you; but you have, and yours might take any course – yes, really any, I should imagine. You are a person who would expect your future to be according to your desires; you would not, would you, suffer obstruction gladly? All I have done, as I said, is, wonder; you are wildly agitated, so take that badly – I cannot blame you.'

'Would you expect me to be calm?' asked Eva, more terribly than she had ever spoken.

'No; but it would have been better if you had tried to be. It is the extreme way you have gone on which made me wonder. You so immediately, I would say almost eagerly, jumped to the very worst, most frightful conclusions. You have worked yourself up and worked yourself up. Any less frightening explanation – and there could be several – as to what may have happened to Jeremy, you have swept aside. If you do fear the worst, why object to taking what would then be the rational course, notifying the police? But no, you prefer to cling to fearing the worst, without aid and without reason. I am sorry, but it is a known fact that people most dread what they subconsciously desire, or, if not desire, could assent to with little trouble. Suppose you do have a lover, or wished-for lover, or wished-for husband, who could come into conflict with the exactions of Jeremy? Might not, then, the little boy be an obstacle, and an obstacle not to be overcome?'

'Words,' said Eva, 'do *not* seem to disconnect from you, Miss Applethwaite.'

'It is simply that I cannot describe people.'

'You are jealous, and wish to acquire Jeremy. I could see that, when we were in the studio.'

The woman pressed the sufficient cat nearer her breast, saying: 'I don't think so.' She pondered, then went on: 'Perhaps I have said too much. Regard me as having been talking to myself; it in fact *is* my habit to think aloud. I wonder what should be the next step; that is, what you had better do? – I am sorry, I should have been glad to help you. Should you, perhaps, return to your hotel and await developments? I cannot believe you have no friends; surely somewhere there must be some who could advise you, or perhaps even throw some light on the matter. I shall remain here, as I do usually. Should I hear anything, or should anything further happen, or should I think of anything, I shall of course –'

'– Thank you,' said Eva.

Anger restored her senses. Rising to go, she now saw what she was leaving – a room, no more. If anything, less: it was largely vacant, uncompleted for ever, as was its owner. Its scant furnishings were memorial pieces. In a corner, a tangle of soiled sheeting, perhaps some abandoned aesthetic purpose, caught what daylight there was; the room being darkened by bile-green walls, to which were pinned flopping sketches, and houses opposite. In the fireplace were (which recalled something?) the white, deadened ashes of a wood fire. Not habitable, this was proper to be the scene of an enormity – as it had been. 'You are right,' Eva said, 'it is time I went.' The woman poured the cat out of her arms, on to its chair, in order to go with her to the street door.

Panic waited till Eva was alone in the Jaguar. Then, as the car moved off, desolation came up with a rush and kept pace alongside. The way downhill, into the bottomless incredulity which is despair, was incandescent with flowering chestnut trees. The Outer Circle swept Eva round Regent's Park, awash in the gold of early evening, running with children. 'Tomorrow, I take you to . . .' Jeremy's seat was not empty, wholly; on its waxen leather something slithered about – one of his puzzles, the favourite lately. The silver bullet in it darted like quicksilver, which it may have been: it bid vainly for Eva's notice, for, unshakable driver, she kept eyes ahead, fixed on nothing but nothingness. After the park gateway, she could, she found, not contemplate any familiar route between here and Paley's. Neither could she expect to endure Paley's – so, instead, swung the other way. But there was to be nothing anaesthetizing about Central London: on the contrary, the car, trapped in tightening networks it did not recognize, began to convey to Eva its own first exasperation and then terror. So, *she* became trapped, in them and in it. She ran it into an alley that said NO ENTRY, stopped, snatched the keys out and made her escape. Though there was, actually, none.

'Nothing has happened, I hope, madam?' asked the porter at Paley's, an hour later.

'I don't know yet.'

· 4 ·

THIS IS WHERE WE WERE TO HAVE
SPENT THE HONEYMOON

Though Jeremy returned, Eva felt it no longer safe to remain in
London. He wandered back into Paley's, that same evening, cool
as a cucumber and in good spirits, round about eight o'clock – he
did not want anything to eat (one might suppose, anything more
to eat) and went straight to bed. Overnight, she made reservations
on a plane to Paris; well before noon next day they were in the air.
They each had with them a suitcase only; she ordered that everything left in the suite at Paley's go down to the baggage room for
storage. Anything edible, to be eaten. Budgerigars, to remain with
the porter's wife. Jaguar, not sure where it had been put: let it be
traced and restored to garage. From Le Bourget she wired to
Constantine: 'GONE AWAY AGAIN OWING TO CONSPIRACY
YOU PROBABLY KNOW OF.' (His behaviour yesterday had been
more than suspicious, incriminating: from lunch-time onward to
midnight he had still been nowhere available on the telephone.)
Eva sent no more telegrams till she and the boy arrived at the
Ritz, Paris – she then communicated with Henry: 'ARE IN PARIS
SO PRETTY WISH YOU COULD JOIN US.' She had no intention of
remaining in this conspicuous hotel, but it was friendly to her on
account of Willy; yes, the place swarmed with memories of him.
She considered it part of Jeremy's heritage. Eva did not think Paris
pretty (she did not know what she thought it, if anything; it had
been there always). The adjective had been chosen to needle
Henry. She had last been here when, eight years ago, she took off
to New York from Orly (the better to mystify pursuers). This time,
she was not sure where to go next.

It was now May. Everywhere was full, she was warned, owing to
the Americans – who are always blamed. Miss Trout obtained a
table for lunch at the Ritz, but once again Jeremy was not hungry.

Part II: Eight Years Later

In the afternoon, they took a taxi over a bridge, then walked from small hotel to small hotel on the Left Bank, till finally she extracted a room from one. Sitting on the edge of this new bed, Eva wrote a compensatory cheque for the sculptress – she then had to go downstairs to procure an envelope. Nothing here went so smoothly as at the Ritz, or Paley's, but she pressured the pessimist at the desk into dispatching for her an addendum to the original Henry telegram – this supplied what was now her address, ending: 'DO COME.' Being at this distance put Eva in a stronger position. Jeremy, at her elbow, watched her indite the telegram with impartial interest; he could not of course read, but could write, being a wonderful copyist; line after line of her copperplate had he reproduced . . . The hotel, grumbling, came across with a stamp for the envelope, but then signified it had shot its bolt: no way of getting the suitcases from the Ritz other than fetching them oneself. Zigzagging across the river continued, therefore, into late afternoon.

Jeremy watched Paris, this further movie. At this hour, it exhausted the resources of Technicolor, and exceeded them. Creamy buildings transmuted to honey yellow as the sun came languidly down the sky, dazzling half of the city out of existence. Viridian shadow clothed such trees as were not in the sun's path. Rainbows of traffic frayed into splintering whirlpools. Flowers spumy like sherbets though more brilliantly chemical in colour effervesced from their artificial settings. Lancing its way through Paris, the steel-bright Seine magnetized leaners over its parapets. It was the wide-open extravagance of the Right Bank perspectives and spaces which most nearly astounded the little boy – who had never seen so much of anything, at once, as he saw of Paris – and, at the same time, their urbanity, their cerebralism, their look of having been calculated to the last centimetre, which most nearly subdued and in the end tired him: too much to grapple with? He was glad to be back *their* side of the river. In the sunken-shadowy hall of the small hotel he looked rather white, pinched. Eva, having watched the suitcases being bumped upstairs (there was no lift), asked: 'Like to rest, Jeremy? Want to sleep, for a bit?' No, he did not. So out they went again, and, arriving on to the Boulevard St Germain, some way up, squeezed through and managed to get possession of two chairs and a segment of table outside the Deux Magots.

It was a wonder Jeremy was not more blasé, considering how

many Paris cafés there are on screens. This one, however, was no less lifelike – he had the courtesy to look round him interestedly. How implacably good, how conciliating his behaviour had been since, first thing this morning, he had been torn from sleep, helpless as a princeling about to be assassinated, to witness the demolition, around his ears, of what had at least equivocated to 'home'. Their continuing on at Paley's, although it charged Eva, day after day, with an unkept promise, had spelled *some* domesticity for Jeremy. He had clutched at the token, later to be exchanged for the real thing. They had in a way kept house, established themselves – their surrounding accumulation of heaps of objects, and still more, imponderables, had quieted, assuaged him and reassured him. And now? All of it swept away!

Nor was it in his power to ask why.

Why, though, was he propitiating *her?* All today, this acquiescent if dazed brightness, and sliding smiles. Paris a spree? No, he knew better. Now, it was true, he was weary – he could no more.

Above all, he must not know she was afraid. 'It's been a long day, Jeremy, hasn't it?' said Eva. But the child did not notice her. Shoals of people were going by, in the violet air. Phalanxes of people were sitting round – the café, springing alight inside, shone out on to their few silences, costive or tenuous, and their accesses of conversation. One knew nobody: Paris was one's own. Was the boy glad they again were alone together: they two only? They were not alone together: an unbridgeable ignorance of each other, or each other's motives, was cleft between them, and out of the gulf rose a breath of ice. A waiter came by. No Orange Crush to be hoped for in Paris, probably? She ordered a *cassis* syrup; for herself, cognac. Eva's habits had changed, in twenty-four hours – this time yesterday, some *ignoto* at Paley's had steered her into the bar and administered cognac: on the house, she was told. It had stopped her thinking. This evening, she needed that . . . Where *had* been Jeremy, this time yesterday? . . . 'Paris is fun, Jeremy?' asked Eva. She still could not get his attention, she touched his wrist. He turned towards her, irradiated by some secret.

Next morning, on her way out to exchange wads of dollar bills flown in from Chicago, last month, on her person, Eva was handed a telegram. 'HAVE SENSE,' it said, 'MIDDLE OF TERM HOW COULD I? HENRY.' This stimulated her, if anything. Henry's known thrift in matters of postage doubled the value of this reaction: anything so costly must be violent – and where *had* he got the money from, eh? Parker? . . . The streets were sweet, as though after a fall of dew. She bought *œillets*, with picotee edges, dripping from the bucket, from the vendor at a corner. She had locked behind her the room in which lay Jeremy, still asleep – the metal-tabbed key rattled in her pocket, knocking against a miniature alloy revolver which had fallen from Jeremy's when she shook out his jacket. (How had he come by it?) Enticing with coffee, the morning was pearly with promise of noon heat. A day for an outing – for instance, Fontainebleau? From thence, a bright-coloured postcard to Cambridge.

The following morning, in London, Constantine got this letter:

Thanks for your affability on the telephone. I made myself known to you, I may now tell you, with a trepidation which I suppose was extraordinary after all these years' uninhibited letter-writing. One can only say, to talk is another thing. The great pleasure my letters to you gave me was bound up with the impossibility of your answering. They could have no come-back, any more than they could be fended off. To be telling you everything about where I was except *where* I was added a fascination to my surroundings (wherever I was) just as telling you all I did except what I was doing gave an extra edge to my line of action. That a day of reckoning could come did not occur to me. It did when I faced up to the telephone. Then, to be let known, and so immediately, that nothing *had* mounted up, that you held nothing against me, that our non-relationship was as ever, unimpaired, static, stable, was a relief. All had been nothing. Life is an anti-novel.

Thanks, also, for putting me in the picture (as you put it) as to old friends. I have contacted Eric, losing no time – I hope you'll think well of me. Almost immediately after our conversation I came to London, found myself an hotel, then telegraphed to the address you gave me: Luton. We met yesterday. He was considerably embarrassed; I felt nothing. I told him, I will do anything he wants, to which he immediately said he's not sure what he wants. (So, where are we?) In that case, I told him, he was seeing me on false pretences; not that I minded, but it was a waste of time. Apart from what he wanted, I said also, what

about those children one heard he had? At once he was on the
defensive, as though baited – as one remembers so well. After
some time, he seemed blindly angry, though exactly with whom
one couldn't make out. You? Me? You and me as a combination
– for he can't get it out of his head that we are or were one. Eva,
after that fandango she led him? As you'll gather, our meeting
was inconclusive. He asked how I was, where I had been. What
I most noticed, seeing him again, was, he is very sentimental.

Yes, and I had a word with Eva. She'd I'm sure been called
to the telephone in the middle of luncheon, not I suppose actually
with her mouth full, though it sounded so. By the time I rang
off, she was still adjusting. Considering, she didn't do too badly.
I must see her; not to would be a pity.

Have there been any of those disastrous consequences you
foresaw, once – of her getting away, I mean? There I did fail
you. On the other hand, I worked more than half in the dark. If
you'd ever been more than partially honest with me, if you'd
ever given me anything like the whole picture, or whole story, I
need not have – or so I think sometimes. But perhaps there is no
whole picture, or story. Or, more likely, you are unwilling to
recognize what it is. I *could* have done better, and that riles me.

I shall be in Reading (15 Roundabout Rd) for not more than
a week. When I have another address, you shall have it. Do not
let Eric have it; I don't want him coming round again. Any
further dealings with him must be through a lawyer. Could you
find one for me? – I should be grateful.

ISEULT

To which he replied:

Dear Iseult,

What should have been one more of your delightful letters
arrived, I am sorry to say, on the wrong morning. I'm fit for
nothing. Eva has bolted again – and not only that, accuses me of
'conspiracy'. That at least was the gist of her telegram. She and
I had seemed to be entering calmer waters. Her return was a
genuine pleasure; since it, she's been accommodating and
rational – I would go so far as to say, affectionate. A halcyon
period of mutual confidence, and planning. A very dear friend
of mine, who met her, encouraged my optimism or euphoria; he

saw nothing in her that could not be put right, and found her in general amenable, he reported. – But now?

You can offer no light on this? If you cannot, I fear I possibly can. You contacted Eva (from what you tell me) with incontinent speed, allowing no time for me to warn her you are about again. The effect on her nervous system could be deplorable; so much so that to it, I must frankly tell you, I trace this renewed outbreak of crazed suspicions. What I am talking about, you should surely know. The notion that you and I are 'in league' in some way gained an overmastering hold on poor dear Eva, at one time, and may not (though one had hoped the contrary) have been quite got rid of. On and off, it has hampered us both in our dealings with her – *I* suffered under it, certainly. Your reappearance set old machinery going – unprepared for it as she was (*not* unavoidably) was. We know her to be a mass of latent nervosity. Had no incident followed, the same day, all might have again subsided – or one may hope so. There was an incident.

On getting her telegram, I went straight round to Paley's. Yes, indeed she had left – with a suddenness puzzling, and, one could see, wounding to that faithful hotel. Had anything happened to upset her? I unearthed this: the little boy had been missing, for an hour or so, at which 'Madam had been very greatly shaken.' He turned up again, fit as a fiddle – but that did it. As well it might. Given the Trout child's probable weight in platinum, it would *not* have been fanciful to suspect 'conspiracy'. The insane thing was, to incriminate me. My best hope of clearing this mare's-nest up is to establish, for certain, who was concerned. I have in mind one character who could be more than fishy. I cannot remember whether or not I told you, during our brief though at that time delightful chat, that Eva'd been farming the boy out, daily, to an artistic person on Primrose Hill? If I did, I cannot, I'm sure, have mentioned the name, or I should remember your laughing – it is too truly rural, it is 'Applethwaite'.

To the eye, Applethwaite is a wash-out. I went to see her (oh, the itinerary of one nightmare evening!). She is the *manquée* who could be 'cover' for anything: chinless women crop up in half those cases, operators pick well. I drew a blank, outright. She has had time to think, she sticks to her story. A Zola-type harlot came and removed Jeremy. This she told Eva, this (she says) Eva accepted. I could not shake her. Someone must try again.

Will you be the one? Should you wish, you could see it as a step towards redeeming your tiny blunder. But also, my reliance on your acumen has been one of the lasting links in our 'non-relationship', dear Iseult. Will *you* go to Primrose Hill and look swiftly round? Just, confront the lady, unnerve her a very little. See if it seems to you she could ever crack. Then come straight to me (I repeat, *straight*) and report? We could, even, have lunch?

Or am I asking too much? If you feel that, say so. But I do wilt under Eva's misdirected hostility. Don't, of course, run into danger – on any account.

Yours
C.

The reply was:

Yes, Constantine, of course if you wish it I will. I would not for anything shirk your trust, but I must say I am put in rather a fix. I simply cannot subscribe to your 'gang' theory: don't you think you've been reading too many stories? Surely professionals don't work so maladroitly? In less than four hours, that little boy of Eva's blandly gave 'them' the slip. Was that not odd?

Must anybody bully the woolly lady? Can you find no other way to make peace with Eva? After all, the boy, like the cat in the song, came back.

ISEULT

In counter-reply:

My dear Iseult,
Do you know, it's you I think who are odd. Is this extra-sensory? What makes *you* say, 'less than four hours'? For how long the boy was missing, I never told you – not in fact knowing.

How do you do your hair, these days? Still showing that wonderful forehead?

CONSTANTINE

Cat-and-mouse again . . .
Their enticing if saturnine flavour made it hard for Iseult to

detach herself from such thoughts, though in a minute she would be needing others. Umbrella up, she advanced on the vicarage through a leaden downpour which rebounded from her silvery raincoat (unlike the yellow Lumleigh oilskin) to splash in over the tops of her matching overboots. The once-familiar village with its flash additions wavered at her through vertical water. A stopped-up gutter on the vicarage porch resulted in cataracts one was obliged to dive through. 'I've come to see you,' she said to Mrs Dancey.

'Do come in!' exclaimed Mrs Dancey, with instant enthusiasm – she never hesitated till later. Now forced to, she scanned her visitor with a pleading wildness. 'I *know* who you are; but –'

'My name's "Arble".'

'Yes, of course! You are not drowned, I hope?'

Across the threshold, Mrs Arble rustled out of her raincoat, tugged off the overboots. 'I'm afraid,' she said, watching the former being hung from a hat-rack, 'that will drip all over your floor.'

'Look how ours do! I'm sorry you've never been here before – I don't think you have? We had always hoped . . .'

'Larkins,' smiled the *revenante*, 'seems so long ago.'

'Yes. The new lady is a keen gardener.' They entered the drawing-room, duskier than outdoors. 'I hope you've been well?' went on Mrs Dancey, conscious of hazard. 'In France, I fancy somebody said? I'm so sorry my husband's out; he will be so sorry. By a coincidence, *we* are just off to France, or rather, Paris. We are taking the choir – that's to say, going with them, not *taking* them; they've saved up – on one of those three-day tours. We're flying there. How they have cut down prices, now they're compelled to! We don't expect to be comfortable, but it should be interesting – best of all, we hope to be seeing Eva. Do sit down: where would you like to? The sofa looks like a stranger without its cover, which has gone to the wash – I seized the occasion.'

Iseult selected a chair whose woolwork was fast unpicking itself: what a pity, it could have been in fashion! 'Oh, then *you* know where Eva is?'

'Yes. And there'll be the little boy – I missed him the day she brought him here. I hear he is a darling, and so clever: all the same how heart-breaking, isn't it?' Mrs Dancey, beset by some vague idea that there had been some paternity-complication, took thought, hoped for the best, plunged on. 'Have you, have *you* seen him, Mrs Arble?'

'I've not yet seen Eva. She has vanished again.'

'Oh, no; Henry knows where she is. You remember Henry?'

'So well. – Constantine Ormeau's worried, though. She rushed off without a word to him, other than an alarming telegram.'

'That was too bad,' pronounced Mrs Dancey. 'Poor Mr Ormeau – when he came to tea he seemed so sincere, sad. Lonely, I thought. But he and our little girl made great friends. At that time, he was looking for you, I think.'

'Yes. What a lot of trouble we all give him. – Henry's now a young man?'

'Yes,' Mrs Dancey agreed, with a troubled air. 'At Cambridge. I do wish Eva would not be thoughtless!'

'How, Mrs Dancey? – May I smoke, by the way?'

'Do, do! I'm sorry we haven't any. What I *am* going to do, though, is make tea. – I mean, telling nobody where she goes.'

Iseult, chucking a spent match into the empty grate, remarked, in a voice as nonchalant as the action: 'She told Henry.'

'I imagine she sent him a picture postcard. But from childhood they have been kindred spirits.'

'They weren't children at exactly the same time.'

'No, not exactly, but Eva's a child at heart – don't you think so? – didn't you always find?'

'Not always,' confessed Iseult, contracting her shoulders.

'Oh, you're *not* cold? A miserable day like this deserves a fire: who would think this was May? But my husband and I are alone, and we're in and out. So long as May isn't like this in Paris! Shall I give you Eva's address? – I shall have to find it.'

'That would be kind. Constantine would be glad.'

'How particularly lucky,' said Henry's mother, 'that Henry sent it!'

'How particularly lucky it came his way!'

For a moment, Mrs Dancey looked at her visitor, not in alarm, more with concern, wonder. Overtones, also undertones, were beyond her. 'What can the matter be?' was her theme song, both in parish and in family life – as a rule, the ejaculation remained in mid-air. 'I *must* boil the kettle,' she argued, 'or we shan't have tea. While I do – look, there are some magazines; some of them may be old, I don't know how old.' She hesitated, flushed, prayed for grace, re-buttoned her cardigan. 'Mrs Arble, will you allow me to tell you, we were so sorry . . .'

'About our marriage?' Iseult asked, in a bright, jarred voice.

'I wonder if anything human *is* ever over?'

'This is. Still, thank you very much.'

'Yes, I see,' replied Mrs Dancey, in such a manner as to make it perfectly clear that she did not. 'How nice, though, that you are back. Are you here long?'

'In these parts? No. Just a sentimental journey.'

'Too bad it's raining.'

'Oh, do you think so? Don't pity me, Mrs Dancey. I just wanted to know if I *could* feel. I can't, I'm cleared. I'm as dead as a doornail.'

'One may,' declared Mrs Dancey, with unusual vigour, 'want to be, but it's wrong to. One never is. I wonder if anyone told you, we lost Louise.'

She went to the kitchen.

Iseult, after a minute, rose and pottered across to the big chipped writing desk, which yawned open, too overflowing to close. Her intentions were vagrant, and not dishonourable – all she wanted to know was, of just *what* junk this havering life was composed. A snapshot, however, was half-submerged in one of the upper waves of the depths of clutter. She looked closer: this could only be Henry. She extracted him, took him nearer the window. 'Yes . . .' she thought, not altogether surprised. He had not (evidently) posed, but been stolen up upon – he flung round upon the aggressor's camera. Instantaneousness, as so often, had done the trick: a very great amount of him had been 'caught'. Temperament was depth-charged up into features which, by their cast, looked as if they would pride themselves on no show of it. Eight years had made the slip of a schoolboy, with his superciliousness, his taunting disregardfulness, into a fellow to be reckoned with – whether or not he was ready to be reckoned with, just yet. 'What an eye,' Iseult ungrudgingly indeed admiringly reflected, 'Eva always did have, from the start. She loved me, once.'

The teacher could not have satisfied more fully the curiosity bringing her to the vicarage. She replaced Henry and followed his mother into the kitchen. 'Could I help?'

Mrs Dancey, rummaging among paper bags in the cake-tin, turned round, startled. She took in the re-entering woman with new enlightenment. 'I see *now* why I didn't recognize you – you must have thought me so very stupid. Your hair's different from how it was, and it alters you.'

Mother says [wrote Henry, a week later] you seemed very well. She felt bad playing truant from the choir, not to speak of skipping the Tomb of Napoleon, but the afternoon with you was like old times, she says. Your hotel is picturesque, she says. She felt she was very greedy at the pâtisserie. So it sounds to me as though everything was now back again on a good banal footing, which was my object. I really can only go on on an even keel. Only one thing misfired: why did only she go to see you, not Father too? – surely the choir could have got themselves round the Tomb of Napoleon, they're not such mutts. What made him shy off? I have a feeling he *has* got wind of something. And you do realize that would never do, don't you? He would be appalled; why, I cannot tell you, though I suppose I in a way know. I'm not sure I'm not slightly appalled, sometimes.

No, I haven't written, I'm well aware of that. For one thing I *am* working like a black, you don't know what it is to be in this torture-house. But also what am I to say? I think it's just as well you are in Paris, to be honest. What happened the other day, just before we went to your train in Cambridge, was my fault, asking that idiotic question. Let sleeping dogs lie, I ought to have thought – but then you see till I asked I was not certain whether there was a dog. We always have been on extraordinary terms.

To do me justice, it wasn't totally vanity (though it could have been). More, and still more like me, I'm sorry to say, a passion for finding out followed by paralysis when I've done so. No, Eva, I'm not going to treat you to a whole lot of adolescent introspection – anyway, oddly enough, that is not my forte: perhaps I am not yet fully adolescent? My trouble is, I don't know how to proceed. Would it be too crude to ask what you want? No, forgive me, to put it like that seems horrible – and, anyway, I quite often think it's conceivable you don't know.

How's Jeremy? Edified, I hope. I must say, in many ways I

envy him; I mean, I'd only too well have liked to have come to Paris, to be in Paris. Mother spoke highly of it (I haven't of course seen her, only a letter). She'll have told you about the sensational reappearance of Mrs Arble, like a voluptuous dryad on our doorstep, two days before they came away? I always told you that one would turn up. She obtained, as you'd say, your address from Mother, with a view to handing it on to your lonely Guardian. How could one foresee *that*? – I am sorry. I hope there've been so far no bad results?

When are you back from Paris? I do want to see you, don't think I don't. Don't ever go right away again, will you? – Here comes Parker, as ever, so I must stop.

Love,
HENRY

On learning from the culpable Mrs Dancey of the leakage as to her whereabouts, Eva had at once pulled out of the Left Bank and removed to Fontainebleau, which Jeremy had taken a liking to. Her postcard informing Henry of change of habitat reached Cambridge too late to deflect his letter, which consequently she never had – ceasing to suppose she would hear from him, Eva adhered to her known principle of leaving no forwarding address with any hotel. In the rack of the cross-eyed Paris one, therefore, the letter probably is still, more flyblown with each day.

At Fontainebleau, one is elevated from tourist status by staying on. She and Jeremy, going about their business, came to be recognizable features of the town. She with her mighty gait and unfinished handsomeness, he with the touching aureole of his handicap engaged first interest, later a sympathy warmed by local possessiveness. They received, correctly, absolutely correct overtures, in and around the hotel they remained on in, in shops and the market, in the selecter pâtisseries and cafés where they partook perpetually of *cafés crèmes*. It was, even, intimated to them by residents who, exercising dogs in the château park, veered past, though nearer each time, the young woman and child, that they were about to become acceptable. Greetings began to be exchanged, to be widened out into conversations. It was in the course of such conversations that a suggestion was first launched and afterwards urged: Eva ought to, nay, must, contact a couple, doctor and doctor wife, who, in this vicinity, devoted themselves to cases such as Jeremy's. They worked by a method they had themselves evolved – its success depended on certain factors, in the main psychic; they were known to be scrupulous in refusing children with whom it was unlikely to take effect. Eva, therefore, made herself known to the Bonnards (as their name was). She returned for a second time with Jeremy, whom, at their desire, she left alone with them. They accepted him.

These people lived some kilometres out of Fontainebleau; one could more quickly walk to them through the forest. Their house with its white doves and weathered jalousies, bound round by a patriarchal wisteria, re-inspired in Eva a lost confidence – she had not believed she could ever again leave Jeremy in others' keeping. Nor was that all: as the month of May went on his lips began to formulate, or attempt to formulate, French words, and he started to accord to the lips of speakers, other than Eva, a level, exacting, scientific attention denied formerly. He had been won over – or, had his going to the Bonnards' happened to synchronize with a disposition to lower his defences? If the latter, what could have been the reason? – what *had* decided him? One could recollect that, since the flight to Paris, in fact since the eve of the flight to Paris, he had, for all his angel amenability, been withdrawn as never before. To be as others, simply to be *as* others, had never tempted him – what, as the terms of his lordly, made-magical life were, could (as Constantine had asked) be the inducement? But now, by what means had the idea of *exceeding* been made known to him, or made itself known to him? . . . He was interacting ideally with the Bonnards, could be on the verge of being one of their miracles – but that they disclaimed miracles. 'He requires now, madame,' said Gérard Bonnard to Eva, in his simplicity, 'only, the company of an intelligent person. He is going through a phase of enlarged desires, of which all possible – I say to you, all *possible* – should be met.'

Eva noticed chiefly that accustomed communications with Jeremy broke down. He no longer obeyed her, not out of rebelliousness but from genuine lack of knowledge of what was wanted. His responses were not less willing, but less ready. To get his attention she had to touch him – though *that*, after all, had been so their first evening after the flight from London, outside the Deux Magots.

The look with which he rewarded her, that done, was bright with immediate amicability, no more.

During the hours when he was at the Bonnards', she pored over French novels, unselectively bought by her, the better to acquaint herself with the language to be his first. Their vocabulary she became able to master, but not their content. When he was not at the Bonnards', he and she cantered on good horses used to consorting with one another into the heart of the tapestry of the forest, or in balmy weather dozed in the glades, at the roots of trees. Or they circulated, brushing their fingertips together as of old, through the mathematical gardens of the château. They went up then down the twin flights, widening apart like reversed antlers, of the exterior staircase. Inside the building, they passed from one to another of the magnetic fantasies in the chains of rooms – the great golden slumbrous Bonaparte bees fascinated Jeremy most; beating his arms, he tried to exacerbate them into swarming. Everywhere indoors was drowned in the green of trees disseminated into a glossy gloom sometimes further varnished by sunshine; underfoot polish became bottomless pools. At every turn they were reflected, or echoed. But his and her universe was over. It had not been shattered; simply, it had ended. It was a thing of the past.

Very early in June, a letter reached Fontainebleau:

You don't say whether you got my other. If you didn't, I should be rather glad; but did you? Why do you keep changing about, I thought you said Paris was so pretty? As soon as one pictures you somewhere, you're somewhere else. Probably you've by now left Fontainebleau. Have you read *L'Éducation Sentimentale*? I suppose hardly. There's a Fontainebleau part. I should not half mind being Frédéric, going for delicious drives in that well-sprung carriage.

Eva, are you annoyed with me? I *could* say, that would be nothing new – would it? But this time, I should be rather shaken if you were. Did I say anything unforgivable in my letter? If I did, I was simply expressing myself stupidly. I cannot exactly remember what I did say. The thing is, I am thoroughly overstrained, everybody is in a frenzy, and I am not having enough to eat. You have no conception what it is like here. (But, of course, you may never have got my letter.) It's the idea of the horrors of a competitive society waiting ahead for one. But to return to my letter – in case you don't know the one I'm talking about, so don't know whether or not you had it, it began about Mother and the pâtisserie. As a matter of fact, it must be the first I've written you for about ninety years, since *l'affaire Jaguar*. Eva, don't run away with the wrong idea. About you, I'm not so feeble as I make myself seem. You are unlike anything that's ever happened to me, and not only that (I begin to realize) but unlike anything that *could*. You are, I mean, on a totally different scale. Without you, everything would be an anticlimax. When I let myself think how I may have bungled things, I feel frenzied.

A telegram came the other day, and for I don't know how long I couldn't open it. It turned out to be simply from Andrew. Term will be practically over by the time you get this – if you get *this*. In *theory*, I can then be anywhere I like, though of course still always bowed under my load of guilt and shame in the form of work to be caught up with. I can raise some money, up to a point – one thing I am rich in, that is resourcefulness. Where shall you be then, so far as you know?

Don't think Father looms too large in my cosmology. He does not really.

How is Jeremy?

I seem to have run out – or run down, like something wound up that gives out. Please do write; there's no fear of *your* saying too much. Write soonish, or it will miss me at Cambridge. It would then I suppose eventually be forwarded to home, where I shall be going unless anything arises to the contrary.

Love

HENRY

In reply:

Dear Henry,

No, I did not have the letter you talk of, but had this one. Am so sorry you say you are unwell. I have not left Fontainebleau, Jeremy is being put right. The people now want him to stay with them and be quite away from me, as an experiment, for 2–3 weeks, so I could come to England, though not for long. Next time, I would advise you to write to Paley's. I shall be calling there although not staying, so as not to be traced.

EVA

Eric again stormed into the Knightsbridge office. 'A nice kettle of fish you have got me into!'

'A thankless task,' said Constantine, to the ceiling. 'Look, I'm sorry, but I'm just off to lunch. – One thought one had everything lined up the way you wanted. Wobbly about the divorce?'

'That's without foundation!'

'You found Iseult in good spirits – well, on the whole?'

'That's my business, isn't it?'

'Largely. She sounded well on the telephone, but I've not yet had the pleasure of setting eyes on her.' Aside, Constantine said to the intercom: 'The car.'

'Don't let *me* interfere with your habits,' said sarcastic Eric, seating himself firmly. He flicked open the perpetual onyx cigarette box, satisfied himself its contents still were Egyptian, snorted. The whole set-up reeked of expense-accounts. 'Can you wonder,' he declaimed, in a general way, 'this country is in the state it is in?'

'No. But one must eat, you realize – don't you in Luton? You know, you time your visits infernally; this happened before.'

'What do you think I do all day?'

'I believe you told me. – Twice round the block, tell it,' said Constantine to the intercom, 'I should then be down. – Now, what is your trouble, Arble, other than indecision? How is Miss Norway standing up to this, by the way?'

'I won't have you drag *her* in. That's no way to speak of her.'

'As you wish. You engaged one's sympathies for her, last time, so very thoroughly, one might say deeply, I admit I don't yet find it easy to leave her out. This is a combustible situation? Frankly, then, take it away; I want none of it. Aren't you being staggeringly incompetent?'

'It upset me again, seeing Izzy.'

'Yes, so I gather. – I'm so sorry, but I have enough on my hands, and have had for some time. Eva's bolted again.'

'Eva's done what?'

'Gone.'

Eric said: 'Can you wonder?'

218

'You interest me. Why? – or rather, why not?'

'Look what she got herself back into. Thieves' kitchen.'

'I beg your pardon?'

'You heard me,' asserted Eric – dauntless if nervous.

Constantine leaned back. With a middle finger, he softly rubbed the site of an eyebrow, meditating. He then whetted his lips. 'Look here,' he advised, 'less of that from you. May one recall facts? Eva's demoralization began at Larkins, with *your* advances. She was morally horrified. Her distressed perturbation wrings my heart, now I have come to know of it. You abused a trust. Your offence against her simplicity does, I must say, sicken me when I think of it. I was blind at the time. She came to me and desired me to remove her – unwilling (perhaps unable?) to say why. I acted too slowly: can I ever forgive myself? She fled, to that, er, tenement in the, er, swamps near Broadstairs. She believed herself safe. You came after her. She was alone. I surprised you there in the house. Followed, the scandal of her presumed pregnancy, the panic driving her to America. Since then, the irreclaimable loss, to her, of any hope of stability, any power to feel or repose confidence. Those who love her have had to face this; we have suffered accordingly . . . No, your, er, oily solicitude for her becomes you oddly. You have also come with it to the wrong shop. Grotesque? – it's worse; it's blatant hypocrisy. And don't act stupid at me, you are stupid enough. What have you to say – if anything?'

Eric said, after consideration: 'You beat the band.'

Constantine inclined to agree. One had not done badly. He pouted out his lips and blew through them slowly.

'Twisting everything round. You be careful, some day.'

'Ah. When?'

'Some day, anybody could kill you. – I *could*,' pondered Eric, not unenjoyably, picking up and weighing the onyx box.

'I must be going, anyhow,' said the other, sliding his chair back over the carpet, rising. 'I am meeting a clergyman. – And next time, pull your own chestnuts out of the fire, will you?'

'Bloody well twisting everything upside down,' re-indicted Eric, though putting down the box.

'And by the way, keep an eye on your wife. She could be in danger of criminal proceedings, I'm beginning to fear. – I'm not offering you a lift, if you don't mind.'

'I wouldn't want one. I have the children with me.'

'You take the cake. Where?'

'Where I left them, with the lady attendant. Well, I had to give their mother some reason for me coming to London again, didn't I? "Business" I said last time. So I said, "I'm taking those two to the Zoo," and so I shall be, shortly. Any objection?'

'None whatsoever, from me. Whipsnade is nearer Luton, it might occur to her.'

'They've had Whipsnade,' said Eric shortly. He heaved himself up – but his visit was not over. Inching open the door, he took a dekko into the outer office: all clear: now was the hour! Homicide abandoned, if ever likely, he let himself go vocally – more satisfyingly. 'You old shocker, telling anyone else off! Look at you and what *you* are, for God's sake! No, you give me the creeps, you and your sort – and so you ought, let me tell you! There *are* limits, or would you not think so? What do you think everyone else is, born yesterday? One day you go too far, eh? You old so-and-so, you and your fancy ways –'

'You are out of date,' beamed the retired sinner. Opening a drawer, he extracted an additional handkerchief: monogrammed. 'Still, nothing like the wrath of an honest man. It also does good to the system, doesn't one find?' During the diatribe, he'd been checking on jottings made on a memo pad: he now pushed the eye-catching pad into position. 'For my secretary,' he vouchsafed. 'One might not be back. – Now, come along, if you don't mind: had you a hat?'

They were under way – or were, till Constantine blundered. In sight of the highly burnished doors of the lift, he remarked, with a frivolous infelicity: 'Yet, one misses Eva!'

That brought Eric violently to a stop. He rooted his heels into the wealthy carpet. A more virulent anger surfaced, from deeper sources. Blood raced to his temples, contusing them; a visible throbbing started behind his ears. His face inflamed as if over a furnace. 'Miss *her*?' he chanted. ' "Sorry" for Eva? She did me in. Who else is at the bottom of all this mess? Who lost me Izzy? I was my own man; now they're all round me like every she-bat in Hell. All was O.K. till *she* bust everything up – deliberately! No, I could have her blood!'

Constantine, stepping ahead, touched the 'down' bell. He then made a deprecating gesture. 'Wha – at?'

'You heard me.'

'I hoped I didn't.'

The lift came. In it, Eric calmed down. Within the few seconds of downward suction, he changed his tune. 'I say –' he began, in a man-to-man tone.

'Well, what?'

'That time at Cathay when you crashed the party – had Izzy by any chance tipped you off?'

'Since you ask, yes. Your wife, after all.'

'That's all I wanted to know. She's a great girl!'

The situation of Eva was as apparent to the intelligent French doctor as that of Jeremy. Doubting it to be as clear to herself, he believed he should make her try to define it for him – there could be gain in at least trying. On the eve of her departure for England, Gérard Bonnard accordingly came to see her, taking the short cut through the forest. The hour was sympathetically well chosen: Jeremy had that day been transferred to the Bonnards', Eva's might be a solitude made less bearable by the Cytherean beauty of this June evening. Finding her, he suggested they stroll in the park, open after the château closed. He was a carelessly jointed big man, with a baggy-skinned face, boyish in outline, and a manner sometimes eager, sometimes abstracted, showing no particular signs of nationality – or of age, for that matter. He had been a figure in the Resistance. He was happy and better than happy with his wife and also partner, Thérèse – now helping the newcomer to bed in a room overlooking the dovecote. Tomorrow, Jeremy would be fending for himself: that was the regime. Madame Bonnard had had to school herself to one kind of abstinence: as to 'mothering'. The Bonnards had no children.

Gérard Bonnard began by thanking Eva for her confidence. They spoke English. 'Also,' he said, 'you are showing courage.' Eva, watching the spokes of sunset shortening over the lawns, said, 'In two weeks, it will be the longest day. Or at least, in England.'

'You have not felt in exile while you were here?'

She shook her head. 'No. I think I was brought here.'

'Are you *croyante*, madame?'

'Sometimes. This evening.'

'May I ask you one thing we have never touched on? You were

honest with us, making no secret of the reason why the child's heredity cannot be known. We have not been greatly hampered by this lacuna – as you know, we are environmentalists, the horrible doctrine of Predestination seeming to us too closely linked with acceptance of the dominance of heredity. It would be irresponsible to ignore, altogether, the physical incidences and recurrences which are part of the physical composition of a heredity – to have known something of Jeremy's could have been to a point helpful, but that we have been able to do without. What is important, and what we are taking into account, is what you have supplied him with instead – the character of what you have given him. From his demeanour, from his assurance, one would take him to be a child in the main line of a powerful family. You are bringing him up to be your father's son – conventionally, one should say grandson. Now we come to what I should like to ask you: had you or had you been given reason to think you could not give birth to a child? Otherwise, what made you prefer mimicry to what could have been the actual continuance of a flesh-and-blood? You were young eight years ago, you are young still. You shrank from something?'

Eva looked waitingly at the doctor, hoping he might assist her to answer. But in return he looked waitingly back at her. She said: 'These seemed the best means.'

'They were drastic, hurried.'

'How should I go to, otherwise, all that trouble? I did not wish, either, to be immoral. I had had disagreeable impressions of love.'

'You say, "impressions" – impressions only? You had not experimented?'

'I was not anxious to.'

'I understand,' he said. 'I will not say that this was a pity: who is to know? – Was there this, also: that you wished (in default of your father) to be Jeremy's father as well as mother?'

'Possibly,' she ceded – not greatly startled.

'Look at the château!' he said suddenly. 'I was born here, everything should be familiar; yet I have never seen what we are looking at exactly as it is at this moment, in this light. I have seen it at other moments, in other lights, which were as beautiful – never being the same. Transfigurations never repeat themselves. One need not be frightened of growing old; to the last, there will always be something new. – Come and look at the reflection in the pool!'

They did so.

'One must not,' he went on, 'judge love too remorselessly. We are at its mercy, but not altogether; it is also at ours. It cannot be as tranquil as this water. It has it in itself to be ideal, yet it is prey to enormities and distortions – which are as agonizing, one must remember, to the lovers as they are, as you say, disagreeable to onlookers. You were compelled, possibly, to be a closer, more constant onlooker than one should have to be? – That is not always a popular position.'

'No,' she said. 'One is sometimes never forgiven.'

'Otherwise, what did they think of you, these people? – those you grew up amongst, and who may have persisted? In so far as they do persist, what are they thinking? Do you feel them to judge you? – This is important. Could you answer?'

'Oh, yes. They agree, I am a liar,' said Eva – though easily, and looking about her at the lovely transparency of the rising shadows without rancour or air of trouble. 'I am not always. For instance, this evening.'

'One is made a liar.'

'I was once told, I am by nature truthful. But on the whole, Doctor Bonnard, I cannot answer – you see, I have made myself not think about what is thought of me, or was. Why is it important?'

'Because one is so much made by it. Whether one resists it or not, it has so much power. It is so hard not to comply with it, not to fall in with it – not to be overcome by it in the very battle one has against it. The way one is envisaged by other people – what easier way is there of envisaging oneself? There is a fatalism in one's acceptance of it. Solitude is not the solution, one feels followed. Choice – choice of those who are to surround one, choice of those most likely to see one rightly – is the only escape. But for some of us, it is an escape difficult to make. Was it for you?'

'I continue going away. But I am awaited.'

'Jeremy,' said the doctor, apparently at a tangent, 'has not yet incurred the ability to lie. We must remember, he is on the eve of doing so. We must all see – you will see, I know? – that if possible he shall never have the incentive. So far, he has been able to conceal, not yet, however, to misrepresent. The day you brought him to us, you told us he had been taken away from you, just before you left London, for some hours. The mystery of what happened in those hours, and of how, still more why, it was affecting him was tormenting you. Thérèse and I have come to feel, and would like to say to you, that you must not allow this to loom too large. We can find no signs of his having been harmed. Whatever was the design of someone else, the child may have, if anything, benefited. What happened could be part of – could even have led to? – the phase he is going through, of which I spoke to you: expanding desires. Can you see it as that?'

Leaving the pool, they ascended the outdoor antler-staircase of the château: at the top, door made fast against invasion by night. Backs to the door, they stood overlooking the scene where they had walked. All was sensuously dissolving, yet was gentle as a sigh, breathless – day, a dying yellow suffusion, was at its last. Wandering lovers were about – some faded trance-like into the distance, but where the pool gleamed two slowly embraced. Some new element entered Eva's silence. Gérard Bonnard asked: 'You are tired, madame?'

'No. I –'

'Not thinking, "Tomorrow, another journey"?'

'I was thinking of the end of it. Of somebody.'

'To be awaited, then,' he suggested gently, 'is not always an undesired thing? *I* should be sad if I were not – that there should be somebody there is precious.' He smiled – that being, by now, more to be heard than seen. 'May I be so happy as to think that you are, after all, in love?'

'Do *you* think so?' she asked, turning to him.

'It is what I hope. In spite of all, it is so very possible to be happy. I think,' said the doctor, looking towards Eva, 'you are framed for happiness – if it could be so simple?' He was a man of few gestures; he now made one. 'It's a matter of genius, possibly: hardly more!'

'This is not simple.'

'He is not simple?'

'No.'

'All the same, *bon voyage!*'

'I am frightened, as though I were about to die.'

'That is unworthy of you, as I know you.'

'Thank you,' said Eva, instantly drawing herself up. 'But this – this beautiful place. I wish I could stay.'

'We must go in, never the less.'

They descended the staircase. He saw her to her hotel, then made his way home again through the forest, this track being so known to him that he could walk quickly through the gathering dark. Jeremy was asleep. Madame Bonnard sat sewing by a lighted window.

The scene of the reunion was a bar.

'And if I did?' asked Iseult, brazening it out. 'She brought him to see us, according to you. No sooner were they in England than they were on our doorstep – or what had been. That we weren't any more at Larkins was the sheerest mischance, as *she* saw it! What had been gone through never occurred to her; nor did, that she mightn't be doing a tactful thing. Her one wish was, one should meet the child.'

'Her intentions were excellent, if extraordinary.'

'So were mine, then.'

'Ah. What will you think?'

'Anything,' said Iseult, agitatedly. About to bite on a tempting fingernail, she saw Constantine wince; she jerked it away. She said: 'He's a nice little boy.'

'Why are you becoming such a tramp?'

'That's how you'd put it, would you?' she asked, giving him an analytical smile.

'That's how it could be put.'

'Well, you had my letters – I'd thought I'd told you. Or didn't you take in what I was saying? I've undergone an emotional hysterotomy, and am the better. No return of the former trouble need be anticipated. My inside's gone. You understand what I mean?'

'Just a little out of my field, I fear . . . Your, er, *appearance* does not give that impression. Why on earth, Iseult, have you adopted it? – when did you?'

'During my travels. You don't like it?'

'The fulminous Latin look? I could tell you who has gone for it – that you know, of course: Eric. Scandinavia's nowhere. He bounced in the other day, all over again, and I'm getting sick of this. I have had enough of it.'

'What made you involve yourself?'

'Philanthropy.'

'Sorry,' Iseult said. '*I* can't help you.'

'Oh, yes you can. Take him away.'

'I must *say*,' she cried, 'you are utterly heartless!'

'You are utterly wrong; I'm a different man. I'm distressed, actually. – What have you got in that parcel under your chair?'

'Oh, yes, Constantine: that reminds me – would you be so kind as to fish it up?' He did so, gingerly placing it on the table. Heavy, he mentioned. 'Yes,' she said, 'a revolver. I was going to ask you: could you keep it for me in the safe in your office? I have nowhere to put it; that's why I brought it this evening. I'm sure you will? I can't very well take it to Newcastle.'

'I'm sorry,' said Constantine, decidedly, 'I'm not going to carry *that* across London.'

'It won't go off,' she said patronizingly.

'Dead or alive, I wouldn't be seen dead with it. It's a ghastly parcel.' It was not a neat job: bulky-knobbly brown paper, thrice-knotted string. 'Why are you going to Newcastle? – which Newcastle?'

'Upon-Tyne. I'll be teaching, as a fill-in. Someone broke down.'

'And you still teach marvellously?'

'I teach,' said Iseult, gone taut. 'Isn't that enough? I don't as I used.'

'One should not undergo emotional hysterotomy – perhaps?'

'That's enough, Constantine.'

'Ah? Sorry.'

'How disobliging you are,' she complained, with reference to the revolver, shifting it on to an empty third chair. 'Then if you won't, I know what I'll do,' she went on, smacking the palm of a hand on to the cushion of hair over her forehead, 'take it round to Paley's, tell them it's Eva's, get them to put it with the rest of her belongings down in the baggage room. It's no business of theirs what is inside. If she turns up again, I can ask her for it; if she never does, there it can stay. It's no longer of interest. I'd hand it back to Eric, but he's better without it.'

'Also, you won't be seeing him.'

'No – of course not!'

'How,' Constantine wanted to know, 'do you know her belongings are in the baggage room?'

'I went in, to see what the place is like. I asked.'

'It surprises me they gave you the information – frankly. Looking as you do.'

'You can't take your eyes off me,' she said coldly.

'Horror, I think,' he said. 'It's not that you've lost your looks, you've thrown them away – gratuitously. What on *earth* is your object?'

'To be different.' Stage-fright had caused her not to take in this bar when she first entered. She now did so. It was in Soho, somewhere. Outside in the street, summer staled away: in here, cracked leatherette was pent up in smokiness. The habitués, sparse this time of the evening, were nondescript. The waiter, if cognisant of their order, did not show it. She asked Constantine: 'Do you come here often?'

'No. Nor shall I again.'

'Yes, you don't seem to be cutting so much ice. Though anywhere else, I suppose, *I* might not do? I so well remember that place where we first had lunch, except where it was? But of course, in those days there was more to say. Wasn't there?'

'Don't be touchy, Iseult.'

'I was being funny.'

'You do realize, of course, that you're jolly lucky I'm not turning you over to the police?'

'Exactly for what reason?'

'Attempted kidnapping.'

Fortunately the drinks came. The interpretation of 'anything' had been vodka. Iseult so badly needed it that for some time she fought a delaying action, lacing and re-lacing her fingers round the glass. Constantine looked sceptically at his brandy before further diluting it with soda. Each, then, watched how the other did. Iseult drained the last of the vodka out of the sleazy ice before saying: 'Still – what about my letters?'

'Immensely interesting. Yes – they were quite remarkable. I have them all, I believe. Do you want them back?'

'No, Constantine. Why?'

'Psychological material, *I* should have thought,' said he, bending upon her a look of disarming earnestness. 'A pity they should go to waste – you should write a book: obviously. Shouldn't you write a book?'

'No.'

He said: 'I disagree with you.'

'What else do you think I was trying to do in France? It was born dead.' She twisted her head away.

'I'm sincerely sorry.'

The bracelets which had been noted by the sculptress were gilt, of exaggerated design. Iseult wore three on her left wrist – she pushed them up it, rattled them down again. 'Talking of France, did you use that address of Eva's I got from the Danceys?'

'No. She has really wounded me too much, this time. The next move – if any – will have to be hers.'

'What the whole of the picture *is* is, Eva obsesses you. You love her, in some preposterous way you don't know yourself. I shouldn't, I suppose, blame you for keeping me in the dark; *you're* in the dark. Still, there it is – isn't it, Constantine? Talking of the Danceys, what, in that case, do you think of all this about Henry?'

'I was not aware,' he said undisturbedly, 'that there was anything about Henry. Rather a lightweight, surely?'

Plucking at a bracelet which had a jet inset, snapping it on its springs, she remarked: 'He knew where she was.'

'*Dear* Iseult, don't jangle your bangles at one! Rue de Rivoli, aren't they? What are their individual histories, you make one wonder? Eat your nails, if you wish, but do try not to flaunt your trophies. You've been plunged in romance, that goes without saying.'

'Yes and no,' she said. 'Do I look like it?'

'You're at pains to do so.'

'Nothing went even as well as it did with Eric.'

To the now weed-throttled lake had been added a flat-bottomed boat – of the type whose absence once had been deprecated by the Dancey children. This one possibly was a left-over from the lads' camping. Floating in the boat in the middle of the lake were Henry and Eva, with a bottle of wine.

The castle was but patchily reflected, owing to lily and other water-leaves being rendered luxuriant by June. The estate was undergoing an interim, the weaving community duped by Constantine not yet having attempted to move in, stupefied, one might imagine, by the amount to be done first. A look of great peace hung over the façade, which had returned to its original air of having nothing behind it. Bluish bloom extended over the sheeny woods. The sun not so much shone as filled the sky.

Where were the swans? Gone.

'They can fly,' said Henry. 'They must have taken off – what a decision! What *was* it like here?'

'I don't know,' she said – meaning, she could not say.

'You're full of inexplicable experiences!'

She tugged a handful of weed out of the lake. 'A very little girl tried to drown herself.'

'Far too experimental a school,' said Henry, devouring one then another of the prodigious strawberries from London. 'But then, so would a honeymoon be.'

Eva picked up a paddle and moved the boat, gently. 'Oh, you mean what I told you, all you children?'

'We had not a cat's idea whether to believe you, I do remember. But then, you were altogether out of our ken, that day – all us children. How dumb with misery we were: frozen! My ears flame with frost-bite, now you remind me!' He flicked at one of them and again looked round him. 'This place is always extreme: either winter or summer.'

'*Oh*, no,' she declared, from the depths. 'Autumn.'

'That time you lost your heart to it?'

'When I never *was* here was spring.'

'Then next spring, why don't we? – no, by then it will be teeming with people. Why can't it stay as it is?' Henry stared rebelliously at the castle, which seemed to be leaning a little back, like a propped-up canvas, against the wall of trees. 'No, I suppose it would fall down. But last time we thought it would, and it hasn't – how tenacious it is!' He refilled a glass and partly crouched, partly reached down the short boat (they were at opposite ends) getting wine to Eva. Both wore bright shirts: hers French, his an unaccounted-for present from Italy. They admired each other, dreamily, as they did the scenery, their voices meanwhile wandering freely, away from them, over the captive lake: impossible to say anything which was not simple. 'I don't think I want to come back,' he said. 'This is too lovely. – Oh, but I *would* like, Eva, to go inside!'

'It's locked, I suppose.'

'Or don't you want to?'

'We'll try, Henry.' The blunt boat pushed an onward way through the leaves, on to which drops fell from the slow paddle. They landed, tied up, made their way round the castle into the entrance courtyard steeply impended over by woods. It was green with silence. Everywhere was deserted. Doors of mouldering out-buildings stood ajar. 'That is where bicycles were stolen from,' said Eva, indicating one.

Henry walked away from her, to stand in solitude, taking all in.

'Mrs Stote, there used to be,' mused Eva, as lost to him as he was to her.

Henry exclaimed: 'My passion for knowing!'

That that be satisfied, if possible, she went over and wrenched at a rusted door-handle: the central portal's. From decorations round it stucco had flaked, crumbled, and, smithereened by falling on to the flagstones, powdered those. More was shaken down, by the useless battle, on to Eva's head, greying her hair – brushing at it, she brushed it in. She grimaced defeatedly at Henry. 'Shall you look like that when you are old?' he asked from afar. Penetrating a network of ferny passage-ways, she rattled at service doors, seeing her reflection in glass panes against internal shutters. Nothing yielded. She returned to the courtyard, saying: 'I'm sorry, Henry.'

'Well, there it is.'

'We could go to the cottage where someone might have the key if she's alive.'

'No, *no*; that's making too much of it.' He took an upward in-ventory of the sightless windows: on this side, there was something intimidating about the stained, sham castle, saturated in shadow. Evening, even at this hour, possessed it, mockingly exaggerating the height to which it tapered beneath the belittling hills. Its inter-ior – for from here there could be no doubt that it had one – could be felt to be full of revengeful unheard echoes. Dungeons within it, even, could be imagined – as though by frivolling with the past the building incurred the past at its nastiest. To top all, this elevation had a constricted look she had not remembered. 'The Dark Tower,' said Henry. 'Let's go back to the boat and finish the wine.'

Vacating the courtyard, they brushed their way back to the boat through growing grass.

'I wish we'd brought another bottle,' remarked Henry, tilting the one there was to see what was left. They did not untie the boat;

she did not get in but sat on the verge, matted with white clover, above it. 'You're more of a bibber than you were, Eva. France, naturally. What did you do in France? – did you fall in love?'

'What a ridiculous question,' she said, bored.

'I'm not so sure.'

'Under the circumstances.'

Measuring out what remained into their two glasses, handing hers up to her, he went on insistently: 'I did wonder – considering how inane I've been. Paralytic! *I* should have chucked myself twenty-five times over! So then why not a *coup de foudre*, in that amorous land? You've seemed remote, somehow – you have, Eva. When you wrote, you wrote a remote letter. All today, it's been as though you were thinking about something, or somebody. Not that everything hasn't been wonderful – still, I wondered.' Leaning over, he sank the emptied bottle, gurgling, into the lake. 'One never knows,' he said, watching bubbles rise.

'You, I was thinking about,' Eva said, giving distance to the admission by directing it to a far-off skyline.

'How can one think about somebody while they're with one? – I can't. I haven't *thought* about you since today started. I, I think I'm a bit dizzy, or off my head.'

'Oh.'

He shaded his eyes. 'You look like a statue, up there against the sky! Whatever I do or say, or don't do or say, do forgive me, Eva! More, everything's gone to my head: this place, you – drink in the afternoon, I should think, too? – Where are the strawberries?'

'There.' Reaching a toe down, she gave a nudge to the punnet. 'But birds have been pecking at them, while we went to the castle.'

'Was that a mistake?' He shifted round in the boat, the better to wonder. There it stood, close behind him – too close to see as a whole. One could measure, however, with what entirety illusion returns. This was a castle for *this* side. A pleasure-ship. It less stood than was – a shimmery image, tethered to its broken watery image down below. 'What do *you* think went on in it originally? No, it is too dreamed-up; it would never do. Would it? But I think it's just as well we couldn't get in.'

Eva had, more or less, vanished from view. She lay flat on the ground. No verdict from her.

'We might,' he said, 'have never come out again.'

'No.'

'Don't go to sleep! – let's walk.' He got out of the boat, she got to her feet; they meandered along the lush, tufted margin of the lake. Meadowsweet fragrant amongst rushes did not drown the honey tang from the trodden clover; stretching, lonely, the castle's neglected lands ran away in inlets into the trees – in the far distance only were any cattle. Soundlessly soft was what was underfoot. 'That day,' remembered Henry, after what had become a becalmed silence, 'all of this was like iron – and so were you, "Miss Trout"! An Iron Maiden.'

Eva rolled a vermilion shirt-sleeve further up, the more freely to scratch a bite on her elbow. Insects were beginning again: which? 'What?' she said, as an afterthought.

'May I drive,' he asked, 'on the way back? I've never driven a Jag.'

'Why wouldn't you let me come in it to Cambridge?'

'Ostentatious. Also, a Jaguar's still a sore subject. My first infamous brush with Mammon. You caused it. What a nincompoop as well as a crook he thought me: Father, I mean.'

'Yet you wish to drive this one?'

'Get the better of one.'

'You could have driven this morning.'

'I was too busy talking about myself.' (He had, certainly, put difficulties on record, and released, for the benefit of Eva, apprehensions, indecisions, mortifications owing to rivalries, and his resentment of various kinds of torment, negative or positive, of which, it could be, he could not have spoken so unguardedly to anyone else. One or two pleasures had been slightingly touched on. She was far from the milieu which gave any of these context. They related, more or less all of them, to Cambridge, being inextricable from his present status, which was given still greater power to hagride him by his too well knowing it to be but too temporary. For – *afterwards?*) 'You're quite good,' he said now, 'at seeming to listen. Though in at one ear, out at the other, I expect, really? And just as well; I'm a brilliant bore. – But I did at least ask about Jeremy.'

'Yes, you did, Henry.'

'I can't get over what's happening; and so suddenly – at the drop of a hat.'

'Not really.'

'Nothing is sudden really,' he said more soberly. 'What *will* he be like, do you imagine?'

'I don't know,' said Eva – this time, not merely meaning she could not say. The torrents of the future went roaring by her. No beam lit their irresistible waters. The Deluge: dead arms flailing like swimmers'. Where were they on their way to being swept to, she, Henry, Jeremy? Who had opened the sluice-gates, let through this roaring? The boy, doing so by the same act by which he heaved the lid from his tomb of silence? Jeremy, whose destiny she had diverted? One does not do such a thing with impunity, the priest had said. The doctor had warned her . . . She absently turned on Henry, at this moment, caverns of apprehension. He, as absently, said:

'Those are Millais wild roses at the edge of that wood. Come over and look.'

On the way, the glassy immunity of the evening lessened. Something began to stir, like a moody breeze. Against an over-grown larch plantation, the showering briar's crimped pink buds and corollas wide-eyed round tawny stamens stood out translu-cently as though painted – yet the wildness of these clear roses scattered about on their thorny trailers was, though without a quiver, breathlessly living, as in no picture. 'They are early,' said Henry of the country childhood. 'It's early for them to be so many. This is an early summer – too early; everything is vertiginous. What's supposed to be going to happen, Eva?'

Behind the roses, the vanishing aisles of crushed, tasselled larch boughs, baffled by want of space, preoccupied her – as had the Cambridge mobile. She felt as she then did. 'Why?' was her answer.

'Why am I asking, or why should anything happen: which do you mean?' Henry asked, with a dogmatic distinctness which was a danger-signal. 'In either case, *you* should know; you are the authority – if there is one? Neither of us seems to know what we are doing.'

'What makes you angry with me suddenly?'

'Nothing is sudden.'

'Then why have you been angry?'

'You shilly-shally.'

'So do you, Henry.'

'No I don't,' he said, furious. 'Or if I do, what else is there to do? *You* precipitate things, then behave as if there were nothing and never had been. You know as well as I do, something started when you came marching back from America. *And* that it got more while you've been in France. But own up to it, cope with it? Oh, no. It's left to me to make scenes. You go remote.'

'I am shy.' It amazed her he should not know.

She emphasized shyness reaching the point of panic by wading away from Henry into the briar bush, less a bush than a tangled prickly terrain of vigorous arabesque trailers and eager suckers: these seized on her skirt and harried and savaged her bare legs. He was agitated. 'What do you think you are being, a nymph in flight? Come *out* of that, Eva; you'll be like Abraham's ram! All I was doing was asking your intentions.'

'Oh.'

'Naturally!' shouted Henry.

She turned about in the briar, prepared to parley. 'Should you be sorry if I hadn't any? How sorry?'

He examined the question. 'I should feel rather . . . flat.' He then laughed wildly. 'I'd consider I had been led up the garden path!'

'Well, then,' said Eva. That settled that. Partly with his aid, she tore and trampled her way out of sanctuary: she bled, in places. Knocking her hair back, she indicted Henry: 'All this, because for a minute I thought of Jeremy – when all today it's been you! What are *your* intentions?'

'I know what they aren't,' he said, goaded, 'and that is, to be one more of your inexplicable experiences! But if not, what? You never seriously have thought we could marry, have you? Or you've never seriously thought we could have a love affair?'

'Not merely love,' said Eva positively, 'of course not.' Licking a finger, she expunged a runnel of blood from round a wrist, before looking him in the face. 'But to marry, yes.'

'That did once flash through my head, but as something crazy. I couldn't let you look absurd – it could make both of us look absurd, even. It would be unheard-of. Your horrible money, my miserable age. It could make me almost another Jeremy. *You* ought to make a tremendous marriage. A dynastic one. Or, I think sometimes, simply not marry anyone: why should you?'

'Why should I never?' she cried aloud.

'I don't know. That's just my idea of you.'

'You, you, you – you would never love me?'

'I don't *know*, Eva, I tell you, I don't *know*!'

She said: 'Let's go back to the lake. – No; will you give me a rose to wear, first?'

She watched him tug vainly at one, then at the next. 'Your hand's shaking,' she said. 'I am very sorry.'

Over the far-off boat was a whirr of wings; there *they* were again, back at the strawberries! Or so Eva saw; Henry walked looking at nothing but the ground. 'I wonder,' he said, 'whether, in spite of all I was telling you this morning, you can conceive what a state I am in and how chaotic it is. *Feel?* – I refuse to; that would be the last straw! There's too much of everything, yet nothing. Is it the world, or what? Everything's hanging over one. The expectations one's bound to disappoint. The dread of misfiring. The knowing there's something one can't stave off. The Bomb is the least. Look what's got to happen to us if we do live, look at the results! Living is brutalizing: just look at everybody! We shan't simply toughen, Eva, we shall grossen. We shall be rotted by compromises. We shall laugh belly-laughs. We –'

'– Your father doesn't.'

'No, but he's in a way mad; that's a preservative. – You remember he once was writing a book? Well, he still is. Every now and then, he comes up against something which makes him have to go right back and re-cast the whole thing from the beginning. It's called "The Faulty Scales".'

'What's it about?'

'Justice. For a year he left it, the year Louise died. – Ought we to go back to the boat and collect the things?'

'What things?'

'The glasses, and so on.'

'Yes. We must not be late.'

They took the boat across to the other shore, where waited the Jaguar. He paddled, she regarded the castle. 'Oh, *don't* look sad, Eva!'

'This, I am seeing for the last time.'

'But that could be true of anything,' he argued. 'We may both get killed on the way back, me driving.'

235

That evidently was not what she had in mind, so did not comfort her. The glasses, Eva's camera (which for some reason had all today been out of the picture, so had not taken any), their two pullovers, which had not been needed, and the big box of excellent cigarettes of which Henry had smoked a few were transferred from the boat to the roomy boot. She unlocked the car; he investigated the dashboard, the gear and so on. 'Which is reverse? You will have to show me.' She handed him the keys, on their jewelled ring. 'Thanks,' he said, jingling them on his palm.

'Henry . . .'

'Hullo?'

'Why is my money "horrible"?'

'It isn't; it's part of your persona.'

'What is my persona?'

'Oh, *bother*, Eva! – What it *is* is, outsize, larger-than-life in every way. That's how you fascinate the imagination. Years ago when you first came cracking into the vicarage you'd already been pointed out as A Very Rich Girl. We had none of us ever seen one – it was like knowing a violinist, or something. There could be a trace of that still, I suppose; one so seldom completely outgrows things. But what harm?'

'You said my money was horrible.'

'Did I? – What could be horrible could be what it could do to me.'

'What would it do to you?'

'Too much. – I said "could" not "would", Eva; but there *would* be danger. I'm such a split-up character. What I don't think I ever have talked to you about, actually, are my ambitions. Perhaps I'm shy of them. It's easier to peeve, and so I do, ad lib. But they do very much exist; I mean, my ambitions. They have great power with me. They are a mixed bag, though. Your money could swamp all but the ones I'm most nearly ashamed of. – Shall we get going?'

They got into the Jaguar, exchanging their places of that morning. Henry, with barely controlled excitement, fitted in then turned the ignition key.

The castle flashed its series of last appearances through gaps in the woods the car began to move through – in vain. Eva, arms folded, leaned back with eyes shut; Henry, so far, drove with a concentration he was endeavouring to make light of. Clearing the last of the rides, they passed through a gateway into the outer world. Up hill, down dale, through the gauzes of midsummer as through the steel-engraving of that January day. After some miles, Henry eased into ease in driving: his triumph was to be felt. 'You are happy, Henry?'

'Outwardly, very.'

A bridge bestrode a quicksilver valley – seen, gone! She sighed: 'What was *that* river's name, I wonder?'

'I wonder,' said Henry, accelerating.

To find out, she unfolded a map. It escaped from her fingers: within an instant the mottled, angular thing had billowed outward all over her body. She stayed passively underneath it. Henry slid the car to a stop abruptly. Slewing under the wheel, he slanted over Eva's erotic counterpane.

'Now you've done it – you'll never find that river!'

'Why not?'

'Because who cares whether you do?'

'*I* do.'

'*I* don't!' He stripped the map off Eva, half-folded it wrongly, chucked it away. 'Eva, I *could* make love to you; it's not that I'm frightened of! The, the reverse. Would you ever like me enough, would you ever let me? I don't think we've ever as much as touched, have we ever – even in the past? So I do sometimes wonder . . . I do now wonder. Or would it all be too very extraordinary?'

'I suppose we shook hands?'

'No, I don't think so. – Or only under compulsion.'

'Henry, this was a wrong place to stop the car, just round a corner; unfair to other traffic.'

'We ought to go on, ought we?' he said, troubled.

'We had better, I think.'

He drove all out. Eva said nothing till a church steeple resembling Mr Dancey's, admonitory reminder of what was coming, rose into view then dipped out again. Then: 'Before we said goodbye, I wanted to ask you –'

'– This is *not* "The Last Ride Together", is it?'

'Unless you kill me.' (The unforgivable driver had flicked an eye off the road.) 'I wanted to ask you if you would act somebody.'

'In a play?' he said dazedly.

'Don't be stupid! – for one occasion.'

'*En*act somebody? Do an impersonation? – of what person?'

'My bridegroom.' She pressed her hands to her temples. '*Appear* to depart with me on a wedding journey, seen off by friends.'

'That sounds loopy. What would be the idea?'

'Getting with me on to a train, seen off at a station. Victoria Station, probably. You would not need to *stay* on the train; you could get off, once nobody was about.'

'Rather poor fun you're master-minding me into, aren't you? Why should I get off the train? And why a train, of all things? – they are so beastly.'

'They are the most formal. And this would be a *train de luxe*, bound for the Continent.'

'Then how should I ever get off, if I did want to? – those never stop. Seriously, Eva, I hate to say so but really you are quite dotty; you're raving dotty. Also, you shake me, rather. The whole thing's too near the bone – *don't* talk like that!'

'Are you shocked, then?' she asked, searching for the answer in his profile. '*I* see nothing shocking.'

'It would be completely spooky. Why do you want what's untrue?'

'One is made a liar. You have refused to marry me, this is the one satisfaction you could give. For all my longing in vain for you, and pain. *Is* this much to ask? For once, one day only, part of one day only, you would at least be mine in the eyes of the world. I'd ask no more, afterwards – I would abide by that.'

'But I might not want you to!' Henry swizzed past a lorry, dangerously near a corner. 'What made you think this up?'

'Our circumstances.'

'When did you think this up?'

'I have been doing so. What worse would this be for you than a charade – a game in a railway station? Why should you deny this thing you *can* do? You don't know whether you love me, you tell me, Henry – therefore, you do not. Love there is no mistaking. I have lived with it, I have felt it, and I can tell you.'

'"Felt it"? You talk as if it was in the past.'

'I shall compel it to be.'

'That's handsome of you!' Henry shot past two Minis, three W.D. lorries, a Pickford van, a cement-mixer in transit which, in travail, had been slowing the line down. Pleased to have got away with this, he whistled. That fatal old fascination of cooking a plot with Eva began to work. 'Your fertile brain,' he commented, 'seems to have jumped two or three snags. For instance, *I* should have to turn up again. *I*'d be left to live with this thing – live it down, I mean. For the rest of my days. Miss Trout's reject. That would not suit me, I am a mass of vanity. Also, to stage an all-out bridal departure wouldn't you first have to fake up some kind of wedding? – or that had you thought of? We'd go through some bogus cere-mony with some villainous unfrocked priest, as in gothic fiction, would we?'

'No; that would not be necessary. Simply, we should be known to be setting forth to be married in Rome, or perhaps Paris –'

'– Or Helsinki or Bucharest or Karachi. Well, that clears that. Seen off with all the works: sobs of emotion, lashings of flowers, digs in the ribs . . . Really, you *have* a nerve, Eva!'

'But you say you won't do this.'

'You have a nerve to think of it. – Now for the seeing-off party: whom would you be proposing to line up? No, you don't need to tell me; I can see it. The entire cast: Uncle Tom Constantine and All. Jeremy to watch himself acquiring a father? – No, it would be roaringly funny,' said Henry temptedly. 'A side-splitting *comédie noire*.' He whistled again.

She gave an unbearable sob.

'*Eva*, what's up?'

'My feelings: you go too far, you hurt them – and endanger my car.'

He reduced speed. 'And what are you doing to my feelings, do you imagine? – with this burlesque.'

'Making a mock of each other? And yet, Henry –'

'– I'm funny because I'm miserable. Sorry about my driving; not so good, is it? I'm slipping – I always begin well.' He drew into the roadside. 'Will you take over?'

'If you would rather.'

He got out, to let her into his place. On his way round the back of the Jaguar to hers, he opened the boot and took out the box of cigarettes. He displayed the box, and had a cigarette already be-tween his lips, though not yet lit, when he cast himself in beside her. 'Helping myself, again – you don't mind?' He reached across for the dashboard lighter. 'Or do you?'

'When have I ever?'

'I'm never certain.'

'All I have's yours.'

'In your feeling, sometimes. Not in reality.'

'It could be. You know I would rather die than have hurt you – Henry.'

He slid a hand about in the air over her knee, then withdrew the hand. The remaining miles to the vicarage began to be demolished silently, evenly; and as evenly, time demolished itself. The landscape insidiously melted into a known one; names on signposts, inn signs, sayings on notice-boards began to talk a familiar language. A green pond, a rustily locked smithy, the bus stop at the mouth of the turn to Larkins, a coppice of sycamore and a mound with no history and away back over the fields the stump of a building were less landmarks than re-tellers of an obsessive story. Back again one was coming, into the web. The innocent theatricality of evening made all this at once more tender and more menacing. 'You're not coming in?' asked Henry, meaning, into the vicarage.

'No, not this time; I have to be back,' she said, meaning in London. 'This is a night I telephone to the Bonnards. They'll be disappointed?' she asked, meaning his parents.

'More, puzzled. – At least,' he added uncertainly, 'I suppose so. Stop just for a minute, will you, Eva?'

The edge of the village: some pretty gardens. The car stopped, but there was nothing to say – or, only their faces spoke. 'Keep the cigarettes, of course,' she finally told him.

'All right. When do you go back to France?'

'I don't know.'

'Why don't you know?'

'Because that depends.'

'On the Bonnards, on Jeremy?'

'Not altogether, Henry.'

'Oh. – Do I see you before you go?'

'That depends also. You want to see me, yet will not do what I want?'

'This is not a "confession", you understand?'

'That was understood.'

'I am an agnostic.'

'Guaranteed conscientious, then. – Sit down?'

'This is not like a room in a clergy-house usually is, is it?'

'I have no idea. I have these one or two rather nice things. – Begin, will you?'

'Strictly, I have no right to your time.'

'My good lady, nobody has any "right" to anything. We subsist on mercy. – Constantine's under the impression you're in Newcastle.'

'I go back tonight. I came to you, specifically to *you*, because your already knowing the story can cut out various explanations. I don't say that was my only reason –'

'We'll take any other as read, shall we?'

'At four o'clock one afternoon a boy was taken from a studio where he was muddling about; around eight that evening he was pushed back into his hotel. It was I who did both; that has ceased to matter. What matters is the intervening time.'

'Go on.'

'He and I knew each other at sight. I appeared to be what he'd been waiting for. One hears of children who meet an unspeakable end being last seen hopping and skipping beside the stranger who is taking them to it. Witnesses, later, say there had seemed to be "recognition" – often, the witness's reason for doing nothing. The sculptress did nothing. For the child's willingness to go with the stranger a blend of guilelessness and adventurousness and liking for the sudden is held unaccountable. But there could also be this to it: fate magnetizes all of us, it magnetizes children particularly. Jeremy's and my case differed from others: I was not (other than factually) a stranger, and what was ahead was not an enormity but a miracle. – Does my acceptance of "miracle" surprise you?'

'No. Though as you know, it is rather a claim to make: I shall expect you to justify it. – What made you want the boy?'

'I had thought about him. Originally, as being my husband's, the result of a galling infidelity. The partner to it would have been my former pupil. The infidelity never in fact occurred – at least, technically. Long after I came to realize it had not, I clung to the possibility that it had. Fundamentally, I had desired that it should. I had gone out of my way to bring it about. – You are accustomed to twisted motives?'

'I meet almost none that are not.'

'The reputed foetus never existed. Her pregnancy had been an invention of my pupil's, designed to inflict pain.'

'Why should she have wished to inflict pain?'

'You met Eva. You could have asked *her* that.'

'I did, in effect.'

'It fulfilled its purpose. Our marriage gave way. The false charge, together with the shock and upheaval, injured my husband, who has deteriorated since. To return to myself: I never quite disengaged myself from the child who, by every showing, had never been. When I was alone, in France, I attempted to reason myself out of this. It eluded reason. That no child *had* been begotten by my husband upon my pupil did not in any way alter my conviction that there was *a* child in the case somewhere. She could have acquired one, either to give substance to her story or for a more characteristic reason: she has a passion for the fictitious for its own sake. – Did that appear to you?'

'It was in the offing.'

'By now, that that *was* the purpose of her disappearance into America is accepted, unquestioned, taken for granted. I, ironically, was the last to be quite certain. That was not till the morning I rang up Constantine from Reading. He ladled out news of friends (I had been away, too). To learn how right I had been was almost unnerving. I must tell you, my interest in the child, the for so long hypothetical child, had always had a particular undertow. It was inextricable from my feeling for Eva. I care for her: would that be possible to guess? Implanted in her there is something which surmounts any harm we have done each other. It is something in which I was instrumental. I am not a teacher for nothing. This survives any failure there was later. – What's that bell, ringing?'

'Eleven o'clock coffee, in the common-room. I'm afraid you are not in a Spanish cloister.'

'I hope I –?'

'No, you are not preventing me from having coffee; our coffee here prevents me from having coffee. When necessary, I percolate my own. – So far, you are giving me the impression that the boy existed for you, emotionally, largely in the context of other people. That was so, or was it not?'

'Not. Or, only initially. I came to conceive of him in his own right, to in some way desire for his own sake. I envisaged him. He was three-dimensional for me before I saw him. Before, even, the fact that he did exist was confirmed by Constantine.'

'Never thinking of him as anything but "him". Why? Never as a duplication of your pupil, as a girl?'

'No. For one thing, a second Eva would have been not only unthinkable but impossible. For another, she belonged in some other category. "Girl" never fitted Eva. Her so-called sex bored and mortified her; she dragged it about after her like a ball and chain. Why should she wish to reproduce it when she chose a child? Also, remember, thanks to her father and Constantine she had grown up apart from women, other than hirelings. She did not need women. Their vulnerability antagonized her – as *I* found. She had had enough of her father's vulnerability. She had watched him being destroyed – if I may say that to you? Eva could not or would not forget her father. There was something she fanatically wanted to redress. That Willy image, it became her object to repair, or reconstitute – whichever you like. The means, as she would have seen it, would be a boy. Acceptable?'

'Convincing. Leave it: go back to where you were.'

'Willingly. My wonder about the boy was nothing so internal as an obsession; it grew outward into a desire to see him I knew I would stop at nothing to satisfy, though for a long time I couldn't see how I could hope to. Can you wonder I seized, without loss of time, at an opportunity handed me on a plate? Unfortunately Constantine blabbed.'

'Yes. He is artless – occasionally. He paid dear, as you know.'

'Yes; I was sorry.'

'You speak of your pupil's invention of her pregnancy as having in it a wish to inflict pain – on you, I infer. You can't have removed the boy without some idea of the inordinate terror that would cause her. You had a reciprocal wish?'

'Not that I knew, not at the time. I seemed to myself to be acting under necessity. Since, I have wondered whether the wish was latent. I still do not know, so I can't tell you. This is where you come in – why I came to you. Would *you* say that it was?'

'Did I, what would you expect me to do? Impose a penance?'

'No; that would be superogatory. My existence as it has come to be has been in the nature of a penance for some years. I have paid up; I should say I owe very little. I've paid up retrospectively for what I have done or not done, done wrongly or done for the wrong reason, side-tracked, or botched. I've paid in advance for anything I may do still. I didn't come here to ask you to absolve me; I have already begun to absolve myself. There are stages in that. Could a stage be final, I should incline to feel it had been reached. The afternoon I spent with the boy, I mean.'

'The "miracle"?'

'I retract that.'

'Do you know, I am sorry.'

'You should be. I dislike your sardonic tone. You are a priest.'

'I cannot get rid of my tone, it is like a stammer. – Will you go on?'

'Understand one thing: when I went to meet Jeremy in the studio, I still was to an extent in a state of shock. Only a few hours ago, you see, had I learned from Constantine that Eva's American child, of unknown parentage, was a deaf mute. To do Constantine justice, he had no reason to know what a blow *that* was! Yet even if Constantine hadn't told me, the terrible over-expressiveness of the child's face would have, almost at the first glance. He had been counting on me. Here we were, confronted, both strangling with hopes, yet – hopeless? You imagine I am too sure of myself: a teacher? Don't think I minimized the agony, the barrier. For him, it was an agony taking him by surprise; he had been protected from it, he had never felt it. Yet it was proper he *should* feel it: the time had come. As beings, we were delighted by one another. We went downhill from the studio and got on to a bus, sitting on the top. *Qua* ride, the ride was no pleasure to him – nothing he saw could tell him more than it had already told him a thousand times. I cannot tell you what satiated eyes he had, or how his weariness of seeing, seeing, seeing without knowing, without knowing, without knowing was borne in on me. Clay was caking on his fingers, and he watched it, gathering his forces. His mind was racing, making him shrug his shoulders and keeping him twisting about on the seat beside me. Questions were furiously, frantically framing themselves inside him, and the knowledge that they were and the answers to them and the impotence to answer were furiously in me. His being in his cage taught me how I am in mine. He may come to speak – when shall *I* do anything else?'

'What you can do, don't denigrate; that is sacrilege.'

244

'Yes. – What I did do was, come at the right time. The rest, he did – the much more, he must do. I made him see *why* . . . What he did to me was illimitable. Genius we had in common, that was the solvent. Yes, I roused his – but he resurrected mine. *Resurrected* mine! Yes. For all I speak of our two cages, between us there was eternal life. He was my salvation – do you see? . . . I'm not of course going to tell you categorically where we went, what we did. I am not daring to tell you how we communicated, or what about, or to what effect. What I do want and mean you to understand is, he and I were in anything but a dream, all those hours: everything was razor-edged actuality, layers deep. While we were in Westminster Abbey, he traced the lettering of the inscriptions on monuments he could reach with the point of a finger as though responsible for incising them for the first time. While we were around Leicester Square into Soho where the evening arcades and bazaars were open he chose himself a present from me, then a present for me. He is aggressive, by the way – for himself he made straight for a pocket-size toy revolver, made of lead or something. He pointed it, consideringly, at me: "Don't do that," I said, "even with a toy." Which reminds me, if he and Eva should open up house again at Paley's, I must remove one that's among her things.'

'That gun you wanted to plant on Constantine. I suppose not loaded; or else is it?'

'I don't know; I shouldn't think so. – It reminded me of Eric.'

'Are you going back to your husband?'

'I don't know. – For me, he chose a red cotton flower: a poinsettia. He wanted me to put it in my hair; but how could I? – already I'd been accosted. When I didn't, he lost interest. Don't imagine he for a moment cared for me, but for that one flash – I was a walking strong-box he wanted to rifle. Would he know me again? – that might cease to matter. We had supper in an Italian café; he ate voraciously, as though getting his teeth into the world . . . How little this sounds.'

'Evidently you are dynamic.'

'I was. – Yes, I am able to be. *You* cannot think that wrong?'

'An inane question . . . You've told me as much as can be told; what did operate, chiefly, you can't tell me. On the strength of what you have, you've made quite a case. You may have done what you think you have – it is not impossible.'

'Father Clavering-Haight –?'

'Well, yes?'

'You can find nothing more comfortable to say to me?'

'In my own way I am conscientious, Mrs Arble.'

'Thank you for hearing me, at any rate. What I wanted to know was, if it sounded credible. I have never spoken this aloud.'

'It sounded incredible enough. Stranger things have happened, I mean to say. The person to watch will be the boy – when he turns up again. Why do you exile yourself in Newcastle? Does or doesn't your husband want you back?'

'There are complications. In a good many ways, I should like to talk to you – but my time's up, I see. Someone else coming?'

'He may not be punctual. A Black Muslim.'

'May I stay till he comes? – For one thing, my husband has two children . . .'

Haymaking was at its height; a mechanized whirring sounded over the country six days a week – when distant enough, it was in a contemporary way poetic. Restricted by the positions of orchards, the operation had about it something not only seasonal but tactical, military: summer manœuvres. The cessation at evening brought with it a humid silence scented by exacerbated grass-roots and mangled wild-flowers. How sweet, how haunting new-fallen hay smells. Its mauve-bronze living shimmer is but a memory. There is something sacrificial in every rite, and in this case the victim was Mr Dancey. His martyrdom now reached its annual peak. By consent, the vicarage windows were made fast; doors to the street and garden were opened sparingly, shut quickly. But the enemy infiltrated.

Henry did little to cheer the besieged household. Sympathetically, his nerves were in a state equivalent to their having been traversed repeatedly by a large tractor. He went nowhere. From the upstairs table on which were heaped his books he saw down, daily, into the well of garden, leaned about in by leggy, unstaked delphiniums, their faint blue drained off by thirsting greenery. The foreshortened pergola sagged each year lower over the moss-grown path. This week-end, the garrison was added to by Catrina, who arrived on her motor bicycle to rally round, also to take part in what Henry designated a bi-sexual cricket match. ' "Mixed",' she corrected, 'sex does not enter into cricket.' 'That is painfully evident.' 'If you're so cross, why don't you go to Italy?' 'Why should I?' 'I thought you said some lunatic asked you?' 'I still might . . .' 'What are you hanging about waiting for?' 'I am working, slightly.' 'You are simply giving Father the heebyjeebies, and at *this* time I think it is most unfair of you.' 'Oh, do you,' said Henry, 'really? He's been sneezing so much, one hardly took him to be conscious at all.'

That had not been the case. Hypersensitivity tautened the sealed-in atmosphere. Within the beleaguered earthworks there went on a second, internal siege, though laid by whom to whom it was hard to say. Father and son, passing each other on the claustrophobic stairs or colliding in doorways, ominously and eloquently hesitated, then went their ways – Henry sheathed, thereafter, in a vindictive melancholy. He could say or do, it appeared, nothing not discordant. By now, the disfiguration of Mr Dancey, his submergence, his inflamed and distorting streamingness, was complete, unsparing – unbearable. Insistently turning his countenance full on his son's, he showed that he saw no reason to spare Henry. (When his children were children, they had thought this funny: he had not minded.) This was a minor suffering, with a chasm beneath. At meals they conversed, though irregularly – or had done so: now, with the imminence of Sunday, Mr Dancey was known to be 'saving his voice'. He was to be left in peace to charge up his batteries, few domestic and almost no parish matters being, where possible, referred to him. The prayerful hush which embraced the family at least created a moratorium – Henry was therefore the more taken aback when, about two on Saturday afternoon, he was intercepted not far from the hall hat-stand. 'Where are you off to, this time?' asked Mr Dancey.

'I hadn't thought. It's still so soon after lunch. Why – is there anything I can do?'

'You can wait a minute.'

'Of course; I'd like to – Father.'

'There is not,' began Mr Dancey, picking a circular out of the bowl on the hat-stand, glancing at it, tearing it slowly across, 'there is not by any chance anything that had better be had out, is there?'

'I don't think anything's the better for being had *out*,' Henry said, though as though in a general way.

'You are as good as telling me,' said his father. 'Not that you haven't virtually, for the past week or so – have you any conception how you've been going on? I don't like this, whatever it is. What is it?'

'Am I being more difficult than usual?'

'Yes. You've become impossible. And I won't have it.'

'I'm having an intrigue, as a matter of fact. – I suppose you saw that?'

'I wonder exactly how senseless you are being.'

'The possibilities are infinite,' said Henry, hysterically echoing round the hall, up the staircase.

'I should be sorry to be anybody concerned with you, at your age. In fact, I'm not sure that I should not be sorry to be anybody concerned with you at any age, as you are now shaping or would seem to be.' Mr Dancey, with passionless accuracy, re-tore the halves of the circular into smaller pieces. 'Now I come to think of it, "shaping" is optimistic; you're all over the place. Do you wish to say who it is?'

'No. I imagine you know.'

'I hope I am wrong. If I'm not, I am unutterably distressed.'

'Shocked,' added the boy – as though in parenthesis.

'Distressed is enough for the present,' said Henry's father. He washed his hands of the papery fragments, casting them towards the bowl; several went fluttering down on to the tiles. 'What were you saying?' he then asked sharply.

'I don't think, anything. – I *am* saying, you don't leave me much to stand on: do you?'

'Don't I?' asked Mr Dancey, looking about him. His son stood like St Sebastian. The father resorted to tugging aimlessly, desultorily, at an ulster hanging from the hat-stand. 'I –' he began. His voice went, with almost a click; there followed an overstrained whisper. 'The fault is probably mine – where did I go wrong? What I meant to say to you was, why not get off to Italy? Catrina tells me you have that invitation.'

'*I* told you. It's odd you never remember what *I* tell you. – And speak of angels!' added Catrina's brother. For here she came, thundering downstairs, off to cricket, bashing a canvas bag about, exclaiming:

'I say, *Father*, about tomorrow, how if I telephoned H.Q. for a lay reader?'

'What, some pious dentist?' jibed Mr Dancey, hoarse and unholy. Braced against that idea, he turned his back on his children and, handsomely, began the climb to his study. Sermon to finish. That done, he continued work on 'The Faulty Scales'. A good session, this time; one of his best – he felt clarified, calmed. He wiped the knife of his mind, as though after a sacrifice. Reservations, qualifications no longer trammelled him. No qualm sent him back on his tracks; no arising misgiving compelled him to re-cast. Straight ahead went Mr Dancey, this afternoon – taking no reckoning of such injustices as are possible in exorbitant love.

'What was that about?' Catrina wanted to know.

'Looks like the beginnings of a paper-chase, doesn't it?' said her brother rapidly.

'What does?'

'Look at the floor . . .'

'Oh, wake *up*, Henry! – Well, *I*'m going.'

'Goodbye, Catrina. Bat hard!'

Having waited till the motor bike had sputtered off out of hearing, he went down the street to the village post office. But that closed on Saturday afternoons. He returned to the vicarage and, whistling, took out his father's car: from the town where he'd been at school, twenty miles away, he got off the telegram to Eva. 'ALL RIGHT, JUST AS YOU LIKE. WHEN?' He signed it. Only on the way back did he recollect, telegrams eliminate punctuation. Would this one be comprehensible? Let it ride!

On Sunday, Mrs Dancey and her remaining daughter went to the eight o'clock. Mrs Dancey then having things to see to and Catrina being keen to scour the neighbourhood to post mortem the cricket match, it was suggested Henry attend Mattins. Always sad to see no one in the vicarage pew. And at this season every soul present counted: during the fine spell inroads were apt to be made on the congregation by free-lance haymaking.

The church atoned for the vicarage by its great beauty, its Perpendicular architecture being almost miraculously untampered with, but for outside – the foolish addition of a spire to the tower. Within, it was lit by so many and such large, wonderfully shaped windows as to seem more than half composed of them, and of these the majority were of clear glass: the interior, therefore, at mid-morning was the home of a daylight it not only contained but, as one entered, shed forth. At the east end only was there extraneous colour; elsewhere, nothing but the green of the lime trees shadowing the gravestones out in the churchyard. By clouds gathering or heavy rain falling, blizzards or thunder-storms the place could be penitentially darkened, but those veils soon were withdrawn. Such was the shadowlessness of the church that it became the more onerous to bring sins here, even to lay them down. For Henry, all this had about it something pre-natal – though he in fact had been born at the other end of England. He could have walked up the aisle blindfold; which was as well, for this morning he did so blindly. He turned into the vicarage pew and made his way down its long, haunted, void length. Having reached the end he slid forward on to his knees, bowed his head, knotted his hands.

A thrush had got into the church. It was adolescent; though full-grown still hardly more than a bloated fledgling. Barely yet fit to fly, it did so with arduousness and terror, hurtling, hoping, despairingly losing height, not knowing where it was to land, if it ever did, or how again to take off, if it ever could. Here or there, it beseechingly came to rest, wings widespread, head twisted over its back, beak agape, a palpitation in its speckled throat. The slithery, imploring scratching of its claws on time-polished stone or man-polished woodwork hardly was to be told from the choked, protesting noises it attempted to utter. ' "Happy birds which sing and fly round Thy altars, O Most High",' thought Henry. The bird however avoided the chancel. Everywhere else, it was – or was not: it blotted itself out for minutes together. Preliminary pealings of the organ sent it to cover; it was quiescent when the choir – still the better for Paris? – filed in, followed by Mr Dancey. The service began.

During it, Henry discovered Louise's prayer-book to be still among those along the ledge of the pew. This was her juvenile, as it were milk-tooth one – superseded at the time of her confirmation by something with red-gilt edges, in red morocco, which, as things turned out, she had hardly had time to use. (Where had *that* gone to?) This forgotten one showed toothmarks at the upper corners of its binding: she had been a chewer, salivating as she did so, which accounted for the corners' discolouration. While there had been Louise, there'd been no occasion to investigate anything she had or did: to each other, Henry and she had been open books. He now (while standing during the psalm) investigated this one. On the fly-leaf was written:

> Black is the raven,
> Black is the rook,
> But to Hell goes anybody who steals this book.
> It is particularly holy,
> So Hell will be particularly hot
> And coal-y.

Those savage lines restored to Henry, for some reason, not so much Louise as the original savagery of loss. Sorrow is anger, of a kind. At his father's sacerdotal, translated figure he neither looked nor avoided looking: voice did *not* seem to be packing up, on the whole was as audible as could be expected. For hayfever reasons, no flowers on or near the altar: nicely arranged ferns. A parishioner read the First Lesson, badly; a second did better with the Second. The thrush came out and rebounded against a window on the other side of the aisle. The Son of God . . . On his knees, later, along with everyone else, Henry thought fleetingly – for the first time since he had sent the telegram – of Eva. What HAD he done? He went ice-cold round the forehead. Stand up for the second hymn (preceding the sermon) 'Jerusalem the Golden'. Milk and honey – *absolutely*, insanity!

Mr Dancey calmly approached the pulpit. He disappeared round the turn of the stairs up to it. He then soared finally into view, with a white movement shaking back the sleeves of his surplice. Something which sublimated his face at the same time made it indistinct to the eyes of Henry. The malady had gone – had it? Not a trace of ravage. The expectant people settled into their places, looking up at the lips. A breath was drawn; the lips opened and moved; not a sound came. Waiting unagitatedly, the preacher, meantime, shed on his people a smile of partly complicity, partly patience. Tension rose, sank, rose in the great light church, about which darted the darkness of the now ceaseless thrush. Mr Dancey testingly touched his throat, waited for it an instant, tried again. Out boomed the great vocal bell. Out swung the syllables of the selected text. '*I hate the sins of unfaithfulness*,' thundered Mr Dancey, '*there shall be no such cleave unto me*.' The thrush, gathering velocity from the distance, catapulted beak-on into the glass of the window above Henry. Like a stone it dropped. Henry fainted, alone in his corner of the vicarage pew.

Eva, since last heard of, had made up her mind to return to Paley's. The removal from that other London hotel where for security reasons she had installed herself, and taking up again of her former quarters, was in fact going on this week-end. The step betokened restored morale; at the same time, there was a reason for it. The decision had been in a way imposed on her. Jeremy was coming to join her, for a week. Madame Bonnard was coming to London for a conference, and would bring him.

This had been suggested, it would not be unfair to say ordained, by the Bonnards. For it happened that the date of Thérèse's journey synchronized with a key point in her and her husband's psychological planning for the child. At the stage they perceived Jeremy to be reaching, the removal of any notion of dissolution from his immediate past had become essential. As to one thing, it was imperative that he be reassured; that being, that the (to him) home from which he'd been reft in London, under, as Eva had told them, panic-engendering conditions, had *not* in fact vanished into thin air. Let it be there, let him find it again. It behoved Eva – as they were confident she herself would agree? – to reassemble the whole thing, or at least reproduce it so far as possible, at top speed (given the shortness of time), to the last detail.

Who was Eva to gainsay these dedicated zealots, these inspired authorities as to Jeremy? That their project might not happen to chime in with Miss Trout's own psychological planning did not, evidently, occur to them – or did not in the case of Thérèse; that it at least *might* have in the case of Gérard, Eva inclined to feel, though that faint protest was her only rebellion. She set about her appointed task, which was simplified by what (she supposed?) could be called good luck: owing to the cancellation of a booking, Paley's top-floor suite could be at her disposition on what was, actually, the eve of Jeremy's arrival, and for a week. Having waited only for the electric whirlwind of cleaners to subside, she took possession that Saturday afternoon. Whereupon, up streamed her belongings from the baggage room: the amount stunned her. She pushed or pulled about, unproductively, or stood at bay amongst, the mountains of stuff, or turned her back on it, prey to a restless lethargy.

At some later time, the telephone rang. Who could *that* be? Nobody. No one. Not a soul had been told she was back. It would be the desk. The budgerigars, borrowed back from the porter's wife, greeted the sound of the telephone with a joyous chorus which continued throughout her use of the instrument. This was *a* hotel desk, but not Paley's: someone spoke from where she had been this morning. (Query: how had *they* tracked her down?) A telegram had come in: what would madam wish done?

'What is it about?'

'You wish it opened?'

'Read it aloud, please.'

That done: 'Will you repeat the signature?' asked Eva, glowering at the budgerigars.

' "Henry", madam.'

'Oh. Then will you re-read the message? – No, wait a minute.' She put the budgerigars away in the bathroom. 'Yes. Go on.'

They did so.

'Is there a question-mark?'

'Not on the form, madam.'

'There was intended to be one, I suppose. – Well, thank you.'

It never rains but it pours . . .

What TIME was it, even? She had lost her watch, she could find no clock. She wiped her confused and it could be agonized forehead. Joy wrenched at her inwardly, in its own way almost like a deathly illness. Act, act, *act* on Henry's decision! There might be no other. Round her lay everything, everything, like a fallen city: huge or little hide suitcases, canvas ones, copperbound tea chests and packing-cases, duffle bags, nylon string bags, cartons with flap-topped lids open at angles, the scooter, over-crammed hampers dwindling to waste-paper baskets, rugstraps, at least one extraneous parcel, objects half-clad in twiddles of paper . . .

The malacca cane being in the nude, she leaned it in its habitual corner. – *What* to do about apricots, with tomorrow Sunday?

Everything must be plausible, by tomorrow.

It was. Eva had made it, and with minutes to spare – she deserved credit. Fatigued, yet levitated, she sat about, waiting for Jeremy, up here in the citified-summery Sunday morning's suspended silentness. In this room was but one outlander: a remaining container, a carton, holding things still to be sorted out, probably jettisoned, such as exhausted picture books, games with pieces missing, over-wound clockwork toys, with on top, intact still, the unappetizing parcel. Out-of-the-picture, the carton was slightly behind a curtain. Tubular roses, pink-tinted creamy stock filled vases with the management's compliments; comatose, the little birds were dotted along their perches. Like a figure wheeling out of a clock, on the stroke of noon Jeremy came in. He greeted Eva with a gay little parody of a French bow.

About his entrance there was already a touch of the executive, however junior. For instance, he was carrying a dispatch case, if of no ordinary kind: of useful size, it was light as a feather – probably? – made of glazed toile, a vermilion tartan, stretched on an aluminium frame and fastened with bright hasps, presumably locked. For an instant, Eva took this to be a present for her, from Fontainebleau; that it was not was made clear by Jeremy's concernedly balancing it on the sofa-cushions, and making certain it was *in* balance, before kissing her. It contained his affairs. (Later, his suitcase made its way in with an unobtrusiveness befitting its lower rank.) After the kiss, he and Eva parted, in order to smile at each other and, as it were, drink one another in – as was appropriate: they had not, after all, seen each other for going on for two weeks.

But it was more than that. They were seeing each other after their first, their one separation since Jeremy had (virtually) been born to Eva. And what was disconcerting was, not that there was any question of disillusionment, on either side, but rather that the minute was reigned over by a startling, because unavoidable, calmness – a calmness to which there was no alternative. One could have called it, a disinfected one. They were glad to be seeing each other again: anything beyond that, anything primitive, was gone. Who knew when it had breathed its last, or where its grave was? Like as they were, they were *not* of each other's flesh-and-blood, and they both knew it. The dear game was over, the game was up.

This the boy underlined, yet perhaps lightened, by a sort of mockery which, clearly, he called on Eva to share. He dealt her a fond, glancing, enticing look, as though to say: 'Both in the same boat, what do we do *now*?' Her answer was not yet ready. He then resorted to everything that was most natural, flung himself on to the sofa, side-by-side with his dispatch-case, and puffed and blew as one is entitled to after an arduous journey. He exhibited pleasure in home-coming like a magazine child. Eva, whose foot-bones ached after the all-but-all-night enslaved activity, reconstructing this, sank into a big chair and kicked her shoes off. Hooking a stool towards her, she swung her feet up. One of her great anti-climatic yawns was torn from her – a lapse of manners: she made a placatory movement of the hand. In return, *he* felt something owing: jumping from the sofa, he worked his way round the whole of the re-construction, with the earnestness of royalty visiting a fair, over-looking nothing. He paid tribute to the exactitude by righting any few flaws in it – returning, for instance, the silver-mounted claw of the greater eagle to the chimneypiece from the top of the escritoire. Passing the budgerigars, he caressed their cage by trailing a finger over its harp-string bars. Coming to a stop at Eva, he conveyed – to a point, almost, enunciated – 'I congratulate you!'

What sort of dupe had the noble Bonnards imagined this boy to be? As stars in Eva's firmament, they declined slightly – a funda-mental misgiving shook her. Alternatively, were their machinations five fathoms deep? This *recherche* for the basic they had made such a point of . . . what of it? Unloading Jeremy on her, for that adduced reason (and at this, of all junctures!), his directors, his psychological engineers *could* have had an undeclarable motive: what? To bring about this undoing. To rid not only the child of Eva but the child and Eva of one another . . . The emotional tumult raised in the budgerigars by Jeremy's greeting became insufferable. She got up and put the birds away in the bathroom.

Now free to devote himself to his affairs, he began to install himself for his visit; when she came back, he was already busy. The dispatch-case was open; he was extracting its professional contents, ranging these on a side table cleared for the purpose. Out first, from the top, came the latest *Astérix*. Otherwise, these were charts, measurement-forms, diagrams, blown-up technical photographs, letter-blocks, a small magnifying hand-mirror and other impedi-menta connected with the twice-daily oral exercises, supervised by himself, which – it *was* understood? – nothing whatsoever during his time in London must be allowed to imperil or interrupt. (*He* would not neglect them!) To the onloooker, Eva, there was about his preoccupation something other than the limpid seriousness of childhood; indeed, alien or even hostile to it. With so much to conquer, he was going to have little or no time to be a child. There was something forbidding – sundering? repellent? – about his centredness, his complacent precision, his assessingness, his anaesthetized rapid handling. He gnawed on a lip, a little – as he might later? These proceedings demarcated his features. A preview . . .? History, one was forced to remember, is forged by the overriders of handicaps, some evident, some not known till the end.

'Oh my *dear*,' she cried to him down the room, 'my dear little boy!'

He came to show her this latest *Astérix*.

After lunch, they would take the Jaguar somewhere: though where? What way out of pressurized London, this fine Sunday? When they were up again from the restaurant, she told him: 'First, you stay with your book; I have to telephone.' To do so, she went to her room.

After some pages, Jeremy looked about him. He lit on the bulge in the curtain made by the carton. Shelving *Astérix*, he went cautiously over and leaned round Eva's door – as ever, ajar. Along the bed she lay like a long log; the receiver was by her on the pillow, and her face was so locked away into it, in either passion or obstinacy, that only the jawline could be seen. So, he safely went across to the carton. He did not require to dig deep; something immediately met his hands. The parcel was as weighty as it was curious; he bore it back with him to the sofa, where he sawed away at the heavily knotted string with his little pocket-knife. What was laid bare needless to say delighted him. He turned it over and over, held it at arm's length, nursed it against a cheek, looked down the barrel, becoming with every minute more loth to part with it. He brought himself to stow it away, provisionally, at the back of the bottom drawer of the escritoire, covering it with a huge used pair of ocelot gauntlets, a leaking bagful of sea-shells, and some other debris. String, wrappings, he dropped back into the carton.

Eva came in and said: 'Let us go out!' They did not after all take the car but walked to the Serpentine, returning for tea in excellent spirits. The wretched carton, more prominent than it had been, caught Eva's eye, as the one blot. 'I *should* like that taken downstairs again,' she told the waiter as he wheeled in the trolley. 'Though I know this is Sunday. In a day or two, tell them, I'll look through it; I do not think, meanwhile, there is much in it likely to be of value. I believe there is a parcel which is not mine; that – tell them – I must also go into, in a day or two.' The waiter, a good friend, himself carried away the carton. Meeting no one to whom the matter could be of interest, he did not transmit the message about the parcel. Its not being there, therefore, was not noted.

Madame Bonnard, of course, had been the person summoned by Eva to the telephone. Taking advantage of the siesta hour, the woman doctor, staying with friends in Nevern Square, had been sleeping, lightly, after her early morning journey and in preparation for the soirée shortly to open the conference. None the less: 'Oh, yes – Miss Trout? I am delighted to hear from you. All goes well?'

'Oh, yes; thank you. And Jeremy is in good condition. It is simply that he must go back when you go, on Thursday; I cannot keep him till the end of the week. So, the escort you had arranged for him, for next Sunday, will have to be cancelled. – Can you kindly do that?'

'*Ah, non!*'

'You cannot cancel the escort?'

'I cannot believe you. You know, this is quite a reversal.'

'Yes. I am going abroad on Thursday, to be married. That will be in the morning. I should like him to be at the station to see us off. *Your* departure won't be till later, when your conference closes?'

'You understand what a blow you may be inflicting? – That you undo the entire good of this visit?'

'I don't think so. This *is*, as you say, "a visit". As I can now see clearly, for me and Jeremy there will in the future be nothing but these; and *they*, Madame Bonnard, will well content him. So, I think he should see *I* see he is free of me; and what better way than this to show him? I am sorry to disturb you after your journey, but time is short: I have to make many arrangements, bookings, and travel-plans, all of which I must communicate to my fiancé, whom I meet at the station.'

Madame Bonnard, with her first touch of astringency (malice, not: malice was not in her), asked: 'Arrangements, might you not entrust to your future husband?' No reaction. She went on: 'Since

– if? – your mind is made up, let us no longer speak of this. And how completely impossible, on the telephone! Simply, Miss Trout, will you let me point out one thing? In a young person, vanity, *amour propre*, and most of all *amour vanité*, can be passions. They can be dangerous. You feel it is now out of your power to injure Jeremy? You insist that he watch your departure with another person? In that event, allow me to warn you. – It is still in your power to offend him . . . You wish me, then, to have his return plane reservation transferred from today week to next Thursday evening?'

'If you would be so kind.'

Sun filled the dust-tarnished glassy parts of the roofs of the temple of departure and streamed through; elsewhere were unpolluted spaces of blue sky. The odours of Victoria Station were fanned by a passage of air: the hour was early, the day young. There was also a dying-down of reverberations, themselves few: the station, for all its resonance, all its immensity, either was always quieter than it once was or was in one of those lulls which descend on termini. The matitudinal rush into London in the suburban section was petering out – and had been in any event remote from Continental Departures, a section having its own functions, dominated by its own clocks. Over platform 8, dedicated to the Golden Arrow, ran a second and lower roof, or glass canopy, which, supported by green-painted iron stanchions, extended some way further towards the Continent after Victoria's major arches ceased. The train was drawn up at its moorings. This was Thursday.

So far, not much was happening. Barely a passenger yet thought of being aboard. Through the Golden Arrow's succession of long windows voluptuous demi-dusk and subdued glitter were hinted at. Yet the train, unsolidified by occupants, had a spectral transparency: one saw through it – beyond was a great dun brick immutable wall. Attendants, buttoned up to the chin, stood officially if not yet expectantly at the ready, some in doors, some on the platform. 'I don't yet know where I am,' said Henry, sauntering up to one of them. Though with nothing to show, he'd been let through the barrier. 'What had I better do? – get my porter to wait?'

'No, I'll look after that case, sir. We can see later.'

'Well, thank you,' said Henry, tipping everybody concerned. He then hastened back through the barrier to the book-stall, where he laid in what constituted a sheaf of cosmopolitan glossy magazines. His family believed him to be in Italy. He wore a light-grey suit, a white carnation. Not only when light-hearted but still more when light-headed does one tread on air, as did he, re-approaching the train, dodging the stanchions, flapping the magazines, angling his way between knots of people. A flash of shadow, a something of the recalcitrance there is about an inaccessible young dancer drew glances after him up the platform. Whom, it was wondered, did *he* belong to? A hand flitted over his shoulder. 'Aha,' said Constantine, 'how are you?'

'Oh – hullo!'

'And where are *you* off to, in such a hurry?' asked Constantine, not only in a benevolent but in what could have been a perfectly general way. 'You are looking delightful, my dear boy,' he went on, examining the carnation. 'As befits the occasion,' he ended, trimly.

Henry rallied. 'So glad you could come!'

'Yes. Yes indeed, so am I. Rather a thin representation, I am sorry to see, so far. Loyal as many of us are, it was short notice. Still, who knows who may not yet materialize? – Jeremy to be with us, do you happen to know?'

'Yes; he'll be coming along with the porter's wife, Mrs Caliber. They leave Paley's in a taxi just after Eva; she will come in a Daimler.'

'A motorcade. Which now should be some way under way. – Tell me, how is Eva?'

'Actually,' replied Henry, at once lightly, confidently and confidentially, 'I haven't *seen* her for rather more than a week; you know how it is. Naturally, we have talked. I mean, on the telephone.' Disengaging himself, to the extent of a step or two, from Constantine, he scanned the perspective, towards the barrier. – 'I say, aren't those Mr *and* Mrs Arble?'

'Not so improbably as one might imagine. – Where?'

The Arbles, spotting their spotters simultaneously, acknowledged that they had – she with a wave, he with a nod – but did not yet join them. Iseult had removed the hair from her forehead; it was confined back by a wide rose-red bandeau, and she carried an armful of red roses, nodding out of the top of their waxen wrappings. With an air of graceful provinciality she, side-by-side with her husband, was inspecting the Golden Arrow, outside and in. He, spruce though informal, wore a check tweed jacket; his hair, as though fresh from a last dash over a basin, was lustrously plastered to his skull: an all-out return of his coppery manly glowingness denoted his being as well content with himself as a new penny. A retaining hand of his was under her elbow; at the same time, he conveyed the impression of having no objection to her having him in tow, to an extent . . . 'And let *that* be a lesson to you, my good Henry,' enjoined Constantine, turning a basilisk eye, with some satisfaction, on the bridegroom-to-be. But further sight of the Arbles was intercepted by a character who advanced, raising its hat, asking: 'Are you by chance Mr Henry Dancey?'

'Yes, I am,' said Henry. 'What made you guess?'

'My name is Denge,' Mr Denge said, as though that answer were self-explanatory.

'Eva – Miss Trout – will be delighted,' averred Henry. He himself lit up, at the historic interest. Otherwise, this party was not being a gala. 'Noble of you, to arrive!'

'Old times are old times. – Running it a little fine, though, is she not?' Mr Denge asked, looking forebodingly at the platform clock.

'Oh, I don't think so!' cried Henry, mastering instant terror – frantically wanting, also, somehow to disentangle himself from Constantine. 'I think I see –' he began, craning his neck, dodging his head. 'No, you don't,' said Constantine, clamping down on that, 'not yet.' Mr Denge, addressing himself to Constantine, said he expected this might be Mr Ormeau? 'And how *is* our young lady?' he put to her former guardian, as likely to be the more seasoned, rock-bottom authority. 'As ever?'

'So it would seem,' said Constantine, irony making him still more affable.

'Pardon me; that's to say *well*, I hope?'

'One assumes, well,' said the oracle, 'on this day-of-days! In point of fact, Mr Denge, I must tell you, I have not seen her, one way and another, since her visit to France. And that lasted some time. She is educating a little boy – as you may know? – which involves her, of course, in many decisions. It was in the boy's interest that she left for France; so far back, now that I come to think of it, as May. Yes, early in May. One regretted seeing her go.

But Miss Trout's decisions – and this I believe you *do* know? – are taken rapidly.'

'Before you can say "knife", virtually,' said Mr Denge.

' "Impulsive", I suppose, is the word,' said Constantine pensively. '–Are you impulsive, Henry?'

'No; I suffer from morbid indecisions.'

'One would hardly have thought so. – Yes,' marvelled Constantine, rubbing lightly at the site of an eyebrow, 'how time flies! *How* many weeks since I've seen her? It could be months, even.'

'No,' said the literal Henry. 'It's not July yet.'

'It shortly will be.'

'By that time, you will have seen her – we hope!' said Henry, who all this time had been going quietly whiter. 'So, as one of my sisters used to say, "Writhe not!" '

'I was sorry about Louise,' said Constantine.

This was harkened to, honourably-speaking inadvertently, though on the off-chance, possibly, that it might furnish a clue, by not so much a group as a drift of people, seven or eight of them, who, questioningly in movement along the platform (which was by now steadily if not yet rapidly filling up) came as though by telepathy to a near-stop. Henry's hymeneal carnation perhaps drew them? They had the waveringness of a phantom company. Of various ages, and both sexes, they shared a tribal likeness. Aunts, uncles, cousins? Each wore a look, or air, which in its own immaterial way was a wedding garment. One or two of the men were decorated by floral buttonholes; women and girls carried ingenuous bunches or fanciful little baskets of garden flowers, hopefully ready to be offerings, in white-gloved hands. They hesitated – then, there being no verification nor hopes of verification, by consent turned away again, to resume their course along the flank of the train, still, always searching from face to face. Henry looked after the last of them. Hoaxed, were they? An unreal act collects round it real-er emotion than a real act, sometimes, he thought.

Beside him, the old warlock inquired: 'None of your people here?'

'No. Haymaking. Hay fever.'

Constantine did not hear him. 'My God . . .' he said.

There stood Eva.

Not far off, in one of those chance islands of space, she stood tall as a candle, some accident of the light rendering her luminous from top to toe – in a pale suit, elongated by the elegance of its narrowness, and turned-back little hat of the same no-colour; no flowers, but on the lapel of the jacket a spraying-out subcontinent of diamonds: a great brooch. A soft further glow had been tinted on to her face; her eyes were increased by the now mothy dusk of their lashes. She was looking unhurriedly, all but abstractedly, in the direction of Henry.

'EVA!'

His sensational dash to reach her left Henry breathless and out of balance. 'I was afraid, I thought you might never come!'

'I am not late?'

Up came the Arbles. Iseult unloaded her roses on to Henry before being the first to embrace Eva, which she did smothering a cry, in which was the accumulated past, against the bride's cheek – so immune, so sculpted by calmness. 'But then, you always were,' murmured Iseult Smith, intelligibly only to herself. Back again into being Iseult Arble, as they drew apart again, she cried: '*And* your brooch! *Yours?* Where was it all this time, Eva?' 'It was my mother's,' beamed the wearer, shining above the diamonds, 'given her on their wedding day by my father.'

'Yes, Eva,' admitted Eric, 'that's a terrific rig-out. It does you justice. Know what I said to Izzy, just now when you hove into sight? – "That's *not* Eva?"' Eva, giving credit where credit was due, said: 'Fortnum and Mason.' He collected her hands in his and fervently crunched them. 'God bless!' he declaimed, with direct emotion – more obliquely adding: 'And no bones broken?' Henry, for whom the morning had gone by so far without a dig-in-the-ribs, now got one from Eric. 'Well, you made it!' said Eric unacrimoniously. (Raising the roses clear of the operation, Henry restored them to Mrs Arble, who tore off their wrappings and bestowed them on Eva.) 'Who'd have thought it,' Eric vociferated, 'that time I had to have that word with your father? "But don't lose heart, vicar," I remember I told him, "that boy could have something!" Neither was I so wrong: eh? Well, well, well. Well, all of the best – and I *mean* that!'

'Thank you,' said Henry.

'Mind, you be good to Eva!'

'I shall attempt to.'

Eva, carrying the roses, moved away up the platform. 'Constantine?'

Constantine, still where Henry had left him, did not advance one step. Cryptically waiting for Eva, he watched her falter. 'Yes, my dear?' he said, encouraging her on.

'I, I, I –' she began, lowering her lashes.

'Well, here I am. – And here's yet another old friend!' He produced Mr Denge, whose hat needless to say was already raised. Mr Denge said: 'Miss Trout, this is a joyful occasion!'

'Thank you,' she said, overcome. – 'Welcome!' she added, by association. She turned to the other. 'Constantine, it has been so long . . .'

'– I have the pleasure of bringing you,' Mr Denge continued, rooting about in an inner pocket, 'half a dozen small coffee-spoons, with the Broadstairs arms inlaid in coloured enamel. Mrs Denge and I –'

'Look sharp, darling,' said Henry, at Eva's elbow, 'you – we – are being given a wedding present.' She did not react, being perturbed, so Henry stepped smartly up and received the prize. 'I'm reminded,' said Constantine, 'that *I* did not come empty-handed, either.' Fishing about behind him, he un-propped from a stanchion a florist's box the size of an infant's coffin, glazed, adorned with bridal rosettes: this he wielded at Eva (engulfed in roses) then Henry (slithering over with magazines) then finally landed on Mr Denge. 'And what,' cried Henry, 'about the rest of the luggage?' Eva's, he ascertained, had already been magicked into its rightful place: Henry coerced or hypnotized Mr Denge into coming away down the train with him to track Henry's suitcase. Off they went. 'That boy is going to be competent, if you let him,' observed Constantine – he and Eva now being alone. (The Arbles had come to a stop two stanchions away.) Eva said: 'Father Tony could not come, then?'

'No. I bring his apologies. Extra busy.'

She looked Constantine in the face. 'He does not approve?'

'I have seen him approve more.'

She brought herself to watch the once-deadly mouth. 'And you?'

'D'you know what, Eva,' he burst out, 'you are looking smashing. A smash hit! Yes. Willy ought to be here. – You are keeping up the insurance on *that*, all right, I trust?' He indicated the brooch. 'Looks twenty times more like itself than it did on Cissie; she was too wispy for it . . . And what,' he went on with barely a change of tone, 'would you expect? I have nothing to say. Nothing to declare. No statement. No; it has been the same all along the line. This is just one thing more: by this time, what matter? This could seem the *comble*; but what is? – what can be? There is invariably more. Nothing is final, I suppose.' He shrugged his shoulders. 'What makes you ask? – a little late in the day, one might have thought. It's a pity I care for you. As a matter of interest, *where* are you getting married?'

She hesitated.

'Leave it!' he cut in instantly – dismissingly. 'If you run into trouble, you know where to find me. Talking of that, where's Jeremy? Wasn't he following you? One sees no signs of him.' He looked about. 'Ha!' he exclaimed. 'Here at least comes the Happy Band, again!' On the return, past drifted the seekers – still seeking, unflaggingly. Was hope dwindling? Mist-like phantoms, the aunts, uncles and cousins in passing by bent phantom eyes upon Eva. Cricket matches and flower shows. They suspected her of being who she was? – impossible to say. One signal only was wanted, one indication: she gave neither. One by one, she suffered them to evaporate. The last of the driblets of wilting flowers being no more, she then turned to Constantine. 'All they know about me is, that I am tall.'

'What are you talking about?'

'I invited them.'

'You were their missing bride? You've behaved infernally. Not that that's any longer any business of mine.'

'I became too shy. I have been lost for too long. All the same, Constantine, am I like nobody? Those were my people; they *should* have known me. My father told me my eyes are like my mother's – are they? I believe my forehead is like my father's: is it?'

Laden as before, but for now being plus the retrieved suitcase, back dashed Henry and Mr Denge. 'The work of a minute!' Mr Denge declared, lifting the suitcase proudly. 'How's the charade going, would you say?' asked Henry, drawing Eva aside. 'My love, my sister,' he went on in a lower voice, still more frantic, 'couldn't we possibly arise and come away? Where's all this stuff to *go*, Eva? I suppose we have seats, reservations? Come on, show me!' She vacillated. Mr Denge, securing an audience, reported excitedly: '*Something* or other's afoot further down this platform! Film either being shot or they're televising a royalty or celebrity: cameras galore!'

'I hope that is not Jeremy,' said Eva, as she and Henry withdrew, disappearing, for what this time must not be more than a minute, into the Golden Arrow. Here were their places. He dumped the magazines, she her roses. The suitcase was whisked away; with it, Constantine's gift.

They missed, thus, what was going on down the platform. It was, of course, Jeremy – who else? His performance attracted more and more onlookers – Mrs Caliber being no longer competent to restrain him. Audience-minded, as are contemporary crowds, see-ers off and travellers stood back respectfully, according space and free play to the child star and not obstructing, they hoped, the rigged-up cameras which, as Mr Denge had, they took to be present and in action, or soon in action – for, how should there *not* be cameras? The boy when first he appeared on the stage, or platform, had been carrying a Gallic scarlet dispatch-case: he went on to put the case down and, at once gravely and with a flourish, unlock it. He lifted out, in a manner evidently rehearsed, what had been its contents – to the accompaniment of a titillated if for the first moment aghast gasp along the platform. He not so much flourished the thing as put it through what *could* be its paces.

'Now, come on,' said an attendant, 'don't you do that!'

'Leave him alone,' said someone, 'he's only acting!' A widespread supporting murmur was gone against only by Mrs Caliber. 'No, now stop that, there's a good little boy! – Half the trouble is, you see, that he can't hear,' she told any few sympathizers she gathered. 'He's as good as gold in reality. Keeping himself occupied all these last days, doing his French mouth exercises all by himself in front of the mirror or when not that playing away at his games, while his mother as could not be helped has been out and about in a rush buying her wedding clothes, and so on. And a child likes to play gunman, it's human nature. Not that he had any business to bring that *here*, though. How was I to know what he had in that little bag? Some goodbye surprise for his mother, I assumed it to be – wouldn't you have? No use asking, because he can't speak, you see. That's another great pity. Not that that's anything but a stage dummy he's got hold of – though how he got hold of that beat me; his mother indulges him. What he's got there couldn't be anything other: how could it?'

Eric knew otherwise. 'Do you see what I see?' he said to Iseult – he and she, loose-ended, having been magnetized into the gathered crowd. He, ahead of her, got the first view.

First, therefore, she only said: 'Yes; that's Jeremy.'

'Yes, but do you see what *I* see?' He yanked her forward.

'Oh, no – no! Oh my God, no – it can't be possible!'

'There you are, however. – Since you pinched it, did *you* fire it off? – Nn – nn? – Then there's one in it.'

'I never thought, Eric. I never really thought –'

'Then it beats me to know what you pinched it for. – *I* let things slide, day after day. That old souvenir. Meant to take it out, have a look at it, do a job on it – never brought myself to. How did you ever know it was in the house, now I come to think? But one thing I am certain of: there was one in it. – Keep still. Don't startle him.'

The boy executed a pirouette. Everybody laughed. He drew in the firearm, looking about with a certain air of design. A child's ballet enactment of a *crime passionel*? Or a boy model, advertising something: 'Little Lord X will shoot up the train, if he isn't given – ?'

Jeremy saw Iseult. But her hair was different – was it not? He sent her a teasing smile. 'Eric, I think I *could* get it away from him,' she said.

Away up there in the Golden Arrow, Henry and Eva remained standing – back they must go, in a minute! They were far from alone; down the long, suave car various fellow-occupants were already seated. In here it seemed, after the platform, silent – to be not overheard, the two had to stand close together. As though the train had started and started swaying, they swayed slightly. 'I'm not going to get off,' he said, brushing his lips against her ear. 'I'm not going to get off this train, I mean. Did you really want me to? – did you imagine I would?'

'I had not thought yet.'

'Hadn't you – *hadn't* you?'

'Though, when I saw your suitcase . . .'

'That could have been a fake, full of bricks and things. – But it isn't, Eva; it isn't. Do you mind?'

Something took place: a bewildering, brilliant, blurring filling

up, swimming and brimming over; then, not a torrent from the
eyes but one, two, three, four tears, each hesitating, surprised to be
where it was, then wandering down. The speediest splashed on to
the diamond brooch. 'Look what is *happening* to me!' exulted Eva.
She had no handkerchief, not having expected to require one – she
blotted about on her face with a crunched-up glove. 'What a coronation day . . .'

'Are you happy?' asked Henry, awed.

'A coronation being living, today.'

'I wish, beloved,' he said, frowning, 'we were in a compartment
of our own, like people going away used to be. Are there no more
of those?'

'I was fortunate,' Eva dizzily told him, 'obtaining any seats.'

'You've got the tickets and so on? Give them to me, then.'

'Why?'

'It looks more lifelike, I mean more usual.' The illusory swaying
of the train became more marked. 'Where are we off to? – where
are we going? What are we doing? – I've burned *my* boats . . . I
can't get over those tears, those extraordinary tears!'

'We must go back, now.'

'To the rest. Yes. – I believe, Eva, we ought to have been standing those wretched people champagne.'

They descended from the train.

'Speech!' shouted Mr Denge promptly. Constantine was in the
act of engorging two pills. He slid the Fabergé box back into its
pocket, saying: 'The Arbles seem to be elsewhere; sorry, Eva, this
makes us rather a small group. News of Jeremy, though – eh, Mrs
Caliber?' Mrs Caliber, only waiting, cried: '*Madam* – yes!'

'Mrs Caliber, where *is* he?'

'I thought I should come and tell you, he's been cutting capers,
over-excited, with many egging him on who should know better,
but a lady in an alice-band succeeded in catching hold of him –
any minute now, she's bringing him along. Though if she coaxes
that thing away from him, as she was trying to, she's cleverer than
I am. All's well that ends well, however. You ought to have heard
those little birds of yours keeping on, this morning, anyone might
have told them it was your wedding day. You're looking your best,
madam, if I may say so. – Is that the gentleman?'

Eva introduced Henry to Mrs Caliber.

'Can't take his eyes off you, can he!' said Mrs Caliber.

'Speech!' repeated Mr Denge.

'Fortunately for Henry,' said Constantine, 'time is limited. In fact, you two had better cut the adieux short and get back to the train now; I take it you don't want a rush at the last moment? Any parting remarks had better devolve on me. On behalf of all, I wish you a pleasant future. The future, as we know, will resemble the past in being the result, largely, of a concatenation of circumstances. Many of our best moments, as well as our worst, are fortuitous. (Let us hope that only the best moments await this bridal pair.) I do not say there is no method of human madness. Our affections could not, I suppose, survive – as they do – were they entirely divorced from reason, though the tie is often a rather tenuous one. Well, bless you, Eva; and bless you, Henry! I regret the wholly secular nature of this occasion, but Father Clavering-Haight could not be with us. Let this sunshine we stand in be a good omen! Things may break well for you; that has been known to happen. Er – life stretches ahead. May a favourable concatenation of circumstances . . . No, here I become a trifle tied up, I think. That is enough. – Henry, you'd better kiss Eva.'

Henry did so, lightly on the cheek.

'Constantine,' asked Eva, 'what is "concatenation"?'

Her last words.

'Well here he comes, running,' said Mrs Caliber. – 'But, oh my!'

Jeremy, at sight of Eva, had twisted free from Iseult – who had not succeeded in disarming him. Making a spurt, he sped like a boy on the screen towards the irradiated figure, waving his weapon in salute. It was the Arbles, hard after him, who then best saw as a whole what happened. Eva joyfully stepped clear of her friends and, unable to take in anything but that this *was* Jeremy, held out her arms. From behind her, there rose above other warnings a great cry of terror from Henry. She turned round in terror to see what was wrong with Henry. That instant, the revolver went off. She fell, while the shot rang round Victoria Station.

Jeremy could not stop running on. A woman bystander to whom nothing was anything had the quickest reflex – she snatched him back before he could fall over the dead body.

MORE ABOUT PENGUINS, PELICANS, PEREGRINES AND PUFFINS

For further information about books available from Penguins please write to Dept EP, Penguin Books Ltd, Harmondsworth, Middlesex UB7 0DA.

In the U.S.A.: For a complete list of books available from Penguins in the United States write to Dept DG, Penguin Books, 299 Murray Hill Parkway, East Rutherford, New Jersey 07073.

In Canada: For a complete list of books available from Penguins in Canada write to Penguin Books Canada Ltd, 2801 John Street, Markham, Ontario L3R 1B4.

In Australia: For a complete list of books available from Penguins in Australia write to the Marketing Department, Penguin Books Australia Ltd, P.O. Box 257, Ringwood, Victoria 3134.

In New Zealand: For a complete list of books available from Penguins in New Zealand write to the Marketing Department, Penguin Books (N.Z.) Ltd, Private Bag, Takapuna, Auckland 9.

In India: For a complete list of books available from Penguins in India write to Penguin Overseas Ltd, 706 Eros Apartments, 56 Nehru Place, New Delhi 110019.

Elizabeth Bowen

THE DEATH OF THE HEART

Sixteen-year-old Portia comes to live with her wealthy older half-brother and his wife, Anna, in London during the thirties. Tormented by the agonies of her first love affair, she is obsessed by the feeling that everyone is laughing at her. And when she discovers that Anna has been reading her diary, she takes a sudden explosive step which pulls everybody up short.

'One of the most sensitive novels written during this troubled century' – *John O'London's*

THE LAST SEPTEMBER

The ambushes and burnings of the Irish Troubles of 1920 seem far removed as, up at the 'Great House', tennis parties and dances continue to divert and flirtations with English officers from the local garrison amuse. Yet a sense of brooding, nostalgic melancholy pervades – the sense of a tragedy coming to its climax in the calm, opulent sunlight of an Irish autumn.

'Written from the heart ... the descriptions linger in the memory with extraordinary persistence, so that in retrospect the story seems to belong to some far-distant half-forgotten phase of one's own life' – Jocelyn Brooke

and

FRIENDS AND RELATIONS
THE HEAT OF THE DAY
THE HOUSE IN PARIS
THE LITTLE GIRLS

KING PENGUIN

☐ *The White Hotel* **D. M. Thomas**

'A major artist has once more appeared', declared the *Spectator* on the publication of this acclaimed, now famous novel which recreates the imagined case history of one of Freud's woman patients.

☐ *Dangerous Play: Poems 1974–1984*
Andrew Motion

Winner of the John Llewelyn Rhys Memorial Prize. Poems and an autobiographical prose piece, *Skating*, by the poet acclaimed in the *TLS* as 'a natural heir to the tradition of Edward Thomas and Ivor Gurney'.

☐ *A Time to Dance* **Bernard MacLaverty**

Ten stories, including 'My Dear Palestrina' and 'Phonefun Limited', by the author of *Cal*: 'A writer who has a real affinity with the short story form' – *The Times Literary Supplement*

☐ *Keepers of the House* **Lisa St Aubin de Terán**

Seventeen-year-old Lydia Sinclair marries Don Diego Beltrán and goes to live on his family's vast, decaying Andean farm. This exotic and flamboyant first novel won the Somerset Maugham Award.

☐ *The Deptford Trilogy* **Robertson Davies**

'Who killed Boy Staunton?' – around this central mystery is woven an exhilarating and cunningly contrived trilogy of novels: *Fifth Business, The Manticore* and *World of Wonders*.

☐ *The Stories of William Trevor*

'Trevor packs into each separate five or six thousand words more richness, more laughter, more ache, more multifarious human-ness than many good writers manage to get into a whole novel' – *Punch*. 'Classics of the genre' – Auberon Waugh